Margaret James was born in Hereford.
She was educated there and at Queen Mary College,
London. While working as a library assistant in Oxford
she met her husband, a research student who later
became a meteorologist.
Subsequently she went to work for the DHSS; but soon
after the birth of her second daughter she decided that
she would like to write. When her younger child
started school she began work on *A Touch of Earth*,
which is her first novel.
Margaret James has also written short stories for
women's magazines. At present she and her family live
in Berkshire.

A Touch of Earth

MARGARET JAMES

Futura

A *Futura* Book

Copyright © Margaret James 1988

First published in Great Britain
by Futura Publications 1988
This edition published by Futura Publications 1994

ISBN 0 7088 3785 9

Printed in England by Clays Ltd, St Ives plc

Futura Publications
A Division of
Macdonald & Co (Publishers)
Brettenham House
Lancaster Place
London WC2E 7EN

'Who loves me must have a touch of earth'
Guinevere in *Idylls of the King*, Alfred Lord Tennyson

Chapter One

'DORCAS? DORCAS! DAMN THE BABBY, where is she?' In a sweat of annoyance and irritation, Ellen Grey looked up and down the muddy village street for the twentieth time, willing her little daughter to appear. 'Dorcas!' she yelled, angrily. She began to walk slowly through the village yet again, calling all the time.

Ellen was late for work already. The rest of the women in her field gang would have been toiling for an hour or more, and Ellen knew that when *she* finally appeared the gang master would take great delight in docking two pence or more from her miserable daily pay of a shilling. And it was possible that he would refuse to find four-year-old Dorcas any work at all.

The little girl was eventually discovered by a neighbour's child, a consumptive creature unfit for even the lightest field work, who spent his wearisome days lounging around the village waiting to die. He had spotted Dorcas in the very act of theft. 'Here you are, Missus,' he announced, triumphantly. 'At the potato bin she is. You'll cop it from Mrs Johnson when I tell!' His little sore eyes blinked maliciously at Ellen, who glared at her informant and pounced on Dorcas.

Hauling her from her hiding place, Ellen slapped her daughter hard across her bare thighs. In amazement, Dorcas dropped the potato she'd been gnawing, and gaped at her mother in fury and mortification. She hit back, kicked her assailant — then, finding her voice again, she opened her mouth and let out a terrific yell. 'No, Mam!' she screeched. 'Go 'way, Mam! Go 'way!' But Ellen picked Dorcas up and tucked her, howling and kicking, under one arm. Still very angry, she ignored the squawking protests coming from the child as she set off for the fields.

Approaching the cart track which led away from the village, however, her rage began to give way to pity for her daughter. 'Tain't the babby's fault,' she told herself as she hurried along. 'Poor little devil, she's had no breakfast; it's small wonder she went poking around the place.'

Ellen set the child down and cleaned her smeared little face with a corner of her rough sacking apron. 'Come on, my biddy,' she said kindly. 'Don't you cry. Here, look — you have this.' She handed her daughter a piece of bread, meant for her own dinner. Scowling, Dorcas took it and began to chew, lagging further and further behind her mother as the two of them walked on. Ellen found that she had not the heart to chivvy the child any more.

The field where Ellen Grey spent the rest of that morning picking stones was in the centre of a valley set among hills so green that, especially after rain, the dozens of shades and hues in the landscape seemed far too bright to have been coloured by nature alone. This brilliance was particularly marked where these same Herefordshire hills abutted newly-ploughed fields of fertile red-brown clay, or were lapped by streams themselves the colour of blood.

On a journey from the old market city of Hereford to the equally picturesque little town of Ledbury, a man's road would take him over the Ashton Lacey hills and past the village of Ashton Cross. And any observant traveller going that way would surely marvel as his route meandered through this veritable rural Paradise, as each new vista opened on to a fresh succession of smiling valleys, every one dotted with quaintly charming hamlets of half-timbered cottages. Each vale was a new haven of agricultural fecundity, displaying either its hopfields or its cider orchards, its arable fields or its lush meadows in which the famous white-faced cattle contentedly browsed.

These pretty fields were, in the main, neatly fenced by tough quickset hedges. But occasionally they were bounded by older, more varied hedgerows, ones which indicated where the larger fields of the previous centuries — of the times before the Enclosures Acts had robbed the peasants of most of their common lands — had been. Among these more ancient boundaries grew great oaks and elms, magnificent horse chestnut trees and huge, sombre ashes.

Such a countryside would seem to be a perfect setting for a community wedded to the land. For here, if anywhere in England,

8

one would surely find a well-nourished, well-clad labouring population; a cheerful peasantry benevolently overseen by a kindly if somewhat paternalistic squirearchy, whose members must surely appreciate that the fruits of this undeniably bountiful red earth belonged to all …

Neither Ellen Grey, nor anyone else in the dilapidated and insanitary village in which she lived, could have easily comprehended this notion. To her little daughter Dorcas, born and reared in near destitution, such egalitarian ideas — could she have understood them — would have seemed quite absurd.

Ellen stood up and flexed her aching arms, rubbed her sore back. The sky was darkening now. 'Dorcas?' She peered through the dusk, looking for the child. 'Time to go home,' she murmured, fatigue slurring her speech. 'Come along with me.'

The infant slipped her hand into her mother's and, her little feet dragging, she allowed Ellen to lead her back to Ashton Cross.

Born one bitterly cold night in November 1850, Dorcas Grey was the third child and first daughter of Ellen Grey, whose husband Michael was a landless farm labourer.

The Greys' home, a small cruck-framed cottage which was pretty enough from without but verminous within, was hardly the best of places in which to give birth. A hovel more fit for keeping pigs in than for sheltering human beings, it was infested with black beetles, and its wattle and daub walls teemed with cockroaches together with a profusion of other insect life. In the loft where Ellen lay the very air seemed to be thick with contagion, stinking of mould and decay. But then the whole cottage was damp, and barely weatherproof.

The winter had set in early that year; there had been hard frosts all over Herefordshire since the beginning of October. Dorcas came into a world of white and dreadful cold, where icicles hung on the broken casement of the room in which she gave her first cry, and the breath from that cry had condensed as steam in the freezing air.

'It's a fine little girl, Ellen. Got a bit of flesh on her; she'll do well.' Wrapped by the midwife in a piece of old blanket and some threadbare linen, the baby had lain close to her mother, gazing up at her with wide, blue eyes. She'd smelled the foulness of the rushlight flickering near her face, and wrinkled her nose in disgust

— but then she had yawned, and slept. 'There — isn't she good?' The old village woman who acted as midwife, who laid out the dead and who doctored all the ailments which came in between, grinned at the baby's tired mother. 'You go to sleep too, my girl,' she advised. 'You've had a hard time of it. I'll see Michael about the half crown.'

When Ellen woke in the chill of the early morning, she found that the baby had made a fist of her little hand and was chewing it hard, making pathetic mewing noises as she did so. Ellen picked her up and fed her, noticing with relief that the child sucked well. 'Perhaps,' thought Ellen, as she stroked the little girl's soft, downy head, 'perhaps this one might live.'

For, although she had no children living but this latest, Ellen had been pregnant when she married. Her stillborn son had been buried in the churchyard a mere four months after her wedding day — and her second son, healthy enough at birth, had died of a cough when just six months old. A succession of miscarriages had preceded the birth of Dorcas; so Ellen hardly dared to hope that this new daughter, born into the same abject poverty as her brothers, would thrive.

In a good week Michael Grey could earn ten shillings, which almost kept his little family from want. Throughout the autumn of 1850, however, Michael had seldom been fully employed, so his wages had been seven, six, sometimes as low as five shillings a week. Unable to sustain life on such a sum, Michael had often risked poaching to feed his wife and himself. There was no food in the house on the night his daughter was born; and, when the midwife had taken a shilling and some odd coppers on account, no money to buy any either.

But, in spite of poverty, illness, starvation and distress, the child came through the winter. Miraculously, she escaped the virulent colds and coughs which weakened or killed more than a dozen young children in Ashton Cross. When the spring finally came, late and unwillingly, Dorcas had become a well-grown, sturdy infant, her rosy little cheeks aglow with good health. Her dark brown hair was growing well, and promised to curl; her beautiful navy-blue eyes were gradually deepening in colour even more, into a brown which was almost black.

'Who's beautiful, my lovely?' Ellen would ask, as she played with the child on her lap. 'Who's my only precious? Who's my little lamb?' It was just as well that her daughter was so bonny, for Ellen had been seriously weakened by almost continuous pregnancy. Now, a series of unnoticed, untreated infections ensured that she would have no more children.

'You going out tonight, Mike?' asked Ellen one February evening, as she watched her husband pull on his corduroy jacket and slip a length of twine into his pocket.

'Aye, my girl, I reckon so.' Michael grinned. 'Seems a pity to waste a good poacher's moon. Me an' Tam Grimshaw thought we'd go up Drayton Spinney. Have a rabbit or two for supper tomorrow, shall we? Or maybe a nice fat pheasant. We'll let old Squire provide our dinner, eh?'

Ellen looked anxious, held her baby close. 'Be careful, Mike,' she pleaded. 'Don't let them take you! You think you're clever — but that new keeper's no fool either. And he has watchers these days, too.'

'Ain't no watcher in the kingdom could catch us.' Michael laughed at his wife's worried expression. 'Cheer up, girl,' he said. 'They'll not run me to earth.'

Michael Grey, like most of his kind, saw no harm in taking game from the woods and fields. Like his friends, he poached as much for sport, for devilment, for fun — to get one back at the ruddy squire — as for food. Fond of a hare when he could get one, Michael was not averse to a pheasant from the landlord's coverts, although raiding these was a risky business. Mostly he just took rabbits, and eggs.

One evening in April he was coming home from the fields when he all but fell over a hare as she crouched in the meadow grass. He seized her, broke her neck with a sharp blow from the flat of his hand, and stuffed her limp body inside his jacket.

That night, the smells of roasting hare coming from the Greys' cottage tantalized their hungry neighbours. Those dining upon bread, lard and ends of cheese became very bitter about the good fortune some folks always seemed to have. They prophesied a bad end for Mike Grey, who got above himself something disgraceful.

A woman whose child — a baby the same age as Dorcas — had died of a septic throat only the previous week, was beside herself

11

with resentment. Twice that year her man had been had up before the magistrates on suspicion of poaching. Yet Mike Grey, the most notorious, the most flagrant covert-robber in the area, never got caught. She had watched Ellen bringing Dorcas home that day and the sight of the little girl, so healthy, had been poisonous to her.

The next day the woman went to the gamekeeper's cottage and laid information that Mike Grey regularly trapped hares. She said she was willing to give evidence on oath that this was so. 'He's a proper thief,' she added, pursing her lips self-righteously. 'He pinches eggs, he takes pheasants — and he's never heard of the ten commandments!'

'Ah, get on home, will you?' The gamekeeper, a labourer's son himself, knew the woman for a malicious scandalmonger. He went on cleaning his gun. 'Don't talk to me about the ten commandments,' he added, 'when you're standin' there bearin' false witness like a good 'un!'

But she persisted. 'If you won't listen to me,' she retorted, 'I'll go to Squire Lawrence hisself. That fellow Grey, he's got an arrangement with a dealer in Hereford market — and he's takin' Squire's game from right under your nose!'

And so the keeper, who had a healthy respect for his employer and who needed to keep his job, had no choice but to have Michael Grey taken up.

Duly arranged and brought to trial, thoroughly overawed by the sight of the justice in all his magisterial splendour, Michael admitted that he had taken hares, had stolen eggs. Imperfectly understanding the nature of the charges against him, he allowed the court to assume that he carried on a trade in poached game. He made no effort to defend himself but muttered and shuffled, finally making a barely coherent plea for mercy.

Scowling at the wretch before him, and taking no account of the lack of any real evidence against the accused man, Michael's judge gathered his robes of office around his fat figure. 'One year at hard labour,' he declared dismissively. It was a lenient enough penalty. Michael stammered his gratitude and was led away.

Her husband thus disgraced and imprisoned, it was some comfort to Ellen to hear that the woman who'd informed on Michael was waylaid by some villagers one dark evening and beaten almost lifeless. But the shedding of this traitor's blood did

12

not feed Michael Grey's dependents and now Ellen was obliged to take whatever field work she was offered — always the most disagreeable, the dirtiest, the most backbreaking tasks — to keep herself and her little child alive.

When Michael came back to her, a year and odd days later, Ellen was dismayed to see the change in him. Formerly a lively, resilient man, whose lopsided grin had been one of the most delightful things about him, her husband was now weak and subdued, broken both in body and in spirit. 'Leave me alone, woman,' he'd said irritably as she'd tried to embrace him. 'Bloody females,' he'd added sourly. 'Be the death of me, they will!'

Michael now slouched around the estate, morose and surly, doing whatever work he could obtain badly, and constantly threatened with eviction by the bailiff, for the Greys were months behind with their rent. He certainly had not learned any of the lessons which imprisonment had been intended to teach him — he still took rabbits and game birds, even trapped hares when the chance arose — but now Ellen boiled his catches in a closed pot.

Dorcas grew bigger and stronger. She walked at ten months. At a year she scratched at the beaten earth floor of her home and grubbed cheerfully in the mire outside the cottage door, happy to chew the black beetles which abounded, together with the worms, ants, snails and anything else which took her fancy. When Michael came home she would climb on to his lap, trailing foul linen across his clothes as she pulled his hair and whiskers, trying in vain to provoke some response from a man staring listlessly at nothing.

One night in late May Michael woke an hour or two before dawn. He sat up in bed and listened, heard the birds and vermin stirring in the thatch above his head. Suddenly, he wanted to be out in the early morning, enjoying the cool, grey dawn which would precede a hot, oppressive day. He rose, threw on his clothes and, leaving Ellen snoring on her back, he stole out. He made for a nearby copse, his steps crushing the grass into dewy footprints as he went.

Stealthily, Michael went into the little wood. He knew that the keeper set snares there and he intended to have a rabbit or two out of them before the watchers' boys came to check them later in the day. He walked down an overgrown path, then plunged into the bracken, pushing his way through it until he came to a little dell.

There were now faint pearlescent streaks in the sky, and the birds were singing their hearts out. He would have to hurry.

Michael grinned as he came across a shining wire snare in which, just visible in the growing light, a fat buck rabbit was threshing in a bloody death agony. Michael eased the loop over its head, smashed its skull on a tree stump, and bundled it inside his coat.

The gamekeeper, coming home wearily from an unproductive night's watching, had his gun loaded and cocked. He saw the shadowy figure of a man — and he levelled his firearm at a point between the shoulder-blades. 'Stop just there!' he warned. 'I'll shoot else!'

Darting a glance behind him, Michael recognized the keeper and cursed. Panicking, he ran, blindly into the heart of the copse. He heard the keeper shout again and then the man fired at him.

A dreadful, burning pain stabbed through the poacher as the bullet hit his thigh. He fell; but managed to drag himself on through the densest part of a bramble thicket. But then another shot caught him in the same leg, shattering the bone and causing him to emit a dreadful, almost inaudible scream. He collapsed in the tangle of thorn bushes and lay prone, gasping, twisting with the convulsions of unbearable pain, still unable to make any sound.

The keeper beat around the wood for a while, wishing he had not sent his dogs back with the other watchers. Finding no one, he retraced his steps to the path, then went home to have his breakfast. 'I'm getting too jumpy,' he told himself. He hadn't seen a man, he decided, as he rubbed his tired eyes. It had been a trick of the growing light — probably a fox or a badger had been crashing about in the underbrush. A human poacher wouldn't have made so much noise.

On his way home the keeper checked the game birds and found them safe in their enclosures, unharmed. He forgot about his early morning encounter in Darrow's Copse.

Michael lay immobile in the brambles. The sun came out. Blood was still seeping from the wounds in his leg, coagulating stickily on his torn trousers; a vast, spreading pool of gore soaked the ground where he lay. He felt sick and faint — and very, very thirsty. He could not move.

The sun grew hotter, and glared down at him through the oak branches; these could give him little protection, being as yet hardly clothed in their summer foliage. He shut his eyes. The pain in his leg worsened and seemed to invade his whole body. To try to ease it, he put his hand into his mouth and bit hard into the palm. After an hour or two, he lapsed into unconsciousness.

Accustomed as she was to her husband taking the odd early morning ramble, Ellen was alarmed when he did not appear for his breakfast. She ran from cottage to cottage, asking the men to give up a bit of their time to help her look for him.

Laughing at her for such a preposterous request, man after man refused. 'Not my job, to go nursemaidin' after Mike Grey,' muttered one sourly. 'Give up an hour to hunt up that idle bugger? Don't be so daft, woman!'

Another, though less brutal, was just as unhelpful. 'There's no call for you to fret, Missus,' he remarked. 'It's Wednesday, in't it? Well – he'll have sneaked off to Hereford market to see that feller he sells his stuff to.'

Ellen wrung her hands. 'He don't sell stuff at Hereford market!' she wailed. 'He never has! Look – he's got a day's work up at the Bartons to go to. Bailiff'll evict us if Mike don't show up! Where can he have got to?'

But no one took any more notice of her. It was not until evening that a search was organized; and, as the moon came up over the copse, Michael's body was discovered in the heart of the bramble thicket. He had been dead for less than an hour – the body was not yet cold. 'Just as well he's gone,' muttered one of the men who helped bring his body back to Ashton Cross. 'They'd 'ave hanged the poor devil anyway, what with all them wires and strings in 'is pockets, an' that rabbit layin' next to him, dead as he is.'

It was easy enough to prove that the keeper's gun had been used to shoot Michael Grey. The man was summoned to the manor house, where he was interviewed – some said congratulated – by the squire. But whatever Mr Lawrence might or might not have said to his gamekeeper, the week after Michael's death dozens of new gin traps – great, heavy cast iron horrors, capable of taking a man's leg off at the thigh – appeared in all the woods and spinneys. The villagers went to gaze on them with respect and awe; mothers forbade their sons to enter any of the landlord's woods, and hoped their warnings would be heeded — for they saw, in their minds' eyes, children's limbs mangled or even amputated by the horrible steel jaws.

Ellen knew nothing of all that, for she lay insensible with grief for a full ten days. She heard with indifference the news that the landlord had told his bailiff to leave Grey's woman in her cottage for the time being, behind with her rent though she was — it was, however, stipulated that she must work in the fields to support herself and the child. Otherwise she was, of course, free to take herself off to the workhouse.

Although urged by her neighbours to be grateful for the landlord's unlooked-for magnanimity, Ellen lay on her bed and called down curses on the whole family of Lawrences, wishing a fate similar to her own husband's on the squire himself. 'I hope all his children do sicken and die,' she muttered, adding that she wished his wife might prove barren ever after. She keened and wailed, beating her fists on the bed-head and grinding her teeth, until all her neighbours agreed that her wits must be gone.

So, since his wife was incapable, the village women prepared Michael's body for burial, and took care of Ellen's frightened, bewildered child.

'Say goodbye to your Daddy,' admonished one old crone, who held the little girl aloft so that she might see into the waggon where Michael, wrapped in a linen sheet, lay. 'Say goodnight to 'im, now!'

Dorcas, not understanding and afraid of the discoloured face of the corpse, wriggled and squirmed — then, finally, bit. She received a sharp slap on the thigh for this, but was then allowed to crawl away to a convenient hen coop and sob in peace.

Another woman now brought along some wisps of straw; leaning over the body, she prised open Michael's hand and closed it again around the few golden stalks. 'There,' she remarked, satisfied. 'That'll show the Lord who our Michael was, that'll excuse his bein' from church of a Sunday! No one could thatch a rick like Mike Grey,' she added reflectively. 'He'll be a sad loss this harvest time.'

Her friend, who was less charitable, grimaced. 'You should've stuck a rabbit's paw in old Mike's other fist,' she remarked acidly. 'Poaching — that's what he got up to of a Sunday! He warn't busy makin' no haystacks!' But no murmur of agreement rose to second those sentiments, and Michael was sent to meet his God holding the emblem of his calling, that of the honest labourer. He was taken to his grave riding in a state he'd never known in life, the brand new blue and red farm waggon plentifully decked with flapping black banners, the whole village following it to the churchyard.

Afterwards, those men who had the money to do so got drunk. The women crowded into Ellen's cottage to weep companionably together, and to pass round a stone jar of spirits. They urged Ellen to bear up, if only for the baby's sake. But Ellen lay supine, heedless. She stared like a mad woman, occasionally muttering to herself; she ignored her daughter, and would take no food.

For a further week she mourned. But then she seemed to make up her mind to carry on with her life after all. She got out of bed, washed herself, tied up her hair with a piece of twine, and went to ask the bailiff if he could find her some work.

Ellen settled down to a life of lonely hardship without complaining. Working on the land all that summer, she wore herself out with physical toil and was usually in a state of such extreme exhaustion that she had no time or energy to fret for Michael, no spare moments to indulge in the luxury of grief for the dead. And, of course, little Dorcas was a living, breathing anxiety who could not be ignored.

Paying another villager a penny or two to mind a child made a great dent in a field woman's daily wage. So, under the shade of an enormous ash tree which stood in the corner of the Big Field, the labouring women had built their own nursery, a stick and wattle enclosure in which half a dozen or so babies and children as yet too small to toddle after their mothers were imprisoned while the field hands worked.

Tiny babies there were at the mercy of their curious elders, who jabbed at their eyes and trod on them; squeals from the pen were invariably ignored by the toiling women, who were usually out of earshot anyway. Sometimes a sullen elder sister, who had not been able to find any paid work that day, would be pressed

17

into supervising this menagerie — bribed, sometimes, by the promise of a penny, but more often threatened with a clout around the ear if she refused.

Clad in flapping linen sunbonnets, their skirts tucked up out of the dirt and their legs encased in gaiters cut from worn-out trousers, Ellen and her companions worked all the daylight hours for a shilling or less a day, going home in the evenings to cook, clean and wash. It was little wonder that women of twenty-five usually looked nearer forty. That summer Ellen's fair skin reddened, blistered and burned, and she developed crow's feet around her eyes as a result of screwing them up against the sun. Her hands became calloused and scabbed, rougher and more worn than they ever were when she'd been the overworked general maidservant at one of the tenant farms before her marriage.

Often the rector, a large, stout man whose skinny wife did not particularly please him, would contrive to pass a group of field women. 'A fine day,' he would bleat, in the unusually high-pitched, squeaking voice which made listening to his sermons a torment. 'A beautiful afternoon!' Staring at the women's swaying bosoms and uncorseted hips, his eyes would roll hungrily in their sockets. 'What a picture you all make,' he would continue, 'as you labour in the Lord's vineyard. Ha ha.'

'Lord's vineyard, my arse,' one of the women exclaimed one day, under her breath. 'What do that bugger know about labour? All he's got to do all day is loaf around the place, makin' up 'is sermons and talkin' to 'isself in Lattin an' Greek!'

'If 'e's not sat up on the bench, sendin' some poor devil off to prison or Botany Bay!' added her neighbour. She glanced around her. 'Has 'e gone yet?'

'Yes. There he goes. Off on another nature ramble, idle so and so.'

'Good. Then I can go and feed our Annie.' The woman straightened up, and stretched. 'I don't know why, but I 'ates it when that old parson's stood there starin' as I'm nursin' her!'

Babies were suckled when a nursing mother felt too full and uncomfortable to continue working. Women who had given birth at around the same time, and who were labouring side by side in the field, frequently took turns to feed one another's children. It was a common sight to see a peasant woman sitting at the edge of the field, simultaneously nursing her own and a friend's baby. Women who had a little milk to spare thought it their duty to offer it to a child whose mother had too short to supply herself. Most babies got enough in the end — and, as a last resort, an infant could be brought up by hand, sucking thin gruel through a sacking teat.

At midday, the whistle would be heard and the women would stop working to go and sit together under the ash tree. As they ate their bread spread with herb-flavoured lard, chewed their dry cheese and, now and then, gnawed on a scrap of salt bacon, a general grumble would be heard that they could do with a bit more meat.

Children no longer at the breast were allowed to swig home-brewed beer from the communal flask which had been kept cool in the shade of the hedgerow. This ensured that they would be comatose for most of the afternoon.

The women would doze and chat for an hour, to be chivvied back to work by one of the bailiffs when the sun was at its highest and hottest. 'I could've done with an hour or two more,' one would moan.

'And my back's that sore,' another would add.

'And my poor legs do ache!'

'And the back of my neck's that burnt since I forgot my 'at!'

But if it was disagreeable to be working in the heat, it was miserable for everyone when it rained. Then, the children in the makeshift nursery were sheltered by covers stretched above their heads, and dry straw was laid on the wet ground — but still the wind and rain drove in, and by the end of the day the children would be as miserable, as cold and as muddy as their tired mothers.

The work the women did was dull and monotonous. While the men did the really heavy labouring — ploughing, hedging and the like — women and children old enough to walk picked stones, planted, singled and harvested roots, weeded, frightened the birds, and tended the hops, for Herefordshire is hop-growing country.

'That's a bad cough, my biddy,' remarked Ellen one chilly autumn morning. 'You got a sore throat, my girl?'

Dorcas hacked and barked in reply. 'Sore frote, Mam,' she wheezed, as she leaned against her mother's shoulder.

Ellen frowned, listened anxiously to her little girl's laboured breathing. Although Dorcas was now a well-grown two-year-old, Ellen feared for her daughter's health if the child were dragged out to the windswept fields every day, to trail after her mother in the bitter cold, picking up stones. Ellen felt she had no choice but to pay a child-minder. 'We'd better go and call on Mrs Lambert,' she said, mentally calculating the shortfall in food which paying a minder would entail.

The minder, an elderly woman who was so poor that her fire of a few sticks could not be a danger to her little charge, was happy to neglect Dorcas in return for twopence a week. So the child spent that autumn and winter cold and usually hungry in the widow's filthy cottage, scrabbling in the mud at the door by way of recreation and play, wrapped up against the chill of the season in a foetid bundle of clothing into which she had been sewn the previous September and from which she would not be released until the following April. 'Mam! Mam!' the child would wail as Ellen left her each morning. 'Mam! Come back! Don't go 'way?'

Her infant's broken-hearted sobs would pursue Ellen as she hurried off to work, wondering, as she went, if there was any point at all in being alive.

When she had passed her fourth birthday, Dorcas was considered old enough to work in the fields on her own account, together with a gang of other village children. In this way she was able to contribute a few pence each week towards the cost of her bringing up. When a child of her age ought to have been at home with her mother, or in the village school, little Dorcas spent long, weary days out in the fields where she scared the birds away from the growing crops; flapping her thin arms to little effect, for the flocks of rooks and crows and starlings only rose squawking when Dorcas and her ragged companions were almost upon them, to settle peacefully again in a different part of the field and unhurriedly resume their interrupted meal. But the exercise helped to keep the children warm, and did earn them a whole fourpence a day.

At other times the children were led out, under the harsh

supervision of a gang master, to get in turnips or swedes for the cattle; either pulling them directly from the fields or collecting them from the great earthen clamps built up in the autumn. The gang master carried a whip, which he did not hesitate to use on any hungry child who stealthily gnawed the roots meant for the cows. 'Put it down!' he would bark at any furtive nibbler, accompanying his order with a stinging cut across the shoulders. 'If I see you do that again, I'll flay your backside for you!'

Dorcas hated those days. She knew that, small and slow as she was, she would be beaten for idleness however hard she worked; and that the older boys would entertain each other by tormenting the younger children. She always ate the piece of bread, meant for her dinner, on the way to the fields; for she knew that if she kept it until midday one of the older ones would take it from her. She longed and longed to go to school, as some of the other village children did — if only to keep warm during the freezing winter months. She never suggested this to Ellen. She knew that it simply wasn't possible — her mother needed Dorcas' small earnings if they were both to live.

They came near enough to starvation as it was. More than once, ill with anxiety about where the next day's food was to come from, and hating to be obliged to go begging at the rectory yet again, Ellen had considered asking the carter to take her and Dorcas to Hereford, where they would both be fed in the workhouse there. 'But they'll take her away from me then,' thought Ellen, as she looked at the malnourished but sweet-faced child on her lap. 'And if I lost my little Dorry, I'd die. I know I'd die. We'll just have to stick it out ...'

In summer, however, things always improved, and then both mother and daughter found it pleasant to be out in the open air, where the meadws smelled so sweet and the birds sang so cheerfully. While other children went sulkily to lessons, Dorcas was happy to go to the fields; when the weather was warm she did not mind her broken-down boots, cracked and ungreased so that they let in water, and always several sizes too large; nor did she fret that her clothes were so shabby. Summer, though, never lasted long enough. After the September hop-picking, the frosts began, and winter came again.

The winter of 1857 was a cruel one. One week in December,

21

when neither Ellen nor Dorcas had been able to work for three days, and had nothing to eat but stale bread, Ellen went up to the manor house to beg a parcel of scraps.

'She got that stuff by showing 'er legs to the stable boys,' remarked one old crone censoriously. 'I hear she was given some oranges an' half a meat pie — you don't get vittles like that for nothing!'

'If I 'ad legs worth showin' — or anythin' else for that matter — I'd do the same,' answered her companion. 'What I'd do for a bit of mutton would shame the Devil hisself.'

Everyone in the village went hungry that winter. Old people died of cold and starvation, young children were killed by the diseases which preyed upon their emaciated little bodies. There was hardly any work to be had, and the people kept themselves alive on rectory soup and parish loaves, all the while cursing the weather, the Squire and the government — and the price of corn.

Some boys had managed to steal a few pounds of apples from one of the barns; and one dull afternoon a gang of them sneaked into a half-derelict, empty cottage, intending to share them out.

Luke Hole, the biggest and strongest member of the group, spread the fruit over the floor and began, very inaccurately, to count the apples out. A crew of his intimates, which included Dorcas and some others from among the larger, fiercer girls, watched. Their empty stomachs churned at the sight of so much food, and their mouths watered in expectation.

Then, a sudden movement startled them; and in through the door came a skinny little girl about five years old. 'It's all right,' muttered one of the boys. He turned back to his adoration of the fruit spread out before him. 'It's only China Jenny.'

China Jenny, a poor, mentally retarded child with the bloated face and slanting eyes characteristic of her condition, came towards the group. She smiled her usual vacant smile; for she was full, as always, of goodwill and friendliness. She saw the apples, and grinned in delight. She leaned forward and took one.

'Put it back, loony,' said Luke Hole menacingly. He glared at her. 'Put it back, I said! Or I'll do for you!'

Not understanding, China Jenny grinned even more broadly. She shrugged her thin shoulders at Luke — then she opened her

22

mouth, and took a great bite of the apple.

Luke Hole leapt up in a rage. 'Right!' he yelled, livid. 'Get the little bugger! Teach her a lesson!' He pointed to two of his particular friends. 'You, Jack! Arthur, and you! Bring her over here!'

Dorcas watched with interest as the two boys dragged poor China Jenny over to a stone trough, which was full of dirty water. 'Duck her!' ordered Luke. 'Hold her under!'

No one would have dreamed of disobeying Luke. The boys did as they were told. They ducked the struggling child three times; three times they jerked her head back out of the water, while she choked, gasped and vomited, not understanding what they were doing to her, or why. Finally, after holding Jenny's head under the filthy water for a minute or more — and grinning around them to the cheers of the onlookers — Jack and Arthur released their victim. She came up blue in the face, her mouth clogged with slime, her eyes almost shut, and she blinked piteously at her tormentors.

'Go home to your Mam,' commanded Luke. 'Home, stupid! Go home! An' tell your Mam to teach you some manners!' When Jenny still hesitated, Jack opened the door and gave her an encouraging kick. She understood then — and so, with the laughter of the children ringing in her ears, China Jenny staggered, weeping and retching, out of the house.

Dorcas Grey was no infant saint. She had teased creatures weaker than herself many times; had thrown stones at half-starved village cats, chased terrified puppies, and been unkind to smaller children without thinking anything of it. She had watched unmoved while kittens were drowned, when boys had toasted live sparrows over fires, when yelping curs had been hung up by their owners and left to expire in a slow and painful fashion.

But while the boys had tortured poor China Jenny, she had watched almost frozen with horror and disgust. Although she'd never have dared to challenge Luke Hole's directives, something about Jenny's plight had moved her to pity, cruel little heathen though she was. As she'd observed the look of anguish on Jenny's innocent little face, that same pity had made her wince with shame.

'Here's your share, Dorry,' said Arthur, breaking into her thoughts.

Dorcas looked at the fruit, felt her mouth water and her stomach lurch with hunger. 'I don't want them,' she muttered savagely. She pushed the boy away. 'You can eat 'em all, you and Jack,' she said. 'And I hope they bloody well choke you!'

Chapter Two

ALTHOUGH THAT WINTER CONTINUED UNUSUALLY cold, the very end of December saw a slight thaw set in; so the field hands could go back to work. Dorcas spent a few days pulling the last of the turnips, a job which she loathed, for it made her hands bleed with wounds which would not heal.

The mild respite did not last long. One morning Dorcas got out of the bed she shared with her mother and looked out to see the fields white with a hard frost which sparkled in the early morning sun. 'We'd better go out,' said Ellen, as they drank their weak tea and chewed their bread. 'If we go up to the manor house, look, one of the grooms might find us summat to do in the stables — cleaning tack or suchlike. Then we'll get a dinner, if we're lucky.'

Mother and child set out. On the cart track which led to the squire's house Dorcas encountered a group of village children. Lounging against a stile, they were waiting to see if the gang master might appear. She decided to wait with them, so Ellen carried on to the manor house alone.

At about half past nine, the gang master rode up on his pony and led a procession of scruffy children trudging the two miles to the turnip fields. But the morning sun, though bright, had so far failed to warm the soil sufficiently for the children to begin work. Unless the ground thawed a little, the roots could not be pulled without damage — and, if they were spoiled, they would rot within a matter of days. While the children ate their bread the gang master debated what to do. Eventually, seeing that the frost would persist, he remounted his scruffy little pony. 'Go on, you lot,' he muttered curtly. 'Get on home.' He rode away.

This was a disaster. The children had walked all the way to the fields, only to be told to go back again without the sixpences they had expected to earn. They stood in the frozen mud, disconsolate — then, miserably, they began the weary slog home, a ragged, dispirited gaggle of little scarecrows, who kicked the sedges moodily as they went.

The group consisted of a number of boys in their early teens and Dorcas. One of these boys, a sullen, disagreeable child at the best of times, needed to take out his irritation on somebody. 'He'd have let us work if it hadn't been for the babby,' he muttered, glaring balefully at the girl beside him. 'Shouldn't be here at all, she shouldn't. Little and useless she is — takes 'er tanner and does damn all for it most days.' He picked up a stone and flicked it at Dorcas, catching her a glancing blow on the temple and drawing a streak of blood.

The other boys snickered, and a couple more bent to pick up pebbles. Realizing that they would all start to torment her soon, and that being pummelled and kicked was the least she had to fear, Dorcas gathered her trailing skirt around her and prepared to run for home. She dodged past her aggressors and made a dash for the edge of the field, where the ground was smooth and there was a well-worn path.

But her feet, bundled up in rags to prevent her chilblains from being rubbed raw by her boots, were numb with cold and would not move as she wanted them to. Her dress, which was far too large for her, kept tripping her up. Yelling and howling, the boys chased her across the meadow. 'Get the babby! Get the babby!' they chanted, excited by the hunt, and now determined to catch their quarry.

Out on his pony twelve-year-old Stephen Lawrence, the land-lord's elder son, had enjoyed his early morning hack and was looking forward to his breakfast. He had turned the pony's head and was making for home when he heard the wild shouts of the boys; so he rode across the pastureland towards the brow of the hill to find out what they were yelling at.

As he breasted the ridge, he came face to face with the ragged little creature struggling towards him; and he saw the look of utter dismay which came over its features when it saw its way barred by a new obstacle. Its pursuers, on the other hand, were jubilant. Seeing their prey thus cornered, they gave a great triumphant whoop of delight; and they shouted to the young squire to hold it at bay.

For a moment, the boy on the pony did nothing. The child whom the others had been chasing now stood stock still and covered its face with its hands, cowering in abject terror only a few feet away from him. Like a trapped animal Dorcas waited help-lessly, expecting at any moment to be torn apart — or at any rate set upon and beaten — by this pack of human hounds which was almost upon her.

'Keep 'er there, Squire!' bellowed one of her pursuers. 'Don't let 'er get away!'

At that, Stephen stiffened, and frowned. Keep her there, indeed! Whom did that rabble think they were addressing? Absolutely disdaining to take orders from a bunch of scruffy peasant children, the landlord's son was suddenly galvanized into action. He spurred his pony on, and cantered in an arc in front of the boys, separating them from their victim.

Furious and puzzled, the gang backed away from the pony's flashing hooves, watched indignantly as the boy on the horse circled their quarry; and, as he rode past them a second time, they were astonished to see him lean over and grab it, hauling it up on to the saddle in front of him. 'Clear off!' Stephen shouted, in the ringing patrician tones which the boys recognized as the voice of authority. 'Go on — move! Go home!' He glared at the boys, who scowled back at him, stood their ground, still defiant — but, all the same, they were helpless to prevent their prize from being borne away. They gazed after Stephen in bafflement, and swore.

The young gentleman immediately regretted his bravado. He wished at once that he'd resisted the temptation to show off his horsemanship to a bunch of peasants, that he'd left the awful thing in front of him to its fate. For the child he'd rescued was now leaning against his melton jacket, smearing it with the mud which its pursuers had been hurling after it. Worse than that, it was filthy all over, literally encrusted with dirt. It smelled so foully that it made him heave.

She — for it was evidently a girl, ragged wisps of long brown hair fluttered in the wind, coming loose from some sort of plait — was crying noisily now, with hoarse, bawling sobs which grated on

27

Stephen's ears. Tattered banners of cloth flapped around her thin body and flicked against Stephen's clean clothes. Her grimy hand, resting on his sleeve, was engrained with something nastier than mere soil. Altogether he was tempted to put her down, to leave her to the tender mercies of the boys, who were still chasing hopefully after them.

But, all the same, he hung on to her tightly — though for what earthly reason he could not have explained. Urging his pony into a gallop, he rode off down the hill towards the village, where he presumed she must live.

He reined in his pony and pointed with his whip to a group of cottages near the well. 'Is your home over there?' he asked, praying for an affirmative; the next sizeable cluster of tenants' houses was seven miles away.

Dorcas said nothing. She had not understood him, had not been able to interpret a sentence which, although spoken in her own language, was uttered in an accent so different from her own that the words might not have been English at all.

Stephen shook her. 'Don't be frightened of me,' he said in a tone of exasperation nicely calculated to make her exactly that. 'Tell me — where do you live?'

The child looked up a him. Screwing up her face, peering at him as if his own features were as bright as the sun itself, she grunted something unintelligible, then wiped her streaming nose on her sleeve. But now she seemed to understand what he meant; and, with a blackened forefinger, she directed him to her own home. Stephen rode over to the hovel she had indicated and dismounted. Lifting her from the pony's back, he set her down at the door. Without having said a word to him, Dorcas ran inside, and slammed the cottage door behind her.

When he was half way up the hill again, the landlord's son turned to glance back to the village. He saw that the little girl had appeared in the doorway of her cottage and was staring after him. Then, even as he watched her, she heaved up her skirts and squatted near the doorstep, relieving herself.

Grimacing in utter disgust, Stephen rode on. Hungry now, anxious to get home to his breakfast, he wondered how people could bear to live as the tenants did, wallowing in such filth. How could they stand being so dirty, why didn't they wash? He wondered, too, how he was going to explain the muck all over his new riding clothes. Again, he cursed his own vanity. The next time he came upon a gang of peasant brats squabbling, he'd leave them to it.

Dorcas stood at the door for a long time, gazing in the direction in which Stephen had gone, reflectively sucking her thumb.

The winter continued bitter. The warmer weather took its time in coming; but, when the spring finally did arrive, Dorcas got her regular change of clothing from the Box, which the rector's wife kept in the vestry. The Box contained cast-offs, clothes collected from the better-off sort of church-goer, which were intended for distribution among the deserving poor. Most of the children from Ashton Cross had at least some of their clothes from the Box — for, of course, labourers' children never had new things.

On the appointed morning Dorcas and a couple of other bedraggled little girls took themselves off to the rectory, to be kitted out for the summer. They found Mrs Collins the rector's wife waiting for them, her pale, protuberant fish eyes as glaring as usual, almost starting out of their sockets. She pursed her lips at the sight of the three village girls. As a good Christian, she heartily despised the rabble from the village as altogether a drunken, heathenish, fornicating lot.

Dorcas stood still while Mrs Collins' maid cut her out of her winter garments, discarding them one by one: the coarse stuff dress, once clean but now filthy and verminous; the scratchy flannel petticoat; and the rough woollen undervest, yellowed and stiffened with perspiration and fit only for the bonfire. Then she led Dorcas to the pump and doused her, before waiting for the mistress to hand out a set of summer garments.

As Mrs Collins' hard fingers poked and stuffed the skinny child into her summer attire, Dorcas stared at her with critical childish eyes. Used to the sight of Ellen's pretty if somewhat grubby face, the little girl marvelled that anyone could be as repulsive as this woman was. For Mrs Collins had such sallow, leathery skin, such bulbous eyes, and such a flat nose with such wide nostrils, that her face seemed more like that of a gigantic toad than of a human being. The rest of her was less reptilian, but just as repellent. Thin and round-shouldered, she was completely flat-chested, straight as a board except for the fact that her shoulder blades stuck out like a pair of incipient wings. Her sparse, greyish-brown hair, the very essence of mouse, was scraped back into a tight, greasy bun; which did nothing to enhance her plain face. Dorcas noticed that she had wiry black hairs on her chin, and several lumpy moles on her cheeks. She was the ugliest person the child had ever seen. Perhaps it was no wonder that she was always so bad tempered ...

Sometimes the eyes of the woman and the child would meet, and both would look away, embarrassed. 'What do you stare at, child?' demanded the rector's wife, fastening a button with an unnecessarily violent jerk.

'Nothing, Madam,' replied the child, stonily.

'Nothing? Then keep your eyes cast modestly downwards, as a Christian maiden ought,' rapped Mrs Collins, wrenching the child's shoulders back and then tying her, far too tightly, into a pinafore which was much too small for her. 'Hasn't anyone even told you that it's impertinent to stare?'

In spite of her exhortations to modesty, however, Mrs Collins had taken a good long look at Dorcas. She had noticed that Ellen Grey's child seemed likely to become something of a rustic beauty, of the brazen, blowsy kind who should be got off into good service in a pious household well before puberty lest she corrupt the young men of the area, and add to the number of peasants' bastards already infesting the countryside.

Clad in a light print dress and carrying a pair of serviceable boots, Dorcas was dismissed. She was relieved that, this time, they had not tied her into a pair of drawers. She hated drawers. They itched, and got in the way when she wanted to relieve herself. She had been given a pair once but, after putting up with the torment of wearing them for a whole week, she had taken them off and hidden them in a ditch, vowing never, ever to wear such stupid things again. After all, Ellen had no use for them and, as far as Dorcas was concerned, her mother knew best about most things.

After her eighth birthday, Dorcas began — at last — to go to school. She had begged and badgered Ellen so much about wanting to become a scholar that Ellen had finally given in. 'Go without your supper, then!' she had cried angrily. 'Do without bread if it means that much to you, if you'd sooner have book learning than meat!' But it had not quite come to that. Ellen had eventually arranged for Dorcas to attend school one or two days a week, free of charge, in exchange for a screw of tea and for running the schoolmistress's errands.

School was a room in one of the more decrepit cottages. Its tenant, a semi-literate widow, had persuaded the rector — and he had persuaded Mr Lawrence — that she was a fit person to undertake the education of peasant children. As the landlord was of the opinion that labourers did not need to be able to read and write anyway, he found this arrangement perfectly satisfactory. Furthermore, he was able to let it be known that on his estate children had the opportunity to acquire an education in a school maintained at his expense.

By dint of a great deal of application and dogged determination, Dorcas mastered her alphabet and learned to recognize all the words which the mistress would scratch on a slate and hold up for the pupils to decipher. She began to hope that one day she might even be able to read.

Ellen was scathing about her daughter's efforts. 'What use is it?' she would demand crossly. 'All this learnin', it's a waste of time — it don't get you nowhere, I can tell you that. I never learned to read, and what use would it be to me if I 'ad? Ain't got no books, have I? Nor likely to have!'

Accustomed to defer to her mother, Dorcas sometimes thought that Ellen was right. School, far from being a quiet seat of learning, was a disorderly place. The bigger boys, always needing outlets for their violent high spirits, often threw their slates across the room and overturned the chairs. There was no opportunity for individual study, for there were no books available to the children — the mistress knew better than to let her precious Bible and few tattered story books get into their dirty, careless hands. But still Dorcas persisted in trying to learn whatever the mistress was able to teach. She repeated the rhymes, poems and passages from Scripture over and over to herself, as if they were magical charms, as if they could somehow unlock a store of learning which Dorcas, for reasons not understood even by herself, longed to ransack. 'I shall do it! I shall learn to read,' she told herself, making herself believe this, making herself concentrate in spite of the racket all

31

around her. 'And one day, I'll have books of my own. I will!'

When the spring came, Dorcas' education halted abruptly. She was out in the fields, with the other labouring children, from dawn to dusk.

If the summer was a good one, and the harvest promised fair, the children were worked until they were half dead with fatigue. June, July and August saw the usual crop of disagreeable accidents, frequently involving exhausted children. Boys and girls were run over by heavily-laden hay wains, or fell from the top of these same carts as they rode home. Cuts and slashes from scythes and bill-hooks were commonplace, as were the gangrene and septicaemia which frequently followed such injuries.

It was always a relief to Ellen when the last load had been taken from the fields, and she and her daughter could go gleaning, collecting the grains which the reapers had missed. Their little sackful had gone to the miller by the beginning of September; in the second week of that month, the hop harvest began.

The hop-picking was a cheerful activity, the province of the women, as the men were now engaged in ploughing and generally setting up the land for the winter. To a little child, those wide Herefordshire hop-fields were like great green forests, for the vines twined eight, ten, twelve feet into the air, casting a yellow-green light on to the pickers below. However cold and wet August had been, it always seemed to turn dry and sunny for the hop-picking. Sometimes the rains of summer had turned the rich, red clay into glutinous, sticky mud, and all the children derived great pleasure from squelching this between their toes. But if the summer had been dry, the paths between the hop-rows would be baked hard into long, red highways, perfect for running up and down.

Dorcas would have little time to play. She stood next to her mother on an upturned wooden box, stripping the fragrant hops from their stems and flinging them into the canvas crib before her. The smell of hops made her dizzy, and her hands were stained yellow on top of their normal coating of grime. 'Don't you dare drop leaves in that crib, mind,' Ellen would warn. 'We won't get paid if it's full of leaves!' And her daughter would yawn.

At intervals throughout the day, the men came round with the cart to collect the hops. They scooped them up, measuring them in great bushel baskets, and they gave the women tokens, which would later be exchanged for cash. As the afternoons wore on the women picked harder, encouraged by their group leader who felt the weight of the tokens heavy in her apron pocket.

Gipsies came to Ashton Cross for the hop-picking. Most Septembers the same half-dozen families visited the hop-fields, but the suspicious villagers never got used to them. The gipsy women were tall and dark, much better made than the villagers. They wore no sunbonnets, and were consequently burned almost black by the summer sun. Their hair was done up in greasy plaits bound around their narrow heads; their black eyes glittered. And they wore bright, outlandish clothes, which were totally unlike the village women's dingy garments. Smelling of woodsmoke and strange perfumes, which were overlaid by a strong stink of the mutton fat with which they pomaded their hair, the villagers avoided them, calling them dirty gippoes.

'Keep away from them gips,' Ellen warned Dorcas. 'They eats children. You go over there and they'll have you in their old pot quick as ninepence, you'll be boiling away along with the rabbits and other stuff they've pinched!'

But her mother's warnings notwithstanding, Dorcas would steal over to look at the gipsies, fascinated by them. Old women too decrepit to work on the hops sat together by their caravans, making crudely-worked lace out of great spools of Lancashire cotton. 'Come over here, my duck,' invited one of these crones one summer evening. 'Have your fortin' told.'

Dorcas, curious, went closer. She eyed the big iron pot simmering on the fire, reflected that it was doubtless full of gently stewing children — and she stopped.

'Nearer. A bit nearer,' wheedled the gipsy. 'Hold out your 'and. I won't touch you,' she added, grinning. 'You're far too dirty!' At this wit, her companions cackled.

Like one mesmerized, the child went two or three steps nearer and held out her grimy little paw. 'Turn it over,' instructed the gipsy. 'Show me your palm — that's right. Ah, now — look! You're going to travel. Not a long way yet — but in years to come, you're going to go over the seas, to foreign lands. An' you'll be with a gentleman. A real gentleman; rich he'll be, as well.'

Seeing Dorcas stare, the gipsy grinned. 'Eh?' she asked. 'Don't you believe me? It's true enough, my gal — it's all there in your hand — and when you're grown up, you'll remember what the gipsy told you!' Suddenly her face became serious. 'You'll have a long life,' she continued gravely. 'And when the time comes — when you're older than me — you'll go to your death by water. Water. Remember that.' She turned to her friends and muttered something in a strange language. The other women nodded and agreed, then one of them laughed.

The sharp sound of that harsh cackle startled Dorcas out of her daydream. Abruptly, she came out of her trance, and fled back to her village, to her mother, to safety. 'Tis all a pack of nonsense,' snorted Ellen, when she heard about her daughter's fine prospects. 'Travel, my foot! Furthest you'll ever go is off to Hereford, when you goes into service! Now don't you start having any nightmares about what them gips said. Told you not to go near 'em, and if they scared you it serves you right!'

Recently, Ellen had started to talk a great deal about service and places. Other women in the village had begun to make rude remarks about great girls of Dorcas' age being too old for babby's work in the fields. Mrs Grey's daughter, they said, ought to be out in the world, sending a bob or two back to her Mam. She was far too big to be pulling turnips now.

Chapter Three

MRS COLLINS, THE RECTOR'S WIFE, frequently took it upon herself to find places in service for the village girls. She had in fact visited Ellen several weeks before Dorcas' tenth birthday to inform her that an excellent place was shortly to become available in Hereford. 'The position is that of an under-housemaid,' she had said severely. 'Your daughter would do well to accept it.'

Ellen had demurred, suggesting timidly that Dorcas was as yet too young to leave home. But Mrs Collins had replied, sharply, that field work was no occupation for a Christian maid about to enter womanhood. 'Only the roughest persons allow their daughters to go out on the land after a certain age,' she said impressively. 'You know what I mean, don't you, Mrs Grey? You would not wish your daughter to become a temptation to others, and a burden to you in her disgrace?'

Ellen did know what she meant — very well indeed. Land-workers had no restraints put upon them; coming and going from their work in the fields, they could indulge in whatever licentious behaviour they pleased. Out in the meadows, they might labour together in mixed sex gangs and talk to each other how they liked.

From casual liaisons babies were born to girls who were little more than children themselves. And Ellen had often observed groups of adolescent boys stealing after one or two girls as these temptresses made their tortuous way home, taking unnecessarily long detours through convenient spinneys. It was common talk that the Ratcliff girls, both hefty lasses of fourteen or so, regularly met up with a crowd of village boys and came home at night tipsy, with their bodices undone and their legs bare.

Dorcas was sent to the rectory to be looked over before the place was confirmed. Mrs Collins read her a long lecture on manners and propriety, which the child heard meekly enough, though with a glitter in her large, dark eyes.

'It is an easy place,' said the rector's wife. 'It will be a good opportunity for you to learn. Other help is kept so you will not be worked hard. And you will be able to get a good situation as a housemaid when your year is up.'

Dorcas simply nodded. She disdained to express any thanks for being taken away from her mother and her home.

The following Wednesday, she was up before sunrise and walking over to the rectory. In spite of the chill of the morning, Mrs Collins had the child stripped and washed at the outside pump. Then she and her housemaid dressed Dorcas in the best from the Box, which happened to be a red velveteen gown of some antiquity and no style at all — but with which the little girl was well pleased, since she liked red. They also gave her a shabby, yellowing nightgown and told her what it was for, together with some drawers, which she was told she must wear, whether they itched or not. 'You may only discard them in hot weather,' said Mrs Collins imperiously. 'And you must wear your undervest at all times. Do you understand?'

Dorcas, now completely sullen, nodded. Then, shivering but now clean, she went home to have her breakfast.

Ellen had made her daughter a meal of bread, cheese and salt bacon, a far better breakfast than either of them was used to. But Dorcas had no appetite. As she mumbled her food tears rolled down her cheeks and dripped on to her dress. She glanced over to the wooden chest in the corner, upon which she had thrown the nightgown; and she saw Ellen's shawl lying folded upon it.

'That's your best shawl, Mam,' she murmured, her voice not at all under her control. 'You can't give it to me!'

'You'll want it, my girl. You take it, and think of me.'

Dorcas began to cry in real earnest then. 'Don't want to go!' she wailed. 'Won't ever see you again!'

Poor Ellen went and put her arms around her sobbing daughter. 'Yes, yes you will,' she said. 'You'll have a holiday at Whitsun like all the other girls — and carter's already promised to bring you home for the day then. And won't you be grand?'

'Will I?'

'Oh, yes! Remember Lizzie Harding? She went off in that old

36

green rag of her mother's — come back in a cashmere gown her mistress give her! Think of that, my biddy. Just think of that!'

Dorcas sniffed at the remembrance of Lizzie. Now known as Elizabeth, she was transformed, almost a lady in her finery while her numerous brothers and sisters still at home went about in tatters which scarcely covered their skinny frames.

Mother and daughter sat together for a few minutes more, until they heard the carter shouting for Dorcas. Was she going this week, or next? With a despairing sigh, Dorcas hugged her mother once again then went slowly through the doorway of the cottage and down the path to the gate.

The carter lifted her up on to the wooden seat beside him, and bade her kiss her mother. Ellen handed up the nightgown and shawl, together with the remains of the child's breakfast. Other women, departing for the fields, stopped to wish her well.

'Be a good girl — keep away from the fellers, they's nothing but trouble,' called one, at twenty-six already the mother of four bastards.

'Won't know you when you gets home again,' cried the mother of the famous Lizzie Harding, hastening off to work with her ragged children running at her heels.

The carter shook the reins and the horse ambled off down the track to take the road to Hereford, some six miles distant. By the time they'd reached the main highway, Dorcas was sobbing fit to break her heart.

The carter let her snivel. When there was a lull in her weeping, he handed her a strip of torn cloth and told her to have a good blow. 'Clear your passages,' he said. 'Then stop that 'orrible noise. Fourth girl I've took to town this month, an' all of 'em dead keen to go 'cept you. What's the matter? Didn't you want to leave your Ma?'

Dorcas grunted, blew her nose, and scowled at him.

The carter grinned back at her, revealing his few green teeth. 'You'll be all right,' he remarked laconically. 'Remember Nell Tranter? Her as always had her head full of lice, an' her arse always showin' through her dress? Well — she come home from Worcester last summer looking like the Queen of Sheba. She did! Petticoats and all, she had! Gentlewoman's companion she calls herself now.' The old man spat contemptuously.

37

But Dorcas failed to cheer up at the prospect of such advancement, so the carter tried a different tack. 'Look,' he offered. 'I'll be back in Hereford this time next week — so if I got time I'll come round to the house where you're going an' tell you how your Mam is, shall I? That be any good to you?'

Dorcas looked at him sideways and, eventually, nodded.

'That's better, then. Now will you stop all that grizzlin'?' He rummaged in a canvas bag near his feet and drew out a few crumpled sheets of paper, which he handed to Dorcas. 'Here you are,' he said. 'Pictures to look at.'

The penny novelette which he handed to her smelled strongly of the herrings it had been used to wrap. Printed on rough, greyish paper, it had smudgy line drawings on every page. Dorcas looked through the text, searching for the few words she could understand; but she soon gave up trying to make sense of the story. She turned her attention to the pictures instead.

A sketch of a plump young woman immediately caught her fancy, for the woman was obviously a housemaid. Stupendously endowed as she was, her gown cruelly constricted her tiny waist and barely concealed her overflowing bosom. But, in spite of the fact that she was almost falling out of her clothes, she resolutely scrubbed the floor upon which she knelt, while a gentleman in fine clothes gazed down at her thoughtfully, fondling a set of magnificent whiskers as he did so.

Turning the page, Dorcas saw an illustration depicting the same gentleman clasping the fair servant around her impossible waist, and attempting — so it seemed — to kiss her, while she turned away in pretty confusion.

Yet another picture showed this same couple, this time kneeling side by side at the altar of some great church.

Dorcas shook her head in bafflement, and let the magazine fall from her hands to the muddy road below.

The day had turned into a fine autumn morning, blue and gold with a smell of burning in the air. Dorcas looked at the unfamiliar countryside passing by her, and listened to the carter's stories of other young girls who had made their fortunes in service. Finally his tales became so preposterous that Dorcas found herself laughing out loud, and telling him that he was a great liar.

She made out the names on the next signpost they passed. 'Is

Hereford as far as London?' she enquired; for no mileages were given.

'Nah. It's only a matter of six miles from Ashton Cross to town. London is more'n a hundred the other way.' The carter looked down at the little girl beside him. 'Hereford's west of the village, see. Other way, there's Ledbury, then you comes to Malvern — then Worcester.'

Dorcas considered these names. 'Was you ever in — er — Wuster?' she asked.

'Been there once.' The carter gazed into the distance. 'Went there with my old Dad when I was about your age. There was a murderer a-going to be hanged, so we took our bread and cheese and we made a day of it.

'Place was that hot it stank like a privy. We couldn't find a place to stand, not a hope in hell of getting near. The scaffold was up high, though, so we all got a good look in the end.

'Murderer was brought out wearin' a blue velvet coat, shirt with ruffles like I don't know what, velvet breeches — the lot. Cheeky beggar waved to the crowd — not a bit afraid, he warn't, not he! There was this woman done up like something the cat found, a-clingin' to the platform, screechin' up at him, "my darlin', my love" — all that sort of flannel. When they strung 'im up she had a sort of fit, an' they had to lug her away.

'Turned my stomach it did. I never been to Wuster since — can't think of the place without seeing that chap again, hauled up like I would a dog, gaspin' his life away. And all those folks watchin' and cheerin', just like it was a puppet show.'

The carter sighed. Dorcas, who had lost interest in his lugubrious narrative some minutes since, suddenly clutched his sleeve; for she'd seen a church spire come into view, 'Are we there?' she whispered fearfully.

'Near enough,' replied the carter, unconcerned. 'Near enough.'

They entered the suburbs of the city, passed the turnpike, and drove along lanes full of apple trees. Here and there was a market gardener's house, but there were also a number of new, red-brick villas, splendid residences the like of which Dorcas, used to decaying lath and plaster hovels, had never before seen or imagined. On reaching the city centre, they found themselves amidst all the noise and confusion of market day.

Dorcas gazed around her, incredulous. People milled about the wide city streets in their hundreds, pushing and elbowing, cursing and chattering. As they entered the High Town, Dorcas shrank back against the carter, convinced that the press of people here would overturn the cart or at least engulf it, and carry her off in an irresistible tide of humanity. 'There's a good crowd, see,' remarked the carter nonchalantly. 'Always is on market day, o' course.'

A flock of sheep was being driven, baa-ing and bleating, through the throng of people, their drovers cursed by pedestrians who slipped and fouled their shoes on sheep mire. The smell of the press of people, of horse-dung, of smoke, of rubbish and sewers, was overwhelming.

Rendered speechless by the sights thrown at her from all sides, gaping in incredulity at the colourful, well-stocked shops, at the beautifully dressed people, and half deafened by the clatter of boots and pattens on wet cobbles and by shrill voices seemingly always raised in anger, Dorcas felt the tears coming back again and would have sold her soul to go home to Ashton Cross.

To the ignorant village child, who had never seen a paved road or a stone-built house before, let alone such things as shops and civic buildings, the shabby country town seemed like Heaven and Hell mixed. The chiming of the Butter Market clock made her eyes widen and the hairs on the back of her neck rise; and the next thing she saw made her grab the carter's arm in absolute horror. 'Who's that?' she managed to articulate, her throat dry with fear.

'That? Where? Drat this crowd, can't bloody well move!' The carter swore at a boy who had run between the horse and the shafts of the cart before looking in the direction in which Dorcas still stared. 'Oh, them's only the old Methodists,' he said dismissively. 'They're here every market day.'

'Methodists?' Dorcas gaped at the tall man on the improvised platform a few feet away from her, at the enormous bearded figure who was thundering such terrible execrations and seemed to have his pale blue eyes fixed solely upon her.

'Aye.' The old man spat. 'A load of loonies they are. Harmless, though.' The carter, finally able to get through the crowd, moved on; but several minutes went by before Dorcas could no longer hear the voice of the Methodist preacher exhorting the market day crowd to repentance.

Glancing to her left as they turned down Broad Street — for the carter had decided to take a detour which would avoid the rest of the crowds — Dorcas saw the tower of a great building. Coming closer, she peered between the houses which surrounded it and stared at it hard, for it seemed to grow, almost, out of the green by which it was encircled. 'Is it a castle?' she enquired, pleased with herself that she'd recognized an example of the type.

'No. Castle was pulled down years ago,' said the carter. 'That's the Cathedral. Pretty ain't it?'

Dorcas shrugged. 'What's a cathedral?'

'A sort of church.' The carter glanced at the child. 'Stead of the rector, though, the bishop takes the services there.'

'Bishop?'

The carter, nonplussed in the face of such abysmal ignorance, gnawed at his gums. 'Bishop,' he repeated tartly. 'Big fat feller, wears a purple velvet weskit and his collar turned back to front. Gaiters on his legs. Got great bushy side whiskers, this one has.'

'Oh — like the Squire!' said Dorcas, feeling that she now understood.

The carter laughed. 'Aye,' he agreed. 'You've hit it there. Very like the Squire!' And he turned into a quieter street, where the noise of the market day crowd was quite inaudible.

Mercifully, the town itself was eventually left behind. Dorcas found herself riding through another suburb of new, square, red brick houses, all of which seemed like little palaces to the wide-eyed, still bemused child. The carter turned into the main thoroughfare again, but then he suddenly twitched the reins, and, leaving the high road, caused the horse to turn left, pulling the cart up a gentle rise to a newly built, double-fronted house surrounded by a large walled garden.

Reining in the horse, the carter tied him to a tree outside the house and then lifted Dorcas down. He picked up her few belongings, and led her, now quaking with fresh terror, down a narrow entry at the side of the house. This brought them to a kitchen door, on which he knocked loudly.

Dorcas tried to conceal herself in the malodorous folds of the man's brown frock, peering out like a frightened rabbit, and as ready to make a bolt for safety. She saw the kitchen door open, and found herself looking up at a tall young woman in a maid's print morning gown.

'G'day to you, Miss.' The carter touched his cap. 'Mrs Collins has sent you this.' He winked at the maid. 'You'll have to get her some milk and a cradle — she's nothin' but a babby!' He disentangled Dorcas from the folds of his smock, and presented her to the maid.

The woman looked at Dorcas, who was biting her thumb and was obviously not going to speak. The child eyed Maggie Stemp suspiciously.

Then Maggie grinned at Dorcas, showing two rows of bad teeth and red, receding gums. 'Come on in, child,' she said, her face a picture of benevolent amusement. 'I won't bite you!' She took Dorcas by the wrist and led her into the kitchen, a large, airy room with a floor, not of beaten earth, but of the most beautiful black and white marble tiles.

Hearing the carter's boots clattering on the slabs as he walked back down the entry, Dorcas slouched against the white-washed kitchen wall. Scowling, she pulled at a strand of her hair, and sniffed in a forlorn and hopeless sort of way while Maggie cut a piece of dough-cake for her, and poured out a glass of milk.

'Well, go on then — eat!' Maggie indicated the food. 'You do eat, I take it?' she enquired. 'Or are you just a bundle of ol' washing, with legs?'

Dorcas glared at her. Offended out of her terror, she grimaced angrily at Maggie. 'New out of the Box this mornin', this was!' she growled, shaking out the folds of the red velveteen dress. 'New!' she repeated, with impressive emphasis.

Maggie threw back her head and guffawed. Tears came into her eyes, and she shook with merriment. 'Oh, dear me,' she said at last, wiping her wet face on the back of her hand. 'You poor little bit of nothing, you!' She observed Dorcas' stricken expression, and made an effort to control her laughter. 'Don't mind me,' she mumbled, still choking. 'I'm sure that's a very nice dress you're wearing. Heavens — you should've seen me when they fetched me from the old workhouse six or seven years since! Bundle of bones and rags I was!'

Dorcas would say nothing more to such a horrible person. She was still glowering morosely at Maggie Stemp when a bell rang, deep in the recesses of the house, and Maggie got to her feet. 'That'll be Madam,' she remarked. 'I must go and see what she wants. Oh, eat up your cake, for the love of the Lord! Sit down here at the table and don't touch nothing but your food 'til I get back. Nothing! Do you understand?'

Dorcas glared at Maggie's retreating back. She gazed around her at the empty kitchen, an amazing place containing two blindingly white sinks, and a huge dresser upon which all manner of china dishes gleamed and various copper utensils shone. There was an enormous oak table and several smaller cabinets; but by far the most impressive sight was the vast black-leaded range, which gave off an enveloping, comforting warmth and a most delicious smell of baking. Dorcas sat down and reached across the table for the cake. She took a bite; found it was excellent, and bit it again. She tasted the milk, and made a face. Not having drunk any since she was weaned, she was suspicious of it — taking another sip, she decided that it was very much inferior to ale. She was still forcing it down when two women came into the kitchen.

'Good day to you, Dorcas,' said the small, dark haired lady who stood by Maggie Stemp.

'This is Miss Lane, child,' added Maggie. 'Say, "a very good morning to you, Madam" — do!'

Dorcas said nothing at all.

Miss Lane smiled kindly at her new maidservant. 'She's extremely small,' she observed. 'I thought Mrs Collins said she was ten — she looks more like seven to me. Poor child, she's frightened out of her wits!' Miss Lane turned to Maggie. 'Tidy her up and find something which will fit her; then you can bring her to me in the morning room. You'd better heat some water and give her a bath,' she added. 'And wash her hair.'

Doras was outraged. About to point out that she was, as it happened, both perfectly clean and decently clad, she had just opened her mouth to say as much when the lady smiled at her again and then turned away, sweeping out of the kitchen in a sweet-scented rustle of silks.

Her initial unmixed terror now abating a little, Dorcas remained at the kitchen table and finished her milk, taking a good long stare at the housemaid as she did so. Maggie Stemp was busying herself in some task at one of the sinks, chattering all the time about her employer, her work, and Dorcas' own good fortune at having come to work at such a house for such a mistress. Dorcas listened intently, never taking her eyes off the speaker for a moment.

She decided that Maggie Stemp reminded her of a scarecrow. In truth, eighteen-year-old Maggie was achingly plain. Nearly six feet tall, very thin and lacking any pretension whatsoever to a bosom, the housemaid's figure was quite undistinguished, as unprepossessing as her face. Maggie's narrow visage was dominated by a high-bridged, large nose; she suffered from a bad complexion, and her teeth were big and crooked, very much discoloured. Her small, mud-coloured eyes, fringed with sparse, sandy lashes, had peered short-sightedly at Dorcas, who had noticed that one of them was disfigured by an unpleasant, weeping stye ...

But then the scarecrow turned from her work to face the little girl — and she smiled. And when Maggie Stemp smiled, her whole countenance took on such an expression of goodwill that whoever saw it would never have called her ugly. That smile illuminated her plain face, and made the beholder's heart lighten.

Now that she was rested and fed, no longer shaking with fear and bristling with hurt pride, the new servant found Maggie's grin extremely comforting. Her reserve began to thaw. She answered Maggie's questions about her home, appreciated Maggie's sympathetic cluckings when the housemaid heard how sad the child had been to leave her mother back at Ashton Cross. 'You come along with me now,' invited Maggie, holding out her large, clumsy, reddened hand.

'Where are we going?'

'Just upstairs. And we'll find you a pretty dress, shall we? You can keep that one for best, if you like.' Maggie opened the kitchen door. 'That's the way,' she encouraged. 'Give me a bit of a smile! You're really a very pretty little girl, aren't you? Hasn't anyone ever told you so before?'

The household in which Dorcas found herself consisted of Miss Lane, a single lady in her middle thirties; her housemaid, Maggie Stemp; her cook, Mrs Butler; and now Dorcas herself. A jobbing gardener came in daily. No men lived in the house, which was large enough to house a sizeable family.

The only child of a successful shopkeeper, Maria Lane was a woman of substantial means and charitable inclinations. She spent much of her time sitting on committees considering the condition of the urban and rural poor, the plight of the heathens in various parts of the Empire, and the misery of fallen women. As chairwoman of numerous charities, Miss Lane raised funds for every conceivable good cause, spoke at innumerable functions and wore herself out doing good.

On his death, she had sold her father's business, and now she lived very comfortably in his house on the interest from his investments. She was, however, no mere fund-raiser. She was well-educated and well read — 'always got her head stuck in a book, she has — wearing out her poor eyes,' said Maggie censoriously. Maggie had no use whatsoever for literature.

Dorcas had been brought to the house to be trained. At the end of a year, she would be free to find herself another, better job. Maggie set about instructing the ignorant, nervous child with great — and infectious — enthusiasm.

Not until several years had passed did Dorcas really appreciate how lucky she'd been to find herself in such a household. At first, the work seemed impossibly hard and totally exhausting. Rising at six-thirty to clean the house, light the fires, prepare the cook's and the mistress's breakfast before she had had anything to eat or drink herself tired Dorcas out. There was so much cleaning to be done — there were wooden parquet floors to be washed, dried and beeswaxed, carpets to be sprinkled with used tea leaves and brushed to a deep-piled finish; furniture to polish to a fine gloss, silver to clean with jeweller's wadding, doorsteps to whiten — and, worst of all, that great iron range to clean and blacklead every single day. To Dorcas, whose own mother's housekeeping had been of the most perfunctory nature, such violent exertion merely to keep what was already clean positively sparkling, seemed utterly absurd. 'It's clean, Maggie! I've polished it till my arms fair ache!' she moaned one morning, as the senior housemaid pursed her lips over Dorcas' efforts to bring the chiffonier in the dining room up to Maggie's exacting standards of shining perfection.

'Call that clean?' Maggie trailed one finger through the barely perceptible layer of dust which disgraced one little moulding. 'It's still filthy! Good heavens, child — what sort of a pigsty were you born in if you call that clean? Eh?' She wagged one finger at Dorcas. 'Do it again — and this time do it proper!'

On wash days it was even worse. The maids rose at six to sort and to wash the household's linen, a back-breaking task indeed. Dorcas scrubbed, blued, starched and rinsed, mangled and pegged out, yawning when she remembered that later on all this lot had to be ironed. And Miss Lane was so particular about her sheets — one little crease would be enough to have her complaining to Maggie, and then Maggie would glare at Dorcas. 'Don't be such a little sloven,' she would say. 'Don't they have such things as irons where you come from?'

But Maggie, a model of efficiency, eventually licked her junior into shape, and turned Dorcas into a housemaid. If they went at it with a will all morning, often their work was completed by two in the afternoon. 'Now we'll go out for a bit of air,' Maggie would announce, grinning. 'Get your shawl.' The maids were encouraged to take an afternoon walk, a thing unheard of in most households, where the servants' only free time was a grudgingly-allowed afternoon off once a fortnight.

Frequently Maggie took Dorcas into town, where the country child gaped at the shops and was afraid of the masses of people moving to and fro. But gradually these small provincial shops began to afford Dorcas enormous pleasure — the sheer variety of goods on display fascinated her. 'Where does it all come from, Maggie?' she would ask, gazing at the sacks of different sugars, the dried fruits, the jars of spices and the endless blends of teas and coffees in a perfectly ordinary grocer's shop.

'What d'you say?' Maggie had no interest in where things came from, only in if they were fit to go into the kitchen of the new house in the suburbs. 'Where does it come from, you say? Well — them oranges comes from the London markets, I suppose. And the sugar comes from the West Indies; look, it says so on the sack. Barbados, I think it is. What d'you want to know for?'

Dorcas couldn't answer that. She would grin at Maggie and turn away to examine something else which had caught her fancy.

She now liked a market day crowd. On a Wednesday afternoon she loved to wander around the High Town, watching the drovers and the farmers, both so different from the smartly dressed townspeople. And she liked to listen to the blarney of the patent medicine men, and to the thundering denunciations of the travelling evangelists, who no longer seemed to be directing their righteous wrath solely at her.

To Dorcas it was a never-ending source of wonderment that a real lady like Miss Lane should do some of her own gardening. Whyever, she would ask herself, should anyone willingly dirty their hands in such a tedious pursuit? Not content merely to dabble in the conservatory, Miss Lane weeded, dug and planted in the half acre of garden which surrounded her house. The daily man did the heavy work, of course — he mowed the lawns, tended the vegetables and made the bonfires. But Miss Lane looked after her favourite flowering shrubs, pruned her own roses and tied up the climbing plants which adorned the garden walls. Her particular pride was her rhododendrons, which grew in specially constructed peat borders, and blazed gloriously in late spring.

Standing in the yard on fine washing days, up to her elbows in soapsuds while she scrubbed the household's underclothes, Dorcas would stare at the mistress fiddling with the new growth on her rambler roses, snipping out weak shoots and tying in sappy new canes. 'Get on with your work!' Maggie cried, one fine summer day. 'Lord bless me, Dorcas Grey — I've never known such a gawper as you are!' She marched over and shut the gate separating the garden from the back yard. 'It's not right that you should stare at Madam like that,' she muttered. 'Have you done that blueing yet? Don't squeeze the bag like that — you'll burst it!'

The year came to an end. No mention was made of Dorcas finding another situation, and she herself had no wish to leave Miss Lane. She dreaded being called in to see her mistress, told that she must now find herself another position. 'Might she let me stay?' the little maid asked Maggie. 'I should like to stay ...'

Maggie grinned. 'She ain't said nothing about you going,' she remarked. 'So don't you mention it, either.'

Maggie Stemp was as good as a mother to Dorcas. It was she who first explained to the child how babies were conceived and born, and who prepared Dorcas for the shock of her first menstruation. The country girl's gormlessness had amazed Maggie. 'You,

47

brought up on a farm, not knowing how a babby is made — who'd have thought it!' exclaimed Maggie, incredulous.

Dorcas shrugged, unable to defend her ignorance. But, as a field hand, she had had little contact with animals and had taken no notice of whatever sexual activity she had witnessed among them. Nor had she had older siblings to frighten her with tales of childbirth or monthly bleeding. Other labourers' children might have observed the necessarily public displays of affection between their parents, and even attended at the births of their brothers and sisters, Dorcas had not. It was only after Maggie had explained the technicalities of human sexual congress that Dorcas understood the reason for the muffled sounds she had heard coming from downstairs in her cottage at Ashton Cross, when Ellen had had a man from the village in 'for a bit of a chat, like'.

Dorcas accepted everything Maggie said without question. 'I won't speak to no errand boys,' she promised. 'I won't have no hugging nor kissing. I don't like men, anyway — they're coarse and they're dirty and they smell.' She grinned complacently. 'Maggie, I'll always stay with you and Miss Lane,' she declared.

Maggie smiled, regretfully. 'That you won't,' she remarked, sadly. 'Some man will come along and like your pretty face — then that'll be that.'

Dorcas, worried, mulled over what she had been told. That business of doing awful things with a man could easily be avoided, but the idea of the monthly bleeding frightened her. It appeared, from what Maggie said, that it was inevitable. But surely it was too horrible an idea to be really true? Maggie might have made a mistake. Dorcas, lying in the big bed she shared with Maggie, pulled the quilts over her head. She decided that even Maggie couldn't know everything. She snuggled into Maggie's bony embrace, and, warm and comfortable, fell asleep.

But Maggie had been right about the horrors to come. When, one morning, Dorcas woke to find herself sticky with blood, Maggie told her that it was long overdue, and helped her to tear up some old linen sheeting into strips. The child cried and cried, doubled up with the pains and cramps which marked her initiation into woman-hood. 'I'm bleeding to death,' she wept. 'Maggie, I'll die!'

'You won't.' Maggie began to stitch several thicknesses of linen together. 'Get up now.'

'I can't!' Dorcas clutched at her stomach. 'Maggie, I can't!'

'Oh, don't be such a crybaby!' Maggie, irked by this display of melodramatics, frowned severely at her junior. 'It'll all be over in a few days!'

'Days? Then I shall die — I know I shall!' moaned Dorcas theatrically.

'Then I hope you've made your will.' Maggie gave Dorcas a sideways grimace before telling her she could stay in bed. 'I'll bring you up a hot brick in a blanket,' she promised. 'You can hold it against your stomach.'

Dorcas spent the rest of the day complaining and fretting, threatening to expire at any minute. By the following morning Maggie's sympathy was exhausted, and she made Dorcas get up. So the girl was obliged to struggle through her daily tasks, bleeding, chafing and sore, uncomfortable and distressed, her stomach in spasm and her head aching, feeling that this common affliction of her sex was rightly called the curse. She suffered and grizzled for three days more. Then, miraculously, the flow slowed down to a brownish trickle and stopped altogether.

It was with enormous relief that Dorcas collected the accumulated soiled towels from their bucket of salty water and boiled them up in a copper pan kept for the purpose. 'There they go — all on the line,' said Maggie cheerfully, as they pegged out the linen strips along with the rest of the washing. 'You're a woman now.' She wrinkled her nose. 'And you're a very smelly one,' she added fastidiously. 'You'd better have a bath, 'cos you stink like a butcher's shop. You'll have all the dogs in Hereford following you!'

Dorcas was not only a woman; she was becoming a very pretty woman. She reached her adult height at fourteen, a good eight inches shorter than Maggie's gangling six feet. She developed a nicely rounded bosom and shapely hips and noticed, not with displeasure, that she had become the object of countless stares, winks and ogles from all kinds of men. She was grinned at in that particular fashion by practically every man she saw, from the delivery boys to the piano tuner, who was at least seventy years old and apparently made of starch and cardboard.

All this attention both gratified and rather embarrassed her. 'What do they stare at?' she wondered. 'Why do they grin at me so?'

She needed to know what she looked like. One morning, when Maggie was out delivering some leaflets for her mistress, who was herself up to the elbows in soil in her conservatory, and the cook was busy with her weekly pastry bake, Dorcas stole up to one of the attic rooms and quickly took off all her clothes.

In the corner of the room there was a large Georgian mirror, propped up against a chest of drawers. Cloudy with bloom and spotting, the looking glass was, Dorcas decided, good enough for the purpose. Standing in a pool of sunlight coming in from the small skylight window, she examined herself from every angle — feeling indefinably wicked and furtive as she did so, but exhilarated at the same time.

She noted the dark smudge of hair which had appeared at the tops of her legs and she wondered if it ought to be there. She eyed her bosom critically, taking her breasts in her hands and testing their weight, pressing her nipples with her fingers and feeling an odd but exciting sensation shimmer through her as she did so. Then she raised her arms above her head and turned around slowly, getting a good view of her bottom and the tops of her thighs. All in all, she supposed she was pleased with what she saw. She unloosed her hair and let it tumble over her shoulders, liking the feel of the silky softness of it caressing her warm skin. Her face, small, heart-shaped and perfectly symmetrical, smiled back at her from inside the mirror, her large dark eyes, straight nose and full, red lips telling her that she was a beauty. She hugged herself in delight. 'You're pretty,' she told herself, blissfully aware that this was not simply her own vanity speaking. 'You're the prettiest girl in Hereford!'

Downstairs a door slammed and, suddenly, Dorcas felt ashamed. She dressed as fast as she could, knotting tapes awkwardly, mismatching buttons. She went clattering downstairs noisily, to get on with her household tasks.

That night, Dorcas did not snuggle close to Maggie. She had suddenly outgrown her need for childish embraces. Maggie seemed to sense it, for she no longer hugged Dorcas to her bony bosom, no longer cuddled her like a little sister. It was now that the inevitable divisions between a very pretty woman and an extremely plain one began to make themselves felt. So, while Maggie and Dorcas remained excellent friends, the physical closeness they had once shared was, by mutual consent, greatly diminished.

Chapter Four

A T ABOUT THE SAME TIME that Dorcas was becoming aware of her physical attributes, was spending time putting her hair up in the most becoming fashion and taking the trouble to trim her bonnets as fetchingly as she could, she was also beginning to regret her own ignorance and almost total lack of education. It worried her that she could not read anything but the simplest road sign or shop advertisement. She longed to read stories, but books and magazines were an impossibility while even recipes were beyond her skill. It was all very well, she reflected, having a face which might break hearts — but to what real use could such an asset be put if she were to remain an illiterate housemaid? She was determined to teach herself to read.

One Sunday, when the family had been to church and the cold midday meal eaten and cleared away, Dorcas went into the silent kitchen and took down one of the cook's stained, grimy recipe folders. She sat with it open on the table in front of her, willing the sense of the words to make itself known to her.

For half an hour she sat there, doggedly trying to decipher a word or two. But the recipe book might just as well have been written in Chinese for all the sense it yielded to Dorcas.

'That's the great "O", and there's "A",' she muttered to herself. 'There's "r", and "p". But what does it mean? What does it say?' The inscrutable words brought her near to tears. She was tracing her finger across the line at the top of a page, unable to make any sense of it at all, when Miss Lane's bell rang. But Dorcas did not hear it. Nor did she take any notice when her mistress came into the room just a few minutes later.

A swish and a rustle of silk by her side made Dorcas start. She stared at her employer, then jumped up muttering apologies. 'I'm sorry, Madam. I didn't know what the time was — I'll bring your tea in now.'

Miss Lane smiled. 'So you are a scholar, Dorcas?' she asked.

Dorcas grimaced, pushed a stray lock of hair back into place. 'A dullard more like, Madam,' she replied. 'I've been trying to understand the recipe. I know my letters — but I can't make out the *words*!' She finished her sentence in a wail of exasperation, and looked forlornly at the battered book in front of her.

Miss Lane raised her eyebrows. 'Such industry,' she remarked. 'Dorcas — spell out this word here.'

Dorcas looked. 'P-a-n-c-a-k-e,' she faltered.

'Quite right. Pancake. Can you not hear the letters telling you so?' Miss Lane turned a page. 'Now, what about that word there?' she asked. 'Make a guess.'

Dorcas considered. 'Salt?' she hazarded.

'Salt, if you say so. S-a-l-t. Is that it? My eyes will not allow me to read such small print. Now — be a good girl and bring my tea-things into the drawing room, and we shall see what can be done with you.'

Dorcas did as she was told. She made the tea, set out her mistress's meal with her usual neatness and efficiency. Miss Lane took a book from her bureau and handed it to her maid. 'Sit down, Dorcas,' she said. 'Look at this while I drink my tea.'

Over the next few weeks, Miss Lane taught her maid to read. It was not difficult — the student was diligent and anxious to learn, the teacher patient and thorough. Very little more than a month later Dorcas could read a page of print almost faultlessly. Interpreting handwriting took somewhat longer, but she mastered it in the end. Finally she learned to write a clear, neat copperplate hand. 'Now you shall be my secretary, Dorcas,' said Miss Lane, whose failing eyesight made it important that she should spare her eyes from small print whenever she could; but whose many commitments and love of literature made this almost impossible.

Mrs Butler the cook, to whom literacy had come hard and unwillingly, was quick to make use of a new pair of eyes. Glad to be spared the bother of deciphering a recipe for herself, she would ask Dorcas to read it out to her. 'Just that bit there, could you, my ducky?' she would ask, almost every day now. 'My eyes ain't as young as yours, see.'

Maggie Stemp, who hardly knew her alphabet and who had been used to regard reading as an utter waste of time, took to buying cheap serialized novelettes and penny magazines for Dorcas to read out to the group sitting around the kitchen fire in the evenings. Dorcas found such stuff tedious in the extreme. Only her affection for Maggie, who would gasp and gape at the more preposterous parts, and ask that they should be read out again, could have made Dorcas endure such rubbish.

But she loved to read aloud to Miss Lane. Her mistress's father had been an avid subscriber to the periodicals, and had actually bought books, real books. The works of Dickens were much in evidence, bound in their serial parts; on winter afternoons Dorcas would be called into the drawing room to read from *Nicholas Nickleby* or the *Pickwick Papers*, Miss Lane's particular favourites. Rejoicing in her newly-acquired skill, the girl read and read until her voice became hoarse, and her mistress would tell her to finish for the time being. 'We'll find out what happens tomorrow,' she would say mildly, as Dorcas reluctantly marked the place and closed the book.

Dorcas was allowed to take Miss Lane's own books away with her, and would lie in bed reading until her candle gave out and Maggie had been snoring on her back for hours. But in vain did the younger girl try to interest her fellow servant in the novels of Fielding or Jane Austen. Maggie's tastes were unrefined, and not even the more salacious passages from *Tom Jones*, nor the more meltingly romantic parts of *Pride and Prejudice*, could wean her from her diet of trash. 'I don't want to hear that old nonsense,' Maggie would announce dismissively. 'Give us a bit more of *The Duchess's Disgrace*.'

'Oh, Maggie!'

'No? Well then — what about *The Heart's True Love*? Or a bit of that murder serial I bought on Tuesday. Makes my skin prickle something awful, that do!'

'Really, Maggie! It's obvious who killed her!' But, to oblige her friend, Dorcas would read out a further instalment of a banal, gruesome, utterly predictable tale until her bedmate's yawns indicated that she had supped full of horrors and was ready to go to sleep. Then, with a comfortable stretch and a peaceful sigh, Maggie would settle down to a contented slumber, prophesying that she would see the ghost of Lady Cecilia as sure as eggs were eggs. Dorcas would then get on with *Persuasion* or *Emma*, undisturbed except for the other maid's grunts, snorts and convulsive jerks.

Maggie's aversion to Dickens became permanently fixed after Dorcas borrowed Miss Lane's bound copy of *Oliver Twist*, to read aloud to Mrs Butler during the long winter evenings. Maggie had sat fidgeting while Dorcas read the first chapter — then, unable to stand it any longer, she had let out a squeal of distress. She had thrown her apron over her head and relapsed into a fit of bitter sobbing, while Dorcas stared at her in astonishment. 'There there, Maggie,' she said, patting her friend's heaving shoulder. 'It's just a story — it isn't true!'

But Maggie's muffled sobs continued, unabated.

Mrs Butler, who had sat as placid and cheerful as ever while Maggie's outburst had been going on, leaned forward and tapped Dorcas on the knee. 'She come from the old workhouse,' she remarked, indicating Maggie. 'Had a hard time of it there, by all accounts. An' you readin' all that stuff 'elped to bring it all back, I 'spec. Couldn't we 'ave something a bit more jolly, like?'

So Dorcas, unhappy to have upset poor Maggie, read the triumphantly ridiculous conclusion to her friend's current novelette; then made her a cup of hot chocolate to help restore Maggie's spirits to their usual high level.

Every summer, Dorcas had two weeks' holiday at Ashton Cross. Her first visit home, after eight months in service, had been wonderful. She could still remember being beside herself with joy as the carter had brought her to her mother's gate, could still feel the warmth of her mother's embrace as she hugged her precious child to her chest, squeezing the breath from her little body. Ellen had been agog to hear the details of her daughter's life in service, had fingered the girl's neat, well-fitting print dress in delight. The fortnight had rushed by, leaving Dorcas to wonder how she would manage to get through the next twelve months without seeing her beloved mother again.

But the second time she had gone home, it had all been so different. She had packed and waited for the carter with mounting impatience, had seen the village come into sight with eager anticipation. 'Here you are, then,' said the carter, grinning. 'Home.'

'Yes. Home.' Dorcas had stared, wondering why she felt so appalled by the sight of it ...

But by the time she had climbed down from the cart, she knew why. It was because she had seen the village for what it actually was: a haphazard collection of decrepit, malodorous slums, clustered around a scrubby, muddy green. And the mother who rushed out to greet her so lovingly was an unwashed, dishevelled slattern, whose embrace seemed likely to defile her daughter.

'Dorry?' Ellen had stood back from her child, looked at her anxiously. 'Anything wrong, my dear?'

Ashamed of herself, Dorcas had shaken her head, and forced a watery smile. She had tried to return her mother's enthusiastic greeting, but she had been shrinking inside.

'Come in then, dear. Supper's all made.' Ellen led the way indoors.

The interior of her once beloved home now looked quite awful to her. Dorcas gazed disgusted at the horrible dirt floor, stared in distaste at the walls down which the condensation streamed and upon which fungus and mildew grew in a hundred fantastic shapes. The cockroaches which lurked in the cracks, the rats who scuffled about the loft and the mice who squeaked in corners revolted her newly-refined sensibilities and she longed for Miss Lane's house, for her clean bed and for real linen sheets. Her mother's bedding, unchanged from one year to the next, stank abominably.

The whole house was uncomfortable to her now. Dorcas, accustomed to regular washing of her clothes and of herself, was constantly aware of how dirty the place was. She could just about manage to keep herself clean but if she tried to wash any of her clothes, the water pot boiled over on to the fire, filling the whole cottage with bitter, acrid woodsmoke and making Ellen curse. 'What did you want to wash it for?' she demanded one day, crossly poking at the blouse simmering on the hearth. 'Twarn't dirty!'

'Yes, it was.' Dorcas snatched her precious best blouse out of her mother's grubby hands. 'And it's even dirtier now,' she added, unable to stop herself.

'Oh.' Ellen returned the garment and wiped her wet hands on her apron. 'Well — since you got a good fire goin', we'll make some toast, shall we? Leave that old washin', eh?'

It was hopeless. Dorcas gave up, and wore the same clothes for the rest of the fortnight.

She was miserable for the whole of that holiday, so much so that Ellen was concerned and asked her if she was sickening for something. Dorcas could not explain that she'd already sickened — that she had become aware, for the first time, of the poverty and degradation of the labourers' lives. During that traumatic visit home, she heard the coarse talk of the men with disgust; she was offended by the sight of so many ragged infants, stained with their own filth; and she observed the casual cruelty of the children, to animals and to each other, with loathing. No amount of maternal affection could compensate for all this — she was bitterly ashamed to have come from such a place.

'I'll never go back to live there,' she told herself. 'Never. I'd sooner die.'

Ellen, on the other hand, took an embarrassing pride in her daughter. Having been a good-looking girl herself, the mother had naturally hoped to see beauty in her child, but Dorcas' looks exceeded even Mrs Grey's expectations. Regular washing, a sufficient diet and habitual neatness had improved Dorcas' face and figure to an extraordinary degree. Her dark brown hair shone; her skin was a rich, dusky, unblemished rose. And something about the set of her features and her grace of carriage made her seem more like a lady than a peasant. 'If only your Dad could see you,' remarked Ellen, tears coming into her eyes. 'If only Mike could look at you! He'd be so proud — that he would!'

Dorcas was in the habit of taking the weekly grocery order in to Follet's store, the shop in the High Town where Miss Lane had dealt since her parents died. In her early years in service, the little maid had merely handed the book over to the assistant and retreated, blushing, without a word.

But when she learned to read, everything changed. She would now linger in the shop, inspecting, comparing, even criticizing goods, making up a great part of the order there and then, basing her judgements on the quality of the produce available. Miss Lane's order was always a worthwhile one, so Dorcas always received as much attention as a pretty girl, with a fair amount of business to transact, could reasonably expect.

When Dorcas was fifteen, Daniel Hitchman came to work at Follet's. A tall, fair-haired, serious young man who had once been apprenticed to a butcher, he had quarrelled with his master and been released from his indentures. He had been taken on by Mr Follet as a general provisions trainee.

Daniel proved to be good at his job. He did not complain about the very long hours he was expected to work, and he was polite to the customers, deferential without being servile, quick and efficient without the obvious haste and brusqueness which customers always found unsettling. He was thus quickly promoted, over the heads of other, older assistants, causing some degree of grumbling behind his back.

'Fancies himself something terrible, does Hitchman,' muttered one assistant, passed over for the pay rise which Mr Follett's blue-eyed boy had recently received. 'Thinks he's it, just 'cause he can slice bacon nice and thin, just 'cause he can joint a ham in five minutes, all neat and tidy. He's going to be a bit too clever one of these fine days!'

But Daniel continued to do well, and was also seen to become a favourite with the lady customers. He in turn was observed to take a fancy to Dorcas Grey.

He made sure that he was always in the shop every Tuesday afternoon, when she came in with her order book. Without actually saying anything, he made it clear that he would deal with Miss Lane's order from then on. So successful was he in intimidating the others that when one day Maggie Stemp brought the order in, Dorcas having a heavy cold, no one went to serve her. She coughed expectantly then stood, puzzled, for a full two minutes until, suddenly, five assistants descended on her in a rush. Daniel meanwhile stood aloof, arms folded; extremely put out by the non-appearance of Miss Lane's pretty servant.

Daniel remained a favourite with Mr Follett; and although his manners disgusted Maggie Stemp he continued to amass a female following of some magnitude. He had a certain magnetism which drew women to him and held them there fascinated. His rare, but inexpressibly charming smile was bewitching. And when Miss Grey came into the shop, Daniel seemed to use up a week's good humour in five minutes. Dorcas, young, innocent and guileless as she was, well-disposed to anyone who was pleasant to her, responded in kind to Daniel's amiability. She returned his smiles, listened to his recommendations, and was happy to spend twenty minutes dawdling with him over business which could have been transacted in half the time.

Daniel found means to brush her hand with his as he invited her to feel the weight of an orange or a lemon, or offered her a sample of some currants or other dried fruit. Scooping up a handful of coffee beans, he would hold them close to her face and suggest that she inhale the aroma. 'Best Brazilian,' he murmured one afternoon, his gaze wandering over her face, noting that today her hair was becomingly curled and that she had a new bonnet on. 'But perhaps you'd like to consider the other varieties? Before you decide?'

'Maybe.' Dorcas found this game quite beguiling. 'Which do you recommend, Mr Hitchman? I'll always be guided by you.'

'Then take the Brazilian. You won't be disappointed.'

'I'm sure I shan't.' Dorcas giggled. 'And you'd better send up six lemons. I'll take your word for it that they'll not be dry.'

'You'll receive the best in the shop,' replied Daniel, smiling in return.

Flattered by so much solicitous attention, Dorcas' already well-developed vanity was stirred. Previously unknown sensations tended to bother her agreeably if her hand came into accidential contact with Mr Hitchman's.

And Daniel had beautiful hands. Strong, hard, very clean, the skin was smooth, and unblemished by prominent veins or hairs. His fingers were long and well-shaped, and in perfect proportion to each other; his nails well-cut and square. Dorcas found herself wondering if the rest of Daniel was just as fine …

Daniel met Dorcas by pure but remarkable chance as she and Maggie strolled on the Castle Green one fine Sunday afternoon. He greeted Dorcas with enthusiasm and even remembered to nod to Maggie. Dorcas smiled back at him so fetchingly that he proposed a walk over to the river, to look at the extent of the recent floods.

Maggie slipped naturally into her role of duenna. She walked along a little apart from the other two and was not surprised to see Dorcas take Daniel's arm when the pair of them reached a low-lying, marshy area. Maggie hung back still further and watched them as they walked across the flood meadows together. 'How nice they look,' she said to herself, 'together like that, side by side!'

She observed that Daniel looked very handsome in his Sunday

clothes. Six feet tall and very well made, with square shoulders and a broad, deep chest, he could have been a soldier. His fair hair was thick, brushing the tops of his ears and falling in straight golden swathes from a neat centre parting. As Daniel and Dorcas turned, and walked back towards her, she studied his face. 'Perhaps he's a bit too heavy round the cheeks to be really handsome,' she thought. 'He'll be fat and double-chinned one day if he doesn't take care. But he has got a nice straight nose, and his eyes are a fine, clear blue — he'll do very well for my Dorry.'

No future arrangements to meet were made, but every Sunday afternoon following that one, Dorcas and Maggie happened to encounter Daniel somewhere in the town. Maggie told Dorcas that Miss Lane ought to be informed. 'Have a word, Dorry,' she advised. 'Before one of them old cats on her Fallen Women committee finds out, and tells her you got a follower. It ain't as if you're doing anythin' wrong, not with me along to look after you. But Madam ought to know about it.'

Dorcas blushed. 'But it's nothing, Maggie!' she protested. 'There's nothing to tell her. What would I say? If you think she should know that we happen to meet Mr Hitchman now and then, couldn't you tell her?'

'All right then.' Maggie grinned at her embarrassed junior. 'I'll have a word.'

When Maggie had her word, Miss Lane removed her spectacles, looked hard at the senior housemaid; then, she smiled. 'Keep a close eye on our little Dorcas,' she said. 'Don't let her go astray!' So the meetings were officially sanctioned and the way for conversation and courtship lay smooth and straight ahead.

But, as far as conversation went, it soon became clear that Daniel had very little to say. While he and Dorcas strolled about together, while Maggie examined the birds, grass and butterflies a discreet distance from the other two, it was only Dorcas who chattered. Her companion merely nodded or smiled in reply. She thought he must be shy. It never occurred to Dorcas, whose mind constantly hummed with a thousand ideas and fancies, that Daniel's brain might be simply empty.

One day she asked him what he liked to read. He screwed up his face and frowned at her. 'I don't read,' he replied at last. 'I haven't the time.'

Dorcas smiled up at him. 'Oh, but you ought to make the time,' she said firmly. 'If you like, I will lend you some of my books — Miss Lane has given me a dozen or more, and I have some which I'm sure you'd enjoy.'

Daniel reddened then, muttered something which she did not catch. He cleared his throat. 'The truth is, Miss Grey,' he muttered, 'the fact is, I don't find that reading comes very easy ...' He looked down at his boots.

Dorcas, overcome with embarrassment herself now, and upset to have put him out of countenance, blushed just as scarlet as he had. 'That's nothing to be ashamed of,' she said earnestly. 'I've only recently learned to read myself and I love it so much that I think everyone else must do so, too. Maggie hates it,' she added lamely.

He stared at her, indignant that she had dared to suggest that he might have anything at all in common with Maggie Stemp. But Dorcas rattled on, regardless. 'Maggie likes me to read to her, though,' she continued. 'Perhaps you'd like it if someone were to read to you!'

She stopped walking then — for, her face on fire, she'd just realized the implication of what she'd said. Her private thoughts and daydreams which had, for some weeks past, filled her mind with visions of herself and Daniel seated on either side of a fire, a cradle at her knee and a child as blond as he was on his lap, had raced on ahead of her. She wished the earth would swallow her up.

They had walked through a small clump of trees. Maggie was a tactful hundred yards distant, out of sight behind some shrubberies. Daniel took one of Dorcas' gloved hands in his, and looked into her eyes. 'I'd like it if you were to read to me,' he said simply. 'I'd like it very much indeed.' Then he bent over her and kissed her, very quickly and lightly, on the lips.

Chapter Five

OLD MR LAWRENCE DIED, LEAVING the whole of the Ashton Cross estate, where Dorcas had been born and brought up and where her mother still lived, to his elder son Stephen. A convinced believer in male primogeniture, determined that his death would not precipitate the division of an estate handed down from father to eldest son for five or six generations, the old squire had left his heir a rich man. But his second son, his wife and his daughter were virtually unprovided for.

Having graduated from university in the summer of 1866, Stephen was gratified that his excellent First now entitled him to a fellowship. He had not, however, made up his mind whether to accept it, for he intended to follow his own inclinations for some years yet. He was therefore very annoyed to be abruptly recalled from his travels in Europe by the news of his father's sudden death.

It had been brought on, he suspected, by over-indulgence and excess; it was almost as if the old man had had a stroke merely to irritate his son. Crumpling the letter from his mother into a ball and flinging it into a corner of the room, Stephen grimaced at his travelling companion, like himself a recent graduate.

'Bad news, eh?' demanded Fred Dawlish, helping himself to fresh bread and coffee.

'My father's died.' Stephen's scowl deepened. 'Damn him.'

Fred raised his eyebrows. 'Oh, steady on,' he remonstrated. He grinned. 'The old fellow hasn't cut you off without a penny, has he?'

'No.' Stephen stared up at the ceiling. 'No, it's not that.' He stook up, kicking back his chair as he did so. 'Fred, I shall have to go home. Can you get back to Athens by yourself? Have you sufficient cash?'

Fred, a younger son who was kept short anyway, shook his

head. 'I'll come back to England with you,' he said. 'Oh, cheer up, man, do! Think of it — how many thousands a year will it be?'

Stephen sniffed. 'I've no idea,' he replied indifferently, and slouched moodily out of the room.

Arriving in Hereford by train, Stephen hired a horse at the livery stables. He rode through the damp, sullen gloom of the English autumn afternoon thinking with longing of the blue skies of Greece, of the towns of the Attic peninsula, of the Ionian islands so lately visited — and of the black-haired, beautiful women.

Especially he thought of the women. He scowled to himself when he reflected that months of celibacy lay ahead, during which he would have to cope with his mother's hysterics, his sister's moaning and his brother's surliness, not to mention his tenants' complaints and his land-agent's officiousness, all without the solace of any female flesh. He was bitterly aware that he'd have to get what exercise he could on the hunting field, which did not compare at all with an hour or two in bed with a warm, willing girl.

It was all as tiresome as he'd anticipated. Mrs Lawrence began to complain as soon as he entered the house; his land-agent was lying in wait for him the first morning after his return. Stephen went into his father's study, where, gritting his teeth, he beckoned to the land-agent to follow him in.

Over the next few days, he tried to think himself into the role of the country squire but without any real success, for his mind was always elsewhere, his thoughts of anything but the Ashton Cross estate. Determined not to shirk his tedious responsibilities, however, and needing something to occupy his energies until he could decently return to the Continent, he sat down with the land-agent and together they went over the estate's books.

To his surprise, Mr Tatlow found that the young man was a quite different sort of fellow from his father. The old squire had been perfectly content to leave the whole management of the estate to his underlings, desiring only that the agents and bailiffs would collect the rents, oversee the tenant farms and keep the peasants in their place. Tatlow murmured as much to Stephen. 'This isn't really a gentleman's task, sir,' he'd said patronizingly. 'I don't think you need actively concern yourself with all this paperwork. I'm here to take that burden from your shoulders, after all.'

Stephen had looked up from a ledger. 'The affairs of the estate *are* my concern, Mr Tatlow,' he replied. 'Now — could you explain this deficit here? There must be some quite simple explanation for five hundred pounds apparently disappearing into thin air. You can tell me what it is.'

Tatlow sighed. The last thing he wanted was a master who understood the running of his own estate, poking, prying, asking more awkward questions. He frowned and racked his brains. Five hundred pounds must have been about the sum he'd needed for refurnishing his house the previous spring. 'The money didn't disappear, sir,' he said unctuously. 'It was used for re-fencing all that common land up near the Barton. It hasn't been entered, sir, that's all.'

'I see.' Stephen looked unconvinced. 'Then perhaps you could make sure that, in future, the books are kept in order?'

With a dogged determination, Stephen read up all the relevant estate records and was relieved to see that, apart from some rather excessive feathering of nests by the land-agent and his cronies, the books were all in order and the profits on the farms much as he'd have expected. The estate was unencumbered by mortgage, and each year a respectable profit was made and invested. Very little money seemed to be ploughed back into the improvement of the estate; the only really heavy expenditure was upon the preservation of game. The last time a tenant's cottage had been repaired at the landlord's expense had been in 1842, after a fire.

No money was set aside for the maintenance of a school, for road-mending or construction, or for the relief of sickness or hunger among the labourers.

Stephen called a meeting of his agents and bailiffs; he addressed them, as they afterwards complained, as if he were the Lord God Almighty and they the servants who had been found wanting. Tatlow began to mutter about making way for a younger man, and asked his wife if she would like to move to the town. He was disgusted when the new squire set about organizing a programme of road-building, to connect all the tenant farms, cottages and villages to the manor house, and the estate itself to the main Hereford to Worcester road. 'You shouldn't commit yourself to all this expense, sir,' wailed Tatlow. 'The estate can't support it!'

'Nonsense,' replied his master. 'Of course it can. And the men will be glad of the work. It will be a novelty for them to have employment through the winter, and I'm sure they'll thank us for it.'

'New brooms,' muttered Tatlow, under his breath. That evening, he drafted his resignation.

Stephen had ridden round the estate and observed that his labourers were, on the whole, worse housed than his animals. He made notes on the building work which needed to be done, and he told the agent to get on with the organization of it. Instead, Tatlow went to complain to his late employer's widow.

'You're mad, Stephen; quite mad,' said Mrs Lawrence that evening. She wept into her handkerchief and called on the spirit of her late husband to witness his son squandering the profits of generations on such ludicrous extravagances as roads and building work. 'It's unnecessary, all this renovation,' she moaned. 'It will only cause the tenants to get above themselves. They're quite happy as they are!'

Stephen made no comment. So she wrote a heart-rending letter to a neighbouring landlord, who later rode over to Ashton, up to his horse's knees in mire, to remonstrate with the poor widow's headstrong son.

'Three years' profits will be swallowed up by these proposed improvements of yours,' announced Mr Challoner, standing before the fire and warming his coat tails. 'Three years' profits, Stephen! And for what? For pandering to the tenants. And will they be grateful? Not at all!'

Stephen shrugged. 'I think, Mr Challoner,' he remarked, 'that before you criticize me, you would do well to look at the state of your own tenants' cottages. The health and happiness of your labourers is, of course, your concern but I can tell you now that I wouldn't allow human beings to live in those houses. In fact, I would hesitate to keep pigs in them.'

'Pigs?' Mr Challoner stared, outraged.

'Pigs.' Stephen rang the bell by his desk. 'I must apologize for the state of the road,' he remarked. 'But I hope that, next year, any visitors to Ashton Cross will be able to travel about the area dry shod.'

* * *

The final proof of the landlord's idiocy was presented to his mother just a few days later. She heard from the rector's wife that Stephen had told his gamekeeper not to proceed with a prosecution against a tenant caught in one of the spinneys with a live rabbit in one pocket and a dead pheasant in the other.

She listened incredulously as Stephen confirmed the truth of this horrible rumour. 'But you can't let him get off like that!' she had moaned. 'Think of the example to the others! Now all the tenants will think themselves free to take whatever game they please?'

Stephen yawned, shrugged. 'The tenants are welcome to every rabbit and game bird on the estate as far as I am concerned,' he replied offhandedly. He hadn't even bothered to raise his eyes from his book. 'No doubt they like fresh meat as much as I do.'

His mother gaped at him. 'I don't understand you,' she replied, completely at a loss. 'The game belongs to us, not them! They can't just steal it, whenever the fancy takes them!'

Her son frowned, shut his book. 'I'm going to give up game preservation,' he announced. 'It's a complete waste of money. Have you any idea how much it costs?'

'Well —'

'I thought not. My dear Madam — I respect your opinions, and I hope I always shall defer to those wiser than myself. But you must realize that I now have other uses for my revenue. I shall find the keepers different work, or recommend them to our neighbours. As for me — I'm a farmer, not a sportsman. What use are pheasants to me?'

Mrs Lawrence had reached for her smelling bottle, quite certain that she was having an attack of nerves. She was sure that she couldn't possibly have heard Stephen correctly. But she had. And over the next few months she was further mortified to realise that not only was Stephen determined to have his headstrong way, but that his brother Henry agreed with what he was doing and was even anxious to help him.

By early spring the repairs and renovations to the estate buildings were well under way. The tenants waited sullenly for wages to be lowered to pay for them all, and they grumbled about the new landlord almost as much as Tatlow did.

But wages did not fall. They went up — only by a shilling a

week, but even an extra twelve pence meant a great deal to a labourer whose weekly wage was a mere half sovereign.

But then the landlord, seeing that the improvements he had implemented were well under way, found he was losing interest in the affairs of the estate. He reflected that it was, after all, his brother Henry who was the farmer of the family; he always had been. It was Henry who had taken an interest in the place ever since he'd been a child — Henry who had, as a young man, tried to persuade his reactionary father to invest in new machines, to try out different breeds of stock. Henry ought to have inherited the ancestral acres which were such a burden to their present owner.

'Might you consider not going up to university?' asked Stephen one evening, as he and Henry walked across a marshy field, back towards the manor house. 'Would you, perhaps, think about taking over the estate instead?'

Henry's eyes had brightened but he had been non-committal. 'This meadow needs draining,' he remarked. 'I'll talk to Tatlow about it.'

'Before you do that, answer my question. Would you like to be the manager here?'

'I'd be willing to help you.' Henry looked hard at his elder brother. 'But as for running the place by myself — I'm not eighteen until May. Don't you think I might be too young for such a responsibility?'

Stephen laughed. 'You know far more about farming than I do,' he replied. 'What has your age to do with it?'

'Not much, I suppose. But the land belongs to you. You're the elder, you inherited it; you have a duty here.'

'Oh, rubbish. You know you could carry out my duty far better than I could. God, Henry, I'll die of boredom if I stay here another six months! It's so damn depressing, all this grey-green countryside, endless bloody fields, rain, mud. I hate it here, I always have, I always will. And you like it, don't you? All these sodden miles of wilderness mean a great deal to you.'

'Yes, I suppose they do.'

'Then you're welcome to them. I make you a present of the whole damned encumbrance!'

'But what will you do?'

'Me? Oh. I'm going back to Greece in April. I'm going to

organize an excavation, that's what I'm going to do.'

Henry gave his brother a quizzical look. Excavation? Digging around in the earth like a common labourer? Searching for buried treasure? Perhaps, Henry reflected, old Tatlow had a point. Perhaps Stephen was a little touched, after all ...

When Dorcas went home for her annual summer holiday in late July, she found that Ellen's cottage had been practically rebuilt. Instead of a hovel, she now lived in a comfortable, weatherproof home.

'It's all his doing,' said Ellen. 'He's had all the houses repaired, and he saw to it that all the men were in work last winter. He's even had them ruddy traps took out of the woods.'

'He? Who do you mean?'

'Oh, I suppose you haven't heard, have you? New landlord, I should have said. Old squire died last autumn, see — didn't you know?'

'Ah.' Dorcas grinned at her mother. 'What's he like, this new landlord?' she asked.

'Like? Seems pleasant enough.' Ellen scratched her head. 'He ain't much to look at, though,' she added. 'And that's a fact. He's one of those middle-sized sort of men, dark — nothing you'd remark on. They do say he's a terrible one for the girls; but I can't say as how he makes my old heart beat any faster than it should!'

Thinking of her own handsome Daniel, Dorcas smiled. 'I've got something to tell you,' she said. 'I'm walking out with a shop assistant these days, and I think he likes me.' She blushed. 'More than likes me,' she continued. 'Indeed I won't be surprised if he asks me to marry him. So what do you think of that?'

'A shop man? Gracious me, child, I won't know you!' Ellen, amazed, got out of her chair and walked around the room, agitated and delighted. 'And you really think — well, why shouldn't he? You're a fine looking girl; you'd be a credit to any man!'

She looked at her daughter complacently, and a great smile broke across her face. 'Oh, I'd be that pleased to know you weren't coming back to live here, to marry somebody like Luke Hole!' she said. 'Bringing up a family of a dozen brats without the means to put food in their bellies, working your fingers to the bone, and all for nothing! Things is better here now than they was in my young day; but it's still a bad life, a hard life, not one I'd wish on anybody. You stick with this shop man,' she concluded. 'Then you won't want for anything for the rest of your days.'

A clear twilight evening a few days later found Dorcas walking down a path to the village, humming to herself and feeling pleased with life. She'd spent a day with an old friend and had thoroughly enjoyed herself boasting about her prospects to a wide-eyed Annie Partridge, who was soon to marry a labourer and tie herself down to a life of poverty and servitude for the rest of her days.

Hearing footsteps on the path behind her, Dorcas stopped to look round. Seeing a man approach, she stood aside to let him pass, for the path was narrow.

A dark, broad-shouldered man of medium height, five or six years older than herself, he was walking very fast, obviously in a hurry. He drew level with Dorcas — smiled — wished her a good evening. She replied in kind, smiled in turn, and watched him walk on. He'd looked a pleasant sort of fellow, she decided. Perhaps he was the new agent. He'd be an improvement on that old misery Tatlow if he was.

Ellen screwed up her face when Dorcas described the man she'd met. 'Straight black hair? Dark eyes? Sort of thick-set, like?' she'd asked. 'Bit sunburnt, was he?'

'Yes, he was very tanned. He didn't look like a gentleman — he was friendly, and he was dressed much too plain.'

'Hmm. I think you must have seen the squire. I heard it from Mrs Lewin, who had it from the housekeeper, who was told by Mrs Lawrence herself, that he was expected home. Come to do a bit of courtin', I understand. Young lady, it is, only child, great beauty, they say. Rich as well. That should be enough for him, shouldn't it?'

Dorcas shrugged, wondering whatever a rich, beautiful young lady would find to like about the rather plain, ordinary-looking man she'd passed on the path that evening. She went on with her supper.

Dorcas' holiday came to an end and she returned to Hereford. Daniel met the cart on the outskirts of the city and they walked into the town together, arm in arm as acknowledged lovers may.

Dorcas chattered unceasingly as they strolled along, Daniel giving her no more than half his attention. Habitually quiet, he seemed more than usually preoccupied that day. 'What are you thinking about?' she asked, suddenly realizing that he hadn't said a word for the past ten minutes.

'Oh, nothing. Nothing at all.'

They were walking down a tree-lined lane when Daniel stopped, leaned over Dorcas and kissed her, drawing away almost as soon as his lips touched her face. 'You will marry me, Dorry, won't you?' he asked, in the tone of one asking for a casual arrangement to be confirmed.

She hadn't dared to hope for this, not just yet. Her face a picture of astonished delight, she threw her arms around his neck. 'Of course I will!' she cried, absolutely thrilled. 'Oh, Daniel, of course I'll marry you!'

He reddened, embarrassed by her enthusiasm. Squirming slightly he tried, even as she hugged him, to back away. He patted her shoulder nervously, then disentangled her arms from around his neck. 'Good,' he said. 'That's what I thought you'd say. Well then — we're engaged!'

In September the carter brought Dorcas a letter from Mrs Collins, telling her that her mother had had a fall, cracking bones in both a wrist and an ankle. The farrier had set the joints, but Ellen needed nursing for a few weeks. Could Dorcas be spared for a month or so? Otherwise, Ellen could go to the workhouse infirmary.

Knowing how much Ellen would hate that, Dorcas went at once to Miss Lane and asked for a few weeks' leave of absence.

Miss Lane looked at her little servant's stricken face. 'Of course you may go,' she told her. 'Ask the carter to wait while you pack. And here.' She opened her cashbox and took out eight half-crowns. 'If you need any more money, write to me,' she said. 'I shan't expect you back here for three or four weeks.'

Within two hours of the carter's arrival in Hereford, Dorcas was seated beside him on the way back to Ashton Cross.

The old man grinned at Dorcas, leering in his over-familiar way. 'Growin' up fast, aren't you?' he demanded. 'Still in your first place, I see. Fell on your feet there, didn't you? Always thought you would.'

'I've been very fortunate.' Dorcas smiled primly at him. 'Very lucky indeed.'

'Ah.' He chewed the insides of his cheeks for a while. 'Your Mam, she ain't too bad,' he volunteered. 'She's in her bed still, but she'll mend all right. Bones'll set. Don't fret about her.'

Dorcas managed another faint smile, trying not to mind the man's proximity. He smelled horrible, and he was sitting on a fold of her dress. She reached for her basket and handed him a bun, which he devoured with evident pleasure. Coughing crumbs, he wiped his sleeve on his mouth. 'You make these?' he demanded.

'Yes. Would you like another?'

'Wouldn't say no.' He snorted. 'Like I always says, there's two things a woman oughter do by instinct, and one of 'em's cook. I 'spect you'd be good at the other thing, too — eh?' He gave her familiar nudge in the side. 'My missus can't do neither,' he reflected gloomily.

Dorcas grimaced, but said nothing. She let her mind wander while the carter droned on, pushing her closer and closer to the edge of her seat in an attempt to get as near to her as possible. She was daydreaming about the rooms over Follet's shop which she and Daniel were to have when they married. She had seen the pattern of chintz she meant to have for the curtains and she was planning the design of covers for her chairs. She fancied red velveteen for her sofa …

Ellen did not look too ill. She was badly bruised, but obviously going to heal. Delighted to have her daughter with her, she retailed all the local gossip. 'We're to have a new schoolmistress,' she said. 'A real, educated lady! That ol' baggage what used to teach you, she fell on her fire she did; drunk on gin, they say. Only happened a few weeks since.'

'What happened to her?'

'Oh, she's in the work'us infirmary now; she won't come out of it, either.' Ellen sighed reflectively. 'Mr Henry's had the place made bigger, you know,' she added. 'And he's even going to get some books. All the children's got to go to school until they're ten, he says — dunno what their parents'll think about that!'

Neither did Dorcas, but she didn't particularly care. She sketched out her plans for the future. 'I'm going to have five children,' she announced. 'Three boys, two girls. And you can live

70

with us — we'll have a villa with proper running water and gas lights, out on the Whitecross Road. Daniel will have his own shop one day, so he'll earn enough to pay for it all.'

Ellen improved rapidly. A week or so after Dorcas had come home she could flex the fingers of her left hand without pain. She came downstairs to sit in front of the fire, while she waited for her ankle to heal.

Mrs Collins, who hated to see anyone idle, brought the invalid a pile of plain sewing to do. Ellen bodged and dirtied it all, leaving Dorcas to sort it all out later, and restitch it properly.

When Ellen could hobble around using a pair of sticks, Mrs Collins came bustling over to the cottage to inform her that Mr Henry Lawrence had decided to offer her work in the manor house. She was not to consider going back to the fields. 'Though why he should make it his concern I don't know,' she remarked. 'As if he hadn't enough to do, what with running the estate single-handed while the young squire gads about, doing no one knows what — but everyone can imagine!'

She eyed Dorcas up and down. 'A fine lady you've become, Miss,' she said waspishly. 'I hope you go to church, and say your prayers? I trust you remember to bless those responsible for your good fortune?'

While Ellen lay at home, recovering her strength and struggling with her plain sewing, Dorcas took occasional walks through the autumnal lanes, watching the hop-pickers, and remembering how much she had enjoyed that time of year as a child although she would have disdained to dirty her hands on yellow hops now. The weather was beautiful: misty mornings gave way to clear blue afternoons, when the sun was as hot as at midsummer.

The landlord had come home to Ashton Cross, presumably to continue his courting of the rich young lady. He rode a black mare, and was considered, by those villagers in the know, to be a fine horseman. Dorcas saw him in the distance now and then.

By the end of the hop-picking, Ellen was almost recovered. Her wrist came out of its strapping, and she could walk well enough with the aid of a stick, which she would probably need until the end of her days now. Mrs Collins visited her one Saturday morning and pronounced her better. 'You will start work at the

71

manor house on Monday,' she informed Ellen. 'You may stay there as a live-in servant until you are really fit again.'

'I'll come back to me own 'ouse, thank you very much,' replied Ellen. 'Carter'll fetch me to and fro. I don't want to stop in that great draughty barn of a place.'

Mrs Collins grimaced. There was no end to the ingratitude of the poor! 'The carter will fetch you at six on Monday,' she said coldly. 'He will leave you at the kitchens, then take Miss here on to Hereford. I don't doubt that her mistress will be wanting her back.' She sniffed. 'A fine time you've had of it, Dorcas Grey,' she muttered. 'I've seen you, walking the lanes and taking your ease while others toil! Your mother has some blankets from the Box here. I'll thank you to step over to the rectory with them this after-noon, if you please.'

Dorcas spent the rest of the morning putting her mother's cottage to rights, then she made a pile of the borrowed blankets and walked over to the rectory with them, lugging them in a great unwieldly parcel. After disposing of her burden she set off for home again.

The weather was still fine, and exertion had made her hot. She took off her bonnet and loosened her hair. Then she rolled up her sleeves and tucked her dress above her ankles, in the way all countrywomen did, in order to save it from the mud and dust. She was just considering a paddle at a boundary stream when she heard footsteps behind her; turning, she saw the landlord walking quickly, about to catch up with her.

He drew level with her, and smiled. 'Another lovely afternoon, Miss Grey,' he remarked.

Dorcas stared at him, surprised that he knew her name, blushing because she was acutely aware of her extremely untidy appearance. She looked just like a field girl. 'Indeed it is, sir,' she muttered, wishing he would walk on. He'd seemed to be in a hurry, after all.

But, far from going on, he slowed down his pace to match hers. He pushed his hands into his pockets and strolled by her side. 'I'm pleased to hear that your mother is better,' he said.

'Thank you, sir.'

'Do you go back to Hereford on Monday?'

'Yes, sir.'

'Your friends will be pleased to see you, I expect.'

'I hope so, sir.' Dorcas began to walk even more slowly. She kept her eyes on the path, willing the man to go on ahead. But then she stumbled against a stone — the landlord put out his hand to save her, caught her arm. She looked at him and for a second, just a second, their eyes met.

Stephen let her go straight away. He satisfied himself that she was not hurt; then he wished her a good afternoon and strode on in the direction of the manor house.

Dorcas watched him go. She reached up and ran her fingers through her untidy hair, annoyed with herself for feeling so disquieted, for she could not stop her heart from pounding, nor her eyes from gazing, as if bewitched, in the direction the landlord had gone. Even after he had disappeared over the brow of a hill, she could still see him ...

She could still see the way his hair grew back from his forehead, recall how densely black it was. She could remember the details of all his features, could even picture the incipient stubble on his sunburned cheeks for, unlike most other men, he'd been clean-shaven — or as clean-shaven as a naturally heavy growth of beard would allow.

And she'd observed that although his clothes were very plain, they were of a quality she'd never seen before. His riding jacket, cut very precisely, had been beautifully made and had even smelled expensive. She blushed when she remembered that she'd recently taken him for a bailiff, in her ignorance assuming that all gentlemen wore much more showy clothes, brightly coloured waistcoats dripping with fobs and seals, extravagant neck ties. She couldn't begin to imagine Mr Lawrence dressed so, nor see him with fancy curling whiskers, or his hair long and larded with macassar oil. But all the same, he was a gentleman. That was obvious. A gentleman; a member of a different species.

After she had eaten a midday meal and cleared it away, Dorcas left her mother dozing in her chair while she rushed about the cottage in a frenzy of activity; tidying what was already neat, repacking her own clothes, and scouring the cottage into an unheard-of state of cleanliness. She felt hot and irritable to a maddening degree. She fetched a bucket of water from the pump and washed herself all over but the touch of her hands on her body made her feel even more unsettled.

A restless night left her in the same feverish state. She fidgeted all morning, unusually silent; she answered Ellen's remarks mechanically, her mind miles away. After picking at a cold lunch, she took herself off for a walk.

The day was cooler than the previous one had been. Dorcas dressed herself in her best winter clothes, put her hair up neatly, and brushed her boots before leaving the cottage to take the path which led away from the manor house. Not a soul was in sight. 'There's no reason for him to come this way,' she told herself, all the while hoping, praying — knowing — that he must.

So it was with little surprise that she heard the sound of horse's hooves behind her, and felt the rider slowing down as he drew closer to her. She turned round to face him.

'Miss Grey? I thought it was you.' He smiled at her, a non-committal, perfectly ordinary smile of polite greeting. He dismounted. 'I've been looking at the fences on the north side,' he added conversationally.

'Have you, sir?' Dorcas coughed and cleared her throat, wondering why her voice sounded so odd. 'Well — it's a nice day for a ride.'

'Indeed it is.' Stephen stroked the horse's nose. 'Can you ride, Miss Grey?' he asked.

'No, sir, I can't. I don't believe I've been on a horse above once or twice in my life.'

'Ah, I suppose you wouldn't have. Well, would you like to try it? Why don't you get up on Minstrel here? There's nothing to be afraid of.'

'Oh, I'm not afraid —'

'That's good. Up you go, then.' Stephen took her by the waist and lifted her, easily, on to the animal's back. 'Since you're a lady it ought to be a side-saddle, of course,' he said. 'But how does it feel?'

Dorcas beamed down at him. 'It's splendid, sir. So high up!' She ventured to pat the animal's neck. 'He seems a very docile horse, sir,' she added.

'She is, she is — very gentle. This horse, incidentally, is a mare.' Stephen saw Dorcas' blush deepen, and laughed at her. 'Would you like to go for a canter?' he asked.

'A what?'

'A canter. A slow gallop. You'll be quite safe.' He smiled encouragingly. 'Sit forward a little, so that I can get up behind you.'

He was in the saddle before she could agree or disagree, and had shaken the reins, causing the mare to move off smartly. Dorcas tightened her grip on his arm, which was holding her against him. She felt the warmth of him, breathed in the muskiness of his clothes and the clean, sharp scent of the man himself. Feeling safe, she relaxed.

Two months of enforced chastity were beginning to tell on Stephen. His personal, if somewhat dubious, code of morality had so far prevented him from chasing after his tenants' daughters; although Heaven knew that plenty of the dishevelled sluts on the estate had grinned at him complaisantly enough over the past couple of months. He felt in his pocket for his keyring, searching for a particular key which he hoped might be there. It was.

Now he looked at the soft, creamy skin of the girl's neck; he saw that her dark hair was smooth and clean. Only that morning he had told himself that a few more weeks' abstinence wouldn't hurt him.

But there was something about this girl. Something about her graceful bearing, about the way she'd smiled at him just now, which had been almost irresistible. She had, so to speak, appeared out of the blue, an answer to a prayer. And she looked forward enough, although she was, he hoped, too young to be diseased. On the whole, she seemed the very person with whom he would have chosen to spend a tedious Sunday afternoon.

Stephen urged the mare on; the animal, sensing her rider's excitement, increased her speed. 'We are going towards Ledbury,' he told Dorcas. 'I know of a house there. Of course, if you wish to go back to Ashton Cross now, I'll take you back immediately. You have only to say. Well?'

The girl said nothing at all.

On the outskirts of Ledbury stood a terrace of tall, narrow houses; once medieval cottages, they were now dignified by a third storey and Georgian façades. At one of these houses Stephen stopped. He lifted Dorcas down and called to a boy who was loitering on the other side of the road, whom he told to take the sweating mare to the livery stables to be rubbed down and kept for an hour or two. Smirking, the boy took the reins and a couple of shillings, touched his cap respectfully to Stephen and gave Dorcas a most enormous wink, which made her flush scarlet. As the boy ambled off, Stephen took a key from his pocket and let himself into the house.

At the sound of the key turning a fat, grinning woman in very bright clothes came running down the passage. She made a ludicrous attempt at a curtsey, and held out her hands for Stephen's gloves and riding crop. 'Mr Townsend, sir!' she gushed. 'What a pleasure! I thought you were abroad!' She dabbed at the corners of her mouth with a handkerchief. 'Them maids is all asleep, sir; lazy baggages one and all. I'll show you up myself.'

Ignoring Dorcas completely, the woman pushed past her and led the way upstairs, showing them into a large, high-ceilinged room where a fire burned in the grate. Except for a wide bed in one corner, there was little furniture. The blinds were down, and the curtains half drawn.

'Can I send anything up, sir?' The woman, seemingly ill at ease, was still dabbing nervously at her face.

'What?' Stephen looked around the room absently. 'Oh — no, nothing. I shall ring if I want you. Off you go.'

'Sir.' The woman bobbed again, looking covertly at Dorcas as if sizing her up. Then she went away, closing the door behind her.

Stephen let the window blind go rattling up, pulled back the curtains and led Dorcas, who hardly knew what she was expecting but who was now shaking with fear, over to the window. He looked at her for a second or two, the undid the strings of her bonnet and threw it on to a chair. 'You're pretty — very pretty,' he remarked; but his face was unsmiling. Still afraid, Dorcas could only stare back at him. And then he let the curtains fall across the window again; he leaned over; and, experimentally, he kissed her.

He held her chin lightly in his hand, and tilted her head upwards, so that his mouth came to rest, quite naturally, upon hers. Only a few inches taller than she was, there was no need for him to push her head back; and the sensation of Stephen's firm, dry lips lying lightly upon her own was unexpectedly pleasant. Dorcas opened her mouth slightly, and he, taking this as encouragement, used his own mouth to part her lips even wider. He licked her teeth.

She felt his arms come round her then; and, as he kissed her still, she heard the sharp snap and rustle as he began to unhook the back of her dress.

He seemed to know how all the different layers of her clothing fitted together. Gradually, taking his time, he undid all the various tapes, hooks, ribbons and ties, easing a terrified but perfectly co-operative Dorcas out of her garments with the air of one unwrapping a parcel. He pushed the bundle of clothing aside with his foot. 'Get into bed now,' he murmured.

She did so, turning away from him while he threw off his own clothes. Then he joined her. She felt him swing his legs into bed, pulling the covers over them both, and he sat up beside her.

Theoretically prepared for what she knew must now happen, Dorcas had nevertheless curled herself up into a self-protecting ball. She'd shut her eyes, and now she waited. And waited. Finally she opened her eyes again to see Stephen gazing down at her. 'What on earth's the matter?' he asked.

She stared at him, eyes wide. 'Nothing,' she muttered, embarrassed. 'Oh — nothing, sir, nothing at all.'

'Indeed. May I touch you, then? When you're ready of course; when you've said your prayers, or finished whatever it is you're doing now.'

'Yes,' she whispered, flinching at his sarcasm. 'Yes, you may touch me. I'm quite ready.' She gritted her teeth.

She was not expecting him to be so careful. She had assumed there would be a sudden, brutal assault. The kissing, stroking and caressing which now began surprised her — she'd not been prepared for the sheer pleasure of it. But, understanding her body far better than she did herself, Stephen took pains to coax her out of her frightened rigidity. He knew where to touch, how to touch, what to say between kisses, and how to make her respond to him. She found herself kissing him back, opening her mouth wide, greedily pulling him closer to her. She was more than ready for him when, having excited her to an almost unbearable degree, he finally came inside her. He broke the lock of her virginity with ease — the pain was sharp, but over almost before she was aware that it had begun. She opened her eyes to smile up at him.

But Stephen, the bulk of his body casting a dark shadow over

77

her, did not smile back. Instead, he propped himself up on one elbow and frowned at her. 'I am not in the habit of seducing virgins,' he told her curtly. 'Why did you come with me today?'

'Come with you?' Dorcas stared at him, afraid again. 'Well, sir, I — I —' Her mouth suddenly dry, she found she could not say any more.

Seeing her look so alarmed, Stephen relaxed the severity of his expression. 'Why did you come here?' he repeated, more gently this time.

'I don't know.' Suddenly ashamed and mortified beyond endurance, she could have wept. She looked away and tried to twist from underneath him.

Stephen obligingly rolled over on to his own side of the bed and examined Dorcas' shoulder blades, for she'd turned her back on him again, and was biting her thumb in an agony of embarrassment. He ran one index finger down her spine, making her stiffen. 'I hope I didn't hurt you too much?' he asked.

'No — not at all,' she lied. 'You — I —'

'You liked it?'

'Yes.'

'Oh, well, that's something, I suppose. Dorcas, please turn round. I don't care to address the back of your head. That's better.' He smiled at her. 'Would you like anything to drink?' he asked, his voice quite kindly now.

Her throat was parched. 'Oh, yes I would,' she replied. 'A cup of water — is there any on the washstand?'

'I dare say there is, but don't drink that.' Languidly, Stephen reached for the bell-rope by the bed. 'The woman will bring tea, chocolate, or whatever you want.'

'No!' Dorcas clutched the bedsheet round her body. 'You mustn't call her!' she cried. 'She'll see that we're — that I'm — oh, for pity's sake, don't ring for her!'

'Good grief, what a puritan you are!' Stephen shook his head. 'You're just a baby, aren't you? I've corrupted a child. Dorcas, it doesn't matter what *she* sees. She's well paid not to see anything at all!'

Dorcas pulled the bedclothes more tightly around herself, and would not look at him.

'Are you desperately thirsty?' asked Stephen, rolling over on to his stomach and reaching for a strand of her hair.

A tremor of excitement rippled through her as she felt his body against hers. 'Not desperately,' she whispered.

'Hungry? Not necessarily for food?'

'I don't know. What do you mean?'

'You know what I mean.' Gently, Stephen eased the sheet away from her and pulled her into his arms again. 'I think you are,' he murmured, stroking her shoulder, letting his hand describe a figure of eight around her breasts then move slowly down her stomach. 'I think you're still very hungry, nowhere near satisfied yet.'

He kissed her face, aware that her lips would now know how to search for his. He stroked her, lightly at first, but then more firmly, making her shudder with desire, making her eyes shine and their pupils dilate. Then, quite suddenly, miraculously, a little whimper of mingled pleasure and pain escaped her and she lay relaxed in his arms, bathed in sweat, feeling as if she could float on air.

But then Dorcas sat up; she wrapped her arms around her lover's neck and, of her own accord, she kissed him. She held him so tightly that he had to unclasp her hands in order that he might breathe. 'Do you mean to strangle me?' he asked, smiling at her now.

'No.' She looked steadily into his eyes. 'I want to be close to you — that's all.'

He laughed. 'You are strange,' he said, and kissed her again. He pushed her on to her back and gazed at her. 'Strange. And beautiful. Very, very beautiful indeed.'

It was past dusk when Dorcas walked into her mother's cottage. Ellen was sitting by the fire gossiping with a neighbour, and was easily taken in by Dorcas' glib lie that she had been up to Beth Lawson's house a few miles away and had stayed for tea. The fact that her daughter's colour was high and that her eyes were sparkling eluded Mrs Grey's notice completely.

The carter came to fetch them at six the following morning. He helped Ellen into the cart, where she lay on a pile of sacking, then he made a space for Dorcas next to himself. 'Only a short lick up to the manor house,' he muttered, dribbling. 'Then it'll be just you an' me, all the way to Hereford.'

'You can stop all that nonsense, Tom Arrowsmith,' said Ellen sharply. 'My Dorcas is a decent girl, about to be wed. She's not one of your field trollops, ready for a roll in a barn with any lad who'll give her sixpence!' She tugged at Dorcas' shawl. 'Any trouble with him, my lass, and you shove him off the seat,' she advised. 'His horse knows the way to Hereford!'

Tom Arrowsmith grinned. 'Don't get yourself in such a state, Missus!' he muttered. Then he laughed, eyeing Dorcas appraisingly. 'I knows when I sees meat for my betters!'

He twisted round to grimace at Ellen. '*You* needn't be so hoity-toity,' he added. 'I remember the time when you didn't mind a bit of a fumble under your bodice, and a hand up your skirt. So there!'

Ellen squawked indignantly at this, then lapsed into silence. Dorcas watched the great hulk of the manor house looming closer through the early morning mist. She was feeling as low as could be — cheapened, embarrassed, defiled, upset — but then, suddenly, her heart lightened, an uncontrollable smile played about her mouth, and she felt like singing. Since the previous evening this see-sawing state of mind had been quite second nature to her.

The cart rumbled on, along the lane past the walled gardens, and thence into the cobbled courtyard surrounded by out-buildings, kitchens and laundry rooms. There was all the early morning stir characteristic of a great house. Grooms were cursing, housemaids chattering, laundry women filling buckets at the pump. Men groaned and rubbed sleep from their eyes; women scolded, and clacked across the stones making the cobbles ring with the distinctive chink of their iron ringed pattens.

The carter helped Ellen to get down, then carried her basket for her while she hobbled over to the kitchen door. Dorcas sat quite still in her seat, waiting, thinking of the landlord, wondering if he was up and gone out in the early morning or whether he slept in some room not a hundred yards from where she was now.

As the carter reappeared and came back across the yard, a valet with a letter in his hand emerged from another door. He stopped by the cart. 'Are you Miss Grey?' he asked.

'Yes.' Puzzled, Dorcas stared at him.

'For you, Miss.' The man handed her a white envelope. Perhaps it was a note for Miss Lane, from the housekeeper? The paper bore the curtest of messages. 'I shall be in Hereford next Tuesday, and will see you in Broad Street at two. SRL.'

Dorcas read this unloverlike scribble over two or three times. Then a wide smile broke over her features as she shook her head, wanting to laugh out loud with delight. The carter, getting up beside her, glared as he eased his rheumaticky limbs into his seat. 'What you got to grin about, eh?' he demanded.

Dorcas put the note safely inside the folds of her bodice and sighed contentedly. But she said nothing.

'Good news, I 'ope?' enquired the carter, nodding at her chest where the edge of the envelope was still visible, tucked inside her gown.

Dorcas started guiltily. 'Oh — that! It's just a message from the housekeeper here, to my mistress.'

'Oh, aye. Course it would be.' The carter sucked his gums and looked knowing. When the cart reached the main road he began to drone a lugubrious song about a maid who went up a hill still a maid and came down it a maid no more. He gargled on endlessly until Dorcas asked him, rather sharply, to stop, for he was giving her a headache.

Miss Lane was pleased to see her secretary again, for she had a vast pile of correspondence to be attended to. 'You look very well, Dorcas,' she remarked. 'The country air agrees with you!' She smiled when her little maid blushed.

The cook and Maggie Stemp grinned at each other when they heard Dorcas singing as she went about her work. Mrs Butler touched her nose and winked at Maggie. 'Thought o' seein' 'er Danny's makin' her lightheaded,' she remarked. 'She wants to be got to church, she does.'

Maggie giggled. 'Only a few months now, Cook,' she replied. 'She'll see 'im tomorrow when she takes the order in an' I 'spect he'll be able to slip outside for five minutes, an' give her a kiss and a cuddle. I'll leave them by themselves this Sunday — I said I'd call round Gilly Towler's. Then they can get on with discussin' their weddin', can't they?'

The two women could still hear Dorcas singing at the top of her voice as she turned out the bedrooms. They exchanged more knowing looks.

Dorcas had rushed into Follet's at five minutes to two that Tuesday, and flung the order book, ready made up, on the counter in front of Daniel. 'I've only got a minute to spare,' she gasped, breathless. 'I've got to get to the dressmaker's by two, to collect Madam's new gown.'

Daniel, who had been looking forward to twenty minutes' unhurried chat with his fiancée, looked gravely at Dorcas' flushed face. He was uncomfortably aware of the other assistants staring and whispering to each other. 'Are you well, dear?' he asked evenly. 'You look very feverish.'

Dorcas made an effort to control her agitation. 'Well? Oh, yes, Daniel — I'm perfectly well. I'm in a hurry, that's all.' She pushed the book nearer him. 'I've written it all down,' she said. 'Look — I can't stay longer. I'll see you on Sunday as usual, shall I?'

Before Daniel could answer, she dashed out again, banging open the glass doors of the shop and colliding with another customer. Daniel glanced up to see one of the other assistants smirking. He glared at the man, then picked up Miss Lane's order book, which he flung on to a pile with some others. He turned his back on the other assistants and savagely applied himself to slicing bacon.

Dorcas reached Broad Street just as the clocks were striking two. She stopped outside a large hotel and rubbed her aching side, trying to breathe normally. Looking across the road she saw Stephen's mare outside the lawyer's office, her reins held by a boy.

At a quarter past two, Stephen himself came down the lawyer's steps. He saw Dorcas, who was trying to seem unconcerned, hovering near a display of bonnets in a shop window. He crossed the road.

Chapter Six

'GOOD AFTERNOON, DORCAS.' STEPHEN STOOD in front of her like a gamekeeper blocking a poacher's escape.

'Good afternoon, sir.' She felt her face reddening even as she spoke and she looked away.

'I have only an hour to spare,' he said. 'Will you come and walk by the river?'

'Of course, sir.' She would have agreed to a stroll through a London rookery with him, had he proposed it.

He did not, of course, offer his arm to her. But he slowed down his usual rapid pace to match her slower gait, so it was obvious that they were companions. Dorcas kept her eyes on the pavement, hoping and praying that she would not meet anyone she knew. She let her feet take her towards the Cathedral, through the familiar narrow streets which led down to the river.

The fields along the river bank were deserted except for a few grazing cattle. Along the towpath sticky red mud clung to the hem of her gown; but she neither noticed, nor would she have cared if she had. Now and then she allowed herself to glance at her companion and found that each time she looked at him the blood rushed to her face.

However could she have thought him plain and ordinary? His dark face and stocky figure were just as a man's ought to be. She looked at his profile, noticed again how heavy his straight, black hair was; and thought that his fierce dark eyes and heavy brows, his hooked nose, his determined jawline and square chin were as handsome as the most classical features could be.

'You stare at me as if you think I shall attack you,' he remarked suddenly.

She jumped almost out of her skin as she looked at him with startled eyes; she shook her head vehemently, making him smile at her. He looked much less forbidding when his features relaxed. She found herself becming less nervous, less tense, and for a second or two she smiled back.

'I expect to go abroad in a few weeks' time,' said Stephen. 'But I would very much like to see you again before I go. That is, if you wish it.'

'I should like that very much indeed, sir.'

'That being so, madam, I consider myself honoured.' He laughed at her solemn little face. 'Oh, Dorcas,' he said, his voice kindly now, 'you do not need to be so formal! After all, when two people know each other as well as I should like to know you, a certain relaxation of manners is permitted.' He looked at her enquiringly. 'You do know my Christian name?'

'Yes, of course, sir.'

'Well, then, you may use it.'

They were a hundred yards or so from the bridge now, past a band of willows which bordered that part of the river, and out into the fields. 'What takes you abroad?' she asked, stopping herself just in time from addressing him as 'sir'; but unable, all the same, to call him by his baptismal name.

'What have you heard in the village?'

'Oh — they all say you wander about the Continent, digging holes in the ground, looking for treasure,' she replied. 'I don't believe it, of course,' she added hastily.

Stephen laughed again, a deep, infectious laugh which made Dorcas herself smile. 'That's what they say, is it?' he asked. 'Well they're right, more or less. That's what I do. I don't suppose they've heard of archaeology, but then that's just the dignified term for digging holes in the ground.'

'You're teasing me, Stephen!' In her disbelief Dorcas had said his name — and the sky had not fallen.

'I'm not teasing you. That is why I go to Greece; why I'm going back there soon, to join my friends who also dig holes in the ground. Listen to me, and I'll explain a little.'

As if he were a teacher and she a student, Stephen then gave Dorcas a short lecture on the aims and methods of classical archaeology to which she listened intently, half believing but half sceptical. 'I wonder —' she began; but now Stephen was in full spate, and did not hear her.

'You can't imagine what it's like, when you finally find what you were seeking,' he was saying excitedly. 'You can't begin to conceive how marvellous it can be, to come across a statue of, say, Athene or Hera, which has been lying in the cold ground for two thousand years!'

His eyes glittered now. 'You can't understand how wonderful it is,' he continued, 'to discover the cornerstone of a palace you *knew* was there, but didn't dare to hope you would find! Oh, Dorcas, I should like to show you the Parthenon, even as it is today, battered by the Sultan's armies, half destroyed! Well — perhaps one day you'll travel yourself.'

He glanced at her; saw that she was gazing at him, eyes wide with interest and surprise. He shook his head. 'I'll meet you on Friday, at about three,' he said. 'Wait for me near the Cathedral.'

Then he turned and walked quickly down the towpath, away from Dorcas, leaving her on the river bank alone. He had not, she realized, asked if she could leave her work, did not appear to consider that she was a servant whose mistress would expect any time taken off so unaccountably, accounted *for*. She was obliged to accept that Friday afternoon was when he had an hour or two to spare, and so that was when he would see her. She wasn't sure if she minded or not. 'I don't ever have to meet him again — not if I don't care to,' she told herself as she walked home.

'Along the towpath? That's a roundabout way, if you like!' said Maggie incredulously, brushing mud from Dorcas' hem. 'You really shouldn't go along the river walk by yourself,' she chided. 'You don't know who you might meet; you could be robbed or murdered or worse, and no one would hear you yell!'

Dorcas had the grace to look ashamed.

'Well then?' continued Maggie, tossing Dorcas' mud-caked shoes into the scullery, 'how was he? Pleased to see you? Did he give you a kiss?'

Dorcas started, coloured — stared at Maggie. 'How did you know I saw him?' she asked, her voice strangled.

Maggie laughed. 'Don't stare like that, you gaby,' she said. 'You look as if you've seen old Nick himself! I was only guessing. I wondered if your Daniel had managed to skive off for half an hour, if you'd been for a little stroll along the river bank together, had a bit of a kiss and a cuddle. That's all.' She grinned at Dorcas. 'Nothing to be ashamed of if you have,' she added. 'You're getting married in the spring, after all.'

Dorcas recovered, and shook her head. 'I didn't go walking with Daniel,' she muttered. 'I took the order in, then I came home by myself — a roundabout way, as you pointed out.'

'Go on with you!' chaffed Maggie. 'Admit it, do! You're as red as a beetroot! Oh, well — Madam wants you to do some letters for her, so off you go. I'll get on with the silver.'

Dorcas was still blushing, thus confirming Maggie's suspicions. 'I'll take her tea in and do her letters while she eats,' she said coldly. 'Don't grin at me like that, Maggie. I won't be teased!'

Dorcas amazed herself by the sheer artfulness, by the absolute ease with which, over the next few days, she spun a web of lies. As she sealed the last letter in a pile she'd finished for Miss Lane, she asked her mistress if she might take an hour off that Friday to visit the grave of an uncle buried in Saint Peter's churchyard. 'I promised Mother I'd try to go,' she said humbly. 'He died a year ago Friday, you see ...'

Her mistress put down her teacup and looked hard at her little maid. 'Your uncle, Dorcas?' she asked. 'I wasn't aware that you had any relatives in the city.'

Easily, a glib stream of fibs poured from Dorcas' lips, about her father's brother who had worked for a shoemaker in Tupsley village, who had been kind to her widowed mother ...

At the conclusion of this rigmarole Miss Lane nodded. 'You may go, Dorcas,' she said. 'Don't stay out long, though — and take Maggie with you.'

Dorcas could hardly contain her delight. She well knew that Maggie had a horror of graveyards, and was confident that the senior housemaid would accompany her into town and agree to fetch some shopping while Dorcas went to pay her respects to the dead.

Stephen came up to her as she was loitering near the Dean's house. He touched her arm, nodding to her gravely, and together they walked through the Cathedral precincts, then turned down a narrow lane adjacent to the choir school. Maggie Stemp, coming out of a jeweller's shop nearby, noticed a lady wearing the same kind of shawl as Dorry's disappearing down an alley with a man.

Taking Dorcas' elbow now, Stephen led her, quickly, through a maze of shabby streets near the river. He stopped outside the heavy wooden door of a tall shuttered house in a quiet courtyard. A brass bell, much tarnished, hung on the doorframe; and now Stephen made it jangle, tapping his foot irritably as he waited for the door to open.

A sour faced maid stood on the threshold. She stared coldly at Stephen. 'Ah, Mr Lucas,' she said tonelessly. 'I had your message. Come in, sir — come in.' Dorcas found that, once again, she was invisible.

She followed Stephen and the maid up a winding flight of stairs, her heart thumping, her mouth dry, afraid again but also excited.

'Is this your house, Stephen?' Dorcas had removed her bonnet and pulled some pins from her hair. Now she was looking round her at the room they were in. She thought that it could do with some redecoration; the plaster was yellow and there were damp stains on the walls.

'My house? No — of course it isn't my house!' Stephen took off his jacket and dropped it on to the floor. He started to undo the buttons on his shirt.

'Well, then how do you —'

He stopped her question with a kiss, and took her in his arms. 'That's nothing you need concern yourself with,' he murmured. He began to unhook her gown, his face buried in her loosened hair.

But she was determined to have an answer. 'The house in Ledbury was yours,' she persisted, as he kissed her face. 'You had a key; the woman spoke to you as if you were the master. Whose house is this?'

Stephen stopped kissing her. He frowned at her, looking at her closely, evidently suspecting some sort of teasing. But Dorcas' face gazed up at him candidly, wide-eyed and completely innocent. 'How old are you, child?' he asked.

'Sixteen. Nearly seventeen. Why?'

'I'd imagined you were older, that's all.' He shook his head, grimacing. 'Oh, this is ridiculous,' he muttered. 'Nearly seventeen — and as ignorant as a baby!' He considered for a moment longer, then came to a decision. 'Put your shawl back on, child,' he said. 'Find your bonnet. I shouldn't have brought you here — you're far too young for this sort of adventure. Go along home now. We won't meet again.'

'What?' She gaped at him, her great dark eyes huge with surprise. 'What's the matter, what have I said? Why do you want me to leave?'

'I don't *want* you to leave, you little idiot!' Stephen shook his head at her, exasperated. 'I want to undress you and take you to bed, that's what I want! Oh, for goodness' sake, child, don't make this even more difficult for me! Don't look at me as if I'd kicked you!'

'But, Stephen —'

'But Dorcas! Listen to me, will you? I like you very much — very much indeed. But I have *some* principles, and I don't simply use women for my pleasure whether they want me to or not. You are too young to know what you want.'

He fastened his cuffs. 'I was misled by your — your general demeanour, shall I say. When I took you to Ledbury, it was because I needed a woman. Don't you understand? And I thought, when you came so willingly, that you'd done that kind of thing before. I was mistaken, of course.'

Stephen's eyes glittered. 'I'm telling you to go, Dorcas,' he said. 'Put your bonnet on and go back to your mistress. Won't she wonder where you are?'

'I *won't* go!' Dorcas glared at him. 'I came here to see you, and I —'

'I came 'ere ter see yew,' Stephen mimicked her. He pulled her shawl more tightly around her shoulders, and placed her bonnet, awkwardly, on the top of her head. 'I'm very flattered that you did,' he drawled. 'And it's been very nice to talk to you. But you really must go now; I have business to attend to in town, and I'm late already. Did you see where I put my gloves?' He glanced idly around the room.

'*Don't you dare mock me!*' Her eyes sparkling with anger, Dorcas pulled her bonnet from her head and hurled it across the room. She threw herself at Stephen and pushed him backwards on to the bed behind him.

'You think you're such a great man, don't you, squire?' she demanded, glaring down at him, her face scarlet with mortification and fury. 'You, with your manor house and your estate and your farms; and your tenants bowing and scraping to you everywhere you go! Oh, I understand you very well! Don't imagine I can't see through you!

'You took me to a brothel, to a house of assignation or whatever it was; and you used me like a whore! But now you're tired of me, so I can go back to wherever it was I came from, can't I? You don't use women? That's exactly what you do! You see yourself as a fine gentleman, don't you, with your drawing room accent and your fancy manners and your fine clothes! Well — you're a wretch. You're a lying seducer, and nothing more than half a man!!'

Dorcas was so angry herself that she'd failed to notice that Stephen's face had now become white with rage. For a second or two, he stared at her in astonishment — then he caught her by the shoulders and lifted her clean away from him. Twisting round, he threw her on to her back and pinned her down underneath him. 'No bloody woman talks to me like that!' he hissed through clenched teeth. He held her shoulders so tightly that he hurt her, then he kissed her with frightening cruelty, wrenching her head back and biting her lips. 'You'll regret what you just said,' he muttered. 'You'll pay for all that, you little slut!'

He kissed her again, forcing her mouth open and letting his whole weight press down upon her, so that she could hardly breathe. But, after a minute or so, he realised that she wasn't struggling to escape from him. He found that, in spite of his anger, he was kissing her less violently; and, what was more, she was kissing him back. He felt her body relax under his; and her arms went around his neck.

Then all his anger evaporated as if it had never been. He shifted his weight from her and sat up. 'Oh, God, you must go,' he said, not looking at her. 'I won't give you another chance.'

'But I want to be with you.' Dorcas leaned her head against his shoulder. 'Don't, please don't send me away.' She took his hand, stroked it, and kissed his fingers; she reached up and smoothed his hair back from his brow. Then she knelt up and put her arms around him, running her fingers around his collar until he looked at her again, until he caught her hand in his.

'You must have bewitched me,' he said, frowning at her as if baffled. 'You must know that I couldn't send you away now; not even if my life depended upon it.' He began to kiss her, gently at first, but then more fiercely, as if he really were possessed.

This time, Dorcas knew better what to do; not at all afraid of him now, she helped Stephen to unfasten her clothes, giggling in delight when he kissed her shoulder, her arm, her wrist, and laughing out loud when he finally lost patience with all her undergarments and pushed her, still half dressed, on to her back again, now almost mad with the need to take her.

The aphrodisiac effect of having such a rich, such a powerful, such a desirable man so voraciously hungry for her went to Dorcas' head like brandy. When, finished, he lay upon her exhausted, his hair damp with sweat and his back glistening with perspiration, she laughed as if she really were intoxicated.

'Dorcas?' he asked. 'What do you find so funny?'

'Nothing.' She looked back at him and gave him the sweet, gentle smile of the utterly complacent mistress who knows that her lover would — at that moment at any rate — do anything in the world for her. And she was blissfully aware of her own power; she knew that he wanted her again, but that he was obliged, against his will, to have at least a few minutes' rest.

They lay next to each other, so perfectly comfortable together that neither of them wanted to get dressed again and go out into the chilly autumn afternoon. 'Your skin, Stephen,' remarked Dorcas, laying her arm next to his and comparing them. 'It's so dark! I always thought that gentlemen's skins were white!'

'Did you, now?' Stephen grinned, displaying his excellent teeth, which were themselves perfectly white, particularly against his tanned face. 'You were mistaken, weren't you? I'm as black as an Indian. And I tan very easily, so I'm darker than ever after a few months abroad.'

'Do you actually go out in the sun?'

'Naturally. How else do you think I dig my holes?'

'But you're tanned all over! How —'

'I go swimming a great deal. In those southern countries, you know, the sea's very warm. Dorcas, can you swim?'

'No. And if I could, I wouldn't swim naked! It's not decent.'

He widened his narrow eyes, mocking her. 'Not decent? I'm naked now — is that not decent, either?'

She bit her bottom lip, suddenly embarrassed. 'I don't know,' she muttered eventually. 'I really don't know.'

'Don't know?' Stephen looked into her eyes, the expression in his own softer than she'd yet seen it. 'Then accept my word for it, it's perfectly proper.' He ran his index finger from her shoulder to her wrist, tracing the contours. 'Now, that's classical beauty,' he murmured. 'But no Aphrodite could rival you. No marble Venus could compare with my sweet Dorcas, clad in flesh and blood. Little goddess, will you kiss me?'

Enchanted, Dorcas did just that.

Later, Stephen took one of Dorcas' hands and examined the palm. 'Not the hand of a maid of all work,' he observed. 'Such a nice little hand — warm, smooth and soft. Someone else must clean your mistress's house!'

Dorcas sat up, squaring her shoulders almost as if she'd forgotten she was naked. 'I am the mistress's companion,' she announced proudly. 'I read to her, I write letters for her — I am indispensable to her.'

'Are you indeed? I see. So you're a learned little trollop, a scholarly jade.' Stephen grinned. 'What a treasure.'

'Don't call me a trollop.'

'Why not?'

'Well, it's —' Dorcas bit her lip. 'It's unkind.'

'Yes, I suppose it is. Well, I didn't mean it, anyway.'

'Didn't you?'

'Of course not. Come here.' Stephen pulled her into his arms and kissed her with real affection. 'I think you've become indispensable to *me*,' he said. He looked around the room. 'Could you find me my gloves?' he asked.

Maggie was waiting for her junior in St Peter's Square, tapping her cold feet and rubbing her red, sore nose. 'Where in Heaven's name did you get to?' she demanded crossly. 'Two hours you've been gone! Two whole hours! You didn't go to look at no grave! You've been to Follet's, that's where you've been!' Maggie folded her arms impressively. 'I shall tell Madam of you!'

'Maggie, I've been nowhere near Follets! Truly!' Dorcas looked up at Maggie with innocent brown eyes. 'Daniel isn't even there on Friday afternoons!'

'I see!' Maggie grimaced. 'You sneaked of somewhere with him, did you? You ought to be ashamed!'

'Oh, Maggie! Don't be cross! I won't do it again, I promise!'

It took all Dorcas' considerable charm to talk Maggie out of her wrath, and the offer of a present of six new novelettes to persuade her out of mentioning Dorcas' truancy to Miss Lane herself.

Dorcas soon abandoned her very half-hearted struggle with her conscience and gave herself up entirely to her passion for Stephen. She set aside all notions of decency, of propriety — even of common caution. Appointments were made and kept at the shabby house in the courtyard. As the days progressed towards Christmas, Dorcas shamelessly exploited Maggie's susceptibility to winter colds. 'Don't come out today, Maggie,' she would say. 'There's a bad fog, and that cough will go straight to your chest if you walk out in this raw air. I'll get all the shopping.'

'Can you manage it?'

'Of course. You stay near the fire, and I'll bring you some balsam from the chemist, shall I?'

And Maggie, touched, would admit that she did indeed feel a bit rough, and agree to stay by the kitchen range. 'Give him a kiss from me, too, Dorry,' she would say.

Dorcas would toss her head. 'I'm not going anywhere near Follet's!' she would retort crossly. 'Whatever makes you think I am?'

As she rubbed her chilblains, another seasonal affliction which made Maggie unwilling to go, outside in winter, the older house-maid would grin at the cook. 'Not call into Follet's, my grand-mother's teeth!' she remarked one cold Tuesday in early December. 'Then why was she lugging all that hot water upstairs before dinner? Why's she wearing her best dress? I reckon old Daniel manages to slip out for ten minutes and give her a hug or two — stands to reason, don't it? Wouldn't be natural if they didn't want a few minutes together!'

And when Dorcas returned from her shopping expedition, flushed (with exertion) and her eyes sparkling (from the cold east wind) Mrs Butler nodded to Maggie. 'Her hairpins is in different to what they was before she went out,' she observed. 'And she ought to tell 'im to shave a bit closer — her face is covered in little scratches, and she can't blame that on no east wind!'

Stephen was becoming far more dependent on his mistress than he would ever have admitted, even to himself. He looked forward to the meetings in the dark, shuttered house with acute anticipation, almost ashamed of himself for being so obsessed.

'Oh, my darling, that was marvellous,' he said one day, as he rolled away from her and sat up. He rubbed his face and smiled ruefully, as if embarrassed by such an admission. 'I do like you, you know,' he confessed, taking a lock of her long hair between his fingers and twisting it around his hand. 'I can't remember ever liking a woman more.'

'Why is that, sir?' Dorcas intensified her Herefordshire accent. 'An' why could that be, squire?'

'Squire!' Stephen gave a shout of laughter and slapped her arm quite hard. 'Don't you dare call me that — I won't take any sarcasm from the likes of you!'

'I'm sorry!' Dorcas giggled. 'Mr Lawrence, sir, I'm that sorry. Don't be angry with me!'

'Oh, shut up!' Stephen considered the woman lying curled up next to him. 'Now, what is it about you that's irresistible?' he asked. 'What can it be? I think it must be that you're so relaxing. You're good at making me comfortable. Dorcas — sit up now.'

She did as he told her, propping herself up on the pillows.

'Now put your arms around my neck,' he instructed. 'Just so.' And he leaned back against her, making himself more comfortable still.

She kissed his ear. 'How's that?' she asked.

'It's lovely. You're so nice and soft, aren't you? No sharp corners. What pretty hair you have!' He reached for a strand of it, pulling a curl straight and letting it spring back into a coil. 'It's quite beautiful. Dorcas, you're a life-giver, you know. I feel renewed when I've been with you.'

But then, suddenly, he twisted round and stared at her intently, his grey eyes narrowed and his forehead contracted. 'And you?' he asked. 'What do you like about me? There must be something. Is it

93

my money? I haven't given you any, and I don't intend to. My face? My figure? That's hardly likely. So what is it, pretty child, that keeps you coming here to be used, as you put it, week after week?'

'I suppose I must love you.' Dorcas looked down at her white arms, so pale against his much darker skin. 'You're as ugly as a Welshman, you're tightfisted and you're completely heartless. Yet I love you.'

Stephen's frown deepened. 'Oh, don't say that!' he muttered crossly. 'You don't mean it, so don't say it. Don't spoil everything. And anyway,' he added, somewhat pettishly, 'I'm not that ugly, I'm certainly not tightfisted, and I'm not entirely heartless.'

He found his watch and looked at it. 'I think we ought to get dressed now,' he said. 'I shouldn't keep you from your grate-blacking or your letter-writing or whatever it is you do. How do you manage to escape from your mistress every Tuesday afternoon, by the way? Where does she think you are?'

It pleased Dorcas to realize, as she walked home through the darkening streets, that she hade once again disturbed Stephen out of his habitual self-possession. 'Surely,' she thought, 'he must have some affection for me? Otherwise he wouldn't have been so annoyed when I said I loved him, or so cross when I teased him? He was like a hurt child when I said he was heartless.' She smiled to herself, aware of her power.

Dorcas was out doing some legitimate shopping when the carter from Ashton Cross called, leaving a letter for her. She found Maggie in a state of extreme agitation over it for the carter, in response to Maggie's enquiry if there was anything wrong at Ashton Cross, had replied that there was plenty wrong. There was such things he could tell her, he said, as would make her hair stand on end — if he had a mind to. And perhaps one day he'd be pushed too far. Perhaps one day he'd say his piece, and damn the squire …

Dorcas took the letter and recognized Stephen's handwriting at once. Her face white, she fingered the heavy vellum envelope for a second or two before tearing it open. Maggie watched her read.

Controlling herself, but not without enormous effort, she folded the paper and tried to speak. 'It's from the housekeeper Maggie,' she managed to choke out at last. 'It's just to say that my mother is much better and is going back to her cottage to live — she's been staying at the manor house, you know.'

Maggie folded her arms and snorted. 'Well!' she exclaimed. 'What a storm about nothing! Old carter, he led me to believe it was bad news!' She looked hard at Dorcas, saw she was still very pale. 'I'm sorry, lovey,' she said. '*I* frightened *you*! Go upstairs and take your outdoor things off, and I'll make you a nice cup of tea.'

Dorcas sat on her bed, still with her shawl wrapped around her, and stared again at her letter. It was a hastily scribbled note telling her that he was obliged to go on a visit to some friends, and that he would see her in the New Year. It had been signed with his initials and was as curt and to the point as a memo to his bailiff. She wondered, bitterly, how her lover could be so casual about it all. She would not see him for at least three weeks. Three whole weeks! It was eternity!

She knew perfectly well why Stephen was going away. It was to see this much gossiped about Miss Marlowe, and to arrange his wedding with Miss Marlowe, God damn her to hell. Ever since the autumn the whole village had been buzzing with speculation about the lady. Now it seemed that an alliance between the master at Ashton and this heiress of somewhere or other was likely to come about.

In her agitated state of mind Dorcas would not have been comforted to know that Stephen had never even seen the woman concerned. All the gossip had been the direct result of his mother's wishful thinking — she had shared her thoughts with Mrs Collins, who had lost no time in spreading rumours all over the estate.

Dorcas had heard that Elizabeth Marlowe was a great beauty. In vain did she tell herself that any woman who was rich, and not actually deformed, was always a beauty. Jealousy made her head throb. She went to bed early, and tossed and turned all night.

Maggie woke her at six, startling her out of a fitful doze. 'You got fleas?' she demanded.

'What a stupid question, Maggie!' Dorcas glared at her. 'Of course I haven't! Don't be so disgusting!'

'Well; summat was making you wriggle,' retorted Maggie calmly. 'It was like being in bed with a ferret, what with you writhin' and squirmin' all over the place half the night. And you grind your teeth, and you talk to yourself!'

'No, I don't!'

'Yes, you do. Look — I have to sleep with you, I should know!'

'You don't know anything! Anything at all!'

Dorcas went through that morning thoroughly foul-tempered. She snapped and snarled at Maggie, who laughed at her, thus making her crosser still.

Eventually she stormed out of the kitchen. She went upstairs and collected a pillowcase full of dirty clothes. Taking them to the wash house, she beat them until her arms ached, sloshing water all over the floor and soaking her shoes. She had just lost the soap for the twentieth time when she heard Maggie cough, and turned to see her standing in the doorway.

'Madam wants to see you,' she said coldly. 'Now.'

Dorcas glowered back at her. 'I'm doing some washing, Maggie — can't you see?'

'You don't usually do any washing these days. Madam's been waiting for you this last half hour. She's got a whole stack of letters, and her eyes are playing her up something terrible; so you'd better leave this to me.' She surveyed the mess in the wash house, noticing the water splashed all over the slabs and the soapsuds all over the walls. 'You *are* out of practice, aren't you?' she asked.

After the midday meal had been eaten and cleared away, Dorcas made her apologies to Maggie and Mrs Butler, and said she would take the grocery order into town, call at the post office for Miss Lane, and fetch Maggie's new Sunday dress from the maker's. As she stood in the hall tying her bonnet strings, she overheard the other two servants talking.

'She's very ratty today, ain't she?'

'P'raps she's 'ad a fight with 'is Lordship.'

'Hmm. She wants to be got to church, that's what it is. All these country girls is the same — 'ot blooded!'

'D'you reckon so, Cook?'

'Aye.' Dorcas heard Mrs Butler giggle. 'She wants a babby, that's what it is!'

'D'you think so? She's only a babby herself!'

Dorcas went out of the house and down the path, frowning. If only everything were that simple ...

'I must forget about him. I shall forget about him! I hate him —

he's used me, just for his own pleasure. He's absolutely loathsome! I'm engaged to a dear, good man. I'm going to be married to him in the spring, and I'm going to live in a nice place above the shop. I shall be very happy.' This was roughly the catechism which Dorcas set herself to repeat whenever Stephen came into her mind.

But when Dorcas was with her dear, good man, it was clear to her what an absolute dullard he was. He had no interest in anything apart his trade. His conversation — on the rare occasions that he made any — was as tedious as a little child's.

He did not kiss her in a loverlike way. All he ever did was dart at her like a sort of bird, and jerk away again. He had no idea how to embrace a woman! So, one day, when he kissed her, she put her arms around him and, slowly, carefully, she kissed him back.

His reaction astonished her. He jumped away as if she were red hot. 'What's the matter?' she asked, puzzled.

'Nothing!' He'd rubbed his face with his hands, blushing. 'You mustn't do that, though, Dorry — don't do that again!'

'Do what, Daniel?'

'Do — that. Only certain sorts of women do — that. Look; when I kiss you — and I like to kiss you, you mustn't imagine that I don't — you ought to stand quite still and do nothing yourself, do you understand? That's how a decent woman behaves, do you see?'

'Yes, Daniel.' Dorcas looked at her hands. 'Yes, Daniel, I see.'

It was hopeless. How could the two men possibly be compared?

In church, where all three servants went on Sundays — more out of habit than out of piety — Dorcas knelt and prayed in earnest. She asked whatever remote deity might conceivably be listening to help her solve her problems, to stop her mind forever turning on a man who did not care a straw for her.

But, even as she prayed, she thought of Stephen. Even as she knelt in supplication, his face was in her mind. She remembered things he'd said to her, and she thought of the warmth of him, of the touch of him. 'You're a life-giver,' he'd told her. Perhaps she was — but she was also certain that she needed him as much as she needed air to breathe.

On the twenty-first of January the carter brought her a letter. 'From my mother?' she asked brightly, her heart thumping for joy as she saw the writing on the envelope.

'Dunno — can't read, can I?' The carter grimaced. 'All I'd say to you though, miss, is watch your step. Better women than you 'ave thought they could get away with it, an' they've all come to a bad end. Think of what your Ma would say, as well.'

'I really don't know what you mean, Mr Arrowsmith!' Dorcas gave the carter a shilling, which he took and pocketed with a very ill grace. 'Now, I have a great deal of work to do,' she told him. 'Thank you again for bringing this.'

Stephen had told her to meet him at the house by the river in a few days' time. Ignoring his peremptory tone, his bland assumption that she was as able as she was willing to leave her work for an hour or two simply to oblige him, she ran upstairs singing. He wanted to see her again! He still thought of her — and he had come back to Ashton Cross! That was all that mattered.

Her high spirits affected everyone. 'The year's turned, that's what it is,' remarked Mrs Butler. 'I 'ates December, too.'

It was easy to persuade Maggie that her mild sniffle would turn to bronchitis if she were to go out that following afternoon. 'I'll get the shopping!' cried Dorcas gaily. 'I'll see the coal merchant! There's no need for you to come with me,' she added, as she bolted her dinner.

Afterwards she rushed upstairs, washed all over, put on her new dress and, wrapping her best shawl around her shoulders, she dashed off with barely ten minutes to spare. She reached the town flushed and perspiring, arriving at the dark, shuttered house just as Stephen strolled down the lane from the opposite direction.

He merely nodded to her in greeting and he hardly spoke for the first half hour that they were together. But, later, he seemed to relax a little. He spread her hair out on the pillow and ran his fingers through it, kissing her as he did so.

She pushed his own hair out of his eyes and tried to smooth away the frown which habitually disfigured his face, creasing his forehead, making him look so cross most of the time. 'Did you enjoy your visit to your friends?' she asked.

'Oh, it was very tedious. They were people I'd never met before, and they were extremely dull. There wasn't a single book in the house worth reading, and there were no horses in the stables worth taking out. I was glad to get back to Ashton, I can tell you.'

'Were you?' Dorcas' heart began to thump. It had all been lies and conjecture, then — there was no fiancée, he hadn't been to meet his intended bride at all.

'I kept thinking of you,' he added, making her spirits soar still higher. 'I've been longing to see you again. You can't imagine how much I've missed you, my dear little trollop!'

Dorcas giggled. 'Weren't there any pretty ladies where you've been, then?' she asked.

Stephen sat up and rubbed his eyes. 'I suppose you will hear about it soon,' he muttered. 'Someone from the village will let you know if I don't tell you. And, anyway, it's not a secret.' He looked at her. 'I've become engaged to be married,' he said. 'The woman's name is Elizabeth Marlowe. Have you heard anything about her?'

Dorcas stared at him, her worst fears realized, her world crumbling around her. 'Only that she's young, rich and beautiful,' she managed to falter, before the tears came.

Stephen sighed, reached across the bed for Dorcas' shawl; he wrapped her in it, and put his arms around her. 'Listen to me,' he murmured. 'The engagement is in the nature of a family treaty; do you understand? My mother and the woman's parents are anxious that we should marry, because there is a similarity in fortune, expectations, and so on. I'd never heard of Miss Marlowe until I met her for the first time three weeks ago. Dorcas — I must marry somebody; and she seemed a pleasant enough woman who is, as you have heard, young and fairly rich.'

'And beautiful,' sobbed Dorcas. 'What is she like?'

Stephen wiped her face with his handkerchief. 'She's a middle-sized woman,' he replied. 'She's neither fat nor thin — I suppose her figure is good. She's fair-haired, very pale. I think her eyes are blue.' He stroked Dorcas' face. 'My dear, dear child,' he said. 'It doesn't matter to me what she looks like. She doesn't compare with you at all!'

'Yet she is to be your wife — while I am just your — your trollop!'

'Oh, indeed you are, Dorcas! You're the dearest little trollop a man could have!' He kissed her wet cheeks and pushed her hair back from her tearstained face. 'Please don't cry so, darling,' he added kindly. 'You know how fond I am of you — I won't ever desert you.'

'You'll marry! You'll marry Miss Marlowe, and I'll never see you again!' Tears began to pour down her cheeks afresh, dripping on to the bedclothes. 'I'll die if I don't see you!' she wept. 'I love you so much!'

'You don't love me. You just say that, as some women do.'

Dorcas pushed him away, glared at him through her tears. 'I love you!' she repeated. 'While you have been away I have tried to make myself forget you, tried and tried to stop wanting you. I have willed myself to hate you, even — I should hate you now, for treating me so! But —'

'But what?'

'But instead, I love you. You make me feel alive! I wish away the hours when I'm not with you! You're in my mind all the time, Stephen. Waking or sleeping, I'm thinking of you. Oh, if only I were a lady! I'd make you love me, there'd be no room in your heart for anyone but me!'

But then, suddenly, grief was joined by anger. 'You're a wretch,' she cried. 'You're a wretch, to be so cruel to me!'

'Don't call me a wretch, Dorcas.' Stephen's eyes glittered. 'Be careful what you say to me. Don't make me lose my temper with you.'

'Wretch,' she repeated. 'Wretch, wretch, wretch!' She laid her hands on his shoulders and shook him. 'All that talk of me being a life-giver!' she cried. 'All those sweet words you've uttered, and all those fancy things you've said! You're just a seducer, after all! I was right about you! You're a philanderer, a betrayer, and a beast!'

'Oh, do be quiet, Dorcas!' Instead of losing his temper, however, Stephen merely yawned. 'You're very tiresome some-times,' he said. 'Very tiresome indeed.'

Dorcas, perfectly well aware that she was just that, and wanting to provoke him into insulting her back, perhaps even hitting her, glowered at him. 'Beast,' she muttered again. 'Devil!'

There was no reaction. She considered calling him a bastard, but, in the end, jibbed at that. 'Pig,' she concluded, with a sniff.

'Pig, eh?' Stephen scowled at her but then, suddenly, he laughed 'You are comical,' he said. He ruffled her hair. 'Funny little thing!'

'Funny?' Outraged, she scratched his shoulder, raked it with her fingernails, deliberately drawing blood. 'I'm not funny,' she cried. 'Don't you dare say I'm funny, you devil!'

'Dorcas, I'll say just whatever I please!' He dabbed at the blood on his arm. 'Put away your claws, darling and listen to me.'

'What, then?'

'I won't be getting married for ages yet. Nothing has been arranged; it's possible that the woman may see someone she likes better and break off the engagement.' He smiled at her. 'I'm going abroad in March or April,' he said. 'I'll take you with me, shall I?'

'To Greece?'

'Yes. I'll show you some of the islands, teach you a bit of the language. Will you come with me?'

'You'd really take me to Greece with you?'

'Yes, if you'd like to come.'

'What would I do about my place? My mistress would want to know —'

'You can tell your mistress you've found another place. I think your place is with me now, don't you?'

Chapter Seven

AS IF IT WERE IN another life, as if it were unalterably ordained, Dorcas continued to walk out with Daniel Hitchman on Sunday afternoons, taking the same tedious promenade around the Castle Green, across the river bridge, along the riverside walk and back into the town centre; nominally chaperoned by a bored, yawning Maggie Stemp.

But Maggie took every opportunity to sit down and massage her chilblains, letting the lovers wander off by themselves. More and more frequently she left them alone for an hour or more, reasoning that if they did get up to any mischief, they were getting married soon enough for that not to matter.

As February went by, Dorcas cut out and sewed some of her wedding clothes, providing herself with a trousseau of plain, lace-edged underclothes, decorous nightgowns, and a few caps. Her wedding dress was being made by a dressmaker in the town and was to be a simple, high cut gown of dark blue silk.

The day of the wedding was fixed. On fine days Dorcas went into the garden to pick the small spring flowers which Mrs Butler meant to crystallize and with which she would decorate the wedding cake. 'I'll make it as fresh and as pretty as the little bride herself,' she said, beaming at Dorcas. 'Just see if I don't!'

'Another parcel for you, Dorry!' Maggie brought in a small package, wrapped in brown paper. 'It's from the people at the dairy,' she explained. 'Open it!'

Dorcas did, took out a blue and white china jug, which was decorated with bands of forget-me-nots. As Maggie exclaimed over its prettiness, Dorcas grimaced to herself. Could she send all this stuff back to the donors? Would she ever have the nerve to call off the wedding? She didn't think so ...

An air of quiet excitement pervaded the house. Dorcas, at the centre of it, was the object of good wishes from dozens of visitors, the recipient of gifts from people she scarcely knew. And, as time went on, she found that the idea of a helpless captive being dragged towards a chasm, into which he will be thrown, occurred to her over and over again.

It was as if all the preparations she was making were, in fact, for another bride. She felt that she was making ready for a funeral.

Once or twice, she nerved herself to tell Daniel the truth. She rehearsed her lines, braced herself for the disgrace which would inevitably follow if he chose to let it be known why they were not going to marry. 'Daniel,' she said to herself, 'I cannot marry you after all. For some months now I have been the mistress of another man. I love him more than life, and he seems to be tolerably fond of me. He has offered to take me abroad in spring. I'm sorry I deceived you.'

Dorcas knew perfectly well that she wouldn't say anything.

One sunny day in March Daniel hired a pony and trap, in which he drove Dorcas and Maggie over to Ashton Cross. She watched him as he drove, noticed that he handled the reins competently. He wasn't nervous or afraid, in fact he was in more of a holiday mood than she'd ever seen him before.

'It's very pretty out here,' he remarked, as they sped past the turnpike and into the open countryside, fresh and green with the new spring. 'The air smells so sweet — doesn't it, Dotty?'

Since they happened to be passing a slaughter yard as he made that particular remark, and the squeals of the butchered pigs drowned out his last few words, Dorcas merely nodded. But then, making a tremendous effort, she smiled at him. 'Didn't you ever come out into the countryside when you were a child?' she enquired.

'No, I didn't. Well — hardly ever. Certainly not after my mother died.' He shook the reins, urging the pony on. 'But I shall do so in future,' he added. 'We'll come out here on Sundays, shall we? We'll show the yokels and the squires that we town folks can do things in style!'

They reached the village at midday. Dorcas, by now accustomed to the contrast between the civilization of the town and the squalor of her own birthplace, looked anxiously at Daniel. But he seemed determined to be pleased with everything. 'They're nice little cottages,' he said. 'The thatched roofs look so cosy, don't they?'

'They're full of vermin.' Dorcas shuddered. 'Give me a decent tiled roof any day.' But, in her heart, she blessed Stephen and his brother over and over again. But for them, she'd be showing her future husband a collection of tumbledown hovels. Nowadays, at least, Ashton Cross looked relatively prosperous; its village street was paved, and its cottages were in good repair. Even if the inhabitants were still as sluttish as ever, she could not be held responsible for that.

And there was Ellen, coming out of her house, her face bright with pleasure. Somehow she had procured herself a decent gown and shawl. She had washed her hands and face and made some attempt to put up her hair. Dorcas climbed down to greet her, a basket of baking held tightly in her arms in order that she might have an excuse not to be fulsomely embraced. 'Mother,' she said. 'This is Miss Stemp. And this' — she took Daniel's hand and offered it to Ellen — 'is Mr Hitchman.'

'Mrs Grey — it's a pleasure to meet you.' Daniel favoured Ellen with his most enchanting smile, she looked overcome with gratification, and Dorcas finally relaxed.

Ellen was, as her daughter had expected she would be, completely overwhelmed by Daniel; by his beauty, which was indeed remarkable, and by his quiet, courteous gravity. Dorcas knew that, after they'd gone, Ellen would brag about her daughter and Daniel for days, but now she was too overawed to natter on in her usual mindless fashion.

She did, of course, retail the latest piece of gossip about the squire. 'Such a handsome young lady she is,' she told her audience. 'Fair as an angel she looks — Mrs Collins says so, and she's seen her picture. Yes, Miss Marlowe's a perfect beauty; and rich, too. I was saying to carter just the other day, she ought to keep the young squire contented, but he said, if any woman could keep Mr Lawrence on the straight and narrow, pigs would grow wings. He's getting very sour in his old age, is Tom Arrowsmith …'

Dorcas blushed — Daniel yawned — Maggie cut more of the cake which she had brought from Hereford. The travellers set out again at four in the afternoon, Ellen taking a most affecting leave of her daughter, holding Dorcas in her arms and weeping over her.

'I'm that proud of you, girl!' she sobbed. 'I'm that pleased — he's a lovely young man, indeed he is — I couldn't be more delighted if you were going to marry the squire himself!'

At that, Dorcas began to cry as well.

Dorcas was, in her turn, taken for a formal meal with Daniel's widowed father, a carpenter who had a malodorous workshop near the tanneries next to the station yard. A small, shrivelled man, he bore no resemblance at all to his golden lion of a son. He treated the prospective Mrs Hitchman with scant respect, remarking that he hoped his son would be more fortunate in marriage than he himself had been. 'Boy's mother worrited the life out of me,' he grumbled. 'Wantin' this, wantin' that — never satisfied, always on the moan. I 'opes as you knows when to leave a man in peace!' He studied Dorcas for a minute or two. 'Well,' he conceded. 'You're young. Can't 'ave picked up too many bad 'abits yet. Eh?'

He slopped his tea into his saucer and sucked it through his teeth. Dorcas, disgusted, pushed her untasted meal aside.

And, on Tuesday afternoons — in spite of everything — Dorcas met Stephen at the dark, shuttered house by the river. She took incredible risks to keep her appointments there. Her wedding gown needed more fittings than any other dress ever made. She forgot essential shopping and had to dash back to town to fetch it. Mrs Butler laughed indulgently at her, telling her that she was like a tabby cat tied in a bag. 'No man's ever 'ad that effect on Maria Butler,' she remarked, grinning. 'Nor likely to 'ave, either!'

March came to an end. Stephen finalized the arrangements he had made to join an excavation in Greece, and was anxious to be off.

He'd spent some time wondering how the other two men, with whom he was travelling, would react if he took Dorcas with him. Fred Dawlish would laugh at him — of that he was certain. He'd ask Stephen what was wrong with a Greek whore, point out that the hetairai of Corinth had appeared to be perfectly satisfactory the previous spring. 'Why didn't you bring your own cheese sandwiches, too?' Stephen could hear Fred asking, in that maddening, sarcastic drawl of his ...

As far as Stephen was concerned, being an object of ridicule was the most dreadful prospect he could imagine. Having as sharp a brain and quick a tongue as any man, he could deal with being directly insulted, could defend himself if physically attacked. He could argue down anybody, get his own way in almost any situation. He had however never learned to cope with being the butt of a joke. Teased, he would bridle and redden, clench his fists and glare. And some of his friends, those with a taste for being punched in the face, took a great delight in pushing their luck just a little too far ...

He decided against taking Dorcas. The more he thought about it, the more stupid the idea seemed. She'd hate all the travelling — she'd certainly grizzle and she'd probably be ill. She was too ignorant to understand what she might be told of the current project; and he wouldn't have the time to be with her very much, anyway. In Greece, she'd be a liability and an embarrassment. Left in Hereford, she'd be so very nice to come back to, so pleased to see him again ...

On the morning of April the second, Dorcas was violently sick. Queasiness persisted all day; the following morning she was sick again. And on the one after that. Maggie, alarmed but not really surprised, drew the obvious conclusion.

'It's a good job you'll be wed by Friday week,' she muttered. She held out a damp cloth for Dorcas to wipe her mouth on. 'He doesn't know, does he?' she asked. 'Well — take my advice and don't you tell him — yet. He might want to stop the whole thing; men are funny like that. Go on, get it all up, you'll feel better then.'

'Maggie, I —'

'Finished? Wipe your face, then.' Maggie frowned reproachfully at Dorcas. 'Oh, Dorry, how could you?' she cried. 'Couldn't you wait? I thought you'd have had more sense, even if he hadn't!' She looked narrowly at Dorcas. 'He didn't force you, did he?'

Dorcas, her mouth full of bile, just managed to shake her head.

'Just as well.' Maggie nodded grimly. 'I'd 'ave throttled 'im myself if he'd hurt you.'

Dorcas hung on to the washstand, and heaved.

Dorcas and Stephen had arranged to meet on the Tuesday of the following week. By the time she saw him again, Dorcas had gone through anger, defeated self pity and conquered bitterness. She meant to tell him, simply and calmly, then to say that she would not see him again, before he had the chance to abandon her.

She arrived at the shuttered house to find him lying across the bed, reading a book. He did not look up when she went over to him; he made no sign of recognition even when she kissed him. So she sat down beside him and waited until he might choose to give her his attention.

He reached the end of his chapter, marked the place and closed the book. He took his time with her that day, and afterwards he wrapped her shawl around her shoulders and told her that she was a dear little thing. 'I have something to say to you,' he announced. 'Before I tell you what it is, though, will you promise not to cry, or make a fuss?'

'I have something to tell you,' she'd replied.

'Oh? What's that?'

'I'm going to have a baby.'

Walking through the streets that evening, Dorcas found that her eyes filled and brimmed over with tears which she had neither the inclination nor the power to brush away. By the time she finally reached home her face was blotched and swollen almost beyond recognition.

Maggie met her at the door, and practically dragged her into the kitchen. 'Where've you been?' she demanded angrily. 'I thought you'd put yourself in the river, that I did!'

She took Dorcas into the scullery and helped her to take off her outdoor clothes. 'I'm telling you, girl; it's no use your weeping and wailing now,' she rapped. 'You must've known what you were doing. I told you all about it when you was a little girl.'

Dorcas sat down at the kitchen table. She laid her head on her folded arms and began, silently, to sob again. Noiselessly, helplessly she wept until her tears soaked through the sleeves of her gown, and a damp brown stain appeared on the scrubbed kitchen table.

Maggie was moved by such distress. 'There, there,' she crooned, patting Dorcas' shoulder. 'I'm sorry I yelled at you — I was worried, see.' She sat down next to Dorcas and stroked her hand.

'Don't upset yourself so, lovey,' she pleaded. 'Tell 'im after you're wed — he'll be thrilled to have a honeymoon baby! Don't cry about what can't be helped. Plenty more 'ave done what you did — an' the sky hasn't fallen yet.'

Dorcas looked up at her friend's kind, honest face. 'Oh, Maggie,' she sobbed, 'I'm so unhappy! I want to die!' She would have liked to confess everything to Maggie, but Maggie hugged her to her bony chest and bade her hush. 'Don't talk about it any more,' she soothed. 'It's too late to do anything about it, and nattering about rights and wrongs won't help. Go on up to bed — I'll bring you up some tea. I'll tell Madam you've got a bad headache; she said herself that you've been looking a bit down these past few days, so if she thinks you've got a cold, so much the better.'

'Maggie, I —'

Maggie shook her head. 'Go on up now,' she repeated. 'Not another word. I'm sure everything will come right in the end. And nothing seems so bad after a good night's sleep.'

Had she taken enough laudanum to make her sleep that night, Dorcas would never have woken up again. As it was, she lay awake until dawn, reliving her last interview with Stephen over and over again.

He had not believed her at first. 'You're pregnant?' he'd asked, frowning, 'Are you sure? I've been very careful, you know; I think it's hardly possible.'

'There's no doubt of it.'

'Oh. Well — is the child mine?'

'Of course it is! Of course it's yours! Whose else would it be?' Dorcas' self control had snapped then — she had begun to cry, unable to stop herself. 'You must help me,' she sobbed. 'I don't know what to do!'

'Well, Dorcas —' Stephen considered for a moment. 'If you're quite sure you're expecting a child,' he said, 'perhaps I could find someone to deal with it for you. There are women who help girls in your situation, I believe — and maybe —'

Dorcas' look of horror made him stop short. 'Oh, you are hateful!' she cried. 'Hateful! How could you even consider murdering your own child? What if I were to die at the hands of one of these women you speak of? And how many other poor girls have you sent to these people who deal with the results of men's philandering, to rid yourself of your own children?'

'I've sent no poor girls to have their children aborted. As far as I know, I've never fathered a child.'

'Well, this child is yours.' Dorcas drew her chemise over her head, fastened the buttons. 'And you want to kill it. Murderer!' She reached for her dress. 'I wish I could hate you,' she muttered.

'But you love me — or so you say. Do you love me still?'

'You know perfectly well that I do. That I must.' She began to pin up her hair. 'Why else would I come to this horrible dirty place, where I don't doubt you've brought girls before? Why else should I meet you here, to be treated like a plaything, to give you an hour's pleasure when you feel the need of it? When you need a woman — any woman?' She looked sorrowfully at him, 'I love you more than I love myself, more than friends or family,' she said. 'I love you more than the air I breathe. Don't you understand me? I can't be any plainer!'

'Then you'd better marry me, hadn't you?'

Dorcas stared at him. 'What did you say?'

'You heard what I said. Marry me.'

'Don't tease me, Stephen. It isn't fair, or kind.'

'I'm not teasing you! I won't ask you again, though. Is it yes or no?'

When Dorcas thought back to that conversation for the hundredth, for the thousandth time, she was unable to decide if her good or her bad angel had been guiding her. 'Is it yes or no?' Stephen had repeated, shaking her by the shoulders.

'I can't marry you, Stephen,' she replied. 'You don't really mean it when you ask me. You can't do.'

'I always say what I mean.' He grinned at her, his dark eyes bright. 'Well — that's settled then. It's time I was a father, I suppose; although you're a little young for motherhood. Ah well. I daresay you'll survive the experience of it!'

Such levity astonished her, convinced her, more than anything else would have done, that he did not really intend to marry her.

She looked at him critically then — took in the too square face, the too heavy features; the wide shoulders and the broad chest; and she reflected that he was indeed nothing but an ugly, lowering

Welshman. Masquerading as a gentleman, Stephen Lawrence was a barbarian whose black eyebrows were too marked, whose eyes were too narrow, whose hair grew too low on his temples. And his mouth was too wide; his nose was too large; his chin was too stubborn.

But all these unprepossessing features were now chiselled into the tablet of her memory and she knew, despairingly, that she could never love any man who did not resemble — who wasn't — Stephen. 'I love you,' she repeated, as if to herself. 'I wish I didn't — I wish I could help myself — but I can't.' She looked at him piteously. 'I love you, Stephen — do you believe me?'

'Yes. I believe you.' He patted her shoulder. 'Put your shawl on, finish your hair while I get dressed. So Dorcas: when can I make an honest woman of you?'

'You really mean to do so?'

'God in Heaven, idiot! Yes! Do you want a declaration of intent, written in my blood? A ring on your finger? Well, you can have one of those. We'll go and buy you one. Now.'

She shook her head, 'I can't marry you,' she said, almost in tears again. 'I can't!'

'Can't you? Why is that?'

'It's obvious, isn't it? I love you too much to make you a joke to you friends and your family — just imagine what they would say! The master of Ashton Cross, tricked into marrying a peasant!'

'Oh, nonsense. I can marry whom I please.' Stephen smiled at her. 'It's too late for you to have silly scruples of that kind,' he said. 'And anyway you're not a beggar maid, and I'm not a duke. It's perfectly acceptable for a farmer to marry a —' he searched for the right word '— a lady's companion. It will be a ten-minute wonder to a handful of people who have nothing better to think about, that's all.' He hugged her close to him and kissed her cheek. 'I know I'm ugly, tightfisted and heartless,' he went on. 'I'm not good enough for you — but will you have me all the same?'

Dorcas took a deep breath, made her choice. 'There is a man in Hereford who wants to marry me,' she said, quickly. 'The wedding is arranged — the child will be born in seven or eight months time. He will never suspect that it is not his.' As she said it, she wished it unsaid.

'*What?*' Appalled, Stephen gaped at her. 'What did you just tell

110

me?' he asked, incredulous. His hand, which had been resting lightly on her shoulder, tightened its grip. 'Dorcas, what on earth are you talking about?' he demanded. 'Who is this man? You've just made that up, haven't you?'

So Dorcas had been obliged to tell him all about her involvement with Daniel Hitchman, with whom her wedding was indeed planned. By the time she was half way through her narrative, the contempt on Stephen's face frightened her and she turned away, unable to look at him, while she faltered on to the end.

'Well, Dorcas.' He pulled her round to face him, caught her chin and held it firmly, made her look at him. 'Well, child — what a scheming little hoyden you are!'

His eyes seemed to bore into her face; she tried to twist away, but still he held her. 'You won't have to look at me for much longer,' he murmured softly. 'So don't turn away now.' He grinned at her with a ghastly, sarcastic smile, making her shiver. 'How incredibly well you have arranged things,' he continued smoothly. 'I can see I've underestimated you. I'd never have thought a mere infant could be half so cunning. But you've run circles round me, haven't you? You must be congratulating yourself on your quite remarkable cleverness!'

He let her go, then. Quickly, he dressed. He reached for his riding boots, pulled them on, and picked up his whip. Seeing her flinch, he scowled at her. 'I'm not going to touch you,' he said, in the same dead, cold tone. 'You perhaps deserve a flogging but I do, as I told you once before, have certain principles. Unlike you.'

Dorcas stared at him, willing him to understand. 'Don't talk to me like that!' she cried. 'You must see that what I propose is for the best! I know you're upset and angry — but, Stephen, think of your family! Think of your own fiancée, poor lady — remember what you owe to her. It's because I love you that I won't marry you! Surely you see that?'

'A woman who is pregnant with my child will not marry me because she would prefer to marry a tradesman.' Stephen shrugged. 'That's perfectly clear to me.'

Dorcas lunged across the bed to grab at Stephen's arm. 'Don't leave me like this, Stephen,' she pleaded. 'Say something kind to me — say anything, but don't look so cold and stern! I didn't mean to hurt you! Everything I've suggested is for the best — you must understand that! Isn't it obvious to you that it's the only thing to be done?'

'Bitch.' Shaking her off, he picked up his coat, put it on. He straightened the lapels, checked his pockets. He favoured Dorcas with one last glance of absolute disgust. 'Bitch,' he repeated, his voice still soft and deadly. 'You didn't mean to hurt me? Liar!' He walked past her to the door, and jerked it open.

The sour-faced maid jumped back from her listening position and fell heavily against the wall, her face a picture of terror. 'As for you,' said Stephen coldly, 'remember that I can have you taken up and sentenced any time I choose. So consider that before you repeat anything you might have heard today!'

He pushed his hand into his trouser pocket and pulled out a handful of loose change. He flung the coins in a wide arc, scattering them all over the landing and into the bedroom beyond. The maid was still scrabbling for the money, pushing Dorcas aside to grab a stray sixpence, as Stephen clattered downstairs and slammed the street door behind him.

Chapter Eight

DORCAS GREY MARRIED DANIEL HITCHMAN in the old city church of All Saints. She carried red silk roses, which Mrs Butler considered, out loud, were unsuitable for a virgin bride. Ellen Grey sobbed noisily throughout the service, and old Mr Hitchman creaked his arthritic limbs during the silences between responses. Dorcas made her vows in a tight-throated whisper — Daniel's voice, when he made his, sounded unnecessarily loud.

The April day had begun bright enough, but when the wedding party came out of the church the sky had clouded over. They all made their way to the hotel nearby, where the wedding breakfast had been arranged, through a light drizzle.

Try as she might in later years, Dorcas could not remember any details of her wedding reception. A blur of faces round a table — her mother, her new father-in-law, Mrs Butler, Maggie Stemp, Daniel's best man, Daniel himself — she supposed they had all been there, but she had no idea what they'd worn, what they'd talked about, what they'd eaten. She vaguely remembered being teased for not eating anything herself. But the whole day had passed in a blur of unreality.

The rooms over the shop which Daniel had arranged for them to have were newly decorated with fresh, flower-patterned papers and white paint. The chairs were covered in a pretty chintz of Dorcas' own choosing; now it made her wince to remember how light-hearted she'd been when she'd selected that particular pattern from the upholsterer's catalogue, months and months ago. When she was so very much younger — when something as absurdly trivial as the design on some material had seemed so important...

Everything was clean and new, unlived in. Dorcas went from room to room, growing more and more depressed; she was glad

113

that Daniel had gone down to the shop for half an hour. She could hear voices coming from the back room, men's voices chaffing and teasing, and Daniel's answering murmur. She flinched as loud male laughter floated up to her.

Daniel had not seemed to mind that she preferred to remain upstairs. He stayed with the other assistants until they all went home; then he locked up the shop. She heard his heavy footsteps on the landing.

'Why are you sitting here in the dark?' he asked kindly as he entered the room. He lit a lamp then drew the curtains against the damp spring evening. He sat down beside her and took her hand in his, rubbed it for a minute or two. 'You're cold,' he observed. 'And you look so tired. I expect you were up early, weren't you? Go and turn down the sheets — we might as well go to bed, don't you think?'

Dorcas went into the bedroom. She pulled back the bedclothes — the fine woven counterpane, the soft wool blankets, the stiff linen sheets — one by one, feeling as little pleasure in these acquisitions as she had when she and Maggie had put the bedroom to rights earlier in the week. 'You'll be able to do it in comfort soon,' Maggie had remarked, coarsely.

Daniel did not come. After waiting for ten minutes or so, Dorcas undressed herself. Attired in one of her new nightgowns, she got into her new bed, wondering why her new husband had not come to undress her; for surely that was part of making love?

But it was another twenty minutes before Daniel came in. He smiled reassuringly as he took the nightshirt she had laid out for him, and went into another room to undress. When he came back he bent over her and kissed her — a light, chaste kiss, dispassionate as always — then he turned the lamp right down. He climbed into bed between the cold linen sheets.

Although the room itself was now in darkness, the rays from the street lamp outside shone through the thin curtains, and the cold white light picked out the objects in the bedroom. Dorcas lay down, and turned her face to Daniel's; she found she could see him quite plainly in the dusk. She could not, however, read his expression. He was looking at her, but without curiosity, and certainly without any obvious desire.

She wondered if she ought to put her arms around him or —

114

perhaps kiss him. Did certain sorts of women kiss their husbands? But then he reached across her, and pulled at the folds of her nightgown.

When she made as if to remove it, he caught her hand. 'No,' he whispered. 'There's no need to take it off. Don't move at all, dear. I promise I won't be long, and I'll try not to hurt you.'

He fumbled with his own nightshirt, tugged up Dorcas' gown and leaned over her.

Dorcas looked up at him, saw that even in the half light his eyes seemed glazed. Forbidden to move herself, she waited for the kisses which never came, waited in vain for some sort of preliminary caress, for some kind of tenderness before Daniel took his wife, before he made use of her in the fashion in which a married man was legally entitled to do.

It seemed, however, that there was to be no hugging. No endearments were to be murmured, no declarations of affection made. Daniel was merely going to do what all male animals do.

Tensed rigid, she shut her eyes tightly. She felt him enter her; he pushed, grunting and breathing heavily now. His face lay against her shoulder, his hair brushed her cheek, but he did not even look at her.

She bit her lip to prevent herself from shouting at him to leave her alone, from begging him to raise his weight from her a little, for she felt she was being stifled.

For a few minutes more the nightmare continued. Then there was silence. Daniel seemed to have gone to sleep. But then he rolled away from her, and lay facing the window. Soon he was really asleep, breathing regularly.

Dorcas lay awake in the darkness, hardly daring to hope that he had not suspected anything. 'Daniel?' She pushed his shoulder. 'Daniel? Will you not speak to me?'

He shifted slightly, raised his head. 'Are you hurt?' he asked drowsily. 'Did I make you bleed?'

'No, but Daniel —'

'That's all right, then.' He lay down again, his arms under the pillow. 'Go to sleep, Dorry,' he murmured. 'Go to sleep now.' And soon he was breathing heavily again.

Relieved beyond expression, Dorcas realized that her wedding night was not, after all, going to end in tears and curses. She had half-heartedly prepared a few fibs about being raped by a labouring man as a child, which she'd hoped might pacify an enraged husband, fobbed off with damaged goods when he'd thought he was getting brand new merchandise. Her very fear must have made her unyielding, she supposed, and Daniel had, she was sure, been innocent of any previous dealings with women. Her husband's inexperience had saved her.

Suddenly, she felt a warm wetness underneath her, and could have cried with relief. Now, she might subsequently declare herself pregnant; and Daniel would have no real cause to suspect the child was not his. She fell into a light slumber, and dozed until morning.

A month went by, and Dorcas found that her clothes had become marginally tighter. She nerved herself to tell him. 'Daniel,' she faltered. 'I know it's very soon — and I might be mistaken — but I think I may be going to have a baby.'

'Really?' Daniel stared over his teacup, then replaced it in his saucer and reached for his wife's hand. 'Do you really think so?' he asked, a smile breaking across his face. 'That's marvellous!'

He had risen from his seat then, knelt beside her to take her in his arms and kiss her almost passionately in his delight.

Overcome by guilt and misery, Dorcas had begun to cry. 'Don't be afraid, dear,' Daniel had said soothingly. 'It's what you're made for, after all. You're young and healthy, you'll be fine, I know! Oh, I do hope you're right about the child!' He had gone down to the shop whistling.

His kindness was so much harder to bear than indifference or cruelty would have been. He made her lie in bed in the mornings, he brought her tea and dry toast, he made her rest in the afternoons, was careful to spare her the slightest hardship. So, in her long stretches of unbroken leisure, Dorcas sewed little garments; she cooked for her husband and herself — that was, when he would let her — and she read.

She read to escape. Novel after novel after novel she devoured, some borrowed from the circulating library, others lugged from Miss Lane's own collection by Maggie Stemp, who warned her gloomily that her eyes would go the same way as poor Madam's. 'She can hardly see to read the headlines in the newspaper these

116

days,' remarked Maggie. 'The doctor says she ought to go to London for some operation or other, but she says she don't want to. I reckon she's scared — I would be!'

For weeks together, then, Dorcas would be Sophia Western, or lucky Elizabeth Bennet, or even poor Clarissa Harlowe. This extending of her personality into the characters of literary heroines helped preserve her sanity in those early months of marriage, when regret, guilt and misery jostled within her to destroy her peace of mind.

Daniel's presence was almost intolerable. He could sit, silent and abstracted, hour after hour, watching her with a faint smile on his placid face, but saying nothing. Sometimes she read to him, but she could tell that he did not attend. Awareness of the wrong she had done him made her dislike his company all the more.

She supposed he was silent simply because he was tired from the long hours he worked in the shop. She told herself that not everyone was as much of a chatterbox as she was. But she looked forward to the birth of the baby as a distraction for her restless spirit.

Maggie was there, delivering books and grumbling again about the effect all this reading was bound to have on her friend's eyesight, on the afternoon that Dorcas felt the first faint gripe of pain and realized the baby was ready to come. As her waters broke spectacularly Maggie went haring off for the midwife, pausing only to say to Daniel, as she rushed through the shop, that the child was on its way. 'Early! He's early!' she had said, emphasizing the word.

The midwife came in her own time, relaxed and smiling. 'He's coming a bit before he's due, ain't he, my ducky?' she asked. She slid her practised hand inside the young mother, whereupon she confirmed that the baby was indeed well on its way. 'You're a good seven months, aren't you, my pet?' she enquired, perfectly well aware that she had just examined a woman at full term. 'Well — you'll be quite all right, so don't you fret. Go to bed now and rest, have a little walk around the room when you feels like it, and I'll come back in a couple of hours' time.'

At eight o'clock that autumn evening, after a comparatively short and easy labour, Dorcas gave birth to her daughter. Although the child was small, she was well made and plump. The

117

midwife gave Dorcas a ghost of a wink. 'A good enough size for a seven-month babby,' she observed archly. She wiped the baby's face and put her to the breast, where the child coughed but then, obligingly, began to suck.

Stroking her baby's head, Dorcas saw that the child's hair was jet black, curling damply in fine tendrils around her little face. The dark, narrow eyes which gazed up at her were, in shape and set, Stephen's own. She even had his frown, a faint but obvious vertical line just above her eyes.

'She's beautiful! Oh, she's absolutely beautiful!' cried her mother, laying the child's little hand on her breast, rocking to and fro and humming to the baby, who continued to stare critically up at her.

'Of course she's beautiful. And just like her mother! Hold her tightly, she won't break — that's right.' The midwife went on to the landing. 'Get Mr Hitchman,' she said to a man busy in one of the storerooms at the foot of the stairs. 'Tell 'im he can come an' see 'is babby!'

Daniel came into the bedroom, into the exclusively female world smelling of blood and new birth, a little hesitantly. He kissed Dorcas on the forehead and looked gravely at the infant she held. 'Can I take her?' he asked diffidently.

Dorcas handed him the shawled bundle, which he accepted almost reverently. He looked at the baby's face. 'She's a treasure,' he said at last. His face broke into a wide smile as he walked across to the window where the lamp would better illuminate the child's face. 'She's a treasure,' he repeated, hugging the child to him now. 'She's the most beautiful thing I've ever seen. Oh, she is — she is!'

He beamed at Dorcas and took the baby back to her. 'I love you, Dorry,' he said simply. Then, blushing at his own delight, he went back down to the shop to receive the congratulations of the other assistants and of old Mr Follet himself, who commiserated and said it was bound to be a boy next time.

The child slept peacefully in her cradle while her mother, exhausted though she was, stayed awake. Dorcas gazed hopelessly into the darkness, watching the night sky for the coming of the dawn. Towards daybreak, she got up and lifted the child out of her enshrouding shawls, and wrapped her in a fold of her own night-gown, holding her baby tightly next to her. Rocking little Anna,

Dorcas felt the tears bubbling up inside her. At that moment, she wanted Stephen so desperately that she thought she would die of grief. But then the baby stirred, searching for milk. Dorcas unbuttoned her nightdress and fed her. As the child sucked, the pain in the mother's chest distracted her a little from her mental anguish. She felt just a little calmer.

The baby thrived. When her mother's milk came in properly she was determined to have all that was going; she rooted and cried constantly for food, clamping her little jaws to the breast and sucking greedily, grunting with satisfaction as she fed. The child's sleeplessness and voracity exhausted Dorcas so much that she was too tired to think, too weary to regret.

At six weeks the baby settled down, consenting to be nursed at regular intervals, agreeing to sleep through most of the hours of darkness. Dorcas lost her pallor of fatigue, and found that she was recovering her strength.

The baby smiled her first smile — at Daniel. 'Wind,' said Dorcas dismissively, as Daniel insisted that Anna was grinning at him. 'Wind — that's all it is. She's just had a feed.'

'No, Dorry, it's not wind. Come and look — she's smiling! She really is; aren't you, my little piglet?'

Dorcas looked. Sure enough, Anna was beaming at Daniel. She was holding one of his fingers in her fat little fist and her mouth was stretched wide in an expression of unmistakable pleasure.

For one so habitually reserved, Daniel's absolute delight in the child was extraordinary. He would pick her up and hold her close to him, crooning to her, lulling her to sleep when Dorcas failed — quite oblivious to the dribbles of milk or sick which trickled down his clean shirt front, not caring that sticky little fingers were pulling his hair. 'She's my own little darling, aren't you, sweetheart?' he would ask her, while she beamed and gurgled at him.

The child grew so very like her father that it made Dorcas' heart ache to look at her. The eyes, in particular, were so similar, and the set of the mouth, the cast of expression, were all his. Anna's black hair grew rapidly, but instead of being coarse and straight like Stephen's, it was soft in texture; and curled in ringlets just as Dorcas' did.

Old Mr Hitchman grunted when he looked at his granddaughter. 'She must have been frightened by a black man when 'er were carrying,' he muttered, grimacing sourly at Dorcas. 'The babby's near enough a nigger!'

This made Daniel scowl at the carpenter and retort, sharply, that the child's mother was dark; so what did his father expect her baby to look like?

Daniel's devotion to Anna increased still further as she made it clear that she preferred his society to anyone else's. He would get out of his bed in the night if he heard her so much as whimper, would lean over her cradle and talk softly to her, soothing her back to contentment. 'Sleep, my darling — close your eyes,' Dorcas would hear him murmur. 'Don't wake your poor tired Mama.'

He liked to watch Dorcas feed her, and would snatch a minute or two when he could, in order to come up from the shop to play with her, to rock her cradle if she was fractious, or simply to gaze at her while she slept. The baby did, for a while, bring husband and wife closer together. Although he remained taciturn and usually undemonstrative, Daniel was not sullen — and he walked out with his wife and her child on sunny Sunday afternoons with his face a picture of modest pride, which quite touched Dorcas' heart.

It was now that she began to feel real guilt. This was not the self-indulgent, rather comfortable kind of guilt she had imagined she'd felt during her brief period of intensive church-going almost a year before, in which she had wallowed as luxuriously as a pig might roll in the mud of its sty. This was real regret, coupled with heartfelt, bitter remorse.

'I injured him quite deliberately,' she thought. 'I betrayed him repeatedly, I deceived him without a thought. And I've had the arrogance to blame him for what he can't help, I've despised him for what is really reticence and modesty, I've looked down on him because he's just an ordinary, working man.'

Daniel, she reflected, might be uneducated — but he did his job well. More than well, it seemed, for Mr Follet had been hinting that he thought of early retirement, and that he had Daniel in mind for his manager. As for Daniel's treatment of Dorcas and her daughter, what could be more loving, more affectionate, more kind?

'I shall learn to love him,' Dorcas told herself. 'I won't mind that he's dull. I won't even mind that he takes no interest in me as a woman, that he doesn't know how to love me when we're in bed together. He can't help his nature, after all. I'll be a pattern mother. I'll be the kind of wife he wants.' For a year or two, Dorcas almost succeeded in fulfilling her intentions.

She found it very hard to do without close physical contact with another adult, without demonstrative affection of any kind. As a small child she'd curled up in bed with her mother, safe in Ellen's warm embrace — then she'd shared a bed with Maggie, had been kept snug and cosy in her surrogate sister's company. But, more than that, Dorcas remembered the almost other-worldly bliss of being made love to by a passionate man, by a lover who had seemed to care as much for her pleasure as he had about his own. Recalling these experiences with an almost tangible longing, she sometimes willed Daniel to turn to her, to kiss her as a lover should, to make her feel wanted.

But their sexual congress, however, remained abhorrent to her. Daniel did not expect or want any response from his wife. When he desired her he would simply take her without any preamble, forcing his way inside her while she lay under him, half-suffocated in the voluminous folds of her nightgown; hating him, wanting to push him away, but feeling some sort of obligation to him which entitled him to use her like that.

'He'd never have married me,' she told herself sometimes as she lay awake, distressed and feeling brutalized, longing and longing for Stephen. 'He would, at best, have set me up in some house or other miles away from my family and friends, where he would have kept me as a pet until he tired of me. Then what would I have done, disgraced, abandoned and alone, burdened with a child? It's better as it is. Much better.'

She had chanced to read, some months back, that Stephen had married a Miss Marlowe, of Stone Lea in the county of Shropshire. She had screwed up the copy of the *Hereford Times* and cried; had felt ill for days, as if her jealousy was literally eating away her heart. 'Perhaps at this moment he's kissing her,' she thought, as she lay awake at night. 'She's lying next to him now, he has his arms around her, his middle sized woman with fair hair, and whose eyes, he thinks, are blue! Whose figure he supposes is good, but who does not compare at all with me! Oh, I hate him! God, I hate him!'

121

Old Mr Follet retired, making Daniel his manager. Dorcas now had money for pretty clothes; she could furnish her rooms above the shop in the newest provincial fashion, could entertain the wives of other tradesmen in the area to tea in the afternoons, where all the women would discuss the shortcomings of their servants. For, of course, Dorcas now kept a maid, and sent out her washing.

People grew ill, and died. Ellen developed a fast-growing cancer which first made its presence felt one autumn taking her, and everyone else, by surprise. Over the winter, the pains in her chest worsened. She took to her bed for a fortnight but then died, still relatively plump and hearty-looking. Her lungs had simply ceased to function.

Dorcas grieved, feeling guilty that she had not nursed her mother as she had intended. But she took comfort in the fact that she had sent money, had engaged a village woman as nurse, and had provided everything necessary in the way of clothing, fuel and food for an invalid.

The last link with Ashton Cross was thus severed. As she watched the sexton shovel earth over her mother's coffin, as she accepted the condolences of Ellen's neighbours and friends, Dorcas was glad that she would now have no reason to visit the place of her birth ever again.

Keeping her looks and figure, Dorcas was vain enough to be gratified that she could still attract the same stares of appreciation which she had first noticed when she was fourteen. She put up her thick, shining hair in a becoming pleat; she wore small, ribbon-trimmed hats which set off her pretty features to perfection; she had her bodices made very tight, in order to show off her narrow waist and full bosom. 'Dorry, my love, you're a picture.' Daniel, pausing to look at his wife as she pinned on her hat one afternoon, gave her a smile of absolute adoration. 'You're the prettiest woman in the city!'

Dorcas smiled back, glancing in the mirror for confirmation. 'He wouldn't have had cause to be ashamed of me,' she thought. 'I wouldn't have been an embarrassment to him ...'

Daniel, the golden youth, ran to fat. His features, once as near to classical perfection as any human being's could be, became obscured by folds of red, mottled flesh, which hung on his jowls and over his starched collars, making him look as if he were choking. His stomach bulged over his trouser band. Even his hands, his once beautiful hands, looked bloated.

He spent most of his waking hours in the shop. Anna liked to be there with him — as a toddler she would sit under the counter at his feet, tucking her dolls into empty boxes, stealing sugar pieces from the blue sugar sacks next to her, happy to be close to her precious Papa. 'Are you there, piglet?' Daniel would ask, feeling a little hand on his ankle, hearing a giggle from among the bags of dried fruit. He would bend down and offer her a piece of apricot, which she loved; or some marzipan, which she adored. 'Cupboard love,' he would remark, as she grinned at him. 'Cupboard love!'

But it wasn't cupboard love at all. An occasional look, a smile from him, was all Anna needed to keep her contented for hours together. If the shop should chance to empty, he would crouch down on all fours to give her a kiss or pinch her cheek, while she laughed in delight. 'Oh, Papa!' she would giggle as he tickled her cheek. 'Dear Papa! I love you, my Daddy!'

Daniel had opened a counter for the sale of all kinds of bacon, ham, sausages and the like; and he bought and butchered the pigs himself. Anna conceived a violent dread of the cold outhouse where the pigs hung, their blood dripping into white enamel bowls and splashing on to the mossy stone paving. She refused to go anywhere near it.

Dorcas, too, felt uneasy when she passed the place where the cadavers were. She hated the smell of raw flesh which, quite naturally, emanated from the place — she loathed the trays of guts, the bowls of offal soaking in salt water, the dishes full of blood. But worst of all were the pigs' heads, which seemed to mock her, grinning as she hurried past the place; their mean little eyes still bright, their blond eyelashes, so like Daniel's own, still attached to their half-closed lids.

One evening Dorcas had cause to go down to the shop. Crossing the yard to fetch in some washing and passing the place where the carcases hung, she glanced across to the outhouse and saw the tail of Daniel's coat in the doorway. Something made her walk across and peer inside.

The butcher was leaning against one of the suspended corpses, his face pressed very close to the dead animal's flank. While its severed head seemed to watch him from the table where it lay, one of Daniel's hands ran caressingly up and down the pig's newly singed body while the other delved inside the guts of the animal, drawing out its organs and slopping them into a bucket.

Daniel seemed to be murmuring, almost singing, to himself; and the rapt pleasure upon her husband's face made Dorcas go cold. His eyes were glazed, sleepy with satisfaction, his mouth was curved in a smile of quiet contentment. His whole expression was so strange, so entirely inappropriate to his rather messy task that Dorcas felt her skin prickle. She was suddenly afraid ...

'Daniel!' The sharpness of her tone startled him out of his reverie. He turned to look at her, guiltily she thought; and the dreaming look was wiped from his features as suddenly as if a cloth had cleaned it away.

'Dorry?' His voice was low and caressing. 'What did you want? What is it, my dear?'

Later on that evening Daniel went into Anna's bedroom, ostensibly to say goodnight, although the child had been asleep for the past hour or more. Dorcas followed him on pretence of tidying away some of her daughter's clothes.

She saw Daniel stroke the face of her sleeping child, saw his great red butcher's hand caress Anna's rosy cheek; she saw the same dreaming expression which she'd seen an hour ago in the outhouse, appear on his face again.

She told herself not to be so fanciful, so foolish. But she knew then that she was afraid of Daniel Hitchman.

Chapter Nine

ELIZABETH MARLOWE WAS THE ONLY child of doting elderly parents. Born when her mother was forty-five and had long given up any hope of children, Elizabeth had been spoiled from her cradle. From her earliest days her most freakish wants had been readily supplied, for her parents could not bear to hear her cry; and nursemaid after nursemaid was dismissed because Miss Elizabeth could endure no discipline or correction. By the time she was eighteen she was spoiled beyond any hope of redemption. She had also become — perhaps unfortunately — extraordinarily beautiful.

The most remarkable thing about her was her white-blonde hair. This had been fair in infancy, which is common enough; but in Elizabeth's case it had retained its flaxen beauty into adulthood. Her face was oval and her complexion completely flawless, no adolescent blemishes having dared to spoil it. She had a straight nose, a soft, neat mouth, and a pretty chin. Her blue eyes, shaded by pale lashes, were rather small.

Below this lovely face was a figure little short of perfection. A shapely bosom gave way to a fashionably tiny waist, and thence to voluptuous hips; while her limbs were well formed and in exact proportion to the rest of her. 'My dear, you are beauty personified,' her mother had told her. And Elizabeth had reflected complacently that this was no more than the truth.

She had known she was an heiress ever since she could remember. When she was sixteen, talk of marriage began, and visitors came to the house in rather larger numbers than before. But two seasons came and went and still Elizabeth was not engaged. A duke's son, invited for the shooting and encouraged to murder all the game on Mr Marlowe's estate, had proved singularly obdurate. 'Nothing on earth would induce me to marry such an empty-headed, unspeakable bitch,' he told his father. 'It wouldn't be worth it, even to save the estate from mortgage!'

For the Marlowes were rich; far and away richer than the Lawrences, who were merely country gentry, of ancient and established family, in a very comfortable way. But Emma Marlowe was gradually brought to realize, with some bitterness, that money wasn't enough; that her family lacked the social cachet to attract a member of the affluent aristocracy.

She had almost decided that an eldest son of some impoverished earl would do when she remembered her friend Jane Lawrence; pretty little Jane, who was several years Emma's junior. Her husband had died not so very long ago, leaving a tidy estate covering a decent area of Herefordshire to a young, eligible elder son just down from Oxford. 'And,' thought Emma Marlowe ruminatively, 'he might be a pleasant young man. If he takes after Jane, he'll certainly be handsome.'

There was a long-standing friendship between Mrs Marlowe and Mrs Lawrence. They had met just after Jane had married, when the new Mrs Lawrence had been the youngest daughter of a baronet with ten thousand pounds of her own and the expectation of more on her father's death. Emma, on the other hand, the only child of an unsuccessful attorney, was thirty-five and not particularly pretty; although she possessed a kind of high-spirited charm which attracted men's attention.

Through Mrs Lawrence, who had a new bride's taste for match-making, Emma had been introduced to Henry Marlowe, a childless widower of forty; a man of means, but not, then, of riches. Drawn to Mrs Lawrence's lively friend, over the next few weeks he got to know her, and decided that he had been too long without a woman to warm his bed. He thought that Emma looked a well set-up, saucy piece who appeared to know what was what. He made up his mind.

'Well, Miss Emma?' he had demanded one evening, clutching at her knee and shaking it, discerning a satisfying wobble in Emma's well-fleshed thigh, 'shall we be man and wife?'

Poor Emma was desperate. She accepted the older man, and tried to provide him with what he wanted.

Mr Marlowe's speculations had prospered. He bought and

invested well, eventually owning mines and factories in the North of England. The death of an elder brother brought him property in Worcestershire and Shropshire. He became, and remained, very rich.

Elizabeth heard with indifference that her mother had invited a certain Mr Lawrence, together with his younger brother and sister, down to the Shropshire house for a month or so. 'They are bound to be lively,' said Mrs Marlowe hopefully. 'They will be company for you, my love — they will raise your spirits.' Elizabeth, who had no interest in books, music or handicraft, tended to become bored and fancy herself depressed during the winter months.

Stephen made his visit to Shropshire at his mother's insistence, fully aware that she hoped he'd come back an engaged man. His brother and sister seemed eager to go to Stone Lea and it seemed to him as good a way as any to fill in a few weeks of a dreary English winter, before he set off for Greece in the spring. He was bored and irritable at Ashton. He wondered, idly, if this Miss Marlowe might be worth looking at.

He met her, and was unimpressed. Although he could not fail to notice her beauty, he was far from overwhelmed by it — liking dark-eyed, dark-haired women as he did, he thought blondes rather insipid. This whaleboned, smirking, pink and white puppet, whose skin was so white and translucent that the veins showed blue and prominent on her temples and bosom, did nothing at all to his pulse-rate; and, looking at his brother Henry, Stephen realized that Elizabeth had made no conquest there, either.

Elizabeth, however, accustomed as she was to instant admiration, found that she liked the look of Stephen; was, unaccountably, drawn to him. Affronted that he did not find her particularly appealing, she discovered within herself a desire to have this one mooning about the house and drooling in vain. So she set out to charm him.

Stephen was never averse to the company of a pretty woman, and Elizabeth was on her best behaviour. She asked him all about his work, revealed that she had long been fascinated by what she called the romance of archaeological excavation, and seemed entranced by what he told her of Greece and Italy.

'I should like to travel myself,' she murmured — a downright fib, since she had never wanted to go further afield than Eastbourne, and hated train journeys, which made her clothes dirty and filled her hair with smuts. 'Mr Lawrence,' she went on, wafting perfumed sighs in Stephen's direction, 'you do make all these far-away places sound so fascinating! I would dearly love to visit — where was it — Crete? Rhodes? The very names breathe magic, do they not?' And she favoured her victim with an enchanting smile.

Then old Mrs Marlowe, who had herself been rather taken by the young man's dark good looks — admittedly most unlike Jane's fair features, but attractive all the same — took to flattering him outrageously. A man of Stephen's self-assurance and vanity found a combined attack hard to resist.

An afternoon spent together in the drawing room was enough. Having told himself that he must marry somebody, some time, Stephen decided that Elizabeth Marlowe would do as well as anyone. He went to sit beside her on her sofa, and, pushing aside her hideous needlework asked, 'Miss Marlowe, would you like to marry me?'

Elizabeth, who had received half a dozen unsatisfactory proposals before, was rather taken aback by the bluntness of this one. 'Well, Mr Lawrence,' she murmured. 'You do take me by surprise!' She began to go through a routine of pouts, grins and smirks, demurs and flutters which made Stephen smile, in spite of himself.

Misunderstanding the reason for his smile, Elizabeth brought her performance to a pretty finale. 'We have known each other for a very short time,' she said. 'I do, however, feel that I'm well acquainted with your heart. So I think that, in answer to your question, I must say yes.'

She rose from her sofa, batted her eyelashes at him. 'I must go and tell Papa,' she said.

Stephen watched her go. 'Acquainted with his heart', indeed! Stupid girl. Such a woman, he thought, would hardly take over his life. She was obviously such a half-wit that he doubted if she would have the determination to oppose any wishes of his. She appeared to have no opinions of her own — she seemed likely to be biddable, bendable — and she would probably have plenty of children to keep her occupied while he went his own way …

Elizabeth reflected on her conquest — as she chose to imagine it — with pleasure. She liked and needed admiration. So a husband, and a dependent husband at that, would provide a delightful novelty and a far better audience than her own adoring parents, than a silent mirror or a stupid, goggling servant. A husband could, after all, be tormented and teased — indulged, perhaps, now and then — then tormented again. Elizabeth looked forward to marriage.

Stephen Lawrence married Elizabeth Marlowe on a fine September day in 1868, in the small church on the Marlowes' Shropshire estate. The family had acquired the gift of the living when they had bought up the land.

The wedding was a splendid occasion. The best society of three counties attended. The bride looked so meltingly beautiful, such a dream of white lace and gauze veils, that her husband was, temporarily at least, the envy of every man there.

But, even as the bride and groom made their responses, there were murmurings that there must be more to this marriage than appeared. Why on earth, it was asked, should a splendid creature like Miss Marlowe throw herself away on a mere country squire, a man without great wealth or any really important connections, a fellow whose rents must be a quarter of his father-in-law's?

'She must have fallen in love,' said one lady guest, eyeing the bridegroom with approval.

'With that blackamoor?' Her companion sniffed derisively. 'I can't imagine anything less likely. Look at him — he's no more than five feet nine if he's that. He has the figure of an artisan, he's as dark as the devil — I'd say he was positively ugly.'

'Oh, I don't know. There's something about him when he smiles, wouldn't you say? But I do know what you mean.' She sighed. 'All that money — I wonder what he'll do with it? Lucky man. I wonder if she could be — ah — enceinte? It doesn't show if she is, does it?'

The other woman shuddered. 'Don't, Celia. The very idea!' She turned to her own husband, a tall fair man whose pale complexion belied his excellent health and sound constitution. 'Shall we go and congratulate the bridal pair, Robert?' she asked.

* * *

The tenants from both families' estates were given a holiday, and a feast. At Ashton Cross hundreds of gallons of cider were consumed, and bloated, inebriated labourers' children staggered home that evening with parents themselves hardly able to walk. It was a wonderful day, to be talked of for years to come.

Mrs Lawrence senior made way for her daughter-in-law by removing herself to a small farmhouse on the edge of the estate, taking with her a selection of the best furniture and the more valuable paintings, together with her unmarried daughter. She made herself snug for what she hoped would be a peaceful old age.

Henry Lawrence lived for a week in the company of his sister-in-law before he removed himself to the Dower House, where he lived alone, absorbed in the business of the estate, until a tea merchant's daughter married him and set about presenting him with a child each year.

Elizabeth's new home was a square Georgian manor house, an elegant, well-proportioned red brick building about a hundred years old. Solid and unpretentious, it looked like what it was: a country gentleman's home, the property of a prosperous farmer. It had replaced a medieval building upon whose foundations it stood.

There was nothing showy about the place, for it possessed no fine pillars, no portico. Elizabeth loathed it. In a few years' time, she decided, she would have it remodelled and refaced. She expected to come into several thousand pounds in her own right when she was twenty-five, by which time she expected to have brought her husband well under control.

This was a task which now looked a little more difficult than she'd originally anticipated. It had taken only a few weeks of marriage for her to understand that Stephen was as strong-willed and stubborn as she was herself, as fond of his own way, and as impatient of restraint.

After a few weeks more, she decided that the best way to bring him to heel would be to act coldly towards him; to make him realize that she was no man's chattel. Particularly when the man in question was a mere country squire, a fellow of no consequence whatsoever. She stopped smiling at him, became positively cool, and waited for him to panic.

Stephen, well aware that he was no Adonis but assuming, reasonably enough, that his wife had married him because she liked him, was puzzled by her haughty behaviour. But since he was at the time very preoccupied with plans for a visit to Italy, he took very little notice of his wife's sulks. She would have to be more positive ...

'I really must have my own private bedroom,' announced Elizabeth one morning. 'In fact, I rather think I shall have my own apartment. You may visit me, of course,' she added condescendingly. 'When it's convenient.'

Stephen, who had been reading a letter, raised his eyebrows. 'Visit you?' he asked, looking up and frowning. 'This is my house — I shall go where I please when I please, with or without your consent.'

Elizabeth smirked, glad to see him needled. 'Of course you shall,' she murmured. 'But surely even a wife is entitled to some privacy?' She took his hand and laid it upon her bosom, rubbing the palm against her breast. 'You would be welcome in my bedroom at this moment,' she whispered, deciding that if he showed any interest in taking things further, she would snub him. That would teach him to be such a dogmatic boor.

Stephen looked at her, and then at his own hand, wondering vaguely why its proximity to Elizabeth's lovely chest was causing not the slightest answering stirring in his own. 'I can't come at the moment,' he replied dismissively. 'I have to see the bailiff at ten.'

'The bailiff?' Hardly able to believe her ears, Elizabeth gaped at him, checkmated. 'You can see the bailiff later!' she cried.

'No, I can't.' Retrieving his hand, he took out his watch and wound it up. 'I'm afraid that, delightful though it would be to idle away an hour with you, I must go and meet Mr Thornley now.'

Elizabeth stamped her foot. 'Go, then!' she snapped. 'But don't think I shall be languishing for you when you return!'

She flounced out of the room, ran across the landing. He heard the key turn in the lock of the first floor drawing room as, shrugging, he went downstairs. He wondered again why he, who since early adolescence had been able to see at least some charm in most members of the female sex, should be so absolutely unmoved by the sight and presence of his own wife — a woman who was undeniably, positively beautiful. He shook himself. He was still

131

hankering after that little bitch in Hereford, he supposed. 'Mr Thornley!' he called to the bailiff, who was standing in the hallway. 'Come into my office, please.'

Elizabeth sat in her bedroom and sulked. She wondered what to do next. Getting out a sketchbook, she began to make plans for the continuing transformation of the manor house, reflecting, as she did so, that it was just as well her father had arranged things so that she retained control of most of her own fortune. The young squire would need her money one day. When that time came, she'd make sure he had to grovel for it.

On her first visit to Ashton Cross, Elizabeth had walked through the fine rooms of the manor house with the housekeeper, clicking her tongue in distaste. The new mistress disliked most of the elegant Regency furniture that she came across despising it as old-fashioned rubbish; and she was amazed to find that the rooms were still decorated in the powdery greens, pastel blues and pinks, papered in the finely striped wallpapers fashionable over fifty years ago. The hand-blocked Chinese wallpaper in the breakfast room was particularly awful, she decided.

She made a mental note that all the eighteenth-century fittings should give place to something of a more solid, substantial nature. As the rooms were, they seemed empty and cold. 'They need stronger colours, more upholstery, bigger pieces of furniture,' she'd announced.

'Do they?' Stephen, busy scribbling something at his desk, hadn't even bothered to glance up.

'Yes, they do!' Elizabeth glared at the back of his head. 'And that's what they will have!'

She had heard that tartan wallpaper was all the rage — not to mention tartan wall hangings, curtains, rugs. The reds and greens of a nice Dress Stuart — was it Dress Stuart? — would be ideal, for the rooms needed richness. A few months after her wedding, the new bride had ordered most of what she wanted, had instructed workmen, hired carpenters; and the manor house was being redecorated and refurnished to reflect the ostentatious taste of a vulgar, uneducated young woman with more money than either style or sense.

Her husband was rather disappointingly uninterested in her improvements. 'Oh, do what you like,' he'd said, when consulted again. 'Leave my rooms alone completely — that's all I insist upon. The rest of the house is yours.'

The domestic staff seemed, for some reason, to take against their new mistress. 'Bitch she is,' remarked a housemaid. 'Nasty faced bitch! Kicked over me coal-scuttle on purpose she did, all over that white rug the master had sent from Greece! Could 'ave said she was sorry!'

Elizabeth was, admittedly, curt with the servants. She certainly took a great pleasure in reducing young housemaids to tears. The older domestics, less prone to worrying about what their employers said to them, merely made remarks about a stuck-up, sour-faced puss. Elizabeth's personal maid, a tall, gaunt, swarthy woman, was treated with suspicion; her entry into the kitchen could silence a babble of voices within seconds.

Gradually, it became clear that the new husband was, to say the least, indifferent to his bride. Obviously bored and restless at home, unable to settle to anything, he prowled aimlessly around the house like a leopard in a cage, scowling at his wife's transformations. When he went hunting, he left before dawn and often did not return until twenty-four hours later, when he was deaf to enquiries about where he'd spent the night. His manservant said he would be surprised if the master didn't take himself off to Europe soon. 'He means to go,' he revealed. 'I heard him say so to Mr Henry — an' he'll go whether *she* wants him to or not, I can tell you that!'

The servants seated around the kitchen table leaned forward. 'He won't leave her here by herself, will he?' The housekeeper looked at Stephen's valet interrogatively. 'They've only been wed a matter of months — he can't 'ave tired of her already! And he must have spent thousands on doing up this house, just for her. Surely he don't want to leave her here all alone! Not his new bride!'

The master's servant grinned. 'I don't think he can wait to get away,' he murmured. 'When she's talking to him, going on about new this and new that, yapping about new carpets new chairs, he don't pay her no heed at all — he just goes on with his reading or his writing. I've seen him get up and walk out of the room when she's in the middle of a sentence!'

The valet leered. 'It's my belief,' he added, 'that she don't give him what a wife ought, or at any rate, she don't give it willingly!

I've been going downstairs some nights, taking my time, seeing everything's all right for the morning, and I've heard him talk to her. He might have let her refurnish this house but she don't get her own way all the time, you know. If the master decides he'll have his way, then he has it — whether Madam will or no!'

Elizabeth had deceived herself when she'd imagined she would be able to impose her will on her husband. He had no interest in her money, that was now perfectly plain. More disappointingly still, her body had proved to be totally useless as a bargaining counter.

Assuming, at first, that Elizabeth expected him to *be* a husband to her, Stephen had taken his wife to bed on her wedding night more or less as a matter of course. He'd been nowhere near mad with desire for her but he had nevertheless been considerate and careful, had taken great pains to give her some pleasure, and had certainly done nothing to alarm, offend or upset her.

It had been hard going. Even as he kissed her pale face, she had sighed resignedly, like one undergoing a painless but particularly tedious kind of operation. And he had tried, without success, to banish from his mind the idea that he might as well be making love to a dead sheep for all the interest and enthusiasm his bride displayed.

He finished, and looked at the pallid doll who lay beside him. 'I hope I didn't hurt you,' he said, as much to break an awkward silence as because he was really concerned.

Elizabeth sighed again. 'No,' she said languidly. 'You didn't hurt me. After all — it's what I must endure now, isn't it?'

'Endure?' Stephen frowned at her. 'I don't require you to endure anything,' he said. 'If you find this whole business distasteful, there's no need for us to repeat it.'

Elizabeth yawned. 'I understand my obligations,' she replied condescendingly. She sat up. 'I like you to kiss me,' she added decidedly. 'I may come to like that other thing too, when I become accustomed to it. Might we try again? It will be less disagreeable, perhaps, now that I know what to expect.'

Stephen grimaced. 'Certainly we might try again,' he replied, stifling a yawn himself.

After this unpromising beginning, things went very badly wrong. Elizabeth, a strange mixture of innocence and forwardness, naivety and calculation as she was, began to take the initiative in such matters. She would on occasion be sullen for days but then she would smile, stroke Stephen's face, and seem to want him.

Sometimes, then, all went well but more often she would tell him, suddenly, that he must stop — that he hurt her — and, angrily, she would push him away.

Such freakish behaviour lay outside Stephen's experience. At first he was genuinely concerned. Unwilling that his wife should be hurt or upset, he had been kind and patient, had left her to herself if this was what she appeared to want, had merely hugged or kissed her when she'd become tearful; had offered the simple physical warmth of an embrace.

But he found that, try as he might, he could feel little affection for someone so wayward and inconsistent as Elizabeth was. There was nothing about her which he could like. He decided that she was a leech — a spoiled child, a taker who gave nothing in return. Being in her company, listening to her aimless babble about what she wanted to buy next, literally gave him a headache; and a night spent with her left him heavy-eyed and unrefreshed.

Eventually, Stephen's patience was exhausted; he left her more and more to herself, only remaining in her company when she actually sought his. And when, one night, he realized that she had been teasing him quite deliberately for the past half hour, he had lost his temper with her quite spectacularly . . .

After kissing him with apparent passion for some time, after taking him in her arms and almost dragging him on top of her, she had, quite suddenly, turned her face away from him. 'That's enough for the time being,' she had said, laughing at him. 'You may go to your own room now.'

'What do you mean?' He'd stared at her, incredulous. 'I can't stop just like that!'

She giggled. 'Of course you can!' she said, sniggering. 'Oh, *do* get up! I hate all this, you know I do!'

'I don't know anything of the sort! And last week, you —'

'Oh, last week, last week!' Elizabeth grinned up at him, a complacent smile on her beautiful face. 'That was *last* week, wasn't it? Tonight, I'm tired. So would you leave me alone now? Could you be so kind as to go away?'

'No.' Stephen glowered at her. 'No, I couldn't.'

* * *

She had not imagined that he could become so angry. Up until then, he'd sometimes been morose and occasionally he'd been positively sullen. He'd never been violent, though. Surely he wouldn't — he couldn't —!

Elizabeth felt him reach for her hands; first one, then the other. He grasped her wrists together, then jerked her arms above her head, holding them there. And then, quite doggedly, he went on with what she'd encouraged him to begin.

She was frightened now. 'Don't!' she'd beseeched, struggling, trying to squirm from under him. 'Don't, Stephen! I'm sorry I teased you! Leave me alone — please!'

'Shut up! Shut up, shut up, shut up!' In a towering rage now, the remembrance of a dozen previous occasions like this one crowding into his brain, Stephen slapped her face hard. Then he did as he pleased with her.

He had been so furious with her — and with himself — that he decided that he could have nothing more to do with her. He understood now how it was that men came to murder poor, innocent, defenceless women...

But by this time, Elizabeth had conceived.

That spring, Stephen set off for Italy, alone. He stayed away until the autumn, did not write to his wife, did not appear to be concerned when he was informed she was pregnant.

He returned from the Continent to find Elizabeth hugely swollen with what the doctor said was probably twins. She greeted her husband politely, affectionately even — but he could not help seeing the hatred in her eyes.

Pregnancy had made her ill with misery and fatigue. She had not intended to have children at all, or at least not until she was ready for them, but that man had forced himself upon her. Now, her beautiful body was bloated, her ankles were puffy with fluid which would not disperse, her veins seemed engorged with blood and stood out prominently on her legs and breasts. Her head ached constantly, and she thought with dread of the ordeal ahead of her. 'I'll make him suffer,' she vowed over and over again, repeating the words to herself like a charm, clenching her fists. 'He'll suffer as much as I do one day — I shall see to that. I won't die — I must live,

136

to have my revenge!'

The doctor had been right. When Elizabeth went into labour, it took her only a few hours to give birth to a fine, healthy little daughter.

But its sibling refused to be born. All that day and through the following night Elizabeth's weakening cries echoed around the manor house; cries unheard by her husband, who had gone out hunting and who did not return home until the following morning. With reproach in her eyes, his mother informed him that a doctor had been sent for, from Hereford.

'Indeed.' Stephen had shrugged in the infuriatingly indifferent way in which he so often did these days. 'I'm going to have a bath,' he said. 'Madam — there's no need for you to wait here. I'll send a message when there's any news.'

'News? You're heartless, child — heartless!' Mrs Lawrence looked angrily at her son. 'That poor woman is suffering the torments of Hell in order to give birth to your child,' she continued. 'And all you can say is that you're going to have a bath!'

'Well, I need one.' Stephen shrugged again. 'I'm dirty. Minstrel took us through Adderley's Brook, and it was deeper than I'd expected it to be. Look at my boots.'

'Your boots!' With a snort of disgust, Mrs Lawrence turned away from him and began to climb the stairs intending to give aid and comfort to her daughter-in-law. She heard her son shouting for his valet, and wondered how she could have bred such a callous monster.

The doctor, a pompous little man, officiously confirmed what, to the exhausted midwife, was already obvious. 'Stuck in the birth canal,' he announced cheerfully. He pulled a forcep blade from each of his two coat pockets and fitted the instrument together, tightening the screw with grubby fingers. 'Well, ladies,' he said beaming around him. 'There's no need for any more fuss. I'll soon have Mrs Lawrence delivered now.'

The women were obliged to hold Elizabeth down as he brought the child, already blue and seeming lifeless, into the world.

Gently, the doctor blew into its lungs, inflating the little chest. In spite of the midwife's assertion that the baby was dead, the doctor persisted and, five minutes later, the child inhaled a feeble gasp of air for itself.

Smiling in triumph at the anxious women, the doctor handed the baby to the midwife. 'He'll do,' he pronounced. 'Wrap him up and watch him through the night. The girl is bonny. Let the mother rest.'

Pleased with the successful conclusion of his efforts, the doctor went jauntily downstairs to be congratulated by the supposedly anxious father. He found Stephen half asleep in front of the drawing room fire, stroking the ears of a pet labrador, an empty brandy glass in his hand.

'A long drawn out business,' remarked the doctor, complacently, helping himself to brandy which he had not been offered. He sipped his drink reflectively. 'Don't you worry about your wife, sir,' he went on. 'I've seen worse — far worse! Why, a month ago — but I don't suppose you want to hear about that.'

He grinned, man to man. 'I can tell you, sir, that the more they scream, the better it is for them. Women are made to take it, after all; God designed them for the purpose! Do you know, I don't hold with all this chloroform nonsense. It's meant to hurt a little. Pain helps the delivery along, you see.' He swallowed the rest of his brandy and placed the glass on the sideboard.

Still getting no response from the children's father, the doctor moved a step nearer Stephen; he put his hands together at the fingertips, and beamed ingratiatingly. 'They are all well,' he said. 'Go up and see them.'

Unable to stand the doctor's chatter any longer, Stephen got to his feet and went up the stairs. He found Elizabeth awake, lying back on her pillows, long strands of sweat-dampened hair sticking to her face still, blue smudges beneath her eyes. 'How are you?' he asked, well aware that he did not feel or sound anything like as concerned as he ought to be; but unable to feel any interest in her or the children.

She gave him a look of utter hatred. 'Go away,' she said. 'I don't want to see you. And if you ever touch me again, I swear I shall kill you.'

He hesitated for a second then he went, slamming the door behind him.

Molly Crowley came to nurse the babies. A strong, healthy village girl of about sixteen, she had been delivered of a still-born child

138

only a matter of days since, and her milk was therefore coming in nicely. After examination, Mrs Andrews the housekeeper pronounced her suitable; so she was put to feed the landlord's children straight away.

When Elizabeth's own milk came in, she cried with the pain of her hard, engorged breasts. She refused, however, to alleviate her sufferings by taking one of the babies from the wet-nurse. Instead, Elizabeth's milk went to waste, soaking her sheets and linen, until eventually it dried up, unused. Her body began to forget that it had ever carried two children. Her waist became slim again, her bosom regained its former beauty, and the bulging veins in her legs disappeared back into the flesh.

Judith was a healthy child, grew fast and became devoted to her nurse, hardly being aware who her mother was. Always hungry, she was weaned at six months, but she still depended on Molly for frequent comfort feeds; so at the manor house Molly stayed.

Since neither her father nor her mother seemed interested in their daughter's welfare, Molly took Judith out with her, tying her to her back while she worked in the fields, earning a little extra money. She also took the baby for long walks in the countryside, showing her trees, birds and flowers. When summer came she kept the squire's daughter at her mother's cottage for days on end, without Judith's parents appearing to notice, or to care if they did.

'Who's my babby?' Molly would ask, bouncing Judith Lawrence on her lap. 'Who's my best biddy?'

'Mum! Mum, mum, mum!' Judith replied, grinning a wide, baby's grin and pulling Molly's hair with her fat little fingers. 'Mum!'

'That's right, my ducky!' Molly beamed at the squire's little girl. 'That's right, my lamb!'

While his sister thrived, John remained feeble and sickly. He retched Molly's milk and was put on a diet of thin gruel, sucked through muslin, which was given to him by whichever of the maids thought to do it. He coughed day and night, cried wretchedly as if protesting against such heartless neglect. Elizabeth took no heed of him. His father, of course, left such matters entirely to women.

Husband and wife, though living in the same house still, now had very little to do with one another. Initially, they had shared a bedroom but after the birth of his children, the husband had all his belongings removed to the top floor of the house, while his wife made the first floor her own.

The babies became toddlers. Judith grew into a pretty, dark-haired little child with her father's stubborn determination and her mother's wayward temper. John struggled into his second year still feeble, still prey to a racking cough, but apparently going to hang on to life. Molly Crowley was the only fixed star in the children's universe — other adults came and went merely as a blur of faces to the twins.

Stephen, who already spent most of his time away from Ashton Cross was, one summer, invited to go to Germany. He accepted the invitation, for he was very keen to meet the team of archae-ologists who hoped to set up a big excavation in Turkey the following year. Leaving no doubt in her mind that he meant to go anyway, Stephen asked his wife if she would like to go to Germany with him.

'Germany?' Elizabeth had opened her china-blue eyes wide and stared at him incredulously. 'Whatever would I do in Germany? No, I don't want to go. And I think you ought to stay here with me and the children, not go gadding off again.'

'I'm going to Germany, Elizabeth. Then I'm going to Turkey. It's all been agreed.'

She had laughed at him then. 'Agreed!' she mocked. 'Oh, Stephen — are you going to spend your entire life hobnobbing with fools like yourself, with people who think it's a man's work to scrabble in the sand and play in the dirt? Isn't it time you put this idiotic enthusiasm behind you and settled down to be a farmer, a country gentleman — which is after all what you actually are?'

He'd been so angry with her that he hadn't trusted himself to reply. He had gone so white that Elizabeth, alarmed, had looked nervously round for her maid to see if she was within calling distance.

But then, she rallied. 'If you insist on continuing to be so irresponsible,' she said, 'if you are determined to have your own way all the time, if you intend to take no notice of your son, daughter or your wife — then you will find that I can be difficult too. If you do go to Germany this summer, you needn't expect to find me here when you come back! I shall leave your house,

Stephen. I shall take my children with me and you won't ever see them again.'

Her blue eyes glittered with malice. 'I'll ruin you,' she told him. 'You won't be able to hold your head up in society after I have made public what I have suffered and endured from you!'

'Do as you please.' Stephen glared at her. 'Say what you wish. But don't imagine that your threats or fancies can influence me!'

Stephen went to Germany, alone. Before he went off to the Near East he arranged for his brother to have power of attorney indefinitely, for he either could not or would not give any indication of when he meant to return. Eventually he received a lawyer's letter, to which he replied through his own solicitor. He was subsequently informed that his wife had left his house.

Soon, a white tide of legal correspondence ebbed and flowed between the representatives of husband and wife. The terms of the marriage contract were set aside. In return for retaining control of her own fortune, Elizabeth agreed to make no further financial claim on her husband. A separation was agreed. Animosity between the Lawrences and the Marlowes flared.

Stephen stayed away from England for several years. He told his brother to move into the manor house, which would suit his ever-growing family far better than the cramped Dower House did. For all practical purposes Henry became master of Ashton Cross. The tenants almost forgot that Stephen existed.

Chapter Ten

DORCAS HITCHMAN, THE MASTER GROCER'S wife, the mother of a beautiful little daughter, the chairwoman of the Charitable Ladies' Sewing Guild for the Improvement of Orphan Girls, and the city's most indefatigable organizer of fund-raising for almost any worthy cause, prospered. The half-starved peasant brat, the nervous, ignorant little servant girl had been replaced by a self-assured, pretty woman, who was the mainstay of the Christian Mothers' Fellowship and of half a dozen equally worthy institutions.

Old Mr Follet died at last, leaving the business to his middle-aged spinster daughter. *She* immediately scandalized all the old women of Hereford by having her hair cut short and, when she was just a few days out of mourning, by laying aside her garments of dull greys, blues and browns in exchange for new ones of brilliant aniline greens, magentas and purples.

Miss Follet sent for Daniel and announced that she intended to visit cousins in the United States; she hoped he would take over full control of the shop. 'I know I can rely on you, Daniel,' she had said, staring at him with a new-found boldness born of bereavement. 'We will see a lawyer, make everything regular — you will have full authority here.'

Scarcely able, these days, to contain her own high spirits, Miss Follet looked enquiringly at Daniel. She'd hoped to see that her trust in him gave him some degree of gratification.

He appeared, however, to be unmoved. His jowly face remained expressionless and his great heavy shoulders had shrugged only slightly as he'd agreed to what she had proposed. He stood near the window of the small office, almost entirely blocking out the light.

Miss Follet coughed, unnerved by his menacing presence.

'That's settled and agreed, then?' she asked, her voice now tremulous, her former confidence completely gone.

'I think so, Ma'am,' replied Daniel tonelessly.

'Good. Ah — Mrs Hitchman!'

Miss Follet's relief was almost comical. She was pleased beyond expression to see Mrs Hitchman, bright, neat, pretty Mrs Hitchman, standing there in the doorway. 'Miss Follet?' asked Dorcas. 'Will you come upstairs and have some tea with Anna and myself?'

'Hitchman's a fine fellow,' thought Miss Follet, as she followed his wife up the stairs. 'I don't think, though, that I would care to be married to him. There's something about him that's just not very comfortable.'

She looked at Dorcas, going gracefully upstairs in front of her; she noticed her trim waist and straight back, saw that her beautiful dark hair was neatly and elaborately braided. 'She's a good looking woman,' continued Miss Follet to herself. 'Clever, too. I wonder what she ever saw in him? I suppose he was handsome enough once, in a bullish sort of way. And she was only about seventeen. Then there was the baby, too — I'd forgotten the baby. 'How is Anna, Mrs Hitchman, dear?' she enquired out loud, as they reached the top of the stairs and walked on to the landing.

'Very well, I thank you, Miss Follet,' replied Dorcas, opening the door of her sitting room, and ushering the older woman inside.

Anna, busily sorting out scraps for her album and pasting garishly coloured pictures on to its pages, was lying on the hearthrug. She rose to her feet, and, naturally courteous, she gave the visitor a charming smile and held out her hand. The three of them settled round the fire to enjoy a pleasant half hour of tea and conversation.

Miss Follet had with her a book of engravings, and she was full of the sights she meant to see in America. She revealed that she had longed to travel ever since she could remember, and would now go round the world if she could afford it.

'Mama would like to travel, too,' remarked Anna, handing a cup of tea to the visitor. 'She will, one day — a gipsy told her that she would go and see faraway places. Isn't that so, Mama?'

Her mother bent over the teapot. 'Fancy you remembering

143

that, Anna,' she murmured, as she poured hot water on to the leaves; very well aware that a flush was reddening her cheeks and neck. 'It's so much nonsense, anyway — all this fortune telling!' Dorcas looked up and smiled at Miss Follet. 'I've no wish to go abroad now,' she said. 'I have everything I need here, so why should I wish to go anywhere else?' And she changed the subject firmly to talk about Anna's progress at school.

Left in charge of the business, Daniel now spent very little time in the rooms above the shop. Some days, he came upstairs only to eat and to sleep. Anna still enjoyed his undemanding company; she still went downstairs to sit under the counter, but now with her books instead of her dolls. If the shop were closed, or empty of customers, she would stand next to Daniel as he worked, and chatter to him — not, it seemed, expecting him to answer her, but quite happy if he ruffled her black curls or absentmindedly stroked her cheek by way of a reply.

But one day, as she watched him joint a ham and smother the pieces in golden crumbs, he had suddenly contracted his brows and frowned down at her.

She looked at him with concern. 'What's the matter?' she'd asked, for his face was white, and now he was muttering something to himself.

'The matter?' he murmured, not looking at her. 'Anna — can you go away and play now? Go and help your mother — go out of the shop.'

'But why?' Anna touched his hand, found it was clammy. 'Did I say something to upset you?'

'No.' Daniel looked hard at Anna then, blinking as if he wanted to make certain that it was really her standing next to him. 'No, you haven't upset me,' he continued, whispering. 'But you must go away! Please, child — go!' He clutched the knife he was holding as if he meant to crush the handle.

'But you're ill, Papa.' Anna covered his hand with hers. 'You've gone pale, and you're shivering. Shall I fetch Mama?'

'Yes. That would be best.' Daniel's voice was still soft, but there was a feverish quality in it now. 'Fetch Mama.'

Dorcas came hurrying down the stairs, to be half-dragged into the shop by her anxious daughter. Daniel looked up at them both, and smiled. 'I felt dizzy,' he explained simply. 'I'm better now.'

While Dorcas stood in the doorway looking at her husband, puzzled and a little afraid, Anna went over to him. She took the knife out of his hand. 'You have a headache, Papa,' she said gently. 'Your head hurts — I'm sure of it. You work much too hard. Can't you leave all this' — she indicated the pile of hams still waiting to be carved — 'until tomorrow? Or tell one of the other assistants to do it?'

'What did you say? Oh yes, I can leave it until tomorrow.' And, as meekly as a little child might have done, Daniel allowed Dorcas and Anna to lead him upstairs.

Maggie Stemp told Dorcas that Miss Lane had almost completely lost the sight of one eye, and that the other was failing fast. 'She hasn't said anything, Dorry,' began Maggie. 'She don't complain, dear, sweet lady that she is, but I'm sure that she'd take it as a great kindness if you would come and read to her, like you used to.'

So, once or twice a week, Dorcas and Anna walked out to the big square house in the suburbs to visit Miss Lane. While Dorcas read, Anna spent her time very happily in the kitchen, being made a fuss of by the cook and the housemaid, who stuffed her with cakes and sweets. On fine days she could romp in the once immaculate garden, now going wild. She could pick bunches of roses which hung down in great, luxuriant, untended swags from the walls, having long since broken their restraining wires. She could swing on the branches of the rhododendrons.

Mrs Butler, a virgin of fifty-two, was at last prevailed upon to marry. She had long had a follower, a Mr Anderson, who was as short and thin as she was large and buxom. He was a cobbler in a very small way of business, who had a neat cottage on the outskirts of the city, where he followed his trade and worked in his garden, growing the enormous vegetables which he brought as tokens to his beloved.

He had, years ago, realized that Mrs Butler would never leave her mistress but had, by degrees, talked her round to considering his proposal that she would marry him, would live with him, but would continue to work for Miss Lane on a daily basis. Mrs Butler, worn down, had finally agreed.

The new Mrs Anderson confided to Maggie Stemp that she was glad to come to Miss Lane's house, if only to get a bit of peace. 'He's that rabid!' she said complacently. 'He's that greedy! I've only got to park my body for a minute before he's on at me to come an' have a bit of a lay down!' She giggled girlishly. 'I'd never 'ave thought he had it in him!'

But, apart from his sexual rapacity, it seemed that Mr Anderson had no faults worth the name. He was generous, obliging, and disposed to let his wife have her own way in everything. 'Dunno why I didn't take 'im years ago,' she sighed. 'Much too late for a babby now!'

She glanced through the open kitchen door to see Anna running up the garden path with Miss Lane's terrier, Trip. 'Just look at that child,' she exclaimed, gazing wistfully at the landlord's daughter. 'Goodness me, if she won't be a beauty one of these days! She'll break hearts, Dorry — you'll see!'

When she was just turned eight, Anna caught typhoid fever and, for one terrible week, it seemed that she would not now get the opportunity to be a beauty or to break any hearts; except, of course, those of her stricken parents.

'I've told her and told her not to go down Gunnet's Lane!' wailed Dorcas, beside herself with fear for her child's life. 'I've told her not to play with those dirty Williams children, not to drink the water from the pump in Mrs Williams' yard! Oh, Daniel — she's going to die!'

Just as anxious as Dorcas was, Daniel embraced his wife, tried to comfort her. But there was nothing he could say to console her, nothing he could do. For days Anna hovered between life and death, dreadfully weakened by constant voiding of blood-streaked stools, burning with a high fever, pulled this way and that by the violence of the disease.

Daniel, for the first time since Dorcas had known him, was content to leave the shop to its own devices while he sat at the child's bedside. He bathed her hot face and limbs with cool water, he sponged the terrible spreading redness which crept over her chest; and he tried, with all the patience of the tenderest of nurses, to get some cold liquid down her parched little throat.

He was as gentle as any mother with her. He changed Anna's soiled sheets, he combed her tangled hair, and he washed her;

wiping her face and hands with the greatest of careful solicitude, not minding the foul smell of the disease, not caring that he was spending twelve hours out of every twenty-four in a room which reeked of death and mortal decay. He sat there, patience itself, for hour after hour, nodding in his chair and talking softly — to himself or to Anna, it was difficult to discover which — long after Dorcas had retired to bed and fallen asleep, worn out by anxiety and grief.

But Anna recovered. Daniel was with her on the morning the crisis passed. He had taken Dorcas in his arms and cried when he realized that the fever had at last abated, and he wept on his wife's shoulder afresh when Anna knew him again, when she called him her Daddy. Now, he could hardly wait for her stomach to be strong enough for all the delicacies with which he planned to tempt her. He ordered foodstuffs from London of such high quality and such irresistibility that the little girl, once recovery was established, put on weight fast and became as rosy and pretty as she had been before.

Anna's recovery either caused or coincided with — afterwards, Dorcas could never decide which — a change in Daniel's behaviour which very much concerned his wife.

It had always been his habit to retire to bed at ten, to fall asleep almost immediately, and to lie as one dead until the following morning. He would rise at five, have his breakfast alone, and go down to the shop, long before either his wife or Anna was stirring.

About a month after Anna's recovery, however, he woke one night at about two in the morning. He dressed stealthily and went downstairs. He let himself out; Dorcas heard his footsteps ringing upon the cobbles as he walked down the road which led towards the lower end of the town.

Wondering if she had been dreaming, she got out of bed herself. Looking out of the window she saw her husband's unmistakable, bulky figure disappearing into the night, which was bright with stars. Perplexed now, she went back to bed and fell into a light doze; she waited, between sleeping and waking, for him to return, which he did at four o'clock.

Daniel undressed noiselessly, and slid into bed. He was breathing heavily, as if he had been running. There was an odd smell about him, too, reminiscent, somehow, of the sweetish odour which hung about the cold store where the pigs' carcases, awaiting butchering, were kept. Dorcas frowned. Surely he hadn't been making sausages in the middle of the night, jointing bacon by the light of the moon?

Dorcas feigned sleep until her husband got up an hour later, and went down to the shop.

The following night, Daniel went out again.

Dorcas decided to say nothing to him. Perhaps, she reasoned, he could not sleep — and the cool night air might have calmed his nerves, shredded as they were by the weeks of anxiety and distress which he'd suffered over Anna. Perhaps his nocturnal rambles soothed him, letting him sleep soundly on his return. Soon, he'd feel no need to go out in the dark.

But Daniel continued to go out in the dead of night, at least once or twice a week. Finally Dorcas could stand it no longer. 'Daniel,' she asked him one Sunday morning, when Anna was out playing in the yard, 'Where do you go in the middle of the night, all by yourself?'

He had raised his bland, expressionless face from the contemplation of his breakfast plate and looked at her for a minute, saying nothing. She was about to repeat the question, more sharply this time, when he said, slowly — weighing his words — 'I find that sometimes I can't sleep. There isn't any sense in disturbing you with my tossing and turning, so I go out for a walk. That's all.' He spoke the last two words in a tone which invited no further questioning and Dorcas, hearing Anna's tread on the staircase, let it go at that.

But, a practised liar herself, Dorcas could well recognize the glib tones of evasion when she heard them. She said nothing more to Daniel, but she racked her brains to find a way of discovering where her husband went on his night-time prowls. To another woman? Daniel? It seemed hardly likely.

Dorcas came to the conclusion that her husband was overworked. She offered to take over some of the paperwork which burdened him grievously — and she did this so readily, and performed her duties so efficiently, that Daniel was pleased with her. 'I can't do sums,' he admitted, scanning her neat columns of figures. 'Would take me an hour to do what you manage in ten minutes. Look — take the accounts over for me, and I'll pay you the regular clerk's wage, whatever it is. Dorry, will you do that?'

'Certainly.' Dorcas, flattered and pleased, nodded. 'I'll do all the paperwork, if you like,' she added. 'Letters and such-like — it would be a pleasure.' So Dorcas kept the books and attended to the correspondence, filling ledgers and account sheets with the neat, old-fashioned handwriting which Miss Lane had taught her, and which was very different from Daniel's laboured scrawl.

Daniel praised her for her efforts, paid her as promised, and did not ask what she did with the money she received. 'He *is* good to me,' she thought one day, as she took Anna into a fabric shop to select the dress materials which her wages enabled her to buy. 'If only he wasn't so silent, if only we could be companions to one another, we might even be happy. But we could never talk. I never know what he thinks. What about this, my pet?' she added, aloud, to Anna, 'Pink suits you — you're so dark.'

Anna looked at the unravelled bolt of fine woollen cloth which the salesman was earnestly recommending. 'Papa hates pink,' she remarked, frowning. 'He says I look nicest in blue.' She pointed to a cheap, blue-flowered cotton print. 'I'll have some of that,' she said.

Dorcas held it against her. 'Yes, that's very nice,' she admitted. 'But, Anna, you don't have to have what Papa likes. If you fancy the pink you have it. I wear pink, after all.'

Anna bit her lip. 'No,' she muttered. 'I'll have the blue. Papa will like the blue.' And that, as far as Anna was concerned, was that.

They walked home together in silence, Dorcas faintly annoyed that Anna had insisted on that particular material; and more than a little disgruntled because it had been such a point with Anna that she should gratify Daniel. 'It's always more important to her that she pleases him than that she pleases me,' thought Dorcas, looking at her daughter. 'If I'd insisted on the pink, we'd have had such a scene …'

Dorcas worked hard for her wages. When Anna was at school she saw to the books, she packed orders, she rolled up her sleeves and polished the brasswork which adorned the shop counters, and she tidied the storerooms. She was not allowed to serve in the shop, which she would have liked to do, for Daniel did not approve of female grocery assistants. 'No, Dorry, my dear,' he had said, quite firmly. 'This isn't a milliner's shop. It wouldn't look right. Not here.'

Late one night, after the last customer had gone home and Anna had been in bed for some hours, a man came into the shop. He pushed past Dorcas, who had come downstairs to help Daniel lock up for the night. She had fastened one of the great mahogany and glass doors and was about to bolt the other, when he barged through it, practically forcing his way in.

He glared at her, and she flinched as she smelled the raw alcohol on his breath. 'Hitchman's wife, are you?' he demanded.

Dorcas stared. 'Yes, I'm Mrs Hitchman —'

'Right, then. Get your man. I want to speak to 'im. Now, I mean — will you move, woman?'

Dorcas gaped at him, uncertain what to do and very much afraid of the tall, filthy, thickset ruffian in front of her. He was unshaven and ragged, his face was scarred and pitted, and his clothes reeked of the tannery where, she presumed, he worked. If he worked. She was still staring at him when Daniel came into the shop, wiping his hands on a blood-streaked towel.

Tall and bulky as he was, Daniel was at least as big as this other man but he paled when he saw him, the colour draining rapidly from his usually ruddy cheeks. Dorcas heard her husband catch his breath as the man, his features split in a wolfish grin, came loafing towards him. He stopped within a foot of Daniel and spat on the clean marble floor.

'*That* for you, Hitchman,' he said, wiping his mouth on his sleeve. 'But, anyway — a man's got to have a drink, so I've come to tell you that Mr Jenks says there'll be a fine one for you tonight. And he said there'd be a half-crown in it for me, too!' The man held out his dirty hand.

Daniel shot a look at Dorcas, and his eyes narrowed. 'You'll get nothing from me,' he muttered. 'Clear off — and tell Jenks that I don't want to see you here again. Ever. When Jenks has something to tell me, he can come here himself.'

Although his voice was so low, Daniel had sounded so menacing that the man suddenly lost all his bravado. Confused, he stared at the butcher. 'But Jenks said,' he began peevishly. 'Oh,

150

come on, master. A shilling! Sixpence?'

As the man hovered, wheedling now, Dorcas saw her husband clench his fist. 'Go away!' he snarled, his voice harsh and threatening. 'Clear off! Now! Shall I have to throw you out?'

The man hesitated; then evidently decided that Daniel was too large to be tackled successfully. He turned and stumbled through the open door, into the lamplight, swearing softly to himself as he went. Dorcas shut the door after him, and turned the key.

'Daniel — who was that man?' she demanded. 'Who is Jenks? What did he mean, there'd be a fine one for you tonight?'

Daniel stood abstracted, as if in a daydream. 'Mmm? What did you say, Dorry love?' he asked, at last.

Dorcas took hold of his arm, and shook him. 'What did the man *mean*?' she cried, beside herself now. 'Daniel — answer me! Stop looking like that!' For Daniel was staring sightlessly past her, obviously still in a world of his own. Finally he looked down at her, his great bulk shadowing her completely. He gave an exasperated sigh and put one heavy arm around her narrow shoulders.

'Jenks is a dealer in foreign stuff; in tea, coffee, and cheap Frog wines,' he explained. 'He sells at low prices to wholesalers, who re-pack his rubbishy goods in new cartons. I suspect he evades excise duty. I've told him before that I'll have nothing to do with him.'

Dorcas looked up into his heavy face, unable to read the expression there. 'Shall we put the counters to rights?' she asked, at a loss.

'Yes. Have you locked both the doors?' Daniel tried the locks to make sure they were secure. Then he began to put up the rough wooden shutters which protected the shelf goods from mice.

Dorcas looked at his broad back and saw that his shirt, between his shoulder-blades, was damp with perspiration. 'A dealer in foreign goods,' she thought. 'A very likely story.' She continued to watch Daniel. 'Liar' — she felt her lips form the word. 'Liar, liar, liar.'

Chapter Eleven

IN THE EARLY 1870S, FOREIGN governesses were quite the thing; even a quiet backwater like Hereford had its quota of women of fashion, who liked to be in the vanguard of change. Mrs Amy Matthias, the Dean's wife, was one of them; and she took great pleasure and pride in the fact that she had employed a real French governess before anyone else in the city. Although, of course, everyone was importing German, French and even Italian women *now*.

When it happened, Marie-Jeanne d'Aubier had been with the family at the Deanery for rather more than two years. Being foreign, she was, quite naturally, a bit odd. One of her peculiarities was her fondness for taking solitary strolls around the Cathedral precincts, either in the gathering dusk or the pearl-grey dawn. A keen amateur water-colourist, she said she liked to study the light. And she had even stolen out at midnight to observe the stars shining down on the ancient, beautiful church.

Her mistress, finding out about it, had emphatically forbidden her to do such an outrageous thing again. 'It's improper and unsafe to wander about in the dark on your own,' she'd admonished. 'I'm surprised that you ever considered such a thing! Think of your own welfare and reputation, if you think of nothing else!'

Miss d'Aubier had treated this caution with absolute contempt. 'A little market town, a place where nothing ever happens — how could there by any danger? she muttered to herself. 'As for propriety — these English are so proper that most of them are more like stuffed dolls than warm-blooded humans.' She had resolved to go out just whenever she pleased.

In spite of her skittish, emotional nature, however, Miss d'Aubier was a good teacher, and the Dean's wife thought highly of her talents. Her two charges, little girls of eight and ten, mimicked her outlandish Breton accent, and laughed at her fanciful style of dress; but they were very fond of Marie-Jeanne. She was not strict, she enjoyed a silly joke, and she appeared to worship the Virgin Mary — an interesting aberration to the two little Anglicans, who had been taught to despise such Romish nonsense but who were intrigued by incense, confessions and penances all the same.

There was, consequently, real sorrow and distress at the Deanery when Marie-Jeanne died. Poor Mrs Matthias wept with dismay when three policemen and a grim-faced inspector brought the news to her that fine June morning. Who would have thought of such a thing? In the very Cathedral grounds themselves, near the choir school, of all places!

The governess's body had been discovered by the two workmen currently engaged in repairing the stonework on the parapet of the cathedral. They had gone to fetch their ladders and tools from the place where they had left them the night before, and had discovered more than they had expected beneath the tarpaulin.

There was no sign that the woman had struggled with her murderer. Her face wore a half-smile; her eyes were open in surprise. She had evidently died at once, of a stab-wound through the heart.

This was dreadful enough. But the aspect of the crime which really fascinated the city people, which doubled the locksmiths' business overnight, was the way in which the killer had dealt with his victim's corpse.

Miss d'Aubier had been gutted like an animal sent to the butcher. She had been slit from neck to navel, her body opened and her entrails removed; these had subsequently been scattered bloodily all over the grass upon which she lay. The police surgeon opined that this had been the work of some crazed doctor — there was no doubt in his mind that a member of the medical profession had been involved, for the cut had been neatly made with a knife honed to razor-sharp precision, and, before they'd been tossed aside, the woman's internal organs had been carefully detached by someone who understood anatomy.

It was asked if Miss d'Aubier had a lover. Some said yes, others no, of course not; Mrs Matthias admitted to having wondered. A stonemason came forward to state that he had seen a woman of her build and appearance in conversation with a tall, well made, fair-haired man only the previous evening. But police enquiries failed to trace such a man; the description was too vague.

On the night that the governess died, Daniel had gone out at ten o'clock and stayed out until two the following morning. He told Dorcas that he had been to visit his father, who had needed some paperwork done urgently, and that he had stopped to help the old man finish a particular order. 'I'm out of practice with a chisel, as you can see,' he said, grinning ruefully, displaying a mass of cuts on his left hand. 'Can you find me some iodine?'

As she dressed his injured hand, Dorcas was puzzled. There were so many cuts — surely he wasn't that clumsy? Even if he were out of practice?

When the news of the murder broke, as it did in full and frightful detail later that week, Dorcas had thought at once of Daniel. She remembered the intense pleasure he took in his butchery, she thought of him gutting pigs in the cold-store — and then she imagined the poor eviscerated Frenchwoman, dead in the Cathedral Close.

She shuddered, and tried to put the connection out of her mind. As if he would even contemplate such a thing! She was making a bizarre concidence, which existed only in her own mind, out of the whole thing. There were at least a dozen master butchers in Hereford, all of whom could no doubt have made a good job of gutting Miss d'Aubier.

For a few days, Dorcas managed to be calm. She reasoned with herself, she told herself to set her ludicrous suspicions aside. But then, when she saw Daniel carve a side of bacon into neat joints, subdivide these into immaculate slices, with the knives which she knew he always kept polished and very, very sharp, she felt quite ill with dread. And when she saw him take Anna on to his lap, when she saw him caress her child, stroking her and absent-mindedly rubbing his hands up and down her sides, it was as much as she could do to keep her seat, to prevent herself from jumping up and snatching the little girl from him.

At other times, however, as she sat at the desk at the back of the shop from which she could watch Daniel sorting, weighing, passing a remark or two with a customer, arguing with a supplier,

154

she would think to herself, 'I must be quite mad. What earthly reason is there to suspect such a monstrous thing of him?'

But then she would see him whetting his knives again; would see the pleasure he took in carving a side of ham, and then she would be afraid. When he wanted her at night, she would lie rigid with terror and disgust, unable to rid her mind of her suspicions. She imagined that he smelled of blood ...

At one o'clock one summer morning, Daniel got up, dressed, and stole silently from the house. Dorcas heard the click of the latch, heard him lock the outside door. She got out of bed and went to the window.

Daniel was accosted by a man who had come out of the shadows of the market hall, and who now took hold of his cuff. As her husband shook him off, Dorcas saw the other man's face, momentarily illuminated by a shaft of moonlight which darted from between two clouds.

Dorcas was sure she knew the man. Suddenly, it came to her. He was the ruffian who had come into the shop late one evening a year or two back. He was the cringing bully who had demanded a half crown, a shilling, a sixpence. Peering into the gloom, she saw Daniel shrug now, and heard the chink of coins. The man loafed away and Daniel made off in the direction of the Kington road, leading out of the town.

Dorcas went back to bed. In the morning, she decided, she would go and see her father-in-law. He could confirm that Daniel had visited him on the night that the governess was killed. She had to set her mind at rest.

In his pocket Daniel carried a bundle containing two of his sharpest knives, each painstakingly honed to paper thinness, and a small meat saw, all carefully wrapped in oiled cloth. He walked quickly down Eign Street, then turned up a footpath by the railway goods yard. He made his way to the new burial ground on the outskirts of the city.

A large, heavy man, he was nonetheless nimble on his feet, and he vaulted the low boundary wall which surrounded the place with ease. He walked to the small chapel inside the cemetery, to the place where the dead from the surrounding parishes were brought in their coffins to spend their last night above earth,

155

before the service and interment early the following morning.

Daniel knocked sharply on the chapel door. 'Jenks?' he muttered. 'Jenks! Damn you, man — open up!'

Jenks had heard Daniel's footsteps crunching on the gravel, but, since the clouds had now covered the moon, he had not been able to establish if they'd belonged to the visitor he'd been expecting. He peered around the door anxiously, a little, wizened, elderly man.

'Mr Hitchman, sir! Come in!' He pulled Daniel inside, and closed the door. He rubbed his bony hands together and grinned, his face monkey-like in the light of the single flickering candle. 'It's a nice one tonight,' he said, gesticulating towards the coffin lying on a trestle table before the little altar. 'Oh, yes — a very nice one indeed!'

'It had better be,' remarked Daniel grimly. 'You had me up here a few weeks ago, remember, and all you'd got was an old man dead of gout!'

Jenks looked aggrieved. 'That one was an alderman!' he whined. 'There was gold rings on him! Surely you didn't miss them?'

'Rings!' Daniel sniffed derisively. He nodded towards the coffin. 'Well?'

Jenks fished in his pocket, and pulled out a screwdriver. 'Oh, you'll have no cause to complain tonight,' he said, with a leer. 'It's a woman this time. Young, pretty — rich, I imagine she must have been. Look at the workmanship on this.' He patted the coffin lid, then got to work on the screws.

Daniel watched him. 'Nothing infectious, I hope?' he asked gruffly.

'Oh, no.' Jenks removed the last screw and lifted the coffin lid. 'Nothing infectious. Look — what a beauty, eh?'

In the coffin lay the body of a young woman of twenty or so, her stomach distended with her unborn child. 'She had a sort of fit,' said Jenks. 'Took ill all of a sudden she was — dead before the doctor could get to her. Too late to save the babby, it was. Her husband, sir! Wept, he did — never seen a man cry so! Gave me a golden sovereign, asked me to watch over her tonight — said I was a good fellow. There'll be men here to bury her at eight.' Jenks sighed ruminatively and looked sideways at Daniel. 'Eight, I said, sir,' he repeated.

'I heard you.'

'Yes, well, just thought I'd make sure.' Jenks grinned. 'Look at her hands,' he said. 'That diamond's worth a shilling or two. I've left her just as she was, sir.'

Daniel eyed the corpse. 'Be quiet, Jenks,' he muttered. He lifted the woman's hand and wrenched the ring from her finger, then thrust it into Jenks' coat pocket. 'Now go away,' he said thickly. 'And no spying on me — d'you hear me? If I catch you hanging around, I'll break your stringy neck for you and screw you down with her — there's room for your skinny body, and they'd never notice the extra weight.'

Jenks opened his mouth to pass some comment on that, but then he saw the expression on Daniel's face and he changed his mind. He felt the younger man take him by the collar and manhandle him out of the chapel. 'You might think you have something on me, Jenks,' Daniel remarked, as he pushed the old man out into the night. 'But remember that I have enough on you to make it a hanging matter!'

Having got rid of Jenks, the butcher closed the door firmly behind him. Sweat was beading his forehead now, and he could feel his shirt sticking to his shoulder-blades. He took off his coat and rolled up his sleeves. He moved the candle so that he could see the corpse clearly. He unwrapped his knives.

Jenks made a pretence of walking away, noisily treading the gravel, but then he crept back along the grass verge, skirted the chapel walls, and, reaching the single window, climbed on to a box he had placed beneath it.

He was, however, such a small man that he was unable to see what Daniel was doing. He doubted if Hitchman could be merely stealing jewellery for it would have taken less than five minutes to despoil the young woman of her other rings, her gold necklace and her small pearl earrings. He must, therefore, be doing something to the body itself. But what?

Jenks did not like to imagine. It was bad enough to be an accessory to robbing cadavers — so if Hitchman fancied himself as a resurrection man, if he was replacing the corpses with sandbags and lugging off the bodies to sell to the medical men, then Jenks wanted to know nothing about it. Stiff with cramp, still unable to make out what was going on, he finally got off his box and loped away into the silent darkness.

Half an hour later, Daniel screwed down the coffin lid. He wiped his knives. He cleaned the saw, and wrapped all his instruments in their cloth. Then he pulled down his sleeves, fastened his cuffs and put on his coat. He let himself out of the chapel and closed the door behind him.

Silently, Jenks trailed him along the tree-lined path, out of the cemetery before he returned to the chapel to check that all was in order for the morning. In the warm night air the smell of corruption almost overlaid the contending scents of sweet oil and other embalmers' materials. Jenks shuddered. After making quite certain that all was as it should be, he left again as soon as he could.

Daniel, walking home in the darkness, found that it was all coming back to him yet again. Those familiar smells of recent death, of hastening decay, had again taken him back almost twenty years ...

He let his mind conjure up a picture of his mother as she had been at twenty-three, before the cancer, which had ravaged her pretty face and eventually killed her, had begun its dreadful work.

He seemed to hear her voice again. 'How's my Danny?' she asked as she leaned over him, tickling his face. 'Is my pretty boy awake yet? Or is my darling still dreaming?' Her silliness had been charming — it still hurt him to remember that he'd loved her for her childishness, for the fact that she'd been a playmate to him as well as a parent.

But then it had appeared, that small red mark on her neck which seemed to grow and grow, a festering sore which developed into a hole in the flesh, a foul-smelling wound which wept and became ulcerated; which would yield to no medication and caused her so much pain that she cried with the agony of it.

Adults, especially when they are in distress, easily forget how much a little child can take in. Mrs Hitchman, while keeping her ravaged face concealed from everyone else, tended to forget that her little son was her shadow, and was with her most of the time, watching ...

On the day he saw her changing the dressing, saw her discard the stained lint and bandages, he had observed the way the disease had now eaten into the very bone of her jaw. He had gazed, appalled — but fascinated. 'It hurts, doesn't it, Mama?' he had asked, pity for her almost choking him.

'Yes, darling; it hurts.' Poor Mrs Hitchman had bent down and hugged him; and he'd seen the wound at close quarters. It was horrible, but he could not take his eyes off it, all the same.

Six dreadful months later, Mrs Hitchman was dead. A merciful release, said her friends and relatives — and for once this platitude was no more than the truth. Her husband, a surly fellow several years older than his wife, had seemed to be philosophical about his loss. Perhaps jealousy of the closeness between mother and son prevented him from feeling any pity for her sufferings. At any rate, he left his wife's relations to make all the funeral arrangements, and went out to work as if nothing was amiss.

On the morning of the funeral, Daniel had stolen into the kitchen, and had clambered on to the table upon which the coffin lay. He gazed down at her, wishing he dared creep inside the casket, under the shroud, to lie there beside her. But then, he did what he'd come to do. With shaking fingers, he had removed the cloth which covered the left half of his mother's face.

Maggots! He gagged in horror. The wound was already infested with them; the creatures were already eating her, burrowing into her cheek. Had they been there while she was still alive?

The smell of death, and the stink of the chloride of lime in which the sheet that wrapped his mother's body had been soaked, went to his head like fumes of brandy. He kissed her, allowing his lips to graze the edge of the wound.

'What's he doing in here?' Suddenly, there was a commotion all around him — women scolded, men exclaimed.

'Danny! Danny, you naughty boy, what have you done?'

'Look! He's disturbed the winding sheet!'

'Oh, Daniel! Go to your bedroom, now!'

Daniel had stared round at the grown-ups. 'I wanted to kiss her,' he'd said calmly. 'I wanted to!' Then, suddenly angry, he broke away from the woman who held him. 'She was mine!' he cried, fiercely, bursting into a violent storm of tears. 'She was mine! And she'll always be mine! For ever!'

Daniel reached the town and put his hand in his pocket, in order to muffle the rattle of metal against metal. He knew he was not satisfied yet. There was still a desire to breathe in that sweet scent of death, to finger damaged tissue, to touch torn skin or to tear it himself if no wounds were there already. But now, added to all that, there was a fresh but incomprehensible urge, a new desire. Daniel now had a need to slice living flesh; to bathe his hands in blood still warm from the heart.

The butcher fingered his knives again; he remembered the reek of decay which had so recently hung about his child, he recalled the stench of her bad flesh. While he sat at her bedside he had closed his eyes and inhaled the smell of Anna's disease, almost able to see the inward corruption become manifest in the outward flesh.

He shook his head. 'I don't understand,' he muttered. 'I love her — why do I want to hurt her? I don't understand, it doesn't make any sense to me.'

But then, as he reached the shop, he realized that there were still plenty of other women. There were those whom he loved — his wife, his child, who were clean and perfect — and there were the others. The whores and the harlots, dozens of them, miserable wretches just like that one who'd grinned at him in the Cathedral Close a few weeks since. It didn't matter what was done to any of them.

Thus his supposed daughter's illness was instrumental in finally tipping Daniel Hitchman over the edge of reason. The associations and memories revived by Anna's fever now engendered an irresistible surge of unnatural desires, which the butcher was unable to control; and which hurled him, helpless, into a bottomless chasm of insanity.

Dorcas had recently made a few pounds of various jams; so, wrapping three jars up in a cloth, she put them in a basket. Then she called to Anna, and the two of them set off to visit her father-in-law.

She found him busy in his workshop, and as surly as usual. He watched her unpack her gifts, mumbled his thanks; then told her that if she had nothing better to do, she might think about making a hard-working man some tea.

Dorcas did this, then took the tray into the workshop, where she found Anna chiselling a spare piece of wood and being told not to cut herself. 'She's good with her hands, is the babby,'

160

remarked old Hitchman, seeing Dorcas come in. 'Takes after her Dad, o' course — he'd 'ave made a fine craftsman if the idle devil could've been bothered.'

'I didn't think Daniel had much interest in carpentry.' Dorcas laid down the tray and poured out three cups of tea. 'Anna,' she added irritably, 'do be careful!'

Old Hitchman sniffed. 'He might not be interested *now*,' he muttered. 'Not now he has a wife and a child to provide for, wantin' this, that and the other mornin', noon and night. But he could have made a success of this trade, believe you me. Made them carvin's up there when he was fourteen, he did. And he made a set of bowls — beautiful they were. Oh yes. If he warn't tied down to that dratted shop day and night, he'd have an interest in carpentry still.'

Dorcas felt her head beginning to spin. 'Would he?' she whispered.

'Aye, he would!' Mr Hitchman glowered balefully at his daughter-in-law. 'Though I suppose you wouldn't like that, would you, my lady?' he sneered. 'It'd make too much mess of them nice clean rooms of yours, wouldn't it?'

Her heart now banging against her ribs, Dorcas sipped her tea. 'How do you think Daniel is looking these days?' she asked.

'How's he looking?' Mr Hitchman slurped his drink from his saucer, letting rivulets of tea splash on to his leather apron. 'I dunno how he's looking. Ain't set eyes on the bugger since Easter!'

'Easter?' Dorcas frowned. 'He came to see you a week or so ago.'

The old man grinned at her, wiped his hand cross his mouth. 'That what he told you?' he asked. 'Well, I ain't seen 'im. He must've come when I was out. Anyway,' he muttered, getting up, 'I can't stop here gossipin' with you all day. Tell the good for nothing so and so that his Dad hopes he is well — and that if it ain't too much trouble, to get hisself round here one evenin' next week. I got a bit of finishin' he could do for me. He ain't got arthritis like I have.' With that, he got up and stumped out into the woodyard, where he could he heard still grumbling to himself as he searched for the piece of timber he wanted.

Anna laid down her chisel then, and looked up at her mother. 'Shall we —' she began. But then she peered more closely at Dorcas. 'Goodness, you're as white as white,' she observed, concerned now.

'Do you feel ill, Mama?'

Dorcas shook her head. She couldn't have described the awful, crawling sensation she felt just then, not even to herself.

Between the murder of Miss d'Aubier and the time Daniel had first begun to go out on his midnight rambles an interval of nearly two years had elapsed. The anxiety and strain of worrying about it all now began to tell on Dorcas. She grew thinner, and permanent dark circles appeared under her eyes. 'It's old age creeping up on me,' she had said, when Maggie Stemp, come to take afternoon tea with the grocer's wife, had asked her what was troubling her.

'Old age, my backside.' Maggie looked affectionately at her friend. 'You're not ill, are you, Dorry?' she asked. 'You haven't any problems here? It's not Daniel, is it?'

'No,' Dorcas shook her head. 'Honestly, Maggie; there's nothing.'

'Well — I think there's something fretting you.' Maggie took Dorcas' hand. 'Won't you tell me what it is?'

Dorcas sighed. 'I've had a summer cold,' she said. 'It's left me feeling low. You know how these things drag on and on.'

Maggie felt that this was not the whole story, but she decided not to go on about it. 'Have you heard about that fellow?' she asked, changing the subject, as she thought, completely.

'Fellow? What fellow? What are you talking about, Maggie?'

Maggie was gratified to find Dorcas still ignorant of the most sensational news of the week. 'They've caught him!' she said complacently. 'He's a foreigner; a medical student. They're going to charge him with the murder of the Froggy woman!'

'Really, Maggie? You're not making it up?' Dorcas leaned forward and shook Maggie's arm. 'It's not just gossip?'

'No! It ain't just gossip!' Maggie was affronted. 'It's in the newspaper today; Madam got Cook to read it out. 'Man held. Charges expected soon.' That's what it said, in big black print — letters as big as my thumbs!' She sniffed. 'Go and buy a *Hereford Times* if you don't believe me!'

'Oh, Maggie!' Agitated now, Dorcas got up and walked about the sitting room. 'Oh, I could kiss you!' she cried. 'If you only knew what a weight that is off my mind!' She stopped pacing, and rubbed her eyes wearily as she tried to smile. 'Oh, I've been so silly!

You can't imagine how stupid I've been!'

Maggie snorted. 'Is that's what's been making you bad?' she demanded. 'Well — I don't see what you got to worry about, big strong husband as you've got to look after you, and all! It's poor, defenceless women like us as should be scared, with no man to protect us if murderers break in and stabs us in the guts before we can so much as yell!'

At the idea of anyone murdering poor defenceless Maggie Stemp, six feet tall and grown stout in middle age, Dorcas actually laughed. She went to look out of the window now feeling lighter, happier and more at peace than she'd been for months.

Euphoria, however, gave way to depression when Daniel's behaviour became even more eccentric. He seemed to be in a sort of daze much of the time. He went out most evenings now, and often stayed out until two or three in the morning. He was absent-minded and appeared to talk to himself. And at tea time he would make a point of taking ten minutes away from work, would come up to the flat above the shop and sit Anna upon his lap, kissing her, stroking her with his great red butcher's hands, as if feeling her for the proportion of fat to meat ...

Dorcas found such behaviour sinister in the extreme; but then reproached herself for ridiculous fancies, and wondered if she were going mad. The fact that Helmut Tellmann, a medical student from Bavaria who had been on a walking tour of the Wye Valley, was still in police custody, did little to ease her agitated mind.

Anna could not help observing the tension between her parents She, with her childish partiality for Daniel, decided that Dorcas was often unnecessarily curt, if not downright unkind. She seemed, too, to expect her husband to do so much; while *she* appeared to spend all *her* time sitting about the house, reading, always reading, Daniel worked. 'She's so irritable,' thought Anna censoriously, enjoying the feel of the long word rolling around her tongue. 'She's sharp all the time. I wonder how he stands it.'

Anna flinched for Daniel whenever Dorcas was abrupt with him; the child felt the hurt which Daniel apparently never felt for himself. For he never retorted in kind, or was ever anything but gentle with his wife.

Sunday, when Daniel did not usually work, was Anna's favourite day. Together he and she could go walking, could perhaps take her kite to fly in the fields alongside the river, to get away from Her for a couple of hours. Together they could both relax. Not needing to talk to each other, they would walk hand in hand for hours in complete but companionable silence, perfectly at ease.

But now and again, Daniel did speak. 'Your mother's a princess,' he announced one evening, during one of their leisurely strolls along the river's green bank.

'She's a *what*?' Anna grinned up at him. 'No, she jolly well isn't!' she giggled 'She grew up on a farm!'

Daniel squeezed Anna's hand. 'I know where she grew up,' he replied gently. 'But to me, she's a princess. The first time I saw her, I thought, she's the woman for me, the only one in the world. Do you understand me?'

'No, I don't — not really.' Anna frowned. 'Mama's very ordinary,' she remarked. 'And sometimes she's so cross that I'd rather be anywhere than with her.'

Daniel gazed across the river, looking at the Cathedral which had just come into view. 'She's very special, your mother,' he murmured. 'Very special. And the wonderful thing is, she'll always be mine; for ever.' He looked down at Anna. 'And so will you,' he continued.

Anna nodded, and tugged at his hand. 'Come and help me fly my kite,' she said. 'Forget about Mama for ten minutes. Then we'd better get home; otherwise we'll be late and be in more trouble — she'll scowl at us all through tea!'

Dorcas, alone in her sitting room that same evening, stood looking out of her window across the deserted street, refusing to worry about Anna or to fret that it was nearly dark now. But where had Daniel taken her, and why was he keeping her out in the cold? She tried, for the thousandth time, to see a way out of the trap she felt she was in.

'Can I talk to him?' she wondered. No. It wasn't possible. What could she say? 'Daniel, tell me — did you kill that woman? Was it you who slit her body like a pig's, was it you who spread her entrails all over the Cathedral Close? Tell me, too, where you go at night. Confess that you did not go to your father's house on the evening Miss d'Aubier was killed. Admit that you did not cut your hand on those chisels — you're a capable, experienced carpenter.' Oh, that was no use!

She beat her forehead with her closed fist. 'Oh, God,' she cried out loud. 'God in Heaven, I must talk to someone! But there's nobody! Nobody at all!'

And then it came to her like a revelation. Of course! She ought to have thought of him months ago! She would write to her late mother's landlord, she would write to Stephen Lawrence. She would ask *him* to advise her! As the lord of the manor, he was the obvious person to turn to in distress. He was an educated, sensible man; now married, with a wife and probably half a dozen children of his own, he would help her, surely! He would understand her fears for Anna — he would know what she ought to do. If only she could see him for an hour, it would ease her heart to talk to him. And he did not know Daniel — he would have no preconceived ideas about him. Stephen Lawrence would tell her what she must do!

But, having conceived this plan, Dorcas now hesitated. What would he think if he received a letter from her after such a number of years, especially when he had left her for the last time in such anger? He would be bound to think she wanted money, whatever she said. As for being the lord of the manor, that was irrelevant; it wasn't the Middle Ages now. It was even possible that he'd have forgotten who she was, since she'd been only one of a whole series of women with whom he'd amused himself more than ten years ago. If she wrote to him, he might write back to Daniel, telling him to keep his wife under proper control.

'But I must talk to someone,' thought Dorcas wretchedly. 'I must — before I really lose my reason. There isn't anyone but him and surely, as a landowner who looks after his tenants so well, as a good-hearted man, he'd think he ought to help me?'

She had thought about it all for a second, for a third time and had finally dismissed the preposterous idea of writing to Stephen when she heard voices on the landing. Anna and Daniel came in, both flushed from running, laughing together — a father and daughter just come back from a harmless afternoon walk, and hungry for their tea...

The following day Dorcas heard a newsboy shouting in the

High Town outside. 'Tellmann released! Special edition!' he yelled, slurring his words after the manner of his kind. 'Tellmann released! Special edition!'

Dorcas got up from her chair, and closed the accounts book upon which she had been working. She ran down the stairs into the street, where she bought a newspaper. It was true; Helmut Tellmann and been allowed to go. There was, apparently, insufficient evidence to bring a prosecution against him, and the murder of Marie-Jeanne d'Aubier remained unsolved.

Dorcas hurried back upstairs and into her sitting room. Seizing a sheet of writing paper, she hurriedly prepared a new pen, sat down, and started to write.

'Dear Mr Lawrence,' she began. 'I hope you will forgive me for presuming to write to you.' She bit the end of her pen. That looked wrong — it was stilted. But she pressed on.

'There is something I should very much like to discuss with you,' she continued. 'It is a matter of great urgency.'

She stared out of the window for a few seconds. Restraint was necessary; she would simply annoy him if she wrote what she wanted to write, if she implored him to come to Hereford straight away, to meet her — where could he meet her? — and tell her, just tell her what to do! 'I do understand that you may not wish, nor even be able, to see me,' she added. 'I shall, however, hope that you will do so, and shall ask for a reply to this letter at the Post Office in Broad Street, a week or so from now.'

Reading the letter back, she realized that it sounded all wrong. But she signed herself 'Dorcas Hitchman', added 'Grey' in brackets; she sanded the paper, pushed it into an envelope and stamped it. Not allowing herself to wonder what her own reaction would be if she were to receive such an odd letter, she forbade herself to change her mind yet again and went out to post the letter. 'He'll most probably ignore it,' she thought, as she made her way home. 'He'll think I want money — he'll tear it up and throw it away.'

A month went by; two months. Dorcas called at the post office regularly, rationing herself to one visit a week, hoping desperately that Stephen would write to her. But no letter came. The clerks got to know her, and then she became anxious lest Daniel should hear that she loitered in the post office, waiting for a letter which never arrived. Finally, she gave up in despair.

Then, one cold, wet autumn day, she was passing the post office when one of the counter clerks came rushing down the steps and almost knocked her beneath the wheels of a passing cab. As he steadied her, apologizing profusely, he recognized her. 'Mrs Hitchman, isn't it?' he asked. 'Odd that I should run into you like this, so to speak! Your letter's come.'

She gazed up at him, frowning. 'What did you say?'

'I said, your letter's come!' He grinned. 'I assume it's the one you've been waiting for all this time. Been here a fortnight or more it has; it'll be going back to the sender tomorrow if you don't fetch it!'

Suddenly galvanized into action, Dorcas muttered her thanks and dashed up the post office steps.

The letter had indeed come. As the clerk handed her the stiff, white envelope she saw the familiar handwriting and her heart thumped. She practically snatched it from the man's hand, and then she went over to one of the writing stands provided for members of the public. Her fingers shaking, she slit the cover and pulled out the single sheet of paper inside.

Dated the twenty-seventh of the previous month, the letter was postmarked Oxford. Obviously hurriedly written, it was short and to the point.

'I have been abroad for the summer,' she read. 'Your letter was not forwarded to me, so I received it when I arrived back in England last week. I hope that the matter of which you wrote is not so urgent that it cannot wait until the nineteenth of November, when I shall be in Hereford. If you still wish to speak to me, you could come to Hindley and Featherstone's chambers on that date, at about three in the afternoon.

'I shall be here in Oxford until the seventeenth. If you so desire, you may write to me at the Mitre, in the High Street.'

He signed himself, simply, 'S R Lawrence'.

Dorcas read this curt note through two or three times, learning it by heart. Then she stuffed it inside the sleeve of her gown and walked slowly home, her original purpose in going to that part of the town forgotten.

She let her mind conjure up a picture of Stephen, which she

immediately blotted out. He wouldn't be the man she remembered. He probably looked very much like his father now; they'd been of the same build, the same colouring. And she thought of the old squire as he'd been at the last harvest supper she'd attended; a red-faced, ugly man, with sparse grey hair and blackened teeth. Dead drunk, he'd been leaning on the arm of his valet, leering at one of his housemaids.

Dorcas arrived home and tried to think calmly. Now, it seemed unbearable to live a day longer with Daniel, to have to sleep with Daniel, to be touched or kissed by Daniel. His very presence, taciturn and threatening, made her shake with fear. It was surely only a matter of time before he realized that she suspected him: then what would he do? And what of Anna?

Anna, Anna, Anna. The name beat like a drum in Dorcas' brain. What if he should harm Anna? Recently, dreadful nightmares had filled her sleeping hours, visions of a carcase suspended upside down from the hook which pierced its feet, its head over the bucket placed there to catch the blood.

But the corpse was not that of a pig. It was that of a child, of a naked female child from whose head the curling black hair still hung. And Dorcas watched as Daniel slid his hands over the dead flanks, caressingly, almost lovingly. Then she watched him take his knife and saw him slice open the stomach, and —

At that point she always woke up, sweating and terrified; sometimes to find Daniel lying peacefully beside her, but more often to find him gone.

The day after she had received Stephen's letter, Dorcas was packing up a bundle of linen for the laundry when she found that one of her husband's shirts was spattered with blood. This was not particularly unusual; he often splashed pigs' blood on to his sleeves. But this was a Sunday shirt, his best; and the whole front was patterned with sprays of brown droplets. Worse than that, the cuffs were stiff with dried gore.

As far as she knew, he hadn't butchered any pigs that week. So where had that blood come from? Whose was it?

Dorcas handed the bundle to the delivery boy and went to her bedroom. Taking her letter from its hiding place, she re-read it for the thousandth time. Working out the dates, she realized that Stephen would be in Oxford for four days more.

She was seized by an irresistible desire to see him at once. Could she go to Oxford? She considered this possibility. She thought, 'Oxford is on the railway line from Hereford; goods coming to the shop from London are usually brought by way of Oxford. I could go to the station, get on a train, be there in a few hours. I could be with him.'

She grimaced to herself, trying to decide whether this was a stupid or an excellent idea. She imagined Stephen's wife coming down the stairs from her hotel room — for his wife was certain to be with him, after all — and this fine lady, clad in silk and furs, would turn to a servant and say, 'Tell my husband that there is a person to see him.' Or perhaps she'd be ordered to leave. She remembered how terrifyingly Stephen frowned when he was angry, as he'd surely be if suddenly confronted in this way ...

Dorcas went out for a walk, going she did not know where, thinking, thinking. If she went to Oxford, she could take Anna with her. The child, sworn to secrecy, would think it a grand adventure. They could go early in the morning and be back late the same evening. Daniel could be told they'd been to Ledbury for the day, had met the carter at the turnpike, as they often did.

Dorcas walked to the station. She bought two tickets, one for herself, one for Anna. At six the following morning, mother and daughter left home for the railway station where they waited for one of the Great Western Railway express trains to London, stopping at Oxford.

Anna, who had expected to meet grumpy old Tom Arrowsmith at the Ledbury Road turnpike, and to spend a dull day playing with Annie Luke's stupid children, was wild with excitement. A train ride! Honestly? Where to? Oxford? Where was Oxford? Further than Ashton Cross? Anna jumped up and down on the platform, practically squeaking with glee.

As the train pulled out of the station, Dorcas relaxed, but then she began to curse her folly. Daniel would certainly find out that they'd been to Oxford. A child of ten could hardly be expected to keep such a thing a secret, especially from the one person to whom she confided everything. However would Dorcas explain herself to him? A sudden uncontrollable urge to take a train ride, for the first time in her life, in the winter, seemed to indicate — if not actual madness — then an oddly unbalanced frame of mind. Her clothes were going to smell of smoke and be covered in smuts. 'Oh, God,' she thought. 'Whatever shall I do now?'

As the train rattled through the Cotswolds, Dorcas began to wonder if she would ever dare to go home. She looked at Anna, who was gazing out of the window enraptured, her eyes flashing, her black curls tossing as she bounced up and down on her seat, still full of excitement. Surely Stephen had only to see her, to look at his beautiful child, to want to help her?

Anna ate her sandwiches and sucked her orange. The Oxford clocks were striking one, a series of unsynchronised chimes echoed around the city as the engine, on time, pulled into the grimy, smoke-stained station.

The spires of the city looked unreal and insubstantial, as if they had been cut out of paper and then pasted against the clear blue November sky. At a loss where to go, Dorcas asked a man for directions to the centre of the town. The two of them, mother and daughter, made their way through the wide streets.

They gazed at the blank, grey stone walls which seemed to rise up everywhere. Was this a city full of prisons? And now they noticed a group of men, clad in flapping black gowns, walking from one of these fortresses, but attracting the attention of no one but themselves.

It seemed such a huge, confusing place! To give herself courage, Dorcas put her hand in her pocket, and fingered her letter, wondering what to do next. As she stood, lost, in the middle of Cornmarket Street, a middle-aged woman stopped by her and asked her if she might direct her anywhere.

'The Mitre?' asked Dorcas hesitantly. 'I believe it's an hotel?'

'Ah yes — that's right.' The woman grinned. 'Go towards the tower on your right then turn left and carry on down the High Street. You'll come to it. You can't miss it — there's a sign outside.'

Without waiting to consider further, Dorcas took Anna's hand and made for the High Street at once. She found a road absolutely full of these blank, grey stone walls, but she also found the place she was looking for. She pulled Anna inside, and asked the servant if she could leave a message for a Mr Lawrence.

As she said the name, a thick-set, black-haired man in plain dark clothes, a man who had been standing with his back to her reading a newspaper, turned round. He started at Dorcas, who, now aware that someone was gazing at her, looked up.

She saw the face which had remained with her, waking and sleeping, for more than ten years. He was very sunburned. His forehead was scored with a few deep lines now, and his hair and side whiskers were touched with more than a hint of grey. But Dorcas knew Stephen at once.

Chapter Twelve

IT WAS OBVIOUS TO DORCAS that Stephen had recognized her, but she could not otherwise read his expression. He frowned but then he recovered from his surprise and came towards mother and daughter. He held out his hand to Anna. 'Is it Miss Hitchman?' he enquired gravely.

Anna took his hand, bobbed and smiled. 'Good afternoon, sir,' she said politely. She turned to her mother. 'Who is this gentleman?' she asked.

Somehow, formal introductions were made. Stephen seemed to talk the most, mainly to Anna.

Dorcas felt her heart lighten a little. He surely saw that the child must be his. He must see his own features mirrored and softened in his daughter, for they were so astonishingly alike.

The porter was eyeing the trio with curiosity. Stephen glanced across at the man, then looked back at Dorcas. 'Mrs Hitchman,' he said clearly, 'I am very glad to see you again. Perhaps you and Anna would like to walk out for an hour or so?'

Dorcas took her cue. 'Thank you, Mr Lawrence,' she replied, painfully aware that there was an uncontrollable tremor in her voice. 'I'm sure we would like that very much.'

The three of them went out into the weak winter sunshine of the High Street. They walked along in silence, well apart from each other, until they came to a shop which sold toys and stationery. Stephen stopped outside it, pushed open the door and led them inside.

'Now, Anna,' he said, 'if you choose a top, a whip and a hoop for yourself, we can take them to a meadow near here and you can show your mother how well you can use them.'

Anna looked up at Dorcas, who nodded. Her dark eyes wide and shining with pleasure, the child then picked out a red painted top, a whip with a yellow handle, and a light metal hoop. Stephen carried the hoop for her while she clutched the other toys, hardly able to believe her good fortune.

They reached Christ Church Meadow, round which adjacent to the college of the same name, there stretched a broad gravel walk. About two hours of daylight remained, in which Anna would be able to master her new toys. She rushed off down the path, bowling her hoop. She would obviously be contented for some time.

Stephen looked enquiringly at his companion. 'I assume that Anna is the reason you wished to see me?' he asked mildly.

'You don't doubt that she is yours?' Dorcas, who had sat down on a convenient bench, did not dare to look at him.

Stephen sat down too, but well away from her. 'No, Dorcas,' he replied eventually. 'No, I don't doubt it.'

He was so much less abrasive than she'd asumed he'd be. Prepared for sarcasm, anger, or at best a cold, sardonic politeness, she was gratified beyond words to find that ten years had softened his manner to an unbelievable extent. He still frowned, but it was easy to see that this was simply his habitual facial expression, not an indication of any particular annoyance. He no longer fixed her with the sharp, narrow-eyed stare which she remembered. His demeanour was gentle, even kind.

But he did not smile, either. Dorcas reflected that this was just as well. Given the slightest encouragement she'd have thrown her arms around him and not been able to let him go. 'What did you wish to discuss with me?' he asked.

'I need your advice.' Haltingly at first, but then more fluently, Dorcas told Stephen about her suspicions, her anxieties, her fears — especially about her fears, for Anna's safety. 'Daniel's mad,' she said tearfully. 'Mad — I can see it in his eyes. And he frightens me so much that I'm now beginning to doubt my own sanity. I'm sure that he killed that woman! But of course I have no proof.'

She twisted her hands in her lap, screwing her wedding ring round and around. 'I'd stake my own life that he was responsible for that awful thing,' she muttered. 'And now that I know he'll do anything, I'm so afraid — for myself, certainly, but more so for Anna, who is not his child. If he ever suspected as much, what might he do to her — or to me? I'd meant to return to Hereford

173

tonight, you see — I'd meant to lie to Daniel about what I'd done today, and I hoped that Anna would keep my secret. But she tells him everything! And now I'm here, I'm scared to return home. Oh, what shall I do?'

'Do?' Stephen thought for a while. 'You're telling me that you wish to leave your husband?'

Dorcas bit her lip. 'I don't know,' she replied. 'But I'm afraid to go back to Hereford; I can't go back, and I won't. Could you — forgive my impertinence, you've already been more patient than I'd dared to hope you would be — could you perhaps lend me some money so that I could take lodgings for Anna and myself somewhere? Just for a while, until I can find myself some work? It shouldn't be difficult to do that — I can sew, I can keep accounts, I can keep house. I ask for nothing but a loan, and I'd pay you back, every last farthing ...' She tailed off, and looked at her hands.

Stephen said nothing for a few seconds. 'Well,' he began hesitantly, 'I could arrange some lodgings for you; there'd be no difficulty about that. But I don't think you've really considered the seriousness of the step you are intent on taking. You have run away from your husband. You propose — no, Dorcas, don't interrupt me, for you must properly understand this — to put yourself under my protection.

'Your husband will then have a real grievance against you. If, on the other hand, you return to Hereford tonight, you can go back to your home and no one need ever know you considered leaving it. I'm sure you can explain away today's excursion somehow. I can arrange for you to see my lawyer, who could advise you.'

Dorcas shook her head. 'So you won't help me,' she murmured.

'It's not that I won't help you; it's not that at all.' Stephen looked at her earnestly. 'Listen to me,' he continued. 'Can't you talk to your husband about your fears? Are you even sure that your suspicions are well founded? If you are, why don't you go to the police? They would have him watched — I'm sure they would be interested in his night-time rambles! In the meantime, could you not go to some respectable lady for a visit? To your old employer, perhaps? To someone at Ashton Cross?'

Dorcas looked down the path towards Anna who, now proficient with her new toys, was happily chattering to a girl of

174

her own age who was walking with her nurse. 'I know I should either have it out with Daniel, or go to the police,' she replied tonelessly. 'I've thought of everything you've said. I could go and stay with Miss Lane, but he'd find me, I know he would.'

Dorcas brushed her hand across her face. 'Oh, God — I don't want to involve or compromise you!' she cried. 'That was certainly not my intention! But I'm not going back to him. I'd rather go to the workhouse here. If you can't or won't help me, that's what I shall do. I'll say I've lost my memory. They'll think I'm mad and they'll soon be right, soon I shall be! But whatever happens, I'm not going back to Daniel!'

Stephen shrugged, ran his hand through his hair. 'I see,' he said calmly. 'Very well, then, I shall arrange some lodgings for you and the child. But Dorcas: this is on the understanding that a message will be sent to your husband, at once, to tell him where you are. If he wishes to come here, you must appreciate that no one can forbid him to do so. If he wants to see you, you must meet him.'

'But —'

'Dorcas, you have no choice in the matter!' Stephen grimaced. 'I shall, of course, instruct a lawyer to be present when we meet,' he added.

'We?'

'Naturally.' Stephen shrugged again. 'I am involved now, whether you wish me to be or not. So, Dorcas, before we do any of this, you must consider again and be quite sure that it is what you want. Are you sure?'

Dorcas nodded. Grateful beyond words, she wanted to reach out and take his hand; but she contented herself with a smile.

He did not smile back. He rose from his seat and walked away from her, calling to Anna; who came running up the path, bowling her hoop.

A message, composed by Stephen — for Dorcas was far too nervous to put any suitable form of words together — was telegraphed to Daniel. For the first time that day, Dorcas felt a twinge of concern for him. Would he be worried? Would he think they'd been kidnapped, or worse? Would he go trudging to Ledbury, frightened for her and for Anna?

Then she thought, 'Let him worry. He's caused me enough

anxiety; let him think whatever he likes.'

Stephen left Dorcas and Anna at a shop where they could buy what was necessary for the night, while he went to engage some rooms for them at a decent lodging house near Magdalen Bridge. When he returned to collect them, he found that Anna was growing querulous and irritable. Hungry, and tired, she wanted to go home.

'It's too late to catch the train now,' said Dorcas, forcing a smile. 'Mr Lawrence has arranged for us to stay here tonight. Shall we go and see the place? And have something nice to eat?'

Anna shot Stephen a look of suspicious distrust, but said nothing. She did, however, consent to walk up the High Street between her parents, and she allowed herself to be shown into the small bedroom prepared for her. Stephen said goodnight to mother and child. Then, slowly, he made his way back to his own rooms.

As he walked down the High Street, Stephen realized that it was late, well after six; the sky was dark, and the moon was rising now. In half an hour he was expected at one of the colleges, where he was to dine, and speak. He had meant to spend the afternoon going over his notes — but now he would have to speak impromptu, to translate from German without any preparation, to talk for an hour or more from a great disordered mess of data which he had not had time to sort out.

'It doesn't matter,' he thought to himself. 'Half of them will be drunk, and the other half will have no interest in me, in Schliemann, or in Troy.' He shivered, feeling the cold of the evening, and hurried on.

The sight of Dorcas, appearing like that out of nowhere, had seriously upset him. It had only been by a great effort of self-control that he had managed to stop himself from reaching out to her.

She, on the other hand, had been so obviously worried and abstracted, so beside herself with concern for the safety of her child — his child — that she'd spoken to him with no more warmth than if she'd been a distant acquaintance. And he had been so mesmerized by her that he had allowed her to place him in an embarrassingly compromising situation — as the evident protector of a woman running away from her husband on a totally

176

ludicrous, completely unsubstantiated pretext.

For she could prove nothing against him. The man was probably an ordinary shop-keeper, a dull-witted fellow fond of a visit to an alehouse; nothing more sinister than that.

But then Dorcas had seemed half crazy with fear, had been almost deranged as she'd talked; and that worried him. Concerned for her, he did not know what to do next. But, as he climbed the stairs to his rooms, he knew that letting her go was not a possibility.

'Bring me some hot water, please,' he called to the servant hanging about on the landing. 'And can you do something about this?' He handed the man his gown, which had lain crumpled and forgotten at the bottom of a trunk. 'I'd like it sponged and pressed. Now.'

Stephen washed, dressed himself in evening clothes, and, feeling more settled now, dashed out to Balliol where he talked fluently about the recent archaeological discoveries in Asia Minor. But his mind was elsewhere, even as he answered questions.

He was making plans for Anna and Dorcas. Whatever happened now, they were his. He would never let them leave him again.

The telegram had perplexed and frightened Daniel. It appeared to come from his wife, who told him that she and a certain S. Lawrence would see him, at his convenience, at some hotel or other in Oxford. Oxford? Whatever was she doing there?

At first, he thought it must be an elaborate practical joke. He went back upstairs and made up the fire in the sitting room. He thought about walking to the turnpike on the Ledbury Road for he was looking forward to seeing Anna, to having her on his lap, to hearing her chatter about what she'd done that day.

It was past midnight when he finally accepted that neither his wife nor his supposed daughter was coming home. He dozed, and woke in his chair at five the following morning, cold and stiff. Very worried now, he took some money and the shop keys, which he slipped through his chief assistant's letterbox. He made his way towards the railway station, still wondering what on earth was going on.

Daniel arrived in Oxford early that afternoon. He made his

way to the address given on the telegram. When Stephen, who had been out all the morning, walked into the hotel, the hall porter told him that a fellow apparently the worse for drink had come in, asking to see him.

way to the address given him on the telegram. The hall porter told Stephen, who had been out all the morning, that a fellow apparently the worse for drink had come in, asking to see him.

'There he is, sir, in the corner,' said the porter. 'I told him you were out but he said he'd wait. Shall I have a couple of the men remove him?'

Daniel was asleep, slouched in a hard chair. Stephen looked at him, saw a big, well-made man, handsome but run to fat far too early in life. Though he looked dishevelled, he was, on the whole, well-dressed and he appeared to be perfectly respectable. Unshaven that day, a bristle of fair whisker was evident around his chin.

Stephen thought for a moment. 'Can you let me have a sheet or two of writing paper?' he asked the hall porter.

'Certainly, sir. Here.'

'Thank you.' Quickly, Stephen scribbled a note to Dorcas, asking her to come at once. Then, on another sheet, he wrote to a lawyer's office, asking if a solicitor and clerk could be sent over as soon as possible. He gave the notes to the porter's boy. 'Be as quick as you can,' he said, handing the boy a half-crown. 'If Mr Fawley won't be seen out of chambers, tell him I shall be calling upon him in half an hour.' Stephen watched the boy go. If his solicitor should refuse to come to the hotel, he would make them — Daniel, Dorcas and Anna — go with him to the lawyer's office. He would have matters cleared up once and for all ...

Stephen went over to the sleeping man and touched him lightly on the shoulder. Daniel woke with a start. He rubbed his bloodshot eyes and gaped blearily at Stephen. 'Mr Hitchman?' asked Stephen. 'Will you come upstairs?'

The seated man grunted. 'Who the devil are you?' demanded Daniel in reply.

The two men sat facing each other across Stephen's cluttered sitting room, Daniel eyeing the crates of books, disordered piles of papers and trunks full of clothes, with great suspicion. 'Have you had anything to eat today?' askd Stephen, breaking a heavily-charged silence. 'Would you like something brought up for you?'

Daniel, who was parched and famished, shook his head. 'Damn your something brought up for me,' he muttered. 'Where is my wife? And my daughter? I tell you this now — if they've come to harm, I'll break every damned bone in your body!' He glared at Stephen; he clenched and unclenched his fists, his eyes bulbous with barely controlled rage.

Just then the door opened, and the porter showed Dorcas and Anna into the room. The child stared — then she ran straight to Daniel, who hugged her fiercely, feeling her body for injury. Satisfied at last that she was unharmed, he sat her upon his knee and held her there.

'You can see that the child is well,' said Stephen. 'I don't think she ought to remain here while we talk; so let her go downstairs and stay with one of the maids.'

Scowling, Daniel considered this; but then he slid Anna off his knee. 'Aye — all right,' he said grudgingly. 'She can go.'

Meekly, Anna followed the hall porter out of the room and he closed the door behind her. But no one in the room noticed when, a minute or two later, the door opened a fraction, nor did they observe the flash of white underskirt as Anna slipped behind the sofa.

The child noticed that her mother was standing close by Mr Lawrence's chair. She could not see Daniel but he had been speaking as she came into the room. 'Well, Dorry?' she had heard him ask. 'What's the meaning of all this? Why are you here, and who's this fine gentleman you seem to know pretty well? Aye, yes, he's told me his name; but what's he doing here with you and the girl? Eh?'

Dorcas was at a loss to know how to reply. She looked helplessly at Stephen. 'I have sent for my solicitor,' he said. 'You and Mrs Hitchman can talk when he comes.'

But Daniel was in no mood to wait for any lawyer. Faint, now, with hunger, light-headed from lack of proper sleep, he cursed Stephen and demanded to know, at once, what his wife was doing in Oxford. 'You may be a ruddy squire,' he growled. 'You may be a gentleman — ha! — but you'll answer me now, d'you hear me?'

Stephen folded his arms and said nothing.

Dorcas looked from one man to the other. 'Don't look so

angry, Daniel,' she pleaded. 'You know that I lived on Mr Lawrence's estate when I was a child. I came here to see him because I needed his advice.'

'Advice? What about? *I'm* the proper person to advise you!'

Stephen looked at his watch, wished Mr Fawley would hurry up. 'Mr Hitchman,' he began calmly, 'your wife came to see me because she is worried about you. She came to me simply because I am an old friend. Now → will you wait for my lawyer before you say anything else?'

'Lawyer be damned!' Daniel got up, lurched unsteadily over to where Stephen was sitting, and glared down at him. 'Listen to me, you!' he barked. 'I'm not one of your bloody tenants! I don't have to pay any heed to what you say, I don't have to cringe and grovel to you! I'll have an answer out of you this minute, curse you, even if I have to beat it out of you!' He grabbed Stephen's lapel and shook it roughly. 'Why is my wife here with you?'

Stephen became very white. He stood up and scowled at Daniel. 'Don't be insolent,' he said icily, removing the butcher's red hand from his coat. 'Sit down, Hitchman! Now!'

Dorcas caught at Daniel's sleeve and tried to pull him back to his chair. 'Daniel,' she beseeched, 'please be calm! Don't do anything foolish! I'm afraid of you when you're like this — but I've been afraid of you for some time now, you know that, don't you? You've something on your conscience — I know you have! You — you've done something terrible ...' Glancing across the room then, she caught Stephen's warning look, and tailed off.

A livid flush appeared on Daniel's face now, but he slumped back in his chair all the same. A grim smile had appeared on his lips. 'My conscience?' he rasped. 'You talk to me about conscience, do you? Well — what about your conscience, eh?' He glared at Stephen. 'And what about your old friend here — what about his conscience? Is he maybe more than an old friend? Perhaps he's a very *good* friend?'

Stephen rose from his chair, walked over to the window and looked across the High Street. 'I think you've said enough, Hitchman,' he remarked.

'That's right, gentlemen, I have.' Daniel got to his feet, caught his wife by the wrist. 'Dorcas — find Anna. There's been enough of this playacting and we're going home. You can explain yourself when we get there. And your explanation had better be a good one — I tell you that now!'

Dorcas twisted out of his grasp. 'I'm not going home with you,' she said.

It took Daniel a few seconds to take this in. He stood in the middle of the room, swaying slightly, looking from Dorcas to Stephen. 'Not going home?' he demanded. 'What do you mean, you're not going home?'

'I mean what I said.' Dorcas looked down at the floor. 'I — I'm not going back to Hereford. I can't — I won't be your wife any more ...'

Daniel looked hard at her, and grimaced. 'I see,' he said. 'Your good friend here — this fancy gentleman of yours — he's enticed you away, has he? That's what it's all about, is it?' He saw Dorcas blush; and he laughed, a horrible, mirthless laugh grating to the ears. 'Very well, Dorcas, stay here. Stay with your friend. It doesn't matter to me! But I shall take my daughter home, and you'll never see her again! I'll make bloody sure of that!'

He stumbled over to the door and tugged it open. 'Anna!' he yelled. 'Anna! Come here!'

Dorcas ran in front of him then, and slammed the door shut, leaning against it. 'My daughter stays with me, Daniel,' she said. 'You won't take my own child away from me!'

'Won't I, though? Just watch me!' Daniel looked into her face with such contempt that she flinched as if he had struck her. 'I can do as I please,' he muttered softly. 'Don't you understand — my daughter is mine! There's no power on earth can take Anna from me! I'll take her home with me if I wish and you can't prevent it!' He made her meet his eyes. 'I think I hate you,' he hissed. 'So get out of my way, before I really lose my temper!'

When Dorcas did not budge, he put out his hand to drag her away from the door. But Dorcas stood firm. 'You can't have Anna!' she cried. 'She's no daughter of yours! She's — she's — oh, for God's sake, Stephen, can't you stop him?'

Daniel stared at his wife in astonishment. Then, suddenly, he wheeled round and looked hard at Stephen. He couldn't help but see the resemblance now; the dark eyes and hair, the set of the features, that characteristic frown. He looked back at Dorcas. 'Harlot!' he cried. Then, his eyes pleading, he asked, 'It's not true, is it? Dorry — she's my child, isn't she? Anna's my daughter?'

Unable to meet his eyes, Dorcas shook her head.

Daniel, looking capable of murder now, glared at Stephen. 'So, you — gentleman?' he rapped. 'Is the woman telling the truth? Or is she mad? Out of her mind?'

Stephen shrugged, almost imperceptibly; but said nothing.

A man winded by a blow in the stomach looks much as Daniel did then. He stared at Dorcas with real loathing now. 'When?' he began, talking to himself. 'Where?' Then he realized. 'A seven month baby,' he muttered. 'You married me — you were carrying his child — and you must have known it! And I — I must have been blind, stupid, — I never thought, I never even suspected! Oh, you, you — there's no word to describe what you are!'

Tears were now running down Dorcas' cheeks; she cried out of simple weakness, out of sheer emotional exhaustion. Daniel gazed at her. 'You may weep, whore,' he said coldly. 'You'll weep more before you've done! How long will your bloody gentleman keep you before he tires of you a second time? He's deserted you before — left his rubbish for an honest man — and he'll weary of you again. You're not young any more.'

Still Dorcas stood there, barring his way. 'I loved you, Dorcas,' said Daniel. 'I always looked after you well, you wanted for nothing. I worked hard for you and the child. Don't make me hurt you now! Move, damn you!'

But then a sudden movement behind the sofa caught Dorcas' eye; and she looked around just in time to see a flicker of blue disappear into the gloom. She went across the room and drew the frightened child out of her hiding place. 'Did you hear everything, Anna?' she asked.

Pale as death, Anna could only nod. She wrenched herself out of her mother's grasp and ran across the room, out through another door, slamming it behind her.

Daniel stared after her. 'You'll suffer for that, wretch,' he said. 'You'll suffer — you and your fine friend here. Anna's still mine in name and in law. You can't prove otherwise. I'll have her back, I swear it. And if you try to stop me taking her, I'll have your friend's name in all the newspapers in the land!'

Desperation now made Dorcas brave. 'You won't!' she cried. 'And if you try to take Anna from me, I'll ruin you!' She looked directly at her husband; she spoke clearly and slowly. 'I'll see you hanged,' she continued. 'I know where you go at night, you see. And I know what you did to that poor woman!'

As she spoke, Daniel's inflamed face gradually lost all its colour; and, recklessly, Dorcas bluffed on. 'I know everything, I tell you! I know! And if you ever try to take my own child away from me, I'll go to the police and I'll inform on you! So try it if you dare!'

A spasm passed across Daniel's face. 'You don't know anything, whore,' he mumbled. 'You don't know anything at all!' He lifted his hand to lash out at her but, as she shielded her face with her arm, Stephen came up behind Daniel and caught his wrist. With a sudden jerk, he twisted the butcher's arm behind his back, and held him.

Daniel winced. He coughed, he choked; he glared at Dorcas with absolute hatred. But then he seemed to realize that he was beaten. 'All right, gentleman,' he muttered. 'You can take your hands off me, I won't hurt the whore! She's mad, quite mad, and you're welcome to her!'

Daniel tried to wriggle free, but couldn't. 'You can have her!' he cried, his voice now cracking with pain. 'Didn't you hear me? I make you a present of her — there's no need to break my bloody arm!'

Stephen felt Daniel's body relax so he let him go. Daniel grimaced; he rubbed his arm, and flexed his fingers. Then he opened the door and went quietly down the stairs, passing the lawyer and his clerk on their way up.

Someone must have taken Dorcas and Anna back to their lodgings. Someone must have brought them some tea, lit their lamps, and later served them with some supper ...

Dorcas, still dazed and light-headed, did not sleep at all that night. In the narrow bed across the room she could hear Anna tossing restlessly, talking to herself in a troubled sleep. The following morning neither could bring herself to begin a conversation with the other, and at breakfast they avoided one anothers' eyes.

Dorcas expected Stephen to come, or at least to send a message. But she heard nothing at all from him. She supposed he must be going back to Hereford soon, either that day or the next — back to his wife, to his children; if he had any.

She realized then that since they'd met again he'd said nothing about himself. It had been she who had talked and talked, who had been so wrapped up in her own anxieties that she hadn't made even the most commonplace enquiry after his welfare.

Perhaps he would simply go back to Hereford and leave her there. Perhaps he'd gone already. She looked in her purse and found that four sovereigns and a few odd coppers stood between her and destitution. She would have to find work, and soon ...

After Daniel had gone and he had asked the porter to take the lady and her daughter back to their lodgings, Stephen had shut himself up in his bedroom, opened a bottle of brandy and poured himself a large tumblerful. As he drank it down, he began to feel better. He lay on his bed and thought about Daniel Hitchman's wife, swirling another glassful of the golden liquid around his glass as he did so.

He wondered if she'd been aware of his desire to take her in his arms and kiss her until she fainted. *Had* she known how much he wanted her? Longing for her gripped him even now, so much so that he rolled over on to his stomach and buried his face in the pillow, moaning softly under his breath.

When he'd received that silly letter from her, he'd assumed straight away that she wanted money. He had decided, therefore, to see her at his solicitor's office, to deal with her once and for all. He'd wondered, vaguely, what she looked like now and decided that she was probably fat, red-faced and blowsy, overdressed; her teeth rotten or missing, her once pretty features coarsened and plain. Country girls, lovely at sixteen, soon went to seed ...

But she hadn't been like that. She'd stood before him, the same sweet-faced, charming girl of his remembrance and unbidden dreams, dressed plainly and neatly, in dark, well-fitting clothes. She was nothing like the vulgar, lower middle-class matron he'd imagined her to have become.

And then there was the child. She'd smiled at him with her mother's lovely smile, which displayed her small, white teeth, the front two marginally overlapping in the same way that Dorcas' did. Sitting up, he rang the bell by his bed.

'Sir?' The servant, appearing almost immediately, looked curiously at Stephen.

'Can you bring me something to eat?' Stephen stared back at the man, making him drop his gaze. 'Anything will do. I don't care what.'

The servant nodded, and left.

When he returned, bringing a tray of supper, he found the gentleman asleep. Stephen slept until five, then he got up, ate the stale, curling sandwiches, and drank a great many cups of coffee. Putting on his coat, he went out.

'I want you to find me a larger house now,' he informed the land agent, whom he'd commissioned to look for a small house in North Oxford. 'Something with six or seven bedrooms, good sized servants' rooms, and a garden. There must be a large garden.'

Then he walked into college.

Having recently taken up the offer of a fellowship, Stephen had been looking forward to a relatively quiet existence as a university teacher, of a routine of lectures and tutorials, interspersed with some fieldwork of a less intensive nature during the summers. He wondered, now, how his career prospects would be affected if he were to set up house in Summertown with a mistress — for every one would assume that Dorcas was his mistress, even if he gave out that she was his wife — and a ten-year-old child.

'Oh, damn it all — other men have their harlots,' he told himself, as he walked up the staircase to the rooms which had been allocated to him. 'Jarret's had that woman in Kidlington for years; and Charlton's notorious for his affairs.'

He reflected that the Master of his particular college was notoriously misogynistic, and that stories of moral laxity among his Fellows seemed to elicit no more violent response than 'Damned women again! Don't know why they bother. Can't stand 'em myself!'

Everything would be all right, he decided. And if college didn't like it — well — that was too bad.

Stephen let another day pass before he went to see Dorcas again. He found his daughter sitting primly in her landlady's parlour, sifting through a pile of cheap magazines which she'd found there. She stood up when he entered the room and looked at him with blatant dislike and mistrust. 'I shall fetch my mother,' she said coldly as she left the room.

The three of them walked to the meadows, where Anna was told to run off and play. She went sulkily, reluctantly, dragging her heels and deliberately scuffing her shoes in the dirt. Stephen and Dorcas found a bench, and sat down upon it, at opposite ends.

'You must tell me what you would like me to arrange for you,' said Stephen stiffly. 'I shall, of course, provide for you and the child. But you mustn't imagine that you owe me anything if I do. You're not to feel obliged to me.'

Dorcas studied her gloves. 'You're very good,' she said, equally stiffly. 'That's much more than I deserve or want.' She looked earnestly at Stephen. 'Mr Lawrence,' she continued, 'all I desire is that you lend me a little money for a short time, until I've found work. Then you'll be doing more for me than I have any right to expect.' She managed a faint smile. 'I heard that you were married,' she added. 'Is your wife well? Have you children?'

'I have two, a boy and a girl. They live with my wife. I never see them, since Elizabeth and I have been separated for the last seven years or more.' Stephen rubbed his face with his hands. 'I'd assumed that you knew that.'

He was looking straight ahead of him, so he did not see the astonishment on her face. 'I spend some of my time abroad,' he went on. 'My brother manages the estate — I go there twice, perhaps three times a year. I'm about to take up a teaching post at the university here; next summer I shall be organizing an excavation in Greece.' Still he did not look at her. 'And,' he concluded, 'since I once promised to take you there, you shall come with me.'

He kept his eyes fixed on the water meadows in the distance; but he felt the light pressure of Dorcas' gloved hand on his arm. Then he looked at her, and saw her smile; saw that a little colour had come back into her pale cheeks at last.

A week or so later, Stephen took Dorcas and Anna to look at a new, red-brick house in the Banbury Road, to the north of the city in a district usually known as Summertown. Anna, who had been very out of spirits since Daniel had gone, had looked almost interested when she heard that name. 'A Summertown house,' she had said. 'That sounds pretty.'

The house had not turned out to be as pretty as its location suggested. It was a square villa of no architectural beauty — a home built, on speculation, for a bank manager or any professional man with a large family. Commodious and modern, fitted with the latest conveniences and connected to all the mains services, it was a charmless place.

They had walked around the uncarpeted, empty rooms, which still smelled pleasantly of recent carpentry and drying plaster. 'Are we to live here?' Anna asked her mother, when Stephen was out of earshot.

'Yes — I think so.'

'With him?'

'Yes, of course!' Dorcas sighed. 'Anna, he is your father — you do realize that, don't you?'

Anna shut her eyes. 'Don't say that!' she muttered. 'Don't talk about it!' She looked at her mother then, her dark eyes unforgiving and cold. 'If you want me to like him, I'll try,' she said. 'But he's not my father. I'll never call him that. And you mustn't say he is!'

Dorcas grimaced. There was nothing she could do with Anna until the child came round; and that would be in her own time. She hoped it would not take too long. 'It's a lovely house,' she hazarded, in a conciliatory tone. 'It's so big — you'll be able to have a nice large bedroom, much bigger than that poky little place you had at home!'

Home! Dorcas bit her lip as she saw Anna wince. And they waited in silence until Stephen, who had been talking to the house agent, came back upstairs to find them.

They returned to the centre of the town in mid-afternoon. Anna was hungry; so Stephen took them to his rooms for tea. After she had eaten, the child yawned, then dozed, then fell fast asleep.

'Poor little thing,' remarked her mother. 'She hasn't slept at all well since we left Hereford. It's not to be wondered at.'

Stephen went over to his sleeping daughter and pushed another chair against hers. He lifted her legs on to it, then covered her with his coat. 'Will she sleep for a while, do you suppose?' he asked.

'I expect so. Could you carry her across the road to our lodgings? Then I could put her to bed.'

'She looks comfortable enough there. Leave her, let her rest.'

Stephen leaned over Dorcas and kissed her, full on the lips. He took her hands and pulled her to her feet.

He closed his bedroom door on Anna, lit a lamp by the bedside, and took off his jacket; he loosened his tie, then put his arms around Dorcas. She, both unwilling and unable to resist him, laid her head on his shoulder, breathing in the familiar scent of him, an intoxicating blend of clean sweat, soap and tobacco, which she remembered from ten years since and which still made her dizzy with desire. She was aware of her own arms wrapping themselves around his neck and of him kissing her face.

But then she stopped him. She put her fingers on his lips, and drew back to look at him. 'I — I didn't intend this to happen,' she said. 'I don't expect — I didn't come to this place hoping for anything but advice from you. I knew you were married — I didn't have any thoughts about — ' She bit her lip, and stared down at the floor.

'I know you didn't. It was obvious. Won't you look at me, darling? That's better.' Stephen took both her hands in his. 'Dorcas, I asked you to marry me once, and you turned me down. I can't offer you marriage now, but I do offer you everything else a husband ought to give his wife. Will you stay with me?'

'But your own wife — perhaps she might want to return to you! I'd imagined that you intended me to be your housekeeper, to look after you and Anna. That's all I thought you'd want of me, after the way I behaved towards you!'

'You thought that, did you?' Stephen smiled, more than a little sardonically. 'My dear Dorcas, when did you last look in a glass? Did you honestly believe that I would be content to have a woman with your face, with your figure, with your innumerable charms' — here he laughed at her — 'walking about my house, and never want to touch her?' He slid his hands up her arms, curved them around her shoulders, brought them at last to rest, lightly, upon her breasts. 'You know perfectly well that I can't even look at you without wanting you. You must be aware that these past few days have been very difficult for me; when I saw you standing before me in that hotel lobby, it was as much as I could do not to fall upon you and ravish you there and then.'

Dorcas, feeling her own body stiffening with longing for him, telling her to take him in her arms, shrugged her shoulders helplessly. 'We're married,' she whispered. 'We're both married —'

'I don't imagine that I shall ever see my wife again. We dislike each other. I don't consider myself at all accountable to her. Nor am I accountable to your husband, since he was so foolish as to say he made me a present of you.'

'Mm — ' Dorcas looked at him, earnestly. 'Stephen, I want you to know that I made a terrible mistake when I married Daniel. I've been punished for it over and over again. I didn't realize what he was like at all, you see — I hardly knew him, we'd only ever walked about the city together, and before we were married we were never left alone. We never — I was never unfaithful to you. I always loved you, no one but you.'

Stephen took her hands, placed her arms about his neck. 'It doesn't matter now,' he said soothingly. 'Really, it doesn't matter at all.'

'But it does! When you called me a bitch and a liar, it wasn't undeserved; but I'd never considered Daniel at all while I was with you. It was as if he didn't exist. Do you understand? I accused you once of using me. Well — I used Daniel.'

'That's all finished with now.' He kissed her again. 'Darling, come to bed.' He began to loosen her hair, to unhook the back of her gown, kissing her with greater and greater urgency as he did so, opening her mouth with his and teaching her, once again, how to respond to being loved.

It was like waking from a bad dream, like walking at last through a doorway into a spring garden, like coming home to comfort and warmth after a long and arduous journey. She'd almost forgotten what it was like to be touched by a lover's hands, to be kissed by lips which desired hers; but now she found that remembrance was flooding through her, showing her what to do, telling her to kiss this man back, to take him in her arms and love him as he was loving her. Stephen was waking her from a ten-year nightmare; slowly and carefully at first, but then with increasing passion. When he finally took her, she feared he must break her apart. He grasped her shoulders so hard that she felt her bones grind against each other; and her flesh seemed to melt against his.

But she welcomed the pain of it. She clung to her lover so tightly that she found, afterwards, that her fingernails were encrusted and sticky with his blood. When at last she relaxed, bruised, spent and exhausted from the violence of the past half-hour, she hugged Stephen still, pulled him down upon her again. 'You've brought me back to life,' she whispered. 'Dear, dear Stephen, you can't know how much I've missed you!'

'Can't I?' He raised his head and looked at her. 'You're just as I remember you,' he murmured, as he studied each feature in turn. 'You're still the same beautiful girl that I've seen in my imagination so many times, quite unchanged.'

'I can't be! I'm ten years older — I have crow's feet around my eyes now!'

'You're exactly the same as you were at seventeen.' He laughed with sheer happiness then, gathering up a great mass of her hair in his hands, he buried his face in it before he let it fall again, tumbling around her face. 'But I've become an old man,' he added. 'Look at my hair; it's nearly white.'

'What nonsense, Stephen!' She smiled up at him and ran her hands through his thick, straight hair, black in her remembrance, but now definitely streaked with more than a little grey. She touched his neck and let her fingers travel down his chest. 'You're right, though,' she remarked, giggling. 'You have aged. Even the hair on your chest is grey! And Stephen, you're so tanned you look like a workman!'

'I *am* a workman!' He kissed her arm, which was very white against his sunburnt skin. 'I dig holes, don't you remember? I've spent all summer in southern Greece, digging holes!' He laughed again, his pleasure at being with her so overwhelming that it seemed to illuminate his whole face, to make his steel-grey eyes glitter with an almost incandescent intensity. 'Don't you know, darling, how perfectly delightful it is to be shovelling away in the hot sun, getting covered with mud and dirt, and sweating like a pig?'

'Delightful?' Dorcas grimaced. 'It sounds horrible.'

'Yes — well — most of the other fellows would agree with you there! *They* just sit around yelling orders, and watching the natives lugging baskets of rubble about; making sure they don't pocket anything to sell back to us later. But, you see, I always want to join in — I want to touch anything they find first, before it's even moved, while it still has the clay on it, while it's still cold from the earth. Even if it's just a piece of burnt brick or a shard of pottery.'

He looked at her closely. 'You don't understand, do you? You think I'm quite mad.'

'I think you're perfect.'

'Do you?' Stephen kissed her, very lightly, on the lips. 'I love you,' he said. 'I've missed you, but I didn't know how much until just now. Darling, your face is rubbed raw — I've hurt you; I'm sorry.'

'I love you.' He'd never said that before. And although Dorcas now realized that her lips were tingling and her cheeks were sore from the violence of his kisses, she felt her heart shudder with pure delight. 'Kiss me again,' she said, putting her arms around his neck and pulling him close to her. 'You didn't hurt me at all. I've been in Paradise.'

He pushed his hair out of his eyes. 'So have I,' he said. 'My darling, so have I.'

Anna, waking in the darkness, sat up, rubbed her eyes, wondered where she was. She rose from her chair and stumbled over to her father's bedroom, for she could see a faint light coming through the slit between door and frame. Gently, she opened the door.

By the light of the bedside lamp she could see her mother. She was lying in bed, her arms around her companion's neck; a sheet covered her from the waist downwards, but she was otherwise quite naked. Dorcas lay on her back, her long hair spread out upon the pillow. That man, who was also without any covering and whose heavy, sunburnt body seemed to shine in the lamplight, lay on his stomach next to her, one arm across her mother's bosom, his hand cradling her breast. They were both sound asleep.

Anna caught her breath and looked away, upset and disgusted. She shut the bedroom door on the sleepers, hoping that the sudden click would wake them; then she groped around in the darkness until she found some lucifer matches and a lamp. She felt tears prickle her eyelids, but she blinked them away and, when her parents joined her ten minutes later, she was sitting demurely in her chair, perfectly self-possessed again.

She could feel their happiness radiating around her as they walked down the dark, deserted High Street; and she felt so desperate then, so lonely and utterly forsaken, that she wanted to sit down in the gutter, and howl.

Things happened so quickly. At the beginning of December, hardly more than two weeks after they'd left Hereford, Dorcas and Anna moved into the house in Summertown. At first Anna found it strange, almost frightening, to be living in such a large place, having been used to the cramped but cosy little rooms above the grocer's shop.

She was left to herself much of the time. That man was hardly ever there during the daytime; she supposed he came home at night, but she didn't often see him, and they never had a conversation by themselves. He was apparently some kind of teacher — but of grown men, not of children. Dorcas had explained this as far as she understood it, which wasn't very far at all …

On the rare occasions that he was in the house, he didn't take much notice of Anna. He seemed to understand that she was ill at ease in his company and he made no efforts at all to ingratiate himself with her; for which she was grateful. Once or twice he asked her what she was reading. But that was all.

Anna had nothing to remind her of her former home. Then, one day, she happened to see a copy of a book which she had owned back in Hereford, a rather childish version of fairy tales. She persuaded her mother to buy it for her. It was, after all, a link with home, so she read it time after time, as if learning it by heart. When she came across passages which she had recited to Daniel as the two of them sat by the fire in the early evening of a peaceful Sunday, she felt tears come into her eyes. But she would not shed them. She refused to cry.

'Do you like to read, Anna?' Stephen asked, seeing her curled up with that same book on three of four separate occasions.

'Yes, I do.' That was another problem — she didn't know what to call him. She wouldn't call him sir. Mr Lawrence was obviously wrong and he was apparently Dr Lawrence, anyway. That was how everyone else addressed him; another mystery which no one had bothered to explain to her. But Papa was, of course, out of the question.

'Would you like some more books?' he asked, breaking into her thoughts. 'You must be rather tired of that one.'

'Oh — I'm very fond of it.'

'May I see it?'

Reluctantly, Anna handed it to him. He flicked over a few of the pages; and he handed it back to her without comment.

Then, a couple of days later, he came home with a great boxful of books for her. Opening it in her room, she found that it contained dozens of story books, all filled with pictures, of the expensive kind which she'd seen and coveted but never thought she would ever possess.

When she had thanked Stephen for them, he had smiled at her and said he was glad she liked them. She had to admit to herself that he looked far less ugly when he smiled — she even felt herself softening towards him, just a little. But she was determined to have him all the same, and she would *not* be bought off with presents.

Anna enjoyed going shopping with her mother. It appeared that they could buy whatever they wanted — clothes, books, furnishings, linens — anything the Oxford shops had to offer. Dorcas spent and spent, and in the evenings she pored over catalogues, looking for even more things to buy.

The little girl had never had so many clothes, never dreamed that she would accumulate so many toys. She supposed that *he* paid for it all, so she asked for far more than she wanted or needed, and found, to her surprise, that it was generally forthcoming. It made her happy to squander his money, and she would have been mortified if she'd heard him remark, 'She's a very moderate little girl, isn't she?'

For Stephen thought his daughter a model of restraint, not greedy at all by the standards of the children from his own social class.

Relations between Dorcas and Anna went from bad to terrible. Things had become very awkward indeed when Anna noticed her mother sign herself D.E. Lawrence, a name to which, as Anna had witheringly pointed out, Dorcas had no right at all.

It had been very gratifying to see her mother blush. 'It is my name now,' she had murmured, not looking at Anna. 'Your father wishes me to be known by it. And,' she added, 'he would like you to think of yourself as Anna Lawrence now.'

'Why?'

Dorcas had blushed even redder. 'Because you are his child, of course,' she replied. 'All children are known by their father's name. Anna, he loves us both, we belong to him — we should be happy to take his name!'

'I'm Anna Hitchman!' Anna glared at Dorcas. 'I always shall be. And your husband loves us both, we belong to him, so his name is mine!'

Then there had been an argument, at the end of which both mother and daughter had been in tears. 'Don't be so difficult!' Dorcas had cried, beside herself with annoyance and distress. 'You're Anna Lawrence now! You must understand that once and for all!'

'I'm not Anna Lawrence! I'm NOT!' Then Anna had allowed all her pent-up misery to explode in a violent flood of tears. 'You took me away from my father!' she sobbed. 'I hate you! I hate that man! I want to go home! Did you hear me? I want to go HOME!'

But she finally accepted that Oxford was now her home. She stopped referring to Daniel as her father. She even tried writing her new name in a few of the books which Stephen had given her. In the hopeless way in which a child, who knows he has no choice, eventually bows to the inevitable, Anna accepted her fate and tried to make the best of things.

She even got used to that man. Resolutions not to speak to him were broken, and when he smiled at her she found herself smiling back. 'I don't have to like him,' she told herself. 'I don't have to speak to him unless I want to — he doesn't seem to notice whether I do or not.'

And it began to matter to Anna that he should notice and that he should like her, whatever she might privately think of him.

Chapter Thirteen

IT WAS THE MOST PECULIAR Christmas Anna had ever spent. There was no visit to church, and on Christmas Day there was no special Christmas dinner although the meal provided was, as always, rich and plentiful enough. In the afternoon, that man brought round a pony and trap; in which, well wrapped up against the cold, he drove Anna and Dorcas to a house in the countryside. There, a family party was being held. There were some other children present, together with dozens of grown-ups. Dorcas, Anna noticed, looked very ill at ease. But that man, of course, knew everyone there.

'They were some friends of your father's,' replied Dorcas later, when Anna questioned her about the revolting people with whom she'd been obliged to spend the afternoon of what had, up until then, been her favourite day of the year. 'The man who spoke to us was Dr Carson; he teaches at the university.'

'He was horrible.' Anna grimaced. 'And those children he said were his daughters were horrible, too — they stared.'

'Did they?'

'Yes. They stared at us both. I shan't go there again!'

'Anna, if your father wishes to take you —'

'I shan't go there again!' Anna stamped her foot. 'He might be able to tell you what to do and how to behave,' she cried. 'But I don't have to do as he says! And I won't!'

Dorcas sighed, was about to remonstrate with Anna; but just then the door opened and Stephen came into the room, with a large cardboard box in his arms. 'Sit down, Anna,' he said calmly. 'And then you can open your presents.'

She glared at him, and then the familiar feeling of resentment, inextricably mingled with a desire to have him say something kind to her, to smile at her, flooded through Anna's heart. 'Smile at me,' she thought. 'Please! Don't look so solemn! Don't frown so!'

Just then, their eyes met; and it was as if he'd heard her unspoken pleading. Stephen knelt by the fireside and unfastened the box. He took out an elaborately wrapped parcel. 'Open it,' he said. It was an order; but, miraculously, he smiled as he spoke.

It wasn't too bad after that. Anna opened everything in the box, and ten minutes later the floor was a litter of wrapping paper, ribbons, new clothes, paints, crayons, books, handkerchiefs, fancy soaps and confectionery — more presents than she'd ever had in her life before.

Too busy examining her gifts to notice that her mother had gone out of the room, Anna glanced up a minute or two later and found that she was alone with the monster. He looked at her gravely. 'I know it's all very difficult for you,' he said kindly. 'I know it's very strange here.'

'What?' Blushing, she stared up at him, wishing he wasn't so difficult to understand. Why did he drawl so? Why couldn't he speak normally, why did he say 'auf' instead of 'off', 'glarse' instead of 'glass', 'vay' instead of 'very'?

He crouched down again, his face level with hers. 'I said, I know things are difficult for you. And I'm sorry that you're unhappy.'

'Oh.' Anna's blush deepened. 'I'm not unhappy,' she lied.

'Aren't you?' He got to his feet. 'That's good,' he said. 'I'm glad to hear it.'

Dorcas, who had given her cook and housemaid the rest of the day off, pushed open the door just then and entered the drawing room; she was carrying a laden tray. 'Tea?' she enquired, her smile fixed and far too bright.

'Please,' Stephen took the tray from her. 'Anna — have some cake.' It was another order.

'I don't want any, thank you,' she said defiantly. 'I'm not hungry.'

But, by the end of the day, Anna, who had been encouraged to drink a glass or two of wine and warm water, felt rather less miserable. Almost relaxed, she sat between her parents on the wide sofa, warm before the drawing room fire, comfortably nodding off; her head drooped, and finally leaned against her father's shoulder. She was vaguely aware of him carrying her upstairs and laying her, fully dressed except for the shoes which she felt him pull off her feet, under her eiderdown.

She woke early the next morning, her clothes crumpled and her head aching; but feeling unusually light-hearted. Somehow, the house didn't feel so alien that morning. And when she heard that man's heavy tread on the stairs, she did not grimace. 'Today, it's the Feast of Stephen,' she thought, and almost giggled. She didn't mind him being there quite so much today.

December passed by, became January; February became March. Round about the middle of April, Anna noticed that her mother was looking rather pale nowadays, and observed that she spent the afternoons with her feet up on the sofa, resting. 'Are you ill?' she asked one morning, not over-solicitously.

'No, not ill.' Dorcas smiled feebly. 'You're going to have a brother or a sister,' she said. 'Will you hate that?'

Anna, inwardly shocked, shrugged with counterfeited indifference. 'I'm glad you're not ill,' she replied. 'He says he'll take me out riding today,' she added, firmly changing the subject. She'd think about her mother's condition later, she decided.

'Did he? That will be nice. Where are you going?'

'I don't know. To the countryside, he said.' Anna looked concerned. 'Will I be safe?' she asked anxiously. 'I've never sat on a horse in my life.'

Dorcas, remembering the feeling of warm security she'd experienced while cantering along the country roads on Stephen's black mare, smiled reassuringly. 'You'll be quite safe,' she said decidedly. 'You'll enjoy it, you'll see. Your father's an excellent horseman, you know.'

Stephen took Anna up a high hill, just outside Oxford, and pointed out the various colleges, churches and other landmarks. Without thinking, she leaned back against him, wriggling her shoulders against his chest, making herself comfortable. She laid her hand upon his arm. 'What's that?' she asked, pointing with her other hand.

'The Radcliffe Camera. It's a library.'

'Oh. And that?'

'St Mary's church.'

'Where you never go.' She twisted round and looked up at him. 'Are you a pagan?'

He laughed. 'I'm not sure how to answer that,' he replied. 'I'll think about it, and tell you later. Shall we go for a gallop?'

'Very fast?'

'Very fast indeed, if you like.'

Anna's desire to see the landscape zipping past her overrode her usual determination to say nothing, do nothing which would gratify him. 'Please,' she replied.

'Hold tight, then.'

She clutched his arm, which was clasped firmly around her waist; she felt the warm strength of him holding her safely against him; and she relaxed. A second later, the wind was lashing her face, tugging at her hair. 'Did you enjoy that?' he asked her, a few minutes afterwards.

She looked up at him and grinned. 'It was marvellous,' she said. And she bit her lip, annoyed with herself for being so delighted by something he had done for her.

Eventually the spring gave way to summer, and in due course the time came to go abroad. The journey by rail across Europe was delightful to Anna, who felt she could happily spend the rest of her life in a railway carriage, watching different countries flash by. She was also glad to find that there was enough time allowed for some sight-seeing on the way to Athens.

Dorcas, although she was tired with the oppressive fatigue of pregnancy, found the energy to go and see the things which Stephen wanted to show them. Happy just to be with him, she politely agreed that the Alps were lovely, and she calmly admired the beauty of Venice — but she was always glad to get back to the hotel, to go to her room and rest, preferably with Stephen lying beside her, reading or making his everlasting notes.

Often, however, Stephen was out with Anna, who made a far more lively and responsive companion. She was enraptured by everything; she gawped, open-mouthed, like a tourist, and she found constant cause for exclamation and question. 'What's that?' she would ask. 'Who are they? Papa' — for she had now given in on this point and sometimes called Stephen Papa, telling herself that she might as well, for convenience's sake; and he didn't seem to mind — 'can we go up that tower? Go inside that house? Can we?'

'Certainly,' was Stephen's invariable reply. He found her enthusiasm charming, and went out of his way to bribe concierges and caretakers into showing him and Anna around any number of private houses and shuttered castles.

Her father noticed, too, that Anna had an ear for languages, for she appeared to understand simple sentences in most European dialects after only a few days in any particular country. She took every opportunity to talk to hall porters, flower-sellers, chambermaids; to anyone who would talk to her.

And Anna came to know Stephen — that man, as she still privately thought of him — much better. As they went walking together she could not help gradually developing a real regard for him, clever, generous, interesting as he was. While *he* knew everything, he talked to her as if she, too, were grown up; he asked for her opinions, listened to what she had to say, explained things she did not understand. He bought her books, crayons, paper, paints. It seemed that she had only to ask, and he would provide. 'Water-colour paints!' she exclaimed delightedly, as she opened a box he'd brought back to the hotel for her one day.

'Yes, that's right.' Stephen took out the instructions leaflet, which was printed in Italian. 'But you can mix these with oil, water, use them dry as pastel colours — you can even stir them up with a yolk of egg, if you like, then you'll have a nice, glossy finish.'

'Egg?' Anna frowned. Eggs were for eating, not for wasting. The shopkeeper's child knew that.

Stephen, realizing what she was thinking, laughed at her. 'You don't need to use egg if you don't want to,' he said. 'Why don't you fetch some paper and see what you can do?' And he got up and walked into her mother's bedroom, closing the door firmly behind him.

Anna was not naturally ungrateful, and it soon became necessary to please him, to take as much trouble to oblige him as he obviously did to oblige her — to earn that charming smile he'd given her on the day she'd thanked him for those first few books. She had to impress him, make him admire her ...

Stephen, for his part, found Anna an intelligent, biddable child who seemed likely to repay any efforts he might make to educate her. He noticed, too, that relations between Anna and her mother were very strained and he felt that if the child were happy, everything would be well. He succeeded in making Anna happy. But in doing so he also widened the gap between Dorcas and her daughter to an almost unbridgeable degree.

'She's a charming little girl,' he remarked, as he lay by Dorcas' side one evening, contentedly winding a lock of her long hair around his fingers. 'And she's so like you!'

'Is she?' Dorcas sniffed. 'Am I moody, sulky and difficult, then?'

'Anna's not at all difficult!' Stephen laughed. 'She's the most delightful companion and a proper little chatterbox, just like her mother!'

'Really.' A sudden spasm of jealousy gripped Dorcas around the heart. 'Do you think she's pretty?' she enquired.

'She's beautiful,' replied Stephen, turning over and falling asleep.

When the family arrived in Athens, Dorcas found that there was a cool, white house prepared for her, women to wait upon her and to look after her. She had nothing to do but sit with her feet up and sew baby clothes.

Stephen would now be away from her for days together. Anna, too, practically disappeared, going off on secret expeditions with the gardener's boy, with whom she conversed in an arcane blend of both their languages, gradually becoming far more fluent in his than he did in hers. Anna's favourite outing was to make the long, hard climb up the hill which she could see from her house, to visit the yellow temples which stood at the top of it, and to gaze at the statues there; which were still beautiful, despite having been mutilated over the centuries by Turkish soldiers at target practice.

Although she was, at her own insistence, taken to the site of the excavation, Anna found little to interest her *there*. Deep holes in the ground, horizontal exploration shafts, tunnels, bits of powdering masonry and jagged stonework were extraordinarily dull. She could not understand why her father came home sometimes hardly able to speak for excitement. He would sit far into the night, scribbling page after page of notes. She would hear her mother asking him if he meant to come to bed at all, and his muffled reply of, 'You go, darling — I must finish this' — whatever 'this' was.

200

After all, he never found any treasure. The site yielded no gold ornaments, no jewels; there were no splendid suits of armour, no swords or breastplates to be admired, so Anna failed to see what Stephen and the other men who came to the house became so worked up about. They would sit around the dining table drinking gallons of horrible red wine and chewing their way through huge meals, eating with their mouths open, arguing in two or three different languages — for there were French, American, German as well as English archaeologists digging up great areas of Greece at that time — about the significance of this, the importance of that. Sometimes one of them lost his temper and stormed out, followed by derisive laughter from the others.

'They're all very boring,' remarked Anna to her mother. 'They shout and yell and carry on so. What does it matter anyway?'

Dorcas yawned; she could hear Stephen's voice hectoring some other man, and she smiled what she was aware must be a treacherous smile. 'Goodness knows,' she replied placidly, keeping her eyes on the door into the dining room. 'But your father thinks it matters, so I suppose it must.'

It was so hot. But Anna discovered that, while her mother complained and wilted, *she* enjoyed the heat on the dry, scented air, which hit her as soon as she opened the shutters each bright blue morning. Her father, she noticed, was just the same — the hotter it was, the harder he seemed to work, as indifferent to the high temperatures as the lizards which darted about the rocks.

Dorcas frowned at Anna's sunburn, and said that the child was getting so tanned that she would soon look like a little African. Her father merely shrugged his own sunburned shoulders. 'She's just a little rosier, that's all,' he replied. 'And she's so pretty that I think some extra colour in her cheeks sets her off to perfection.' He smiled at his daughter. 'Leave her alone,' he told Dorcas, and went on with his breakfast.

He'd said she was pretty! That was splendid. And he'd disagreed with her mother, which was even better still. Anna went out that day without her hat; she tied back her hair so that the sun could tickle the back of her neck and kiss her ears. She went up to the flat roof of the house and took off all her clothes except her chemise, lay spreadeagled in the sunshine so that her arms and legs would bake golden grown, dark against the white of her clothes.

She was never at a loss for things to do. In the stagnant pool a few miles away from the house, where the gardener's boy and his friends went on those soporific afternoons, Anna learned to swim. She wandered about the city alone, and no one seemed to notice if she went missing for hours on end. She could now chatter away in modern Greek to anyone. Her collection of pressed flowers was splendid. And she never wanted to go back to dull, cold, tedious England.

The family stayed in Greece until the end of September. Stephen, pleased with the way the excavation had gone, planned to return the following summer if the authorities would let him. But he took very little care to conciliate the Greeks. 'They're a bunch of ignorant Levantines,' he said, and abused them both behind their backs and to their faces. 'They've no interest whatsoever in preserving their heritage, and they're determined to prevent anyone else from doing so.'

Anna sympathized with the Greeks, privately wondering what Stephen's reaction would be if a horde of foreigners started to dig up half of Oxfordshire. But she was wise enough not to say anything about this to her father, who, in his very limited spare time, had begun to teach her Latin.

Dorcas had murmured at this. 'What use will Latin ever be to Anna?' she enquired pettishly. 'What use is it to anyone, if it comes to that?'

'What use? Oh, my dearest, darling simpleton, you mustn't bother *your* charming little head about that!' Stephen had put his arms around as much of Dorcas' waist as he could and kissed her cheek. Then he had made some rather long-winded remarks about the value of a classical education, which Anna had not quite followed, and which Dorcas had not understood at all. But it delighted Anna to have seen her mother snubbed again, and she decided that she would learn this Latin, whatever it was worth or not worth, to please Stephen — and to annoy her.

She mastered the rudimentary grammar of the language without much difficulty, and then set about reading passages from her father's own very tattered copy of Cicero's orations, which she found dull beyond belief. 'Think of it as a foundation, Anna,' he had said, when she pointed out that Cicero's raking over of Catiline's conspiracy was very, very boring. 'Then, when we get back to Oxford, we can read some poetry, which I expect you will find somewhat more difficult. And maybe next year, we'll make a start on Greek — that's much more rewarding.'

Rewarding! Anna sniffed at that, unconvinced. But the determination to irritate her mother kept Anna at her books. An hour spent with her father, reading a page of Livy — for he had at last conceded that Cicero was too tedious to interest a ten year old girl, and had decided that history might hold her attention better than oratory could — was an hour which Stephen could not spend with her mother. And even if Dorcas was in the room where they worked, hanging round his neck and fiddling with his collar, he was still giving his attention to Anna …

The day upon which Anna, leaning over her father to look at a paragraph which he was reading aloud to her, had accidentally brushed his hand with hers, was the real turning point in their relationship. Stephen had caught her hand in both of his, and he held it for a minute or two, rubbing the palm, while he finished the passage. 'There,' he said. 'That's roughly what it means. Write out a fair copy for me and I'll correct it.'

She felt a light pressure on her imprisoned hand — she looked at him, into his eyes — and saw that at that particular moment he looked very gentle, very kind. She could almost see why her mother liked him so much.

'You're a clever girl,' he said gravely. He shook her hand, jerking her out of her daydream. 'Work hard for me, Anna. You could do very well.'

Anna felt such a glow of satisfaction as he said that. She took her books and papers off to her room, to continue the war with Hannibal. And, as she sharpened her pencil, she told herself that she *would* work hard. For this was something from which her mother would always be excluded.

Oxford was red and gold when they returned to the Summertown house. Stephen took himself off to college, where he now had his own rooms, leaving his mistress and child to hire servants and run the house.

In university society there was no place for women. Some dons might marry, if they wished, but many were clergymen who for various reasons could not take wives. A fair number of them, however, had no scruples about taking mistresses instead.

As far as the university was concerned, these women did not exist; for a man's morals, provided he was reasonably discreet, were his own business. His colleagues did not interfere in his private life unless a sensation appeared likely to affect the college concerned, and not always then.

It was general gossip that a Fellow of Balliol had seduced and impregnated the unfortunate servant girl whose case had been trumpeted all over the national press, who had been abandoned by her lover and who had subsequently, in her distress, murdered her baby. While the woman had been sent to prison for her wickedness, her seducer had been shielded by his college, protected from unwelcome publicity — the Master had refused to have the man dismissed from his fellowship or even disciplined for his immorality. The whole affair was hushed up and life went on pretty much as before.

Dorcas was in a more privileged position than that poor, deceived, forsaken chambermaid. She had the status of a married woman, and was, on the face of things at least, accepted as Stephen's wife. In due course she was invited to sit on charitable committees; she became involved with work for relief of the poor; and succeeding in her attempt to refine her rural accent and to polish her rustic manners, she found she could play the role of middle-class matron to near perfection. So she was able to make many acquaintances and a few friends, and she passed her time in Oxford very pleasantly. If she noticed that there was a certain edge to Mrs Dean Vesey's voice when she addressed Dorcas as 'my dear Mrs Lawrence', she very wisely ignored it. She sipped the tea she'd been given with a polite smile, and accepted the position of the Charity Committee's general factotum without demur.

Stephen, who had long since become used to living as a single man, had thought he had no taste at all for family life. He enjoyed the bachelor clubbiness of his college. But now, he began to find that he was drawn to domesticity — and when the atmosphere of port and cigar smoke, of intellectual chat, became at all oppressive, he was happy to leave it for the pleasant society of a mistress who worshipped his shadow, and of a child who had long since passed the sticky, tiresome, uninteresting stage of her development.

The fact that he had acquired this woman and her child in a

rather sudden, unexplained fashion did Stephen no harm at all. 'She's charming, you know. Quite charming!' Alfred Carson, a classics don who himself lived a rather unconventional life out at Garsington, in a huge house with his enormous family, grinned at a colleague. 'The new Mrs Lawrence is perfectly enchanting. A little rustic in her speech, perhaps — but very sweet. And she wears a ring, so perhaps they really are man and wife.'

'Hmm.' The history don, to whom Dr Carson was talking, snorted. 'I always understood that he already had a wife. Some woman from Shropshire. Never set eyes on her, of course — she's never lived in Oxford.'

'Well —' Alfred Carson laughed. 'He always was a bit of a philanderer. Perhaps he's decided to settle down with this lady. She's pregnant, you know,' he added. 'And that child of hers is obviously his — dead spit of him, he couldn't deny it if he tried.'

Both men nodded wisely. 'Caught at last, eh, Stephen?' demanded the history don, as the object of their discussion walked into the room. 'Well, I must say it's long overdue.'

But, seeing Stephen's grimace, he left it at that. It was well known that Stephen Lawrence was far too touchy to take a joke against himself. And, being gentlemen, the dons did not necessarily say what they might think to each others' faces.

Behind each others' backs was, of course, a quite different matter.

Anthony was born early that November. His mother was delighted with him, thrilled beyond words to have a perfect, beautifully detailed miniature of her beloved Stephen. And, after his birth, Dorcas became pregnant again almost immediately, as if making up for lost time — she lolled about the Summertown house, fat and contented, happier than she'd ever been in her life.

From time to time she thought briefly of Daniel, wondered if she'd been completely wrong about him. She became anxious that he might try to take Anna back. 'If he does,' she thought, 'I'll have to fight him.'

But she would have an ally. Anna seemed to spend more time in her father's rooms in college than she did in her own home. They had become almost inseparable since Anthony's birth and

Stephen would not now give up his daughter without a battle royal, of that Dorcas was certain.

When another daughter was born, Stephen suggested calling her after her mother.

'Goodness me, no!' Dorcas had replied, shuddering. 'It's the most ugly name in the world — I hate it, I wouldn't burden a child of mine with it.'

'I rather like it.' Stephen got out of his chair and walked across to the window, where Dorcas stood. He put his arms around her newly slim waist and kissed her. 'It's Greek for gazelle, you know,' he told her. 'It suits you. I must say, though, that I'm surprised your mother thought of it.'

'She didn't.' Dorcas sniffed. 'Mrs Collins suggested it to her,' she explained. 'Whenever one of the tenants had a child, she used to ferret through the Bible, looking for an appropriate name. There are Hephzibahs and Keziahs in Ashton Cross; and the odd Tabitha! If a mother wanted to borrow anything from the Baby Box at the rectory, you see, she had to give her child a good, Christian name.'

'I see. Well then — if she can't be Dorcas, what name is this child to have?'

Dorcas considered. 'Perhaps I could call her Dora?'

'That would be perfect.' Stephen kissed her again. 'I'll speak to Mrs Collins when I next go to Ashton,' he added. 'I won't have her naming all the children on the estate! The arrogance of it!'

The door opened and Anna came in. Neatly dressed, she was wearing a new pink outfit which set off her dark hair and eyes perfectly; and she was carrying a pile of papers. 'I've finished the work you set me,' she told her father, while she looked hard at her mother, who still encircled Stephen's neck with her arms.

He smiled at her, only too obviously taking in her adolescent prettiness. 'You've been very quick,' he said pleasantly. 'Well — shall we have a look at it?'

'Only if you have time.' Anna shot another barbed glare at Dorcas. 'I'm sure you must be very busy.'

'Not at present.' Stephen disentangled himself from Dorcas and motioned to Anna to pull her stool nearer his chair. He sat down, and she plumped herself down next to him, her shoulder resting comfortably against his knee, spilling her folder full of papers all over his lap.

Soon the two of them were deep in conversation. Dorcas, still looking through the window, knew she was firmly excluded now. 'I'll have some coffee sent in to you,' she remarked. 'You'll be busy for the rest of the morning now, won't you?'

Getting no reply from either father or daughter, she went out of the room. She went upstairs to the nursery to play with the babies, and to talk to the nursery nurse, whose opinion of her younger children's intelligence and beauty was far higher than their own father's was.

Had anyone asked her, Dorcas would have said that she was delighted that Anna and Stephen had become so fond of each other. But she was not slow to realize that Anna's linguistic gifts made her, in some ways, a far more congenial companion to Stephen than Dorcas could ever be.

'I wish she'd make some friends of her own,' thought Dorcas crossly, seeing father and child walking down the garden path, hand in hand, chattering away as usual. 'She leaves him no time at all for me ...'

But Anna did make a few friends of her own age. Despite her determination — after that first traumatic visit on Christmas Day — never to go near the place again, she now made regular sorties to the chaotic Carson household at Garsington.

At first, she went as much for the pleasure of the ride with her father as for the company she found when she arrived there. But eventually she discovered that she looked forward to seeing and playing with Muriel and Juliet Carson, whose ages were one year on either side of her own.

'You're learning Greek, I hear,' murmured Muriel one day, as she hung upside down from a rope trapeze suspended from an old apple tree.

'Yes.' Anna reddened, faintly embarrassed. 'How do you know?'

'Dr Lawrence told Papa,' replied Muriel. 'And he told us. Our father thinks you're very clever,' she went on. 'What was it he said? Ah, I know — you have a good brain.' She giggled. 'That's it. Anna Lawrence has a *good brain*.'

Seeing Anna look thoroughly nonplussed now, Juliet patted her arm. 'And you're pretty,' she said generously, seeking to console Anna for her terrible mental affliction. 'Very pretty.'

'Am I?' Anna was scarlet now. 'I'm not really,' she said. 'I'm too dark.'

'You're a pretty gipsy, then.' Juliet grinned at her still upended sister. 'And what are we, Murry?' she asked.

'A pair of dunces!' Muriel gave a shriek of laughter. 'A pair of idle, good for nothing dunces! A pair of ugly, ginger half-wits!' She shook her beautiful auburn curls, brushing the ground with them; then, reaching up, she pulled herself upright. 'If I hang upside down for half an hour each day,' she explained, 'blood rushes to my brain and fills it with red corpuscles, which will enable it to work more efficiently. And so, in the end, I may not be as stupid as I am now.'

'You will.' Juliet sniggered. 'Exercises like that will make no difference to you.'

'Oh? And why's that?'

'Because, you idiot, for them to work one has to have a brain to begin with!'

Juliet cackled at her own wit then began to run, leaving Muriel and Anna to walk over to the house for tea.

Summer holidays were always marvellous. Stephen usually took the whole family abroad for the month of August, coping with the mountains of baggage, the complaints of nursemaids and the querulousness of Dorcas, who was a very bad traveller, with perfect equanimity.

Italy was Anna's favourite place; and the summer conferences, which her father attended there, ensured that she visited that beautiful, sunny land many times. Walking down the wide Florentine streets with her father, strolling in his company across the Ponte Vecchio upon which the jewellers' shops sparkled and invited, was Anna's idea of Paradise.

While Dorcas and the younger children kept themselves to themselves in the hired villa in the hills above the city, Anna and Stephen went out together; in each others' congenial company they looked, exclaimed, criticized and discussed.

'Have you decided what you'd like to do when you're older?'

asked Stephen one day, taking his daughter's hand and helping her down the narrow steps of the church tower which they'd just climbed together.

Anna took her time coming down. She liked the sensation of having her small hand safe inside Stephen's large, square one. Now, as she reached early womanhood, she was beginning to understand what made her father so attractive to women, even to sour-faced Mrs Vesey, who simpered quite sickeningly at him. 'No,' she replied. 'No, I hadn't given it a thought.'

'Would you like to be a scholar?'

'A scholar?' Anna frowned. 'I don't know. Mama would hate that,' she added.

'Oh, she wouldn't mind.' Stephen smiled. 'Your mother's —'

'She's what?' Anna scowled at her father, wondering if he, too, was going to launch into a 'your mother's a princess' routine, into a fulsome paean in praise of Dorcas; because *he* was obviously as besotted with her, as silly about her, as Daniel had ever been...

'I was about to say, your mother's not of an intellectual turn of mind,' continued Stephen drily. 'Nor does she wish to be. But that's no reason why you shouldn't study if you find the prospect attractive.'

Anna looked at him. He didn't seem to be teasing her; in fact, his face was perfectly grave. She nodded. 'I'd like to be a scholar, then,' she said. 'Shall I take a degree? Are women allowed to do that?'

'I'll teach you myself.' Stephen released her hand. 'That will be a pleasure for us both, won't it?'

Dorcas, far from being an intellectual, was — her daughter decided — both insufferably tiresome and mind-numbingly dull. 'You went out without brushing your hair today,' Dorcas scolded, as the three of them sat down to an evening meal that same day. 'You must have looked a sight — whatever can people have thought of you? Oh, I do hate all this oil they use,' she added pettishly, poking at her food.

'I like it.' Anna shovelled her last spoonful of pasta into her mouth, letting sauce run down her chin and splash on to her napkin. 'And anyway,' she added spitefully, 'I have better things to do than brush my hair. My Papa and I have been looking at churches. We've been discussing ecclesiastical architecture.'

Dorcas raised her eyebrows at that as she motioned to the maid to clear away the plates 'Have you indeed?' she asked.

'Yes.' Anna gave Stephen a perfectly adulatory smile. 'It was fascinating.'

"My Papa"! Dorcas grimaced. So it was "my Papa" now, was it. She'd found someone else to worship — Daniel had been replaced at last. Dorcas peeled an orange in silence.

Fortunately, just as her self-esteem was about to vanish completely, Dorcas happened to glance up. She saw that Stephen was looking at her. 'Have you finished?' he asked.

'I think so.'

'Well; it's a little cooler now, so shall we go for a walk? Anna can stay here and help Maria put the children to bed.'

He rose from his chair and held out his hand to Dorcas. 'Come along,' he said firmly. 'Come and see the lilies and the roses. The owners of this place have made quite an English garden here.'

Dorcas was always glad to get back to Oxford, where she felt at home, and where she was happiest. Enjoying her role of mother, she played the place of matriarch in her ever-increasing household to perfection.

After the birth of Dora, Dorcas had left off wearing her stays; and instead of forcing herself into the horribly constricting garments fashionable in the 'eighties, she dressed herself in loose smocks and comfortable skirts. Now, instead of twisting it into a tight chignon, she usually left her beautiful long hair flowing down her back. She looked very relaxed, very pretty and altogether very contented.

Anna despaired of her. 'Oh Mama!' she wailed, seeing her mother come downstairs one morning in yet another concoction which appeared to consist only of a few yards of cotton print draped around her body, 'you do look a sight!'

'Do I, Stephen?' Complacently, Dorcas helped herself to toast.

'Do you what?' Stephen looked over the top of his newspaper and raised his eyesbrows in enquiry.

'Look a sight?'

Stephen considered. 'You look very nice,' he said, indifferently, and read on.

Anna grimaced at them both. At fourteen, she was very much aware of her own face and figure. She spent hours putting up her hair in severely elaborate styles, and she encased herself in whalebone from neck to thighs.

'Mama, you really ought to wear some stays,' she remarked a few days later. 'And you shouldn't eat so much.'

But Dorcas only smiled. 'I'll eat what I please,' she replied.

Anthony and Dora were allowed to run wild. They went barefoot around the house and garden, and were permitted to strip and go naked, like a pair of black savages as their disgusted elder sister said, when the weather was hot. They had their baths together, and they slept in each others' arms every night, either in their own big feather bed, or, if their father was not at home, in their mother's. If Stephen was there, they were firmly banished to the nursery.

They ate what they chose, when they wanted it. Spoiled and demanding, they were exuberant, loving, excessively noisy children who, hardly ever denied anything, grew up with very high opinions of their own importance.

They outgrew their nursery maids and Dorcas decided that they should have a governess. She suggested as much to their father, who was about to go off to Germany for six weeks, and was very preoccupied with his own affairs. 'You find one,' Stephen told her, scribbling something in a notebook. 'Look in *The Times* — there'll be dozens of advertisements there, from no end of worthy young women. Dorcas — have you seen my spectacles anywhere?'

Dorcas did as she was told and she found Fanny Lewson.

Fanny had advertised herself as a governess, but that description was rather fanciful for she was, in fact, barely literate. Her father had been a tenant farmer in Somerset, who had somehow found the money to send his only daughter to school in Chard. There, Frances had learned a few expressions and phrases of what she was led to believe was French; she had managed to grasp the rules of simple arithmetic, but was never able to apply them very well; and she had, in theory, learned to read and write.

When she was fifteen, her education had been cut short, for she had suddenly been sent for to return home and nurse her mother, who took six years to die of a wasting disease which the doctors could neither alleviate nor cure.

She was twenty-two when her father died. Her two older brothers sold the remainder of the lease on the farm and told Fanny that she must make her own way in the world from then on. They gave her ten pounds and a train ticket to Bristol, telling her she'd be able to get work as a lady's maid there.

She lost the money. Eventually she found herself in a house near the docks, where she earned her living. She gritted her teeth and bore what she had to put up with, learning to hate and fear men, and remembering with nostalgic longing the comfortable pleasure of being curled up in bed with another soft, warm schoolgirl, with a sweet-smelling female creature like herself.

But then, one day, she had pleased a sea-captain so much that he had offered to buy her a present, over and above the fee already paid.

'Thank you, sir,' she had said, allowing her rouged lips to break into a whore's false smile.

'What'll it be, then?' The seaman grinned. 'Can you come out for a while, if I pay the old dame for the time you'll have lost?'

Fanny thought about it for a few seconds. 'Can you write, sir?' she asked. 'Can you write a good, gentleman's hand?' For the man had appeared to be a gentleman himself.

'Certainly I can! But why —'

'Then sir, instead of a present would you write me out a set of references, recommending me as a governess? Could you provide me with letters telling the reader that I can write, cipher, and am fit to have care of children? Which I am, sir, since I've been at boarding school myself, and have had a good education.'

The man had been disposed to be obliging and he had written out a splendid collection of testimonials. Fanny had kissed him with sincerity and, the following week, she had left the house by the docks and started on her career as a governess. In due course she arrived at the Summertown house.

Dora and Anthony had adored Fanny Lewson right from the start — and she loved them. Fond of a noisy romp herself, liking action better than reflection, Fanny preferred a rowdy game of chase all

212

round the garden to sitting down quietly with a first reader.

In any case, Dora and Anthony had, by some mysterious process of absorption, taught themselve to read. Displaying great forebearance, Anna had taken them through a children's primer and they had gone on from there. Once they could read, they devoured every book they could get their grubby little hands on, particularly the unsuitable ones from their father's study, over which they giggled in furtive delight.

'We can read, you know' announced Dora one wet, grey morning, as Fanny reluctantly prepared to give them their first real lesson.

'Can you?' asked Fanny hopefully.

'Yes,' said Anthony. 'We can read anything. And we do.' He giggled. 'We read Papa's books. Fanny, have you read the life of George Selwyn? It's very interesting. Well — bits are!'

Fanny had never heard of Mr Selwyn, and said so. And then Anthony leaned across her desk and tickled her wrist. 'Come and have a game of catch,' he said. 'It's stopped raining now.'

'Exercise is good for growing children,' added Dora.

'Well …' Fanny was tempted.

Anthony pulled her to her feet. 'Come on, Fan,' he insisted. 'Race you to the apple trees.'

It was hardly a normal pupil and governess relationship at all.

Stephen immediately spotted Fanny Lewson for the fraud she was. On his return from Berlin he had called her into his study and conducted a proper interview with her, in the course of which it became obvious that she was well fitted to be his children's nurse but hardly capable of teaching them anything at all.

But Dorcas was evidently very taken with the woman and he had no objection to keeping a nursery nurse for a year or two more. 'Very well, Miss Lewson,' he said heavily. 'I'll talk to you again later.'

She had left his room quaking and near to tears, sure that she would be dismissed, told to leave the house without delay. Instead, Stephen took no further notice of her. Later on that week he interviewed several other ignorant young women, finally finding one whom he decided might be able to teach his younger children. Miss MacShane was the first of several governesses who supervised

Anthony and Dora's education. As Stephen was to find out over the course of the next few years, teachers of young children were a notoriously peripatetic lot.

Preoccupied with his work, his students and his determination to make a fine classicist out of his talented elder daughter, Stephen tended to treat Dora and Anthony in a vague and absent manner, as if they were a pair of puppies. They didn't interest him. .

He'd always been capable of ignoring whatever he chose not to be aware of. So, if Dora wanted to play under his desk and scatter her toys all around his ankles as he sat there correcting proofs, if Anthony wanted to sit next to his father and draw on a spare bit of paper while Stephen worked, that was perfectly acceptable.

The two small children realized very early on that it was Stephen who made all the important decisions. And, when he said no, then no it was.

'Could we have some kittens?' asked Dora one day, appearing like a rather sticky ghost above a pile of lecture notes.

'Kittens?' asked Stephen, reaching for a book and opening it at the marked place.

'Yes, Papa. Two each — two boy kittens and two girl kittens.'

Before answering her, Stephen made a note of the reference he had been looking for. 'I hate cats,' he said calmly. 'They make me sneeze.'

For the thousandth time, Dora was deceived into assuming that the blandness of his tone meant that he could be persuaded. 'We'd keep them in our rooms, away from you,' she promised, smiling winsomely. She grinned and joggled his arm. 'Why do they make you sneeze?' she asked.

'I don't know, Dora.'

'You could find out.'

'I haven't the time. And, Dora, you can't have any cats in my house.'

Dora looked at him and saw, to her distress, that he was frowning now. So that was that. She went to find Fanny, to weep on her shoulder.

Fanny was a splendid mother substitute. These days she had even adapted her style of dress to match that of her dear Mrs Lawrence, leaving off her corsets and affecting the same dreamy, pre-Raphaelite air, which sat rather awkwardly on a person as healthy-looking and plump as Fanny. Anna could not bear her. She urged her father to get rid of the woman, but to her surprise he resisted the idea. 'Your mother likes her,' he said shortly. 'So she may stay for the time being.'

'But Papa! She can't teach! She's absolutely ignorant!'

'Anna, whom I choose to employ is no concern of yours. Have you finished your essay for this week?'

'Not yet.'

'Well, then I suggest that you go and apply your agile mind to that, rather than to the problems of household management; which you can safely leave to your mother and to me.'

Anna grimaced. She walked back through the drawing room, in a corner of which the children, her mother and Fanny were sitting, encamped there like a group of Red Indians, cutting up and wasting silver paper, and giggling together.

Dorcas was fatter and untidier than ever since Fanny had arrived. 'She used to look so neat and pretty,' thought Anna; who did not begin to understand that Dorcas was, through her children, enjoying a childhood which she'd never had herself. Her personal appearance was no longer the main interest in her life.

Until she was fifteen, Anna attended a good day school in North Oxford, along with the Carson children and various other dons' daughters. Later on, her father taught her. By degrees she became his secretary, his aide; she was the one who always knew where his spectacles were, who could trim an old-fashioned pen just the way he liked it, who could tell him exactly the word he wanted when he was at a loss and too idle to reach for his dictionary.

She already read proofs for him and was determined to make herself indispensable. 'You really cannot spell, Papa,' she remarked one day, after she had found seven mistakes on the same page of a first draft of something.

'I know.' Stephen shrugged. 'I never could.'

'Why don't you use a dictionary? It's there on your desk!'

'I'm too lazy.'

She clicked her tongue and smiled at him. 'It's just as well that you have me to check your work then, isn't it?' she asked, somewhat too cheekily.

But he'd smiled back. 'Oh, it is, Anna!' he agreed. 'It is!

Whatever would I do without you?'

She'd been filled with a warm glow.

Accustomed to the company of clever men of her father's age — or even older than that — Anna hardly ever met any of her own contemporaries. The Carson girls, whose talk was all of men and marriage, bored her now. She preferred the company of her father's friends, who were disposed to make something of a pet of her.

At sixteen, Anna Lawrence was better read than many an undergraduate, and she enjoyed showing off to these ancient Oxford dons. She did not think of them as potential husbands or lovers and seemed totally unaware that half her own charm lay in the fact that she was a young and pretty woman. The men who listened to her so courteously and complimented her so readily might not have been quite so enchanted by an equally precocious young man. Anna, on the other hand, imagined that they were charmed by her intellectual capacity alone.

Soon after her seventeenth birthday, she developed a close but perfectly blameless friendship with a German-Jewish classicist, a balding, short-sighted gentleman of past forty. 'Dr Friedmann's given me some books,' she announced at dinner one evening. 'And he's asked to see some of my poetry.'

'Has he indeed?' Dorcas frowned. 'Stephen, did you hear that?'

'What?' Stephen, who was very unsociably reading a book while he ate, looked up. 'Julius wants to see your work? Well, then — show it to him, if you like.' Anna's father grinned. 'He's a very severe critic, you know,' he added, before returning to his own reading.

This intimacy gave Dorcas some uneasy moments. Anna visited Dr Friedmann at his rooms in college, she had tea with him in the town, she was even seen walking with him in the Parks. Dorcas hated the idea of her pretty daughter being thrown away on such an old, ugly man, a fellow more than twenty years her senior, a foreigner who could hardly speak English properly. She took Anna aside one day and tried to discuss the matter.

Anna, predictably, was incensed by her mother's remarks. 'I cannot understand,' she began witheringly, 'why you take it upon yourself to object to my associating with one of my own father's friends, with a man who visits at this house.'

'It's just that — well, Anna, don't you think that perhaps Dr Friedmann has more than mere friendship in view? If he has other designs, things might become awkward. And on the whole I hardly think he'd be —'

'Honestly, Mama!' Anna had grasped her mother's meaning, and she flushed crimson. 'As if a man of Dr Friedmann's age could possibly have — what did you call them — designs on me! He takes pleasure in my company. He likes to talk to me; that's all! I don't suppose *you* can understand that, as I doubt if you've had a single rational conversation in your entire life!'

'Don't you dare speak to me like that, Anna!' Dorcas clasped her hands behind her back, for she was tempted to slap Anna, hard. 'Apologize now!'

'Oh, I'm sorry, Mama,' said Anna offhandedly. 'But really!'

'Yes, really!' Dorcas glared at her daughter. 'Anna, you may think you're very clever,' she snapped. 'You may have read far more books than I have, or ever shall. But you don't know the ways of the world. You must be careful. And you must always remember that we're not — not, shall we say, quite like other families here. We mustn't draw attention to ourselves. You know what I'm trying to say.'

'Yes.' Anna smiled coldly. 'Yes, I know what you mean. But that's not my fault, is it? It's yours.' And she turned on her heel and walked out of the room before Dorcas could say anything more.

Dorcas had long since accepted that the only time she was ever likely to have Stephen's full attention was when she was in bed with him. During the day he was always busy — and, if at leisure, he would be reading, would only half concentrate on what she was saying. So, one evening, as Stephen lay next to her, running his fingers through her hair, she tried to bring the worrying matter of Anna's friendships with older men to his notice.

'Anna's bothering me,' she announced. 'Stephen, I —'

'Oh, really Dorcas!' He kissed her face. 'I don't want to talk about Anna just at this moment!'

She removed his hand from her arm. 'But when can I talk to you about her?' she demanded. 'You're hardly ever here during the day, and if you are at home you're busy or you're about to dash off to a lecture or something. How is she ever to meet anyone suitable? Do you know what I mean? Whom can I invite here?'

'You're getting fat, you know,' he replied inconsequentially, patting her bottom. 'Especially around your hips. You're quite a pudding these days!' He kissed her wrist, examined her fingers, then he pulled her across him. 'Good God, what a weight,' he said, laughing at her frown. 'You're twice the woman you were five years ago!'

'I'm not, don't be so rude. Oh, Stephen, do stop that for a minute! Tell me what to do about my daughter — she's worrying me!'

'Well, don't worry about her. She'll meet someone she likes some day, and that will be that. She's only seventeen, though, and she's young for her age. It will be years before she starts to think about getting married.'

Stephen began to unfasten the buttons of Dorcas' nightdress. 'I'm sure she'd tell us if she had met anyone she liked in that sort of way,' he went on. 'Then I'll start to worry about settlements and all that sort of thing. But until that time comes, I shan't fret about it and neither must you.'

'Do you love me?' she asked, half an hour later, as he lay on his stomach, half asleep.

'Of course I do.' He threw one arm across her waist and tried to pull her down beside him. 'Can we go to sleep now?' he asked. 'I've a lecture at nine-thirty tomorrow.'

Dorcas shook him awake again. 'You must talk to Anna,' she said firmly. 'She's keeping something from us — I know she is. I'm so afraid that one day she'll announce that she's going to marry some old man of sixty, who has won her heart merely by complimenting her on some silly Latin verses! Please, Stephen! Will you speak to her before she makes a fool of herself, and of us?'

'Oh, very well.' That was what she thought he'd said. On the other hand, he could just as well have been muttering in his sleep.

Anna would have been furious if she had heard that conversation between her parents as they lay together committing adultery as if it were nothing to be ashamed of.

Long ago, she had decided that if she ever were to marry she would choose a clever, spiritual man, some years older than herself, who would value her for her mind and to whom she could become a valued companion. Not a plaything, as her own mother so obviously was. 'But before I marry anyone,' she thought, 'I have to do something for my father. He might be besotted with Mama, but I'll make him proud of *me*!'

Chapter Fourteen

ANNA HAD BEEN PURSUING THIS high-minded course of action for a year or so when she began to find that one of Stephen's students was on her mind rather more than he ought to have been. Anna, not used to entertaining irrational fancies, simply couldn't understand it.

Thomas George Guthrie was out of the normal, ordinary run of undergraduates. Most of those who came to the Summertown house to see their tutor were either the bored sons of the gentry and the aristocracy, filling in the time between finishing school and getting on with the real purposes of their lives; or they were the earnest sons of the middle classes, in general a set of unimaginative sloggers. Tom Guthrie fell into neither of these categories.

For one thing, he was older than the others — at least twenty-five, perhaps more. His background was possibly middle-class Lowland Scots, but just as possibly not. He was extremely, exceptionally clever. Stephen disliked him intensely, but had to admit to his colleagues that Guthrie was the ablest student he had ever taught, or imagined himself likely to teach.

Dorcas, who ran across him now and again when he came to see Stephen, couldn't bear him. 'He makes my flesh crawl,' she said one day, shuddering as she watched him leave the house. 'Stephen, can't you see him in college? Why does he have to come here for supervisions?'

Stephen merely shrugged, then grinned at her. 'Does he bother you that much?' he asked. 'What's he said to you?'

'Nothing but good morning and goodbye. But — ugh! He's horrible! And he smells — I don't know how you can bear to have him in your study!'

Stephen laughed. 'I must admit that Mr Guthrie's personal cleanliness leaves a great deal to be desired,' he agreed. 'But, darling, I can hardly forbid him to visit his supervisor simply because he doesn't wash his neck!'

Anna was attracted to Tom Guthrie in spite of herself. She found him frightening, which made her determined to confront him, and to conquer her fears. The most unsettling thing about him was his stare; he had small, sharp, black eyes, as dark as Anna's own, which seemed to bore into her face as he looked at her.

But it wasn't that his beauty enraptured her. Far from it, for Tom was not a good-looking man. His complexion was of the sallow, greasy kind, and he had straight, oily, black hair which he wore too long, matting into his beard. A thick-set man of middle height, with long arms and short legs, his friends referred to him as the gorilla. 'When you die,' remarked one, 'you ought to be embalmed and preserved for future generations, for you're the absolute proof that Mr Darwin's theories are correct!'

Tom had looked narrowly at the tall, blond god who'd made this observation, and remembered that he now bore Gilbert Armitage a grudge.

Tom seemed to enjoy Anna's company. At any rate, he sought her out and talked to her. Now and then he would lay his hand upon her sleeve, the lightest touch, to emphasize a point. And then a tremor would go through her — a mild but exhilarating electric vibration, and she would blush. Anna looked very pretty when she blushed.

Certainly, she thought of Tom more than she would have wished. She began to dress, and to do her hair, even more carefully than usual for Tom might call at the house at any time, to see her father, to return a borrowed book, to collect some work, to hand in an essay. She dreaded him seeing her not at her best. The fact that his style of dress — for he was invariably clad in frayed black trousers, a baggy melton jacket, and his shirts were grey from neglect — seemed to indicate that he thought very little about what anyone wore, did not prevent Anna from paying fanatical attention to her own appearance.

She wondered at herself. 'It's not as if he's at all handsome,' she thought. 'In fact, he's an ugly man!' But then she told herself that it was, of course, Tom's mind which attracted her; and was pleased to discover that, unlike her mother, she was above anything as sordid as mere physical lust.

Tom Guthrie was not slow to realize that he had acquired some sort of power over Dr Lawrence's pretty daughter, who coloured so fetchingly whenever he spoke to her. He was not a man to waste anything, and he wondered to what use this influence could be put.

He was half-hearted considering a university career so, if he married the daughter, would the father exert some pressure to get Tom a lectureship? Somehow, Tom doubted it, for Dr Lawrence was quite obviously a perfect example of an upright, Christian family man who would expect a chap to rise by his own merits. 'And he doesn't like me,' Tom reflected. 'He'd probably hit me if I suggested marrying his precious Anna.'

Tom decided, in the end, to go in for politics. He wondered if Anna were the sort of woman fit to be the wife of an ambitious politician — then he decided that if she weren't that already, she could probably be moulded to become so. And, added to that, she was pretty now. It was likely that she'd be beautiful in due course, an extra asset which Tom did not despise.

He strolled down the garden path one morning, intending to speak to her. What was she doing today? Surely she wasn't still messing around with some third-rate translation of Lucretius, whose work it wasn't at all proper that a woman should read? If he married her, he'd definitely put a stop to all that studying nonsense. She'd have her hands full looking after him, his household and his children, after all.

'I'm thinking of leaving Oxford before I take my degree,' he remarked, as he sat down beside her on the garden bench, crushing a fold of her skirt. He looked at her closely, and was gratified to see her redden. 'I really do think I've had enough of the place,' he added cunningly.

'Have you? Well — my father thinks you'll get a very good First,' ventured Anna, looking down at her books and blushing even more, for Stephen had certainly never discussed the prospects of Tom Guthrie, or of any other student, with her. 'Why don't you stay and take the examination? It's only a fortnight or so away, and I'm sure you must be well prepared for it.'

Tom stuck his hands in his pockets, stretched out his legs and smiled at her, a weasel mesmerizing a rabbit. 'I'm going to go in for Parliament,' he announced. 'I shan't need a degree for that.'

'In the Tory or the Liberal interest?' Anna's mind was working furiously: would her father let her marry a Liberal MP?

'Whichever will have me. Does that disgust you?'

'I — well — I don't know a great deal about politics,' she lied, unwilling to admit that Tom's attitude shocked her.

'You wouldn't.' Tom smiled kindly. 'A young woman would find such things well above her head.' He lay back against the arm of the bench and closed his eyes. 'So you advise me to take my degree?' he asked.

'It's not for me to advise you, Mr Guthrie. But it does seem a pity not to, since you've worked for it and since you're likely to do so well.'

'You don't believe in wasting your time, then, Miss Lawrence?'

'No, I suppose I don't.'

'Neither do I, neither do I.' Tom opened his beady little eyes wide and made Anna look at him. 'I would like to think that all the conversations I've had with you were not a waste of time,' he murmured. 'I should like to believe that we've both profited from them?'

Anna squirmed under that gimlet glare. 'I believe we have,' she managed to reply.

That was enough for Tom. He felt he was understood, and he got up to go. 'I shall take my degree,' he told her. 'And when I go to London, I hope you will allow me to write to you, and maybe your father will permit you to write to me?'

Anna nodded. 'I'm sure he will,' she said.

Tom grinned down at her.

Tom took his congratulatory First, the best of the year and, probably, of the decade. Then, having turned down the offer of a fellowship and the quiet, comfortable life which that would have ensured, he took himself off to London. Anna did not hear from him for six months. Then he wrote to her — she replied — and a regular correspondence was established.

Most of his long, entertaining letters detailed the goings-on in political circles, as seen from the point of view of a clever, envious outsider. They were very funny, very malicious and very libellous. In the wrong hands, those letters might well have destroyed his incipient career as certainly as a torpedo would sink a battleship. Anna understood that he trusted her to be discreet and was intensely flattered.

The letters were signed, merely, 'T'. He was not that foolish.

When Tom managed to attach himself to a prominent Liberal peer, Anna began to wonder if she might make a good political wife. When Tom wrote and told her that he was almost certainly being put up for a by-election, she began to think of orange blossom and lace veils.

In Tom's absence, Anna forgot how physically repellent he was and her infatuation for him could expand without check. She tied up his letters in bundles and hid them among her clothes, although anything less like love letters could hardly be imagined. 'Anna Guthrie. Mrs Guthrie,' she said out loud, trying out the name. 'Yes. It sounds quite well.'

Anna gave very little thought to the physical intimacies which marriage would entail. She supposed that she could put up with a certain amount of — that. But she didn't want children; she couldn't bear sticky, beastly little brats like Anthony and Dora, who whined and moaned if upset, and whose happier moods were accompanied by even noisier shrieking, yelling and squealing. Having seen where passion led, she thanked heaven that hers was not a passionate nature.

Stephen observed that his daughter now received weekly letters from that Guthrie fellow, and he decided that he and she should have a private talk before things got completely out of hand. He made his own statement somewhat heavy-handedly; and thus ensured that his daughter would build her walls of secrecy even higher ...

'He's a cold, ambitious man,' said Stephen firmly. 'I don't know what he may have said to you — but I don't consider that Mr Guthrie would make any woman a good husband.' He looked earnestly at his pretty daughter. 'Do you like him very much, Anna?' he asked, expecting a candid answer.

Anna flushed scarlet. 'I hope I've given no one, least of all Mr Guthrie himself, any reason to suppose that I think of him as a lover,' she retorted. 'I shall fetch his letters now so that you may read them all. There's nothing in them which is at all reprehensible but I feel that, since you are so concerned, you should see them all the same. And I shan't write to him any more, if you forbid it.'

'Oh, Anna — I don't forbid it!' Stephen rubbed his face, realizing too late that he'd approached this particular problem in quite the wrong way. 'Since you're here,' he said, 'shall we look at some of those translations you were doing? You're something of a poet in your own right these days, aren't you? Perhaps we ought to put some of your work together and let a publisher see it.'

'A publisher?' Anna, still annoyed, scowled at him.

'Yes. Liebermann is planning a new anthology of classical poetry, with English translations alongside the original texts. Shall we offer Arthur Liebermann a sight of your work?'

Anna, aware that she was being flattered and conciliated now, scowled even harder. 'You and I both know that I am merely competent,' she replied stiffly. 'There's no need —'

'You're much more than just competent!' her father interrupted. 'In five years' time you could be outstanding — far more accomplished, let me tell you, than that fellow of whom you seem to have so high an opinion, Griffiths or whatever the devil's name is! You have a flair, a feeling for language, which he never had. And you must accept, Anna, that upon this particular subject I am something of an authority myself, and that I do know what I'm talking about!'

Tom found more friends and backers in the Liberal party. He'd got himself nominated as a Parliamentary candidate, singled out from among a dozen other outsiders — for it had been recognized that Mr Guthrie was hard-headed, calculating and hard-hearted, thick-skinned enough to fight an unwinnable by-election or two until he was considered experienced enough to go for a safe seat. 'We'll have to do something about his appearance, though,' muttered one old political warhorse to another. 'Can't have the fellow fighting Beechstoke North looking like a ruddy tramp!'

'Smarten yourself up a little, boy,' remarked his patron one day, in passing.

Tom looked up from his desk. 'What?' he asked.

'Tidy yourself up.' His patron sniffed the air. 'Wash a bit more often, why don't you?'

Tom considered this advice and, more or less overnight, he went from one extreme to the other. He went out and bought a complete new wardrobeful of clothes, which included the first of the exotic brocaded waistcoats that were to become his hallmark in his subsequent meteoric career. He retained his whiskers, being apparently chary of revealing too much of his face to the opposition but now, instead of a beard which resembled a tangled collection of knitting mistakes, he wore a neatly trimmed pair of the most magnificent side-burns, oiled and preened to splendid glossy blackness. 'Fellow looks like the bloody Demon King now,' remarked his patron. 'Thinks he's in some damned operetta!'

But, on the whole, it was an improvement; and the pervasive scent of citrus water was a pleasant change from Tom's previous aura of stale sweat.

He was told to find himself a wife. 'It looks better if you're a married man,' remarked the Liberal peer. 'Have you anyone in mind? If not, I can provide you with a list of suitable girls.'

Tom had immediately thought of Anna. 'As it happens,' he said, 'there is someone.' He knew that Anna's father must be a Tory; but he hoped that that might not matter too much. He put her name forward without any idea that she would be found unsuitable, so he was surprised and aggrieved when he was informed that she just wouldn't do.

Tom had spent a pleasant fortnight planning a detailed strategy for bringing Anna to heel, for moulding her to his exact specifications. He assumed straight away that his mentors' objections to the girl sprang from her father's political affiliations, and he prepared a speech defending his choice of bride.

'I am perfectly well aware that her father is a Tory of the most backward, reactionary kind,' he began, looking his patron in the eyes and faintly bothered by the old man's derisive smile. 'But I have had various enquiries made, and I find that the estate he owns is properly managed by his brother. He might be an absentee landlord, but he's mindful of his obligations to his tenants; they're well-housed and fairly well paid.

'All the children on the estate attend a school run at the landlord's expense,' he went on. 'And, what's more, the present squire gave up game preservation when he inherited; so his tenants can have a partridge or a hare when the fancy takes them, and the

226

farmers don't have to put up with the landlord's pheasants ruining their crops.'

Tom paused for breath and saw, to his dismay, that the same sarcastic grin was still twitching the corners of his mentor's mouth. 'Go on, boy,' remarked the peer. 'You're doing splendidly. The place sounds like some damned Garden of Eden; I feel I want to reach for my pitchfork —'

Tom grimaced. 'There haven't been any riots or rick-burnings, there've been no machine smashings,' he continued gamely. 'Not a single labourer went on strike in 1872, although most of them have now joined that fellow Arch's union — and that, I may add, without any opposition on the landlord's part.

'As for Dr Lawrence himself, he's a recognized authority in his field, he's published his work, and he's spoken of as Bennet's successor when that Chair becomes vacant. I really don't see why I shouldn't ask his daughter to marry me.' Tom folded his arms and looked defiantly at the other man. 'I think she'd be an ideal wife for me, whatever you may say.'

'Ah — you do, do you?' The Liberal peer lit a cheroot, and blew out some elegant smoke rings. He stared hard at his protégé. 'Enquiries!' he scoffed. 'You've made enquiries, have you? Well, you're easily satisfied, that's all I can say. I'm beginning to think we might have made a mistake when we backed you!'

Carefully, the old man stubbed out his cheroot, then he leaned back in his chair. 'Scandal, boy!' he said, grinning. 'Scandal! The girl's background doesn't bear examination! And you've made enquiries. Ha!'

Tom had become quite pale. 'What do you mean?' he demanded.

'Well — it's difficult to know where to start!' The Liberal peer shook his head. 'Let's plunge straight in, shall we? Tom: our distinguished friend Dr Stephen Randall Lawrence, celebrated grave-robber, ditch-digger and Latin usher, is an adulterer living in what we usually call sin with some bit of rubbish he first picked up in the course of his somewhat misspent youth. She's one of his tenant's daughters. It seems he had some hole and corner affair with her years ago, and chucked her over when he got married.

'But he didn't get on with his wife; not that we'll hold that against him, for as it happens I can't bear the sight of mine. Instead of behaving like a sensible man, though, instead of keeping a mistress tucked away somewhere or other, he took up again with this peasant, and he passes her off as his spouse.

'It appears that she has a husband still living. Lawrence's wife is a woman of property, an heiress he'd be wise to hang on to. She lives near Oxford, but it seems they have nothing to do with each other.

'So this present menage of his, this cosy little home he's established for himself, no doubt complete with roses all around the door, is not entirely above board, is it?' The Liberal peer laughed. 'But it's all very romantic, wouldn't you say?'

Tom's face was livid. 'What about Anna?' he managed to croak.

'Ah yes — your own true love. Well; the woman who calls herself Mrs Lawrence appears to have produced the child at some stage of her varied career. For some reason old Lawrence sees fit to let the world assume she's his daughter.

'Who she really is, I can't tell you. Odds on she's somebody's bastard; but whose is anyone's guess. Lawrence's and his whore's? Possibly; the dates fit.

'But you see, my dear fellow, she just won't do. Caesar's wife and all that sort of thing.'

Tom winced, blinked his eyes rapidly, tried to adjust his thoughts. 'I don't believe any of that,' he said after a second or two. 'It's totally ridiculous, I've never heard anything so far-fetched. None of it can be true.' He leaned forward and glared at the other man. 'Where did you get your information?' he demanded.

'That's not something I have to tell you!' The Liberal peer grinned. 'Why can't it be true?' he enquired, languidly. 'Good God, man — it's a common enough arrangement, you know!'

'It may be a common enough arrangement among certain sorts of people,' retorted Tom. 'But in this particular instance I just cannot credit it. You don't know the people involved and I do, very well. The man was my tutor for three years; I've met Mrs Lawrence, and I can assure you that she's no dollymop! She's a quiet, sensible, pleasantly spoken lady whose manners are quite unexceptionable!'

He grimaced. 'The whole idea is preposterous,' he went on. 'The idea of Dr Lawrence chasing female haymakers around his estate is one which I find absolutely untenable. He's so — well, he's so damned correct! He wouldn't dream of doing such a thing, that's all I can say!'

The Liberal peer sighed and shook his head. 'Oh, Tom — Tom, my boy,' he soothed. 'What a great deal you have to learn! Well, you're still young, I expect you'll become better acquainted with the world.

'Look here. Your precious tutor is a man like any other, with the same appetites as the rest of us. He's arranged it so that he can have his fun with his baggage, and then throw her over when he's had enough of her. So far, he's managed to do so without raising a storm or ruining his career.'

'I still don't accept —'

The Liberal peer slammed his hands down upon his desk. 'Oh, for God's sake, man!' he cried. 'That whole university is a hotbed of fornication! Half the men of the cloth there are no better than the Sultan himself, and if it's not women they're after, it's their students! It's only we fellows in public life who really have to watch what we do — and if we're discreet — well! Oh, don't take it so hard, Tom! God knows they're all the same on their backs! We'll find you some other girl!'

'I don't want some other girl.'

'Yes, you do. Twenty-six, are you? Twenty-seven? Never had a woman, have you?'

'That's none of your business!' snapped Tom, reddening.

'I thought not. You've the look of a virgin, for all your fancy clothes and swagger!' The Liberal peer looked closely at Tom. 'You're not one of those fellows who's looking for a twin soul, are you?' he demanded. 'Not one of those chaps who wants some sort of spiritual communion with a female? You're not tending towards all this votes for women nonsense, are you?'

'No!' Insulted now, Tom glowered ferociously. 'Women are far too irrational to be entrusted with the franchise!' But then, feeling utterly deflated now, he sighed. 'It's just that I — well, I thought Miss Lawrence, or whoever she is, was fond of me,' he muttered pathetically. 'And I liked her. It is possible to like a woman, you know, without becoming her slave!'

'Oh, I dare say it is.' His patron's supercilious gaze swept over Tom. 'I'll let you see a few names on my list tomorrow,' he said, yawning. 'And now I must leave you — I have to dress for a dinner engagement. Finish that report before you go, there's a good fellow.'

Tom returned to his lodgings in a state of anger, humiliation, and sheer, blind fury. Boiling with a desire to hurt someone, badly, he'd found that kicking a crossing sweeper had done little to relieve his seriously wounded pride.

How dared that woman try to ensnare him! Oh, he had to admit that she'd baited her traps beautifully. She'd listened to his opinions so deferentially, she'd seemed to admire him so much! Yes, she'd been clever, that daughter of a whore and God knew whom! Tom marched into his room and snatched up a sheet of writing paper.

At first, he wrote to relieve his feelings. The letter he finally sent to Anna was, compared with his first drafts — most of which would have been actionable for libel — a model of decorum.

'Madam,' he wrote. 'Certain information has been made available to me, which renders any further communication between us impossible. I am sure that you will understand what I mean.' He paused there, wondering whether to elaborate — wondering if, after all, everything his patron had said might have been a total, if somewhat involved, fabrication. He decided to be brief ...

'Please do not write to me or seek to see me,' he continued. 'I would be grateful if you would return to me those letters which I have sent you over the past year.' Good God, he hoped she would return them! She wouldn't use them — would she? She wasn't clever enough to realize that they could ruin him? He signed himself, 'Thomas Guthrie.'

Anna had picked this letter from among the dozen or so upon the hall table, and taken it up to her room in a state of pleasurable anticipation. She read Tom's curiously brutal little missive over and over, puzzled.

'Certain information'! Whatever could he mean by that? As if her personal affairs were any concern of his!

It upset Anna to have received such an unexpected insult, such an unmerited reproach. She was disquieted for hours, and wondered whatever Tom could have heard about her.

But, within the space of a morning, hurt had given way to

anger. How dared he write to her in that horrible fashion — whatever he had, or thought he had discovered! Then she remembered her vague ideas of marriage to the man and she shuddered, disgusted. A dirty, swarthy goblin, with grease on his cuffs and dandruff all over his shoulders, filthy fingernails and linen to match!

With that curt letter Tom's power over Anna vanished as if it had never been.

She took out the letters he had asked for and called to Anthony. 'Hickson's making a bonfire today,' she told him. 'Go and stuff all this rubbish into the middle of it, will you? Make sure it burns!'

'I heard from Mr Guthrie today,' she informed her father that evening.

'Oh?' Stephen looked up from his plate while Dorcas put her knife and fork down with a clatter, and stared at Anna.

'Yes,' she continued, enjoying this. 'He tells me that he is being put up in the next election. In the Liberal interest, of course. So —'

'So what, Anna?' Dorcas had gone quite ashen.

'So he thinks that in future he should have nothing more to do with the Tory establishment here. That's all.'

Anna picked up her own cutlery and began, calmly, to eat her dinner. She reflected that her father now looked like a man whose appeal against the death sentence has been upheld. The relief on her mother's face was almost funny.

Later, when Stephen and Anna were by themselves in his study, he had covered her hand with his and held it for a moment. 'You did like him, didn't you, darling?' he asked.

Anna looked back at him. 'No,' she replied firmly. 'I liked to talk to him. But I never liked the man himself.'

'Ah.' Stephen grinned, gave her hand a squeeze. 'Good,' he said. 'That's good. You know, my dear child, I always hoped you had better sense than to admire someone like that!'

The Liberal peer noticed that his protege was without much of his bounce and vitality nowadays, and he put this down to the disappointment over his lady love. 'Buck up, now, Tom,' he had said. 'Don't mope over a damned woman — there are plenty more of 'em to pick from!

'Tell you what — finish that briefing, and then we'll go somewhere that'll raise your spirits. We'll get a cab to Covent Garden, we'll call on Ma Mellot. My treat.' He grinned encouragingly. 'That's what's wrong with you, boy, you need some relaxation! Now, what's your fancy? Watching or doing? Black, white, brown or yellow? Boys? Ma Mellot can fix you up, whatever you want.'

Tom pursed his lips and scowled in disgust. He declined his patron's kind offer. He finished his work and went back to his lodgings, wishing he could get the picture of a dark-haired girl in a white dress, sitting on a bench in a sunny Oxford garden, out of his mind.

Chapter Fifteen

I T LOOKED LIKE BEING A pleasant, warm summer again. Another lot of undergraduates had taken their degrees and gone out into the world, leaving Oxford empty and peaceful in the early July sunshine.

Anna had had her first article accepted for publication, and was in consequence feeling very pleased with herself. She didn't really mind having had to submit it jointly with her father, nor did it rankle — very much — that he would get the credit (or discredit) for it. To have an article of hers in the standard *Classics* review, complete with a byline of S.R. and A.M. Lawrence, meant more to Anna than she could have said...

For all that, however, her father had let her down again. Living proof that, notwithstanding his intellectual brilliance, S.R. Lawrence was still subject to the same base desires and bestial urges that most men were, had been thrown in Anna's face a few months previously, when it had become clear that her mother was pregnant.

Dorcas was very large now, and counting the days to her delivery; she whiled away her time sewing little garments, and having endless discussions about possible Christian names with Fanny. She'd given up trying to interest Stephen in suggesting a name for the child soon to be born. 'Oh, you choose something, dear,' he had said absently, when consulted. 'I'm sure you'll think of a suitable name. Dorcas, I can't find my small Greek lexicon anywhere. It's the one with the red cover. See if you can lay your hands on it, will you?' He could be very tiresome sometimes.

But the family was, on the whole, at peace within itself. The two younger children were, by degrees, becoming slightly less noisy and quarrelsome, and Anna and Dorcas had found nothing to disagree about openly for several months.

Stephen was aware that the current professor of Greek would be retiring at Christmas, and that he was in line for the job; which he wanted, very badly. There were half a dozen contenders for this particular prize, but everyone knew that it was between the aggressive, ambitious lecturer who maintained that unorthodox household in the Banbury Road and whose morals were not entirely above reproach, and an elderly, totally respectable cleric by the name of William Archbold; a man who had published virtually nothing, and whose chairmanship of the Cellar Committee occupied far more of his time than his teaching duties did. But Archbold was a close friend of the Master, and a particular favourite of Mrs Dean Vesey, who, as everyone knew, ruled her husband with the proverbial iron rod.

'You'll get it,' Alfred Carson had told Stephen, confidently. 'On merit, you've no competition — no one's published anything like as much as you have, and they can't pretend that you're not the most competent teacher in the university, not when your students got the three best Firsts this year.'

Stephen had sniffed. 'The Master doesn't like me,' he muttered. 'And, as for publications, he doesn't give a damn for research. He despises fieldwork. Now, if I were a serious drinking man, if I were a sodden old bachelor churning out second rate translations of Aristotle — if I were one of his cronies, then I'd stand a chance.'

'You'll still get it.' Alfred Carson grinned. 'It's either you or that dried-up fellow Archbold. I shall resign my fellowship if they give Archbold the Chair. I say, Stephen?'

'What?'

'You like a good claret, don't you? Get George Armstrong to propose you to the Cellar Committee. You can make some improvements there, and then you'll be well in with the Master! You could persuade them to change the college wine merchant perhaps; that muck we had at High Table last week was disgusting, but your fellow always supplies you with some pretty good stuff.'

Stephen laughed. 'All right. Tell George to propose me. And that reminds me — you could come to dinner tomorrow, if you like. I have some excellent St Emilion at the moment, just ready for drinking, and no one at home likes it but me.'

Since the beginning of her friendship with Tom Guthrie, Anna had been in the habit of reading the London *Times*, scanning its columns every morning after breakfast. She was sitting outside on the terrace one bright July morning, pleased to have the paper to herself — for her father had gone off on a lecture tour — and was idly glancing through its pages as she drank a second cup of tea, when she saw something which made her choke. Ashen-faced, she had replaced her half-full teacup awkwardly, letting it slop all over the breakfast tray. She hurried indoors, taking the paper with her.

Her mother, surprised at Anna's evident agitation, followed her.

Dorcas found Anna in her bedroom, sitting on her bed, still white with obvious shock. Breathless from climbing the stairs, Dorcas put her hand to her side and plumped herself down beside her daughter. 'What's the matter, dear?' she asked.

Anna's eyes were full of tears, and it was some minutes before she would say anything. Eventually, however, she handed her mother the copy of the newspaper. 'Page six. Read it,' she managed to tell her, before dissolving into a violent fit of weeping.

Dorcas lay back against the pillows, resting her pregnant bulge against a hump of ciderdown. She ran her eyes down the columns until she came to a short filler paragraph at the bottom of the page.

'Hitchman to hang,' she read. A few short lines reported that Daniel John Hitchman, a Hereford grocer, had been convicted of the murder of Marie-Jeanne d'Aubier, a French governess. She had been stabbed to death then mutilated, and her body hidden in the Cathedral Close; this had happened back in the summer of 1878. The expected date of execution was given. It appeared that the condemned man did not intend to appeal against the sentence.

The bluntness and stark brutality of the reporting shocked Dorcas, who had long suspected Daniel's guilt. She looked pityingly at Anna, who had not been prepared at all . . .

Feeling Dorcas' gaze upon her, Anna glanced up at her mother, her face a picture of anguish. 'I'm sorry, Mama,' she said tearfully. 'I should have prepared you for that more gently.' She looked at her mother's figure. 'Or not told you at all.'

Dorcas said nothing. She sat, unmoved, leaning against the pillows while she watched her daughter give way to a fresh bout of sobbing. 'There must have been something about this in the newspapers before now!' wept Anna. 'If I'd known, I could have done something! Of course he can't be guilty; it must be some awful mistake! He'd never, ever have done such a terrible thing! Never!'

Dorcas, wondering what on earth she could say to her daughter, folded her hands in her lap. She wanted to cry out, 'Oh, Anna, yes he did! I knew he had — I've known for years, I knew the morning he came home smelling of her blood, the morning after he'd killed her; I knew even when that other man was arrested. And, what's more, I'm glad he's going to die — he deserves death for that, and for all the anxiety he caused me, for all the misery I had to endure when I lived with him. He's a monster.'

She reached for Anna's hand. 'Anna, dear, don't cry so,' she pleaded. 'Maybe he did kill her,' she added unwisely. 'It's possible, after all.'

It was the worst thing she could have said. Anna snatched her hand away and glared at her mother in utter amazement; she noticed, too, that Dorcas' eyes were dry, and her expression calm. 'What?' she demanded. 'Are you trying to suggest that the man who brought me up is a murderer? That he stole out of the house where we all lived, and roamed the streets looking for a victim? That he found this Marie-Jeanne whatever her name was and killed her? Mama, it's preposterous — you know it is! My father was a grocer, for heaven's sake — he worked from five in the morning until late at night; when would he have had *time* to go out and kill anyone?'

Dorcas said nothing. 'That wretch isn't your father,' was on her lips; but she bit the words back and tried to meet Anna's hostile stare.

'You'd like to think it is true, wouldn't you?' asked Anna bitterly. 'You'd like to think that there was some justification for leaving him, for treating him so unkindly. Don't think I don't remember how you used to snap at him, nag at him, scowl if he so much as took me on his lap.

'You used to ignore him for hours together,' she went on remorselessly, 'sitting in your armchair with your nose in some silly novel while he tried to get through a great pile of paperwork which you could have helped him do, which you ought to have done for him since he'd just done fourteen hours' work and you'd just been lazing around all day!' Anna, forced to draw breath, glared at her mother. 'You can't deny it,' she muttered. 'Can you?'

Dorcas wanted to take Anna by the shoulders and shake her; to force her to understand what it had been like to be Daniel's wife, to have lived with Daniel suspecting what she did. But she said nothing. She was well aware that almost any attempt at self-defence would simply cause Anna, who was already nearly hysterical with shock and despair, to lose her temper completely.

'He loved you; he worshipped you,' her daughter was murmuring, quietly, rocking to and fro on her bed. 'I used to see him looking at you as if you were some kind of goddess; no man could have adored his wife more than he loved you.

'And all you ever did in return for that unselfish devotion was to grumble at him for putting on a little weight, moan if he smoked an occasional pipe of tobacco in your precious sitting room, glare at him when he talked to me. And now he's going to die a horrible criminal's death for a crime he can't have committed and you don't care! You don't even care!'

Anna, exhausted by her tirade, fell sobbing on to her pillow, abandoning herself completely to grief. Reaching out to touch her daughter's shoulder, Dorcas found that her hand was roughly pushed away. She rose to her feet and walked out of the room, leaving Anna to cry herself into a stupor.

Fanny Lewson had taken Dora and Anthony into the garden. As it was such a hot day, both children were clad in nothing but short holland smocks and their arms and legs, tinted golden brown by the sun, were bare. They looked so pretty, so huggable, that Dorcas bent down and gathered them into her arms, enjoying the delicious warmth of their childish bodies against hers.

They were untainted by the touch of that devil. They belonged to her absolutely. She felt the baby inside her kick. 'I don't care,' she said to herself. 'It's true what Anna says; I don't care at all. I couldn't weep for him — he made my life unbearable. I knew he'd killed that woman, slit her body like a pig's. I'd like to know how they caught him.'

She shuddered. 'He's a beast,' she thought. 'He deserves to die, and I hope they won't be gentle with him.'

Anna hardly spoke to anyone for the rest of that week. Stephen

237

was still away from Oxford, on a lecture tour of Scotland, and was not expected back for at least another fortnight. Dorcas felt hot, irritable and tired, not at all in a mood to humour Anna.

Although she had felt fit and well while she'd been expecting Anthony and Dora, this particular pregnancy had been difficult. Dorcas suffered from headaches, from constant backache, from swollen ankles; excessive heartburn made eating and digesting a misery. In addition to all that, she had a cough which started as soon as she lay down at night and whichever way she lay, she was uncomfortable.

'I'm too old to have this baby,' she said to herself crossly, as she pushed another pillow behind her head. 'There must be no more. Stephen will have to see to it. I don't want to become a grandmother before I've finished producing children of my own'.

Stephen wrote home to tell them that it was cold in Aberdeen, wet in Edinburgh — and, as for Inverness, he never wanted to see the place again. He hated the barren Cairngorms, he said, and feared that if anyone else invited him to agree that those bleak, bare hillsides were bonny he might well hit him. The food of the Highlands was appalling. And his audiences, though they came in gratifyingly large numbers, were unresponsive and he suspected that they were bored. All in all, he would be glad to come home.

The date set for Daniel Hitchman's execution came, another bright, sunny morning. As eight o'clock struck, all the varied chimes of Oxford recorded the event, and to Anna those dozens of individual notes seemed to say just one thing: dead, dead, dead.

Anna and Dorcas both felt a terrible oppression of spirit that day. Dorcas tried — and failed — to summon up some feeling of pity for the criminal. Anna stayed in her room and wept, experiencing the pain of bereavement for the first time in her life, and feeling utter hatred for her mother.

'She's a harlot,' thought Anna, tearing a handkerchief into shreds with her teeth. 'A whore. That's what Daniel called her, and that's just what she is. She must be nearly forty but she still flaunts herself at Stephen, she's always lolling all over him, trying to inflame him; when he has a thousand better things to do than pander to her! She's disgusting. Absolutely disgusting.'

After that dreadful day, Anna found it impossible to speak to her mother. There was nothing to be said except, perhaps, 'I hate you'. The sight of Dorcas, swollen almost to bursting with her lover's child, an adulteress evidently proud of her wickedness, was so repulsive to Anna that she was glad her mother spent much of her time on the drawing room sofa, dozing, out of her daughter's way.

For convention's sake the whole family met around the table three times a day, just as usual. But mealtimes were terrible. On several occasions either Dorcas or Fanny tried to begin a conversation with Anna, but both were roundly snubbed. In reply to any question Anna would only shake her head or give the slightest of nods. If a fuller answer was required, she would pretend not to have heard. She got up and left the table as soon as she could, leaving her mother surrounded by that brood of bastards and hangers-on, as she thought of Fanny and her younger siblings.

'Don't worry about her, Mrs Lawrence, dear,' Anna heard stupid Fanny Lewson say. 'Miss Lawrence is at a difficult age, after all. And she does miss her father so!'

The sultry summer weather continued. By now, everyone was sick of that hazy sunshine, and longed for the relief of a storm; which did not come. There were cases of scarlet fever in the workmen's cottages, a cluster of which lay very near the Summertown house. Dorcas told Fanny Lewson to keep Dora and Anthony at home but their incessant noise made her already splitting head ache so badly that one afternoon she could bear their racket no longer and told Fanny to take them to the Parks.

'Don't take the short cut through Ballard's Lane,' she had said. 'And don't let them play with any other children in the Parks, because of the fever.'

Such were her instructions to Fanny, who wasn't listening, and who did precisely what she'd been told not to do. While their nursemaid sat and read a penny novelette, Dora and Anthony had a fine romp with a gang of other boys and girls.

A few days later, Anthony found that his head ached, that his throat was sore, and that he felt much too hot.

He went to find Anna, who was sitting in the shade, and he grumbled to her, hoping (for he was not a child who learned from experience) for sympathy. He took her cool hand and laid it on his forehead. 'See?' he moaned. 'I'm boiling!'

'Yes, you are.' Anna looked at him with distaste. 'But what do you expect to be?' she asked him, 'when you will run around in all this heat?'

'I haven't been running around!' wailed Anthony, undeterred by his sister's indifference to his plight. 'My head hurts too much to do that! Anna, I'm ILL!'

Anna removed his grimy hand from her clean white dress. 'I'm going out now,' she told him. 'Go and find Fanny. Ask her to give you a cool bath or something.'

'You're always going out. Where are you going?'

'For a walk.'

'Can I come? The exercise might do me good.'

'I think you ought to be in bed. Go and find Fanny, as I told you to.'

Anna got up and walked into the house, leaving Anthony staring morosely after her. He went indoors, wandered aimlessly around the drawing room, then went back into the garden.

He couldn't find Fanny. His mother had been asleep on the sofa, and he hadn't liked to disturb her; Dora was playing some complicated game of her own, and, when he offered to join in, she told him to go away. Finally, he walked off down the garden path, and, to cool himself, he lay down in the stagnant water of the pond, wallowing like a hippo among the water lilies. By the evening he was burning hot — at bedtime, near delirium. Dorcas, afraid, sent for a doctor.

Anthony, of course, had scarlet fever. He was isolated in one of the attic bedrooms, where his mother, her baby due at any time now, nursed him herself and would let no one else near him. For a week he was very ill, and Dorcas reproached herself for her past neglect, terrified that he would die. She wondered, fearfully, what Stephen would say to her if his son lost his life because of his mother's carelessness.

Anxiously, she looked at his poor little face, now crimson with a vivid rash, with a horrible, itching eruption which, by the third day of his illness, had covered his whole body. 'Don't die, darling,' she thought, as Anthony vomited the food she'd spent the past half-hour trying to get down him. 'Oh, don't die! Please don't die!'

She sent Fanny to fetch the doctor again. 'Will he — will he get better?' she asked him, her face grey with fatigue and streaked with tears of anxiety.

He shrugged. 'My dear Mrs Lawrence,' he replied soothingly. 'You're doing everything you can for him. And the child's strong, so —'

During most of that terrible week, Anna was nowhere to be seen but Dorcas did not even notice that she was missing. All her nervous evergy was absorbed in keeping Anthony alive, in willing him to live. And she had to keep an inquisitive and resentful Dora, who was used to having her mother's attention and was annoyed to be denied Dorcas' company, away from the sick-room.

At the end of the week, the doctor returned. 'Well done, Mrs Lawrence,' he said, taking Anthony's temperature and finding it normal again. 'Thanks to his mother's excellent nursing, I think this little chap will pull through!'

He was right. When Stephen returned from his lecture tour later that week, Anthony was well enough to be lying in a garden hammock, bored and bad-tempered, but getting stronger each day. He grumbled that he itched, that his tongue was sore — for the skin which had been affected by the rash was now scaling and peeling. Dabbed and blotched with carbolic oil, he was a horrible sight.

Stephen, who had not returned from Scotland in the best of humours anyway, was furious to see Dorcas looking so haggard and drawn. He lost his temper with Anna, who, he shouted, should have taken charge and engaged a nurse for Anthony. 'Since, however, you obviously felt it was beyond your limited abilities to do even that, you should have sent for me!' he barked, glowering at her. 'Look at your mother! She's half dead with exhaustion! I would have thought I could rely on you!'

Anna had shrugged, but said nothing. She met her father's eyes, matching his scowl with an even better one of her own. Then she walked out of the room, letting the door slam behind her, which she knew perfectly well would enrage him still further.

Seeing that he was about to go after her, Dorcas caught at Stephen's sleeve. 'It was my fault that Anthony was ill,' she murmured, trying to calm him. 'I wanted to look after him myself. I never thought of a nurse.'

Stephen made some muttered observation on the whole of the

female sex, and favoured Dorcas with a glower. 'What's the matter with Anna these days?' he demanded. 'Have you and she quarrelled about something?'

Feeling unequal to the task of explaining the real reason for Anna's state of mind, Dorcas shook her head. 'She's just at a difficult age,' she replied, parroting Fanny Lewson.

'It's not that.' Stephen sat down. 'There's something bothering her at the moment; there has been for weeks. She's quite altered.'

'So are you, Stephen. You've never lost your temper with her like that before.'

'I had good reason to do so just now!' Stephen grimaced. 'Well — perhaps I was a little hard on her,' he conceded. 'I didn't mean to go on at her like that. But really, she ought to have done something to help you! Poor love, you look worn out!' He rose to his feet, fetched a footstool and lifted Dorcas' legs on to it. 'Is that more comfortable?' he asked solicitously.

'I was comfortable already,' she replied. 'You don't have to make such a fuss of me, you know. I'm not ill, just tired. It's the heat. And this baby — Stephen, dear, I want to talk to you about the baby.'

'I've already told you, you may call it what you please.'

'Oh, it's not that!' Dorcas leaned against him and put her hand on his arm. 'We shouldn't have any more children, you know,' she began. 'And we —'

'We what?' He smiled at her. 'I don't mind if you have another dozen,' he said indulgently.

'But I do! I mind, a great deal!' She felt her voice rising, becoming a wail. 'I don't want any more!' she cried. 'Oh, I feel so tired these days — my back aches, and my hands are so swollen that I've had to take my rings off —'

He didn't understand. He simply smiled kindly at her, put one arm around what he could of her thickened waist and laid her head on his shoulder. 'This sticky heat makes us all irritable,' he said. 'Don't worry about it, darling. This time next week, you'll have a new son or daughter; won't that be lovely for you?'

'Will it?' Dorcas made herself comfortable against him, yawned, and fell asleep.

Dorcas eventually had to admit to herself that her baby was now

242

well overdue, although she was still insisting to Stephen that she had miscalculated when she worked out the dates. The weather remained oppressively hot. Dorcas lay in a basket chair on the terrace, waiting, waiting, trying to ignore Dora's yelling and shrieking.

A further week went by. Still the baby did not come. But the change in the weather, long awaited by a tired, hot, dirty city, did come at last. August brought clouded skies, and a fresher wind replaced the sluggish breezes of July. The rain came, bucketing down, smashing summer flowers into muddy ruin, spoiling any number of tea-parties and garden fetes. And, finally, Dorcas' baby decided that it was time to be born.

Dorcas lay in bed all morning, riding contractions, coping easily with the familiar pain. She kept Fanny Lewson with her; willing, obliging Fanny, who was an excellent nurse, who brought drinks and helped the expectant mother take little walks around the bedroom, and who was far more congenial company than the rather bossy midwife whose arrival Dorcas wished to defer for as long as possible. 'It will be all over by the time Stephen comes home this evening,' remarked Dorcas complacently. And she lay back on her pillows, listening to the rain.

But then everything began to go wrong. By midday, the intensity of the pain had worsened, and its nature had altered. Instead of the familiar, expected contractions, growing closer and closer together, there was a terrible, griping knot of agony centred, it seemed, on the unborn child itself. 'Go and fetch the midwife, now,' whispered Dorcas to Fanny Lewson. 'And you'd better hurry.'

The midwife examined her patient, looked concerned, and sent Fanny out again for a doctor. For the mother's face was ashen now, her pulse far from normal, and she had told the midwife that she could not feel her baby moving any more.

Although the doctor came to the house within ten minutes of Fanny calling at his surgery, he was too late. Unable to hear any heartbeat coming from the child in the womb, he set about the dismal process of delivering a dead baby.

He knew he would have to work quickly. The mother was extremely ill now, and he feared fatal convulsions if the baby were not born very soon. Left to herself, the woman might be in labour for hours yet. He decided to dilate the birth canal by hand.

He was as gentle as he could be. He shut his ears to the cries of the woman he was attending, having heard such cries before — on the many occasions when, like today, he had not been summoned in time.

He brought the child into the world and handed it to the midwife, observing, as he did so, that the mother looked half dead herself. 'Mrs Lawrence?' The doctor leaned over his patient. 'Mrs Lawrence, I'm very sorry. It wasn't possible to save the child.'

Dorcas looked back at him, unable to take in what he'd said. Exhausted by the pain of her confinement, she wanted only to sleep.

The doctor stayed with her for the rest of the afternoon, fearing a sudden deterioration in her condition. But by early evening, when the child's father returned to the house, she was sleeping normally. Faint from loss of blood as she was, her colour was better and her pulse rate had steadied.

For the next few days, Dorcas slept, Anthony dozed, and Fanny did her best to keep Dora occupied. Stephen took his work into his mistress's bedroom, sat up on her bed next to her, looking at her anxiously now and then, and making himself concentrate on the preparation of the following year's courses. He would not allow himself to think about a future without her. Sometimes he would take her hand in his, rubbing it as if trying to warm it into vitality — willing her to recover.

Although she wanted only to sleep, he made her sit up and take some food, frowning at her and obliging her to eat a little of each meal Fanny brought upstairs for her. 'Another mouthful,' he would say, severely, holding the spoon in front of her face while Dorcas grimaced and tried to slide back among her pillows, moaning that she wanted to go to sleep. 'Just one more spoonful. Then a drink.'

'Don't!' Dorcas pushed the proffered cup away. 'I don't want it!'

'You must take it!' Stephen, upset and alarmed though he was that she didn't even seem to recognize him, insisted where anyone else would have probably given up. 'Drink it, Dorcas! Now! Then you can sleep all you please.'

Fanny was just as forebearing. She washed Dorcas and changed

244

her nightgowns, devotedly performed the more disagreeable tasks of nursing without complaint. In the end, the university lecturer and the children's nanny — a most unlikely nursing partnership — did, between them, pull Dorcas back from the brink of death. A week after her confinement, she was obviously stronger; and Stephen allowed himself to hope that Dorcas would recover.

'Have you been here all the time, Stephen?' she asked him one morning, as he placed her breakfast tray on the bedside table and began to butter a piece of toast for her.

'For most of it. Why?'

'I thought you had. I was aware that someone was with me, but I wasn't really sure who it was. Stephen — the baby died, didn't he?'

'Yes, I'm sorry, my darling, he did.' Stephen laid down his knife and sat beside her on the edge of her bed. 'Oh, God, Dorcas,' he muttered, pushing his hair out of his eyes. 'I was so afraid that you would die, too! You've been so ill. You've looked at me as if you didn't know who I was. You do know me now, though, don't you?'

'Yes, of course I do. Stephen, don't look so cross — you mustn't frown at me like that!'

'I'm not frowning.'

'Then what is the matter? Oh, Stephen dear, don't cry! You mustn't cry!'

He didn't answer that. He wrapped his arm around her and sobbed into her hair, making the tearing, choking sounds of someone who has not wept since childhood. His body shaking with emotion, he soaked the shoulder of her nightdress with tears.

'Don't cry, don't cry,' she repeated, at a loss for anything else to say. She stroked his hair, patted his shoulder, crooning to him as if he'd been one of her children. 'There's nothing to cry about,' she soothed. 'Nothing at all.'

'Isn't there?' Clearing his throat and making an effort to check his tears, Stephen looked at her pale face. 'Do you really think I have nothing to cry about?'

Dorcas shrugged. 'I'm much better now,' she said placatingly. 'I know I've been ill; but I'm well again now.'

'Good.' He wiped his face with the back of his hand. 'If you had died,' he said quietly. 'I'd have died, as well.'

'Nonsense, Stephen!' Dorcas smiled at him. 'You'll live for ever!'

He shook his head. 'I'd have died too,' he repeated fiercely.

Each morning since his return from Scotland, Anna had met her father at breakfast. On the day she disappeared she had eaten her toast and drunk her coffee with him as usual, had even asked how her mother was.

'She's still very weak, and she'll be so for a long time yet,' he'd replied, as he'd laid a breakfast tray with a plate of hot toast and taken the pot of fresh tea from Fanny Lewson. 'I imagine, though, that she's out of danger now. Miss Lewson, have I got everything?'

'I think so, sir. Shall I take it up to Mrs Lawrence?'

'No; I'll go up myself.'

Anna had looked at him, fussing around her mother's breakfast as if he were a housemaid, and she pulled a face. 'I'm glad she's feeling better,' she remarked. But her father, she knew, wasn't paying attention. He was far too preoccupied with her mother's health to think of his daughter at all.

When he looked back on that morning, Stephen had decided that Anna had indeed seemed rather abstracted. But he'd been too tired and anxious himself to think about Anna's state of mind. And he hadn't known about Daniel Hitchman or about her other well-kept secret.

Leaving Dorcas asleep that evening, Stephen had gone to look for his daughter, meaning to suggest a short walk. He had had time to regret losing his temper with her, and was anxious that there should not be any coldness between him and his favourite child.

He wondered what she'd been doing with herself — he hadn't talked to her at any length for weeks. He hoped she didn't feel neglected.

He went up to her room and tapped on the door. Getting no reply, he turned the handle and went inside.

Anna's bedroom was in disorder. Clothes were scattered about everywhere, her dressing table was a clutter of cosmetic jars, brushes and piles of books. Her wardrobe was half empty; on her bed lay a recent copy of some provincial newspaper.

Stephen picked it up, and found it was the familiar weekly

Worcester journal. Its banner headline, printed in red, invited its reader to learn about the terrible crimes of the Hereford Butcher. Her father sat down on Anna's bed and began to read. ·

Chapter Sixteen

WALTER JENKS HAD REJOICED AND praised the Lord when Daniel Hitchman had been convicted of murder. His delight had been unclouded by the fact that he was now in prison himself, doing six years at hard labour, a sentence which was likely to kill a man of his advanced years and poor state of health.

Jenks had never, up until very recently, been a religious man. He had of course paid lip service to the forms and customs of the Church of England, for his job as a sexton depended upon this compliance. But his true loves in life had always been alcohol and money; and he had not been averse to acquiring the latter by any means presented to him.

He had first made Daniel Hitchman's acquaintance many years back, when Daniel had been just a lad, happy to earn a few coppers by sanding down the coffins which old Hitchman made. 'That boy of yours like to do a bit of shovellin' for me?' enquired the sexton one morning, seeing Daniel at work. 'Bob or two in it for him, there'd be.'

The idea had appealed to Daniel. From the age of twelve, he had been casually employed by Jenks to dig graves.

On the whole, Jenks liked his work. Most of the time it was easy enough; and it had the advantage of a tied cottage which went with the job.

'I'd 'ate to 'ave to do with all them dead bodies,' his regular drinking partner had remarked on more than one occasion. But Jenks had no fear of cadavers; on the contrary, he had what he knew himself to be a little peculiarity, just a small, harmless foible. He liked to unscrew the lids of the coffins — which were often left in the graveyard's own little chapel on the night before burial — and to gaze upon the faces of the dead. If he could help himself to a ring or two, so much the better. No one living would know, he reasoned, and the corpse would not care.

One evening, as he was busy with his pliers twisting a stubborn circle of gold from a woman's finger, Daniel Hitchman came into the chapel behind him. 'What you up to then, Mr Jenks?' he asked affably. For Jenks was panting and straining, cursing both the body and the piece of jewellery of which he was trying to despoil it.

By now, Daniel was a well grown, very good-looking young man of about sixteen, who had been apprenticed to a butcher for a couple of years. He still came to the graveyard occasionally, happy to earn the few extra shillings which Jenks could put his way. But, until that evening, he had only once before looked upon the face of a corpse ...

Hearing Daniel's tread, Jenks had spun round. Relief flooded across his mean little face. 'Oh, God in Heaven, boy — you didn't half startle me!' he muttered, wiping beads of sweat from his forehead. 'I was just — er — tidying the body here.'

'You were *what*?' Daniel laughed. 'You were pinching rings, you mean,' he observed scathingly. He retrieved the pair of pliers which the little man had stuffed into a fold of the shroud. 'Here,' he said. 'Better not bury these. Or what will you do next time?'

Jenks pushed the pliers into his pocket and looked nervously up at the powerfully built lad standing beside him. 'Well, and what if I was helping myself?' he asked in a wheedling tone. 'I'm a poor man, Daniel — a very poor man. And what's one little ring?' He grinned. 'Tell you what,' he added. 'When I sell it, we'll go halves. What do you say?'

Daniel stared at Jenks while he rattled on, his handsome face completely impassive. 'Oh, you can keep your dirty money,' he replied. 'I'm not a thief.'

Jenks had grinned even more broadly at this. 'You're a good boy, Daniel,' he had said. 'A very good boy. I won't forget this. I owe you a favour.'

'Aye, Jenks, you do.' Coming closer to the coffin, Daniel bent over the corpse and stared at it, fascinated. 'What did she die of?' he asked.

Glad to get off the subject of theft, Jenks considered. 'Oh — she had a cancer, I think,' he replied. 'Took her off very quick.'

'She was so young, wasn't she?' Daniel seemed unable to take his eyes off the woman. 'And pretty. Very pretty. My mother was pretty, you know,' he added dreamily. 'And she died young; when I was six, I think it was …'

'Yes, well, that's a shame.' Jenks had picked up the coffin lid with the intention of replacing it and screwing it down again, but Daniel held out his hand and prevented him.

'Poor lady,' he went on, in the same abstracted voice. 'Did she have much pain, I wonder? What did it do it her?' He had reached across now, and was touching the dead woman's greenish, waxen face. 'I wonder where it hurt her?' he murmured. 'It wasn't on her face, was it? Not on her pretty face.' He touched the shroud, plucked at the edge of the cloth.

Jenks shuddered. 'Come on now, boy,' he snapped. 'Move out of the way, can't you?'

'What? Oh — yes.' Daniel came out of his reverie and stepped back, allowed Jenks to replace the lid. The boy was very pale now, and a ghastly smile played around his lips. And, although it was a warm day, the sight of that smile made Jenks shiver with cold.

Daniel left the butcher and went to learn the grocery trade at Follet's shop, in High Town. He no longer came up to the grave-yard to dig graves for Walter Jenks. But, a few years later, when he was married to a pretty, dark-haired girl and was the father of a lovely little daughter, when he was spoken of as heir apparent to old Follet himself, Daniel had paid Walter Jenks a visit. 'You owe me a favour, Jenks,' he had said quietly. 'Do you remember?'

At first, Jenks had assumed that Hitchman was in need of money; that his request to be left alone in the chapel with a corpse awaiting burial was not so much to keep watch over the dead as to plunder the body. So, he had not really understood why Daniel had been incensed when summoned one evening to the body of a wealthy alderman.

'He must have had a few rings about him,' whined Jenks, as Daniel had shaken him by the collar. 'I'll go halves with you on the next one, look — I promise! Next one as has got summat worth havin', I'll split with you!' Half strangled, he tried to jerk himself out of Daniel's grasp. 'Let me go, bugger you!' he gasped. 'You're choking me!'

Daniel had released the sexton, and pushed his face close to the terrified old man's. 'To hell with your bloody rings!' he muttered.

'I don't want them! I want you to send word when it's a woman — a young woman. And if she's pretty, so much the better! Do you understand me?'

Jenks nodded, trembling. 'A young, pretty woman,' he gabbled, shaking with fear. 'Yes, yes, I'll remember that.'

'Good.' Daniel had turned on his heel then and vanished into the night, leaving Jenks mystified.

Jenks was not a squeamish man. He did, however, recognize that a corpse is not usually a pleasant sight. He sympathized with Daniel's aversion to anything but the dead body of a young, pretty woman. 'And,' he thought to himself, 'Hitchman's no fool. They often has the best trinkets and such, little rings as couldn't be taken off, earrings and all that sort of thing,' He rubbed his stubbly jowls. 'Hitchman's not a fool,' he repeated, as if to convince himself.

One night several years later, Jenks had let Daniel into the chapel and gone away, intending to return and lock the doors after Hitchman had gone. As he felt in his pocket for the key, however, he realized that he had left his purse behind. 'Better go back and get it,' he thought. 'Don't want Hitchman helping hisself.'

For some reason Jenks had not gone marching straight back into the chapel. Instead, he had approached it stealthily, and now he peered around the slightly open door. And he stared, appalled, at what he saw ...

By the light of a guttering candle, he could just make out Daniel's heavy figure. The butcher was in his shirt-sleeves, holding a long, thin-bladed knife in his hand. Upon his face, which was illuminated by the candle, was an expression of sheer rapture — it made Jenks' spine tingle, for it brought back a half-forgotten memory. He knew he'd seen that look upon Daniel's face before.

And then, quite suddenly, the knife descended. There was a tearing sound; and, all at once, a warm, sweet smell of blood. The metallic odour of it filled the air until the sharp scent of carbolic acid was overlaid by the unmistakable stench of dead humanity.

Jenks turned away and began to walk quickly back towards his own cottage on the other side of the cemetery grounds. He paused only when he was half-way there, to be violently sick into the long grass. But even then he did not stop long. Instead, he vomited as he went on, leaving a long trail behind him all along the path. Feeling ill with loathing, fear and dread, he almost expected to see the ghosts and demons in which he'd never believed rise up before him. Stumbling and choking, he made his way back to his own safe fireside.

Daniel went home an hour or so later. He trudged away into the darkness, walking heavily past Jenks' cottage. Hearing the young man's characteristic footfall on the gravel near his house, the sexton blenched.

It had taken all Jenks' courage to go back to the chapel that evening. He had forced himself to enter and he breathed a sweet sigh of relief when he saw that all had been left as tidy as usual. Then he had taken his screwdriver and gone to work on the coffin lid. He lifted it away, held the lamp above the casket, and looked down upon the body inside.

It was as well that Jenks' stomach was empty now, that the only result of his retching was a mouthful of sour bile. He stared, sickened, appalled, incredulous. For it had not occurred to him that men did such things.

The body, no longer decently wrapped in its shroud, had been sliced and mutilated in a disgusting fashion. The young woman who had lain so calm and untroubled in death was now wounded horribly, particularly about the face, neck and chest. Her flesh had been cut to bloody shreds; there was a livid purple bruise upon her cheek which might have been a dreadful parody of a kiss ...

Now, the sexton half perceived why Daniel had insisted upon female bodies. 'A woman — a young, pretty woman,' he could hear Daniel saying, in his flat, townsman's drawl.

'God above,' thought Jenks, his legs weakening. 'And to think he was married to that dear, pretty lady. He had a little girl the image of her mother. If his wife had known — did she know? What happened to them? He gave out that she left him. No wonder!'

Feeling desperately in need of some alcohol now, Jenks replaced the coffin lid; with shaking fingers, he screwed it down very tightly. He set everything to rights for the morning and walked unsteadily across the moonlit graveyard. 'How many is it?' he wondered. 'Over the years, that is? Two hundred? Three hundred? More? And I thought he wanted the rings and trinkets!'

He grimaced to himself. 'I'll have to inform on him,' he thought. 'He's got to be stopped. But if I go to the police, what will happen then? They might believe — Hitchman might tell them — oh, Lord!'

That night, for the first time in his wretched life, Jenks prayed sincerely for divine guidance. None was forthcoming. Instead, visions of a pretty face with the skin peeled away from the jawline, with the neck slit and the upper chest a mass of contusions, came to haunt him.

From then on, the knowledge of what Daniel Hitchman did hung like a stone weight about his heart. 'Monster,' he thought to himself. 'Monster, bloody monster. I'll do for him one day!'

Again and again Jenks considered going to the police; but he never did. He could drop Hitchman in it, but Hitchman could do the same for him. In any case, what he had seen had terrified him. If Daniel could wreak such havoc upon a corpse, what might he do to a living body? Jenks broke out in a sweat at the very thought of it, at the idea of what he'd seen in the cemetery chapel that night and would see in his mind's eye to the end of his days. 'Beast,' he would mutter. 'Madman. He'll pay in the end. I'll settle him.'

That spring, the band of evangelists who travelled the Midlands and who visited the city from time to time, returned to Hereford. Members of some extreme Primitive Methodist sect, the group consisted of one very large family; brothers, sisters, husbands, wives, uncles and aunts — and every variety of in-law and step. Dressed like seventeenth-century Puritans in clean white linen, homespuns of grey, brown and black, the evangelists were remarkable for their eccentricity of dress, and they attracted notice everywhere they went.

They habitually earned their living from casual labour on the land, but they would also turn their hands to anything offered to them by way of work in the towns. Decent, sober and hardworking, they never begged. On market days, their leader preached in the High Town, attracting large crowds of both town and country people, who liked a free show and appreciated the fact that after this particular entertainment no one came round with a hat.

This leader, this tall, blond Moses, was a marvellous orator —

and he had a yet more splendid presence. Six and a half feet tall, he had pale blue eyes which looked as if they could see right into the more obdurate heart, he also possessed a powerful, resonant voice, was inspired by Messianic fervour. He would stand four-square, leonine head and massive shoulders above the crowds, thundering out the word of God. And he would call sinners to repentance in a manner which few could resist.

A large group of people had gathered that fine spring day. Walter Jenks, hurrying across the town, found that his way to the left was blocked by a great flock of sheep, and his passage to the right impeded by the gawping throng of human sinners milling around the preacher, who was in full spate and had his audience completely rapt.

'Bloody time wasters, stupid gabies,' muttered Jenks, as he kicked ankles and tried to push his way through the crowd. But, in the end, he could not get through the press, and he had to stay and hear the Word.

The people were not to be disappointed that day. As they were harangued, women swayed and moaned, men looked stricken, children grizzled and wailed. Cursing their follies and wickednesses, beating their breasts, confessing their sins to their next door neighbours, everyone was having a good time and Jenks was eventually caught up in the general fervour.

Entranced now, affected by the atmosphere of repentance, and having heard the promise of pardon if only he would confess his sins, Jenks suddenly found that the weight which had oppressed his conscience for so many years was suddenly too heavy a burden to be borne any longer. In a voice unlike his own, he cried out — and the preacher heard him.

'What do you say, brother?' he asked.

'I have been the chief of sinners!' reiterated Jenks, parrotting the prescribed formula with a fervour which made it new again. 'I have walked in the ways of the Devil hisself!'

There was a sudden, absolute silence. Everyone craned to look at the little elderly man who stood trembling among them.

The preacher walked over to Jenks. He laid his great, square hand upon the old man's grizzled head. 'Speak again, brother,' he said, his blue eyes kindly now. 'Do not be afraid to testify before the Lord of Hosts.'

Jenks hesitated, but he was now in a state of hysterical excitement which overbore all common prudence. He climbed on to the wooden box next to the preacher, and he testified before the Lord — and before the goggling people of Herefordshire — for all he was worth. The people listened to him in silence, hardly able to believe their ears.

'He's a monster!' cried Jenks. 'He's a fiend in human form, a devil incarnate, what passes hisself off as an honest shopkeeper! He does visit the graveyards at dead of night! He does open the coffins! And he does tear the bodies of the dead like a ravening wolf!

'I seen him at his dreadful work — but until this day, I been too afraid to testify against him! But today, by the grace of the Lord, I have found a tongue to speak with and I shall tell what I knows!'

He looked across the square towards Follet's shop. 'Daniel Hitchman!' he shouted, pointing to the place where the devil incarnate was probably sorting dried fruit or weighing out sugar, 'you are a monster! Your hour of retribution is at hand! You are bound for the fiery pit, where you belongs, and has done this many a year!'

Jenks was still calling down curses upon Daniel as he was hustled along to the police station by an excited, chattering mob.

He repeated his testimony before the station sergeant. 'I took his gold!' he cried. 'And he butchered the bodies of poor Christians! Lord have mercy upon me!'

The police sergeant had dealt with lunatics before, so he was unimpressed by Jenks' revelations. Well knowing the man whom Jenks had accused of such incredible crimes — for the sergeant and the grocer played billiards together — he took the sexton aside and asked him how much he'd had to drink that day.

'What's all this about then?' the policeman enquired, not unkindly. 'Mr Hitchman upset you, has he? You can't go around slanderin' decent, honest citizens, you know, and Mr Hitchman could have you prosecuted if he heard what you've just said about him.'

The sergeant turned to a constable standing near him. 'He's a sexton, see,' he explained. 'Got some strange fancies, he has — it comes of having to deal with all them dead bodies, day in, day out.'

He had Jenks taken down to the cells to cool off. The little elderly man hadn't appeared to be drunk but he was definitely disorderly, if not positively deranged. Then the policeman ordered the crowd to disperse.

Disappointed now, the people drifted away, muttering. They were still in the mood for excitement, and a group of them, who had nothing else to do, went to stand outside Follet's shop. Later in the afternoon a window was broken. Buzzing like hornets, little knots of people discussed the business among themselves, asking each other if it could be true. By evening, the whole story, complete with embellishments and variations, was all over town.

By six o'clock a huge, expectant crowd had gathered in High Town, and the people were rewarded by the sight of two rather apologetic-looking policeman coming out of Follet's with Daniel Hitchman between them. They had asked him, very politely, if he'd mind going with them to help clear up one or two things ...

Daniel heard the accusations against him and was asked for his comments. 'It's just a formality, sir,' the police inspector had said. 'I need your official denial before I can charge the fellow, you see. Otherwise, we wouldn't have put you to all this trouble.'

Daniel sighed, leaned wearily against the desk at which he was sitting. He stared vacantly at the sergeant opposite him. 'Jenks hasn't made any of it up,' said the shopkeeper. 'It's all true.'

The inspector, who had been lounging against the windowsill, spun round. '*What* did you say, Mr Hitchman?'

Daniel looked at the policeman, shrugged. 'I said, he hasn't made any of it up.'

'Oh. Well, in that case —' The sergeant gaped at Daniel, too astonished to remember that he ought now to go through the routine procedure of caution and charge. 'You've been doing that since you were a young lad?' he demanded incredulously. 'And you were up at the burial ground last week, on the same errand? Mr Hitchman, I just don't believe you.' He looked up at the inspector. 'Seems we got a right pair here, sir,' he muttered, rising to his feet to allow his senior officer to sit down.

Daniel remained quiet and composed. 'It's just as Jenks says,' he insisted. 'I couldn't help myself, you see — I had to do it, I had no choice. Look in the graves, if you wish to make sure.'

'We will — oh, yes, we will!' The inspector nodded to the sergeant. 'Have him taken down,' he said.

As a constable led Daniel away, the inspector turned to the sergeant. 'God only knows what we'll charge him with,' he muttered. 'There must be half a dozen felonies all mixed up in that. I'd never have thought it of a man like him — of any man, come to that. *Why* do it, for God's sake?'

The graves were duly opened, the bodies found to have been mutilated in the way in which Jenks had described. Amid threats to burn down the prison with Hitchman inside it, Daniel was taken to Worcester for his own safety.

There, a detective sergeant with a good memory studied the notes to Daniel's case; and thought of a Frenchwoman murdered in Hereford some ten years since.

He got hold of the relevant file. He found that *her* body had been carved like a joint of meat — and that *her* killer had never been found. 'Try him with it, sir,' he urged the chief inspector. 'A few questions won't hurt. He could have been an accessory — perhaps he came along afterwards, like some bloody human jackal. If he found her dead, he might be able to take us to her killer. Or perhaps we'll stick it on him, sir.'

There turned out to be no need of subtlety on the part of the police. When Daniel was taken to a room for questioning, he had looked from one policeman to another and a faint, derisive half smile had crossed his lips. 'You don't need to go through all this business of trying to catch me out,' he said. 'I killed her. I was going to tell you so.'

He rubbed his eyes and stared up at the ceiling. 'She was a harlot, you see,' he explained reasonably. 'So it didn't matter what was done to her. She was always walking about the Cathedral Close at night,' he added.'I saw her dozens of times; she used to smile at me, you know — such a smile, the bitch. She was a whore, wasn't she?'

'There isn't anything else you'd like to tell us?' The policeman spoke very softly, afraid of breaking the spell, for Daniel seemed to be in some kind of trance.

'Anything else? No. Why should there be?'

So Daniel Hitchman was charged with murder; and incredibly, he was found fit to plead. He was tried, found guilty and condemned.

He sat through his trial indifferent to the florid speeches of the prosecuting counsel, who was a famous QC brought to Worcester specially and who presumably felt that he ought to give his audience a good performance.

Daniel's defence was non-existent. His counsel, having found his client entirely indifferent to his fate, did not even try to plead imbalance of mind.

When the cap was placed upon the judge's head and the sentence of death passed, Daniel leaned back against the box and sighed. He had not spoken a word at his trial, except to plead guilty. Now he ignored the boos and howls from the public gallery, and, indifferent to the uproar in the court, he simply closed his eyes in resignation.

The people felt themselves to have been scandalously cheated. They'd hoped, at the very least, for a last minute plea for mercy; they'd expected the condemned man — who was as certainly destined for Hell as any individual could be — to cower and tremble, afraid. The jurymen had been extremely provoked by the defendant's tranquillity. Everyone — save, possibly, Daniel — went away from the courtroom that day more or less dissatisfied.

'They ought to 'ave asked 'im what became of that wife and child of his,' complained Daniel's neighbours, remembering that Mrs Hitchman and her daughter had, one day about ten years back, apparently vanished into thin air. At the time, it had been assumed that Mrs Hitchman (a flighty piece, as her neighbours had afterwards agreed) had run away from her rather dull, taciturn husband — had gone off with some other man, taking her child with her. This was a story which Daniel had never bothered to encourage or contradict. He had never spoken about it to anyone, and rumours had, over the years, gained the currency of truth.

Now Dorcas and her daughter were remembered as a dear, sweet lady and a lovely little girl. 'What happened to them?' asked everyone. 'They did ought to beat it out of 'im afore they strings the bugger up!'

But Daniel had nothing to say on the matter. He went to his execution still clutching that particular secret to his heart, and he met his end with the same dulled indifference with which he had gone to his trial.

Afterwards, the hangman wiped his hands. 'A rum 'un,' he

observed to the doctor. 'Never said a word to the chaplain an' never give *me* nothing, not so much as a penny.'

He wiped his nose across his sleeve. 'No one ever give me less'n two bob before,' he grumbled. 'An' I've 'ad gentlemen give me gold, for the promise of a quick trip! Ah, well — p'raps this time I warn't as speedy as Mr Hitchman 'ere would've liked. Serves him right.'

Having checked the body for any sign of life, the doctor turned to the hangman. 'You're a vindictive brute, Marston,' he remarked. 'Here.' He took a coin from his pocket and tossed it to the executioner. Then he hurried away; a medical man with a strong stomach, a veteran of many executions, who had nevertheless been disturbed by that day's business.

The ballad-mongers had been obliged to draw on their own vivid imaginations for details of the Hereford Butcher's last words and final confession. Never had such a sensational murder trial petered out so anti-climactically; and for a while there was talk of sending a petition to Parliament, demanding the re-introduction of public executions. Then, at least, the people would have the satisfaction of seeing justice done, even if the felon could not be guaranteed to play his part in the entertainment with the spirit and style expected of him.

For a few days, the story of the trial pushed agricultural news from the front pages of local papers and broadsheets. But soon enough the whole thing was forgotten. By the time Daniel's body, itself now mutilated and dismembered by medical students, had been buried in the prison cemetery, the murder was old news. Daniel was allowed to rot in peace.

In order that she might read the details of the case, Anna had sent for a copy of the local Worcester paper. At first, she was sickened and horrified, unable to credit what she read. She could not believe that the man whom she had supposed was her father could have done such terrible things.

Appalled, she bit her lips to keep down her rising bile and she thanked Providence that she was not Daniel's child. She well remembered those knives of his, all those blades kept honed to wafer thinness, always kept razor sharp; and she recalled the almost swooning pleasure that Daniel had taken in his legitimate butchery. Many a time she had watched him while he jointed a leg of ham, smothering the pieces with golden crumbs ...

Now she recalled one day in particular, when Daniel had suddenly told her to go out of the shop; when he had looked oddly at her, and gripped his butcher's knife so tightly that she'd thought he would crush the handle.

Every day for a week she took out the newspaper and re-read the story, trying to digest the horror of it. Bit by bit, the raw awfulness of it receded. She became familiar with the idea of what Daniel had done, could wrap it up and store it in the locked cellars of her mind, among other unpleasant memories.

'They mean me,' she'd thought, as she'd read about Hitchman's daughter, who had, along with her mother, disappeared mysteriously about ten years since. She wondered if she ought to let it be known that she and Dorcas were still alive, and had been treated with nothing but kindness by Daniel Hitchman.

But then she reflected that such revelations would do nothing but harm. They would bring scandal and disgrace upon the family in Oxford, they might well ruin the career of her own dearly loved father. And Daniel himself could no longer care what the world thought of him.

Gradually, Anna ceased to think so much of Daniel. She had someone more important on her mind these days. She'd fallen in love.

Chapter Seventeen

ANNA HAD MET JOHN HARLEY in the spring of the year in which Dorcas' fourth child had died and in which Daniel Hitchman had been executed. By the summer, Anna was so desperately, so hopelessly in love that she was certain that any chance of future happiness depended entirely on John. The terrible events of the summer had made her determined. 'Whatever happens,' she'd told herself, 'I'm going to be John Harley's wife.'

Anna and John had met quite by chance. Their relationship had begun and developed so casually and so easily that neither had been aware of the extent to which each had become dependent upon the other. The trap was baited, and the victims sealed inside it, before either Anna or John realized what had happened.

In the habit of spending some hours of every weekday in one or other of the university libraries, Anna was noticed and recognized by many of the undergraduates. As the formidable Dr Lawrence's daughter, she inspired them to keep their distance. So, in the cool silence of the Bodleian or the dim gloom of the Radcliffe Camera, she could read and work undisturbed. There was, after all, no peace to be had at home, where the shrieks and yowls of Anthony and Dora constantly filled the air.

Anna never understood how her father contrived to work at his desk while Dora played some noisy game or arranged a dolls' tea-party right in the middle of his study; or while her mother stood behind him with her arms around his neck, fiddling with his hair and murmuring some nonsense or other. Anna had watched her pestering him only a morning or so since. 'Anthony has such a bad cough,' Dorcas had told Stephen, patting his collar and adjusting his tie.

'Oh? Take him to see a doctor, then,' Stephen had replied,

without even taking his eyes off his work. Then he had caught Dorcas' hand in his and smiled up at her. 'I'd like some coffee, please,' he'd told her. 'In ten minutes or so.'

Anna had taken the book she'd come to fetch and then left the house, reflecting that it was no wonder Stephen made so many spelling mistakes. She wished she had his remarkable powers of concentration. As it was, the racket at home nearly drove her insane.

A few months back Stephen had, despite Anna's protests, written to Arthur Liebermann and enclosed some examples of his daughter's work, with a view to their publication. To Anna's amazement, Mr Liebermann had expressed great interest in Miss Lawrence's translations and had, eventually, commissioned her to prepare English versions of sixteen of the poems in the anthology which his publishing house was then preparing.

'Very well done, my dear,' her father had remarked, reading the letter and beaming at her over his spectacles. 'I'm not surprised though,' he'd added. 'You'd really captured the essence of those pieces I let Liebermann see. You ought to write some poetry yourself, you know — you seem to have a feeling for it.' He picked up some work she'd left on his desk the previous day, and handed the paper to her. 'This is beyond praise,' he said. 'Those last three lines in particular are quite splendid.'

Success had gone to Anna's head. She now had a grand design, a life's work laid out before her. She was going to translate the work of some of her favourite authors into readable but precise English; and she hoped that her renderings would, while capturing the spirit of the originals, become standard texts in their own right.

Anna had realized, very early on, that the cloddish prose translations available as cribs to students would have once been enough to put her off Latin and Greek poetry for life. Had she not had Stephen to encourage and inspire her, she was certain that she would have given up classical studies in disgust. A particularly terrible, stumbling version of the *Aeneid*, published a year or two since, had crystallized Anna's ambitions, and the receipt of her first commission had decided her. *She* would produce work as remarkable for its scholarly accuracy as its poetic beauty. In future years, quotations in English would always be taken from A.M.

Sitting in her usual place one day, her books and paper spread all around her, she'd been letting a line from the poem she was reading roll around her tongue when she chanced to look up. She realized then that she had said the line out loud, for the young man opposite was staring across the table at her, a faintly ironic smile upon his face.

Anna blushed with annoyance and bent her head over her books. But, when she glanced up to find out the time, peering through the gloom at the clock, the young student did the same. Again their eyes met. Grimacing, Anna collected her things together, then walked out of the library into the late morning sunshine, meaning to go home for her lunch.

John Harley, an undergraduate at Magdalen in his third year at university, would be glad when he could finally leave the place. He'd had enough of ushers, of rules and regulations, of work for the sake of it. It had been a terrible mistake to read Greats, and he wished now that he'd opted for another subject.

But his mother had insisted on his taking classics. 'Get yourself a gentleman's education,' she had said firmly. 'Pass your examinations and I shall let you have an annuity to do with as you please.'

Three years ago that had seemed a fair bargain; but now John was convinced that going to university had been a sheer waste of time. He'd decided, however, that since he had to take his degree examination, he was going to do well. He would get an honours degree, not a mere pass. So, while his friends were out on the river or chasing women, were drinking more than they could either carry or afford, John Harley sat in the library, reluctantly poring over his books.

He had noticed the girl before, of course. He knew who she was. The brainy daughter of that awful sarcastic old tartar Dr Lawrence, she looked far too pretty to be as clever as it was rumoured she was. Why a stunning girl like that should voluntarily spend her days cooped up in a library when she might be out in the sunshine, visiting her friends, harassing her dressmaker, wasting her time and money in the mindless fashion in which his own sister did, was quite beyond him. 'What the hell's she doing every day?' he wondered. 'Scribble, scribble, scribble — she's like some demented counting-house clerk.'

John made a point of sitting near to her whenever he could. She made a restful object for his poor tired eyes whenever he had to look up from Virgil, Tacitus or some equally tedious old bore.

She didn't even notice him. He had time to examine her as closely as if she'd been a statue, or a painting. He observed that her complexion was as rich as double cream, saw the hint of rosiness on her cheekbones; he wondered, cut short in a fringe across her forehead, if such long, thick eyelashes made her eyelids heavy. Her hair curled prettily around her face, while the rest of it coiled in heavy braids at the back of her head. Letting his gaze travel past her chin, he began, as a reflex, to undress her; he imagined her figure under all that whalebone, linen and unnecessary corsetry. He rested his face against his hand, and sighed.

The girl glanced up at him sharply. Her dark grey eyes shone, enormous in her heart-shaped face. John smiled at her.

He had the pleasure of seeing her redden vividly, which made her look even more fetching. It was incredible that an ugly old monster like her father should have begotten such a beautiful child, who resembled him so closely — but who, in another way, did not resemble him at all …

Anna, meanwhile, was considering moving all her clutter to another part of the library, for that grinning student was getting on her nerves. She could go up to the gallery, she supposed, but then she'd be yards away from the dictionaries, and she wouldn't be able to see the clock. She grimaced in annoyance, and bit the end of her pen.

A rustle of papers made her look up. John caught Anna's eye. He smiled — and to Anna's complete disgust, she found herself smiling back at him. That did it. She pushed her books into her bag, got up, and marched out of the library. After lunch, she decided, she'd go and establish herself at one of the small individual tables, where the light was terrible, but where she'd at least get some peace.

John made a heap of his books and papers, raced down the library steps, and caught up with her just as she turned into Broad Street.

'Miss Lawrence?' he panted. 'May I walk with you? I'm going in your direction, you see. My lodgings are in the Banbury Road, and I'm just on my way home to lunch. You bag looks far too heavy for you to manage easily, so I wondered — forgive my impertinence …' He was blushing furiously now, and Anna stared at him in surprise.

She stood in the street, looking at him. Embarrassed and annoyed, she wondered if this peculiar young man had been drinking. But then, his nervous smile softened her; she looked at him more closely, saw that he was very young; and, what was more, almost as embarrassed as she was. 'My bag looks heavy, does it?' she asked. 'Very well, then, why don't you carry it for me?'

He seized it from her before she could change her mind, and slung it over his shoulder.

'I don't believe we've met before?' she asked, somewhat sarcastially. 'You're not one of my father's students, are you? I've never seen you at our house.'

'Oh, no. Dr Lawrence isn't my tutor. But I go to his lectures, of course.' The young man drew a deep breath. 'John Harley, Magdalen,' he announced, introducing himself.

Anna nodded in acknowledgement. 'Mr Harley, I'm happy to make your acquaintance,' she said. 'It appears that I don't need to introduce myself.'

'No indeed, Miss Lawrence. Everyone knows you!'

They walked together down Broad Street, John glancing at his companion now and then. She was, he decided, even more of a stunner in daylight. Those dark eyes were fabulous. And she walked with such grace that she seemed to glide.

Her clothes showed off her slim figure to perfection. Remembering Dr Lawrence's bulldog build, John wondered what Mrs Lawrence could be like.

A tall, fair-haired young man of twenty or thereabouts, John Harley had the air of someone who is accustomed to being liked. Talkative, somewhat frivolous and very easy-going, it never crossed his mind that anyone might find his somewhat puppyish high spirits at all tiresome. Anna thought he was an excellent example of the kind of bumptious undergraduate she particularly despised. At that moment, she felt as if she were accompanied by a large, amiable but very stupid Labrador dog.

As they walked on, John chattered like a magpie, telling Anna

265

that his mother had threatened to keep him in poverty for the rest of his life if he failed his degree. 'But I shall surprise her,' he announced, frowning. 'She thinks I'm an idle layabout, just like the rest of the fellows I go around with. But I can work when I choose!'

Anna laughed. John Harley spoke more like a child of Anthony's age than a grown-up man. Even his facial expressions, his furious scowl and his wide, cheerful grin, were the exaggerated mannerisms of childhood. 'Surely,' she said, 'if you take the authors you like best, you can't fail to be interested?'

'The authors I like best?' John Harley grimaced. 'Oh, I can't bear any of them! It's all so much boring rubbish, this Greek and Latin so-called literature. Give me a modern novel any day. And anyway, I'm not a scholar. I'm not cut out for mooning about a college, muttering Horace to myself, and fretting over the interpretation of some obscure passage which nobody gives a damn about anyway! And besides — oh, I'm sorry.' Blushing furiously, John Harley bit his lip. 'I'm sorry, Miss Lawrence,' he muttered. 'I meant no disrespect to your father ...'

Seeing him look so abashed and embarrassed, Anna laughed at him again. 'Oh, I understand what you mean,' she said kindly. 'And in any case, when my father was as old as you are now, *he* wasn't mooning about a college! He was travelling all over Europe and the Middle East. He didn't settle down here until he was well past thirty, you know.'

John grinned back at her, somewhat ruefully. 'Yes, of course, I do know that,' he said. 'Your father must have been abroad for years. You can't have seen very much of him at all when you were little.'

'Er — no.' Anna reddened. 'No, I didn't.'

'I have read a couple of his books,' continued John. 'Look — I'm sorry to have been so boorish. I didn't mean to be rude. I'd like to travel,' he added wistfully. 'I've never been out of England yet.'

'Haven't you?' Anna smiled. 'I've seen the Parthenon,' she announced, with an air of superiority. 'I've been to Italy a dozen times — I've been to Crete and Rhodes and Cyprus. And, of course, to France, Germany, Austria ...'

'Goodness!' John pulled an expression of mock amazement. 'An intrepid lady explorer. Out in the wilds with your butterfly net, were you? Did you go over the Alps on a donkey, all alone except for one faithful servant, who protected you from the wild tribesmen; but who fell down a convenient crevasse when he'd served his purpose? Did you cross the Adriatic on a raft?'

'What?' Anna stared at him. But then she began to laugh. She giggled like a schoolgirl all the way along St Giles.

John was determined, after that first conversation with Anna, that the acquaintance should continue. He didn't know precisely why. Obviously, there was no possibility of any sort of close relationship with her. But there was something about Anna Lawrence which made it more satisfactory to be walking along the Banbury Road with her, carrying her bag for her, than lying in the arms of any other woman in England could possibly have been. And surely even her terrible old father couldn't object to a chap being chivalrous?

A couple of weeks went by. John began to address Anna by her Christian name without first asking her permission, for he was certain that it would have been flatly refused. 'I don't think that would be appropriate, Mr Harley,' he could hear her saying, in that rather over precise, clear voice of hers. He thought of her as Anna, he dreamed about her as Anna. She wasn't Miss Lawrence to him any more.

It became a regular arrangement, after those first few walks together, that John and Anna should finish work for the day at about five and that he should accompany her as far as the Summertown house, stopping a few doors away from Anna's home. As the weather grew warmer, John grew braver. 'We ought to have a walk around the Parks at lunchtime, you know,' he remarked one fine May afternoon. 'Get some fresh air.'

Anna agreed. This was something she did occasionally anyway and it was pleasant to have the company of this lively, good-looking student, who had such a disrespect for almost everything which was precious to her but who, inexplicably, did not offend her.

And, despite his professed distaste for studying, John Harley was becoming more learned by the day. Quite unconsciously,

Anna had either shamed or beguiled him into taking some interest in his books.

At first, he had found the idea of anyone voluntarily reading, let alone translating any of the classical authors, totally incomprehensible. But then he discovered that Anna's own enthusiasm inspired him — just a little. He found he was unselfconsciously discussing his own work with her, and that he was impressed by her understanding. 'You're much more interesting than old Turner,' he remarked. 'I do begin to see what you find so fascinating about it all. But I'll never be a scholar like you. I'm much too stupid.'

'Yes,' she'd agreed, laughing. 'Indeed you are!'

He'd bridled at that. 'It's all very well for you,' he'd retorted, crossly, pulling at a blade of grass at his feet and flicking the seedhead across the ground. 'I expect your idea of a little light reading is a few books of the *Iliad*; and I'm sure you and your father speak Latin to each other at home!'

'Of course we don't!' She looked at him, sprawled on the grass at her feet, and moved along the park bench a little. 'Come and sit here by me,' she invited. 'Don't loll there on the ground like a schoolboy. Now, here's what I think you ought to do this afternoon. Would you like to write out a couple of exercises for me, and I'll correct them?'

He did not reply, so she nudged him with her foot. The contact sent an electric current surging through his body, tingling along his spine and across his shoulders. 'Come along,' he heard her say. 'Your examinations are next month, and you've three years of wasted time to make up for!'

'You're so hard on me, Anna!' John was still trembling from the effect of that first touch; he felt that if he tried to get to his feet, his legs might well buckle under him. 'Can't we stay here for another half-hour?'

'*You* may, if you wish.' She got up from the bench and walked towards the park gates, while John looked after her, thinking what a lovely creature she was and wondering how on earth he was going to convince her that he was the only man in the world for her.

'I think your mother may be pleasantly surprised,' remarked Anna a few days later, as she handed him a folder of the work which she'd looked over for him. 'You're not as backward as you pretend to be, are you?'

He laughed. 'You think I may get a decent degree, then?'

'Oh, yes, of course you will.' Anna looked at him quizzically. 'Why is your mother so concerned about it, anyway?' she asked. 'And what does your father have to say?'

'My mother's a widow,' he replied. 'My father was killed in a riding accident when I was about three. I don't remember him at all. My mother's always tried to be both father and mother to my sister and me. She's attempted the impossible, I'm afraid.'

Anna nodded. 'I see,' she said. 'I suppose you've been indulged from your cradle?'

John laughed. 'I've been spoiled to death,' he admitted. 'That's obvious, isn't it? Do you know, I was never beaten until I went to school. So, anyway — when my mother asked me to take a classics degree, I agreed, to please her.'

'Do you love her very much?'

'Oh, yes — I do! She's adored me and petted me, let me have my own way in almost everything. How could I not love her?'

It was John who first pointed out that Anna was short-sighted. 'I'll have to move from that corner of the library,' she remarked one day. 'I can't read the clock from there, and I haven't a watch of my own.'

'You should be able to see the clock quite clearly,' said John. He pointed across the street. 'Look over there,' he added. 'Tell me what's written on that placard in Blackwell's window.'

'Blackwell's? I can't read anything from that far away!' she snapped crossly.

'"Mr Alfred Gough Lewis, Reader in Law at the University of Edinburgh, will be giving a public lecture at the Sheldonian Theatre on Tuesday, September" — I can't read the date — "at four o'clock. He will present" — shall I go on? You need spectacles, Anna!'

'I don't!' She looked at him, stricken. 'My eyesight's perfect!'

'You're just a little near-sighted,' he replied kindly. 'If you had spectacles, you'd find the world a far more interesting place!' He grinned. 'Tell me, Anna — is my hair black, fair or ginger?'

'Don't tease me!' Anna glared at him. 'I won't wear spectacles!' she cried. 'I'd look an absolute fright!'

'You could never look anything but lovely. And you'd be able to see all the things you're missing now. Just imagine it!'

Gradually, the idea of wearing spectacles became slightly less awful to her. John had told Anna that she could never look anything but lovely, and she found that his opinion mattered to her. Before she'd met him, no power on earth would have induced her to disfigure her face with the things.

Then he began to criticize her clothes, and he got away with that, too. 'You look so nice in blue, you should wear it more often,' he remarked.

'What concern is it of yours?' she asked sharply.

He had smiled at her, affable as always. 'None at all, my dear Miss Lawrence,' he admitted. 'But I am a judge of fashion, you see. I have experience of advising ladies. My sister is about your height, she has your colouring — and she sometimes listens to me when I remark on her clothes. So I am insolent enough to imagine that I can instruct you, as well.'

'Perhaps Miss Harley asks for your opinion?' asked Anna coldly.

'Oh, hardly ever. But I give it, all the same; and she often takes my advice. Anna, look in your glass when you get home; see how well that blue and white print becomes you. Then compare it with the maroon stripe you wore yesterday, and you'll appreciate what I mean.'

'I had no idea that I was being so closely observed! But in any case I shall still wear what I please.'

'Promise me you'll look in the mirror later? You'll understand what I'm talking about, I'm sure.'

'I doubt if I shall.'

'Oh, you will! You'll see how ravishing you are in blue and your vanity won't allow you to wear any other colour again! And so your mother's favourite charity will benefit when you throw away all your pinks, browns and greens. I shall be a universal benefactor, you see; and all sorts of people will benefit from my good taste!'

Anna stared at him for a second, then burst out laughing. 'You're preposterous!' she cried. 'You're the most offensive undergraduate in the whole university!'

'Am I?' He shrugged. 'Well — perhaps you're right about that.'

Anna had, for the past few days now, been taking John's arm as he and she walked around the Parks together. It felt perfectly natural to allow her hand to lie comfortably upon his sleeve. It also seemed natural to stroll in and out of the shade of the green willow trees which grew in clumps along the river bank. Then, one afternoon, as they'd walked beneath the enveloping branches of a tree growing by the river bridge, John had covered Anna's hand with his — and held it.

Anna had never before touched the hand of a man of her own age. The sensation was akin to receiving a succession of mild electric shocks. Indeed, she almost expected her hair to prickle away from her scalp.

John, having caught her hand, held it too tightly for her to struggle free. And he stopped walking, obliging her to stand still as well.

'Anna?'

Her heart banging against her ribs, Anna looked at him defiantly. 'What is it?' she demanded almost rudely.

'Why are you always so sharp?' he asked 'Why are you afraid of me?'

'Afraid of you?' She stared. 'I'm not afraid of you! Whatever makes you think that? Anyway — it's you who's afraid of me.'

'Oh, certainly I am.' John's light eyes looked solemnly into Anna's dark ones. 'Oh, yes, Miss Lawrence,' he agreed. 'I'm afraid of you! I'm afraid of your cleverness, of your beauty, of your reputation. And your father scares the living daylights out of me; I'm shaking now at the idea of being summoned to his room and being lashed by that awful sarcastic tongue of his! Because what I'm about to do will probably warrant a dressing down from him. And it's quite possible that I'll be asked to leave the university altogether.'

Anna was astonished. 'What do you intend to do?' she asked, her voice hardly a whisper.

He replied by repeating his original question. 'Why are you afraid of me, Anna? You're frightened now — you're shaking with terror.'

'I'm not! Don't be so silly! Come along — we ought to go now! I want to get back to the library.'

'And I want to kiss you.'

'*What*? You can't do that! You mustn't — this is a public park!'

'That doesn't matter. And if we were in the middle of Trafalgar Square, it still wouldn't matter. Anna, come here.'

'No!'

But her hand was still imprisoned in his, and she could not escape. And now John Harley leaned over her and kissed her on the mouth.

He had stood back from her almost as soon as he had touched her lips with his. Blushing very red in the way in which fair-skinned people often do, he shook his head. 'I've wanted to do that for such a long time,' he murmured. And then Anna was in his arms while he held her close to him, while he kissed her so hard that he left her breathless and fainting. She was obliged to put her arms around his neck, if only to prevent herself from sinking on to the ground.

'You can breathe at the same time, you know,' he said, relaxing his hold on her a little. He touched her face, and smiled. 'May I kiss you again?' he asked.

Anna blushed as red as he had. It didn't seem decent to say, 'Oh, yes — please do!' But, perhaps fortunately for Anna's self-respect, John did not wait for an answer. He assumed that her silence gave consent.

Anna had always imagined that all kisses were either of the wet and horrible variety — nasty, stickily unwelcome slobbers such as Anthony and Dora offered — or that they were the dry, dusty pecks of affection one received from one's parents.

But John's kisses were quite different. His mouth felt hard and dry, yet soft and gentle as well. He tasted of tobacco and the mintiness of tooth powder, an altogether intoxicating combination. And the sensation of having his mouth on hers was so absolutely delightful that Anna never wanted him to stop kissing her …

Having believed all her life that only harlots positively enjoyed being in a man's embrace, Anna was dismayed to find that she was enjoying being kissed and she was even more alarmed to discover that she was, of all things, actually kissing this man back. 'There,' he was saying, a minute later, 'you can do it now, Anna. What a responsive pupil you are!'

She laid her head upon his shoulder and felt his hand stroke her hair. 'We really ought to get back to the library,' she said. 'It must be long past two.'

'Can't we spend the afternoon on the river instead?'

'No.' She looked up into his eyes. 'No, we can't. You must do as I say — for a change!' And she walked away from him, striding across the grass without a backward glance.

Anna, good at keeping secrets, kept her happiness to herself, locked inside her heart. She looked lovely that summer. Stephen, preparing for a lecture tour, noticed that she looked different in some way; and asked her if there was anything she wanted to talk to him about.

'Nothing,' she said. 'Why do you ask?'

'It's just that you look — I don't know how to describe it. Happy, but more than happy.' He eyed her narrowly. 'Smug, perhaps?'

Anna laughed. 'Of course I'm smug! Why shouldn't I be? I've just had another article accepted, Mr Liebermann liked my last four translations. I'm almost famous!'

'Hmm.' Stephen nodded, not convinced.

Dorcas, being pregnant, had no time for Anna. She spent most of her time resting, or making a pretence of listening to Dora read; for the child's latest governess had recently given notice and was taking some holiday due to her. As for Anthony, he was now far too advanced in his studies to be a fit pupil for the average governess and, since his father did not have the time to teach him, he would be going to school in September. He seemed pleased to be leaving home, which grieved his mother. She hoped her son would be happy at school — she had heard some dreadful stories about those places …

But Stephen informed Dorcas that Anthony was well able to take care of himself and that she was not to worry about him. 'He and Dora can have the summer to themselves,' he announced. 'I'll find her a new governess for the autumn.'

This news delighted Dora, who, though clever enough, was too volatile to want to do anything as static as studying. She still preferred a riotous game of chase to anything else, and she wore Fanny Lewson out.

Weekends, when John and Anna could not meet, became intolerable to them both. Anna considered if she might invite him to her home.

Almost as soon as she'd thought of it, however, she rejected that idea. Her father would frighten him away for good or, if Stephen didn't terrify him, Dorcas would embarrass him. She would fall over herself trying to be hospitable, she'd hover around him pressing him to have more tea, more cake — and John would immediately see that the supposed Mrs Lawrence was not a lady. Her accent still gave her origins away.

'Why does he glower so?' Anna stared critically at her father, who was sitting at the breakfast table, grimacing at an article he was scanning; she wondered why he insisted on reading while he ate. It was, after all, very anti-social of him. Then she looked at her mother, now gross and swollen in her sixth or seventh month of pregnancy. She wished Dorcas would stop wearing all those horrible Pre-Raphaelite curtains! And her long hair was, as usual, loose. It hung untidily down her back, looped up with one of Dora's ribbons. After the baby was born, Anna decided, she would take her mother in hand. Then she might allow John to meet her.

In spite of time taken off for afternoons walks with Anna, John was fairly well prepared for his examinations, and would now probably get a creditable degree. One warm day he announced that it was much too hot to spend the afternoon cooped up in the library, and he told Anna that he was going on the river. 'And you're coming with me,' he added firmly. 'You need an afternoon away from your books.'

'Do I?'

'Yes.' He grinned at her. 'And, as for me, I'll work tonight,' he continued, seeing that she was about to refuse. 'Set me some work and I'll do it, on my honour I shall! Oh, Anna — it's such a lovely afternoon, and it's my last summer here! I spent all the other two on the river, but *this* year I haven't had a boat out at all. Oh, don't look at me like that! Don't be so severe!'

'We can't spare any time for idling.' Anna folded her arms and looked hard at him. 'Or, at any rate, you can't. You're still hopelessly behind in your work, you know.'

Her sharpness only made him grin even more broadly. 'Anna, that's for me to worry about, isn't it?' he asked airily. 'Oh, why won't you pity me a little? I'm not clever like you. You're perfectly well aware that I have no brains at all. Won't you indulge my whim, just this once? Or think of it as necessary recreation? If I try to absorb any more, my head will split.'

She shook her head at him. 'You're one of the laziest people I've ever met.'

'I know that.' Seeing that she was weakening now, John laid his hand on her sleeve. 'Come on, Anna. I can get a punt down at Magdalen Bridge if we hurry.'

'Well — I suppose a few hours won't make very much difference.' She looked at him sharply. 'Are you a good waterman?' she asked suspiciously.

'Of course I am! I've had plenty of practice, after all! There's nothing to be frightened of,' he added, seeing her frown. 'Provided you can swim.'

'I'm a very good swimmer, as it happens,' she retorted.

'Of course you are,' he agreed. 'You can do everything, can't you?'

They floated slowly upstream, between willow-fringed banks. They drifted under bridges, then shot along the wider stretches of the river until the boat came to rest, quite by accident, beneath the shade of one of the many conveniently over-hanging trees.

John tied up the boat and went to sit beside Anna; he took her in his arms. He kissed her, and realized with some satisfaction that she was kissing him back. But he hated the tight sleeves which bound her arms right down to the elbows, loathed the high lace collar which hid her neck, and wondered why she bothered to wear such a vile garment as the horrible whalebone corset which was now sticking into his chest.

Anna wondered why he didn't slide his hand inside the back of her blouse. If he were to undo the top button, he could touch her neck and shoulders — why didn't he? She couldn't suggest it, of course. And, suddenly, she noticed that he wasn't kissing her any more.

She opened her eyes and looked at him. His thick, fair hair, bleached flaxen by the sun after a few weeks of warm weather, made his face look darker than it was; and his narrow grey eyes were pale in the bright afternoon sunlight. She thought how good-looking he was, was about to lean over and kiss him again ...

'Oh, this is stupid!' Irritably, John reached for his jacket, took out a packet of cigarettes and lit one. 'We can't continue like this,' he added, blowing smoke into the air and frowning at her.

'Whatever do you mean?' Anna stared at him, baffled.

'You must know what I mean.' He bit his lip and scowled at her. 'You're making me mad — you know you are.'

'Oh, I'm *so* sorry!' Offended, she sat up straight and stared into the tree above her. 'I didn't ask you to bring me here, did I?'

'Oh, God, Anna! Don't be like that!' He threw the cigarette into the water and buried his face in his hands. 'Haven't you ever been in love?' he muttered.

Anna considered. 'I don't know about that,' she replied guardedly. 'But I am very fond of someone ...'

'Are you really?' John sniffed. 'And of whom are you very fond, eh?'

'Don't be silly, John,' she replied sharply. 'It's obvious, surely?'

'It's not obvious at all. You're so stiff and formal, Miss Lawrence, that it's impossible to guess what you think.'

He looked so miserable that Anna began to wonder if this wasn't a game after all. 'Do I have to spell it out to you, then?' she asked, rather more gently.

He continued to scowl at her. 'Yes, you do,' he said, sulkily. 'Spell it out, make it perfectly clear to me. Say to me, "John Harley, I love you". Like that. I need to be told simply, you see. I'm not clever like you, as you're well aware.'

Anna burst out laughing. 'Oh, you poor dunce!' she giggled. 'Very well, then — John Harley, I don't just love you, I adore you. I know every feature of your face as well as I know my own — I keep a picture of you in my heart. Do you understand me now? Why don't you kiss me again? Don't you want to?'

He pushed her so hard that she fell over on to her back, flat upon the cushions in the bottom of the boat. '*You're* allowed to kiss *me* !' he cried, leaning over her and taking her by the shoulders. He shook her, loosening her hairpins so that her hair began to work its way out of its braids and was eventually lying loose upon the cushions, a dark cloud framing her face. 'Why do I have to do all the work?' he demanded. 'Please, dearest Anna, kiss me; and tell me that you love me!'

'I love you.' Anna wrapped her arms around his neck and kissed his cheek. She hugged him as close to her as whalebone and stiffening would allow. 'I love you, I love you, I love you.'

'Good.' Smiling down at her, John took Anna's face between her hands, and kissed her mouth. 'I thought that perhaps you did.'

But then he was serious again. He lay next to her, his face buried in her black hair. 'I think you're a sorceress,' he murmured. 'A changeling. A witch!'

It became Anna's waking nightmare that John Harley, who evidently came from the most upper of upper-middle-class backgrounds, should discover the circumstances of her birth. She could imagine his mother, a stout, puritanical widow, still clad in her mourning black or purple, ordering him to have nothing more to do with a girl like Anna. She was insecure enough to believe that he would obey his mother, to imagine that his financial security would be far more important to him than she was.

So John was not invited to the Summertown house; and it did not occur to Anna to wonder why he hardly ever mentioned his own family. It never crossed her mind that his mother and sister might not be the paragons of respectability she imagined.

One does not casually seduce the daughter of a senior classics don. But by now, John had reached the stage when he felt he had to sleep with Anna or go mad. The desire to take her to bed was not however how he explained his feelings to himself.

'You must marry me,' he said, as they walked up the Banbury Road together one early evening, a week before John's final examinations.

'Must?'

'Must.' John was in no mood for repartee. 'Anna, you must say you'll marry me — now — or tell me that you won't. Then I can begin to plan the rest of my life. It you refuse me, I shall see you to your house; then I'll go and enlist for India. Or something.'

'And if I accept you?'

'Which you do, don't you?'

'I must talk to my father about it.'

'Your father?' Panic filled John's eyes. 'Oh, God,' he muttered. 'Don't do that! Or at least not until I've taken my finals — perhaps not even then.'

He shuddered. 'I hadn't thought about meeting your father,' he went on. 'You know I can't be the sort of man he has in mind for you. He's bound to forbid you to see me again when he knows who I am. He'll glare and he'll frown and he'll have me thrown out of the house!'

Anna stopped walking. 'Don't be so silly!' she said, sharply. 'You've never even met him — you don't know what he's like! If he knows I love you, he'll be pleasant to you for my sake. Come and meet him one day. We could go to his rooms in college.' And then you won't see my mother, added Anna, to herself.

'I couldn't do that. Honestly, Anna, I'd make a complete fool of myself, and he'd forbid you to have anything more to do with me. Oh, I know I'll have to meet him sometime, but ...' He laughed ruefully. 'I'll have to prepare myself first. Stuff my head with facts, you know!'

Anna shook her head. 'You're being very stupid,' she said. 'He's a very kind man — gentle, even.'

'*Gentle? Him?*' John gave a snort of derisive laughter. 'Nonsense,' he said. He held out his hand and made it shake uncontrollably. 'You see that?' he demanded. 'That's what an hour with your father can do to a tutorial student. Believe me, it's true — I've seen men come back to college after a session with him, who've needed half a bottle of brandy before they're fit for anything. And you expect me to march into his room and ask if I can marry his daughter.'

'Well, I'm very like him and you're not afraid of me.'

'Yes, I am! Well; I was. Until I found that there were some chinks in your armour.'

'All the same, there's no need to be afraid of my father. Close to, he's quite human. Remember you've only seen him from a distance, at lectures.'

'Lectures.' John grimaced again. 'Another word for torture where he's concerned.'

'Whatever do you mean? I'd have thought he was quite a good speaker!'

'Oh, he is. Your father is just about the best lecturer in the university but the trouble is, he knows it, and he expects his audiences to appreciate him.'

'What's wrong with that?'

'Nothing, I suppose. But he's nerve-racking. He always waits for complete silence before he starts to speak and, once he's begun, he expects us to keep as still as little mice. There's to be no sound from us but the reverent scratch of pens taking down the great man's immortal utterance.

'Listen, I'll tell you something. During my first year, I had a friend at Oriel. And, one day, he happened to whisper something to me while your father was talking. And your father noticed.'

'And?' Anna grinned. 'What happened?'

'Well, your father stopped in mid-sentence. "You find my remarks tedious, sir?" he asked. My friend went quite pale. "No, sir," he said. "Not at all." So then your father said, "Your good manners do you credit. But I'm afraid that I'm boring you all." And he looked round at the rest of us, smiling that horrible sarcastic smile of his. Nobody even breathed.'

Anna was in fits of giggles now. 'And then what?'

John grimaced. '"Perhaps you would like to come and continue this lecture yourself?" your father asked. "Come, sir — don't be over-modest."'

'And?'

'Well — my friend looked a bit sheepish. But your father still had those awful eyes of his fixed on poor Henry, who went down to the lecturer's desk and did as he was told. Or tried to. Your father sat down and wrapped his gown around him. "You can use my scribbled notes if you like," he said. Anna — it was like watching a public execution.'

'More like a circus, I'd say!' Anna laughed out loud. 'It sounds hilarious,' she giggled. 'I do wish I'd been there! Oh, really, John — he was only teasing you! He must have been astonished when your friend actually did try to continue the lecture! I've heard that during Mr Archbold's lectures people eat sandwiches and read the newspapers!'

'Well, they wouldn't try that in Dr Lawrence's lectures, that's all I can say.'

For a while they walked along in silence. 'Have you told your mother that you wish to become engaged?' asked Anna eventually.

'No, not yet. That's another problem. She's got some awful sporty girl in mind for me. You know the sort, wild hair, buck teeth, freckles. Her father's the local MFH, and there's a big estate in Northamptonshire. I can't bear her. Anna: I want to marry you.'

Anna made up her mind. 'Then we'll run away and you can do just that,' she said. 'We'll go and get married without anyone knowing, all by ourselves.'

'We'll do what? Why?'

'Because if we go away together and come back married, nobody will be able to do anything about it, will they? When we get back again, they'll just have to accept it.'

John frowned, as if considering, but then he smiled. 'Anna,' he said, 'you're a genius. It's a marvellous idea! When shall we go?'

'After your exams.'

John giggled. 'To Scotland?'

'Oh, I think so. We might as well be as vulgar as possible, mightn't we?'

'Yes!' John laughed out loud. 'We'll elope!' he cried, grinning all over his face. 'Oh, Anna, you're brilliant! Brilliant!'

Anna was surprised at herself for suggesting such a thing. But she was finding life at home intolerable. Her father, the only rational member of the family, would be going on a lecture tour soon so she would have no one sensible to talk to for four weeks or more. Anna decided that, while Stephen was away, she and John could go

But then, after her father had gone, Anna had received the shock of her life, for she had learned of Daniel Hitchman's conviction for murder. For a week, she had been almost frantic with shock and despair.

Added to that, her two little siblings were driving her mad. Soon another little howler would add to the noise and disorder. Anna felt that if she stayed at home any longer she might well go mad.

John noticed her abstraction, and asked what wrong. 'Nothing,' she'd replied, feeling that it was out of the question to discuss Daniel with him — yet. 'I want to be married,' she said, which was true enough. 'I want to be your wife.'

'I want that, too.' John glanced around him to check that the street along which they were walking was deserted, and kissed her. 'Now that I've taken my exams, I can't think of anything else. When can we go?'

'Soon.' Anna nodded her head. 'Soon.'

John Harley had sat his final examinations in that mood of heightened perception which sexual frustration sometimes engenders in the young. He was fairly certain, as he handed in the last paper, that he'd done quite well. Now he and Anna had nothing to do but lie in the bottom of a boat and kiss each other — and, when doing that became too fraught for both of them, to talk, and plot. 'We'll go in July,' John had said. 'It's dead here then. I'll tell my mother I'm going to visit a chap in Yorkshire.'

But July brought such a crop of calamities that Anna could not steel herself to go, leaving Anthony ill and her mother alone. And, although her brother recovered, and her father came home, Dorcas then lost her baby. 'They're doing all this to spite me,' thought Anna. Gritting her teeth, she wondered what was coming next.

But then, thankfully, her mother seemed to be regaining her strength. Her father took up residence in Dorcas' bedroom, and hardly spoke to his elder daughter for the next week or so. It seemed a good time to leave.

One morning in late August, Anna packed a small valise. She paid a boy to carry a trunk to the station for her, telling the housemaid that it contained some books which her father was sending to London; and praying hard that Stephen would not hear of it. At midday she set off for the station, to meet John.

'He'll hardly notice I'm missing,' she told herself, stifling her conscience with a ruthlessness of which she was quite proud. 'Ever since he came back from Edinburgh, he's spent every waking moment with *her* — he's only spoken to me to find fault!' She lay back in the cab and smiled to herself. 'And in any case,' she thought, 'I'll be back in a few days' time. He won't even realize that I've been away.'

Chapter Eighteen

WHEN STEPHEN HAD FINISHED READING over the newspaper articles which particularly interested him, and when he realized that he had not seen his daughter all day, he became rather worried. Then very worried.

He summoned Fanny Lewson to his study. 'Miss Lewson,' he said, his concern for Anna coupled with his own extreme weariness making him even curter with her than he usually was, 'do you know where Anna is? Did she say anything to you about going out for the day?'

'Miss Lawrence doesn't confide in *me*, sir!' Fanny gave an injured sniff and began to search her pockets for a handkerchief. 'And in any case, Dr Lawrence, I've had no time to talk to your daughter. I've had my hands full trying to keep Miss Dora occupied, and in seeing to the cook, and in looking after the house. I've had to think about a dozen things which nobody ever considers — that is, unless they *aren't* done!' Feeling ill-used and unappreciated, she began to cry noisily into her handkerchief.

'Oh, don't make that horrible noise!' Stephen frowned at her, but more in anxiety than irritation. 'Look — ah — you'd better go and see to Dora now, hadn't you?'

Glad to be dismissed, Fanny shot him a reproachful look; and then she scuttled away, like a frightened rabbit. She wondered to herself how on earth dear Mrs Lawrence could be so fond of such a monster.

Stephen sat down at his desk and began, idly, to scribble on a corner of his blotter. Surely Anna would not have gone away of her own accord? Not while her mother was still so weak, and her brother barely convalescent? He knew that Anna had no great love for Anthony, but nevertheless ...

Ten minutes later, he went upstairs to Dorcas' bedroom, and told her that Anna was missing. She'd opened her eyes and looked at him enquiringly but her eyes were so vacant that he could not tell whether she'd heard him or not.

'Darling, Anna's gone away somewhere,' he repeated, sitting down on the edge of her bed and taking her hand in his. 'Dorcas, did you hear what I said?'

'Yes. I heard you.' Dorcas made an effort to sit up in bed. 'I know what you said,' she continued feebly. 'Oh, I don't know where she is, Stephen — but she's out to punish me, of that I am aware.'

'Punish you? What do you mean?'

Dorcas sighed. 'She read about that man's death, you know,' she whispered. 'She knows what happened now. Oh, Stephen, it's all so difficult to explain!'

'I read about it too.'

'Did you?' Dorcas stared at him. 'Is it a national scandal then? I suppose it must be. It was reported in *The Times* — that's where Anna saw it first.' Dorcas pulled a face. 'I can't think why it was in *The Times*, can you?' she asked. 'I'm sure no one wants to read about the execution of a provincial criminal. Lift me up a little, dear — that's better.'

'What did Anna say to you?'

'Say?' Dorcas considered. 'Well — she was upset, and you know she gets herself into a state when she's annoyed. She says things she doesn't really mean. And she was very angry with me, because I didn't seem to care that he was going to die.' Dorcas grimaced. 'I didn't care!' she said, fiercely. 'I was glad! But I didn't say so to Anna.

'She didn't speak to me for the rest of the day and she's hardly said two words to me since. Perhaps she's gone to Hereford.'

Stephen frowned. He well knew that Anna had a passionate, impulsive nature; and that she might not consider the damage she could do to her family by publishing her relationship with the murderer, merely in order to clear him of one of his imputed crimes.

He considered taking the evening train to Hereford, but then he looked at the woman lying against him and knew that he couldn't possibly leave her. He would have to wait at least until morning. And Anna might have sent word of her whereabouts by then.

'You think she's definitely gone to Hereford?' he asked Dorcas.

'I don't know!' Dorcas shrugged helplessly. 'She may have done. Or perhaps she's run off with some man.'

That possibility simply hadn't crossed Stephen's mind, and he sat for a moment looking quite winded. 'D'you mean Guthrie?' he demanded incredulously. 'Dorcas, she wouldn't have —'

'No, Stephen, she wouldn't.' Dorcas attempted a reassuring smile. 'Not with that horrible little ape. She liked to talk to him and show off to him, but I'm sure she didn't like him in that way.

'But she has been behaving oddly lately. Even before that other business she was looking secretive, and I caught her giggling to herself on one occasion, which you must admit is strange ...

'And she's had some new dresses. I remember telling her recently that it was too chilly for her blue chintz, but she took no notice of me, of course. Think, Stephen. Who could it be?'

'I really don't know.' At a loss for once in his life, Stephen shrugged helplessly. 'I've no idea at all.'

'We'd better look in her desk, then. There might be something.'

Dorcas got out of bed, slid her feet into slippers and walked unsteadily along the landing to her daughter's room. 'Most of her best clothes have gone,' she observed, glancing at the disordered wardrobe. 'Is there anything in the top drawer of her desk?'

Stephen looked. 'No, nothing at all.'

'She's taken her journal, too, then.' Dorcas sighed, wearily. 'Oh, I expect she'll be back,' she murmured. 'Now I must go and lie down again. Do you think you could help me back to bed?'

Stephen picked her up in his arms and carried her back down the passage. He noticed, with some alarm, how light and insubstantial she was. Looking at her face, he saw the blue smudges under her eyes; and the hands which lay upon his shoulder were far too thin, the veins on them showing purple through the flesh. 'Damn Anna,' he thought, suddenly furious with her. How dared she upset him at a time when he had so much else to be anxious about?

'Will you have something to eat?' he asked Dorcas, as he lifted her legs on to the bed and pulled the covers over her.

'No, thank you. Don't make me have any supper tonight.' She gave him a watery smile. 'I just want to sleep. But stay with me, will you? I like to know you're here.'

Well aware that his daughter's disappearance would be general gossip in a day or two, Stephen waited until Dorcas was asleep, then he went into his deserted college and found the porter dozing at his cubby hole. 'Wake up, Timms,' he said sharply. 'I want a word with you.'

Timms came to with a start. 'Dr Lawrence, sir? Yes, sir — there's a letter for you here, come today.'

'It's not that.' Stephen let himself into the porter's lodge and sat down next to Timms. 'I want you to make a few enquiries for me,' he said. 'I wish to know if any of the students have been — ah — seen with my daughter. Walking, perhaps. Or speaking to her.'

Timms stared. 'You mean, sir —'

'Oh, I don't know what I mean!' Stephen glared at the man. 'I wish to know if one of the undergraduates here has been making a nuisance of himself, pestering Anna — do you understand me, Timms?'

Timms gulped. 'I think so, sir,' he replied, still somewhat mystified by this odd request. 'I'll see what I can do for you.'

Very little of what goes on in a university escapes the attention of the college porters. There is not a great deal to do in the long summer vacation. Timms now accepted Dr Lawrence's sovereign and said that he would ask around his brethren. 'If there's any young gentleman sweet on Miss Lawrence, sir, I'm sure I'll be able to point him out to you in due course,' he said confidently.

'I hope you can.' Stephen got up to leave.

Timms opened the door for him. 'Ah, daughters, sir!' he muttered lugubriously. He heaved a great sigh and looked sorrowfully at Stephen, one harassed father understanding the trials of another. 'Got four of 'em myself, sir; always whispering and fidgeting they are, causing their Ma and me no end of worrit. Sooner they're married off the better. Nothing but trouble, daughters!'

He pocketed the sovereign and nodded to Stephen conspiratorially. 'Don't you and your wife fret, sir,' he said. 'I'll ask around, and I'll send up a message as soon as I knows anything.'

'Thank you, Timms.'

Stephen pushed his hands into his trouser pockets and walked off down Broad Street, glowering, damning Anna to the ends of the earth. There was bound to be at least a minor scandal now — Timms could hardly be trusted to be particularly discreet in his enquiries, and when it was observed that Anna was not in Oxford, and had apparently run away from home, the Dean's wife would make as much capital out of it as she could.

He kicked a pebble across St Giles. Anna would regret the trouble she'd caused him! It had cost him very dear to ask the help of a college porter. Had Anna appeared before him just at that moment, he would have taken her by the shoulders and shaken her until her teeth rattled.

Two days went by and nothing was heard. On the third day a note, an ill-written thing scribbled by Timms on college writing paper, was brought to the Summertown house. The porter asked Dr Lawrence if he would call at the lodge; or would he like Timms to step up to the Doctor's house? For Timms had something to impart.

Stephen gave a shilling to the boy who had brought the note. 'Tell Mr Timms I'll see him in college this afternoon,' he said.

Timms had made detailed enquiries and come up with a possible solution to the mystery of Anna's disappearance. 'I had this from old Fred Forsythe, sir,' began Timms. 'He's the head porter at Magdalen, you know. He's heard that there's a chap by the name of Harley been seen a-strolling in the Parks with Miss Lawrence. That's all, sir,' he added, seeing Stephen's face grow thunderous. 'There ain't any reason to suppose there's anythin' between 'em; they've only been seen together once or twice. But I thought I ought to let you know, sir, you being so concerned.'

The porter tapped the ege of Stephen's desk. 'Fellow by the name of Harley, sir,' he repeated. 'Took his degree this summer.'

'Thank you, Timms.' Stephen pushed another sovereign across his desk. 'You've been very helpful. If you hear anything else —'

'I'll let you know at once, sir.'

Timms stumped off down the stairs and Stephen sat back in his chair, thinking. Harley. A familiar name, but not one of his tutorial students, he was sure of that. He'd have to go over to the records office and look at the man's file.

When the clerk placed John Harley's record before him, he saw that Timms had been right. The man had graduated that summer, with a better than average degree. His academic record had been totally undistinguished and his degree result the effect of a sudden panic, which had paid off rather well. Stephen turned up the young man's personal details.

As he read, the room began to close in around him. As he saw the names, it seemed to him that the clouds scudded over the sky and completely obscured the sun. As soon as he'd seen the name of John Harley's mother, he knew what had happened.

'John Randall Harley,' — yes, those had been the child's Christian names. 'Father, deceased.' Of course, she would have said that. 'Mother, Elizabeth Jane Harley, of Stanton House, Stanton St Nicholas, Oxfordshire.'

Stephen sat at the table with the open file before him, his head beginning to spin, his throat closing up as if he were being strangled, his blood turning to ice in his veins. He told himself, of course it can't be the same woman. Just because it's the same name, that doesn't mean it's her — it's merely a coincidence.

But her mother's name had been Harley. She had, he remembered now, taken a house in Oxfordshire after she'd left Ashton Cross.

Unwilling, still, to accept such a terrible possibility, Stephen leaned forwards against the desk, his left hand supporting his head, turning the pages of the file with his right. It was all there, of course it was. The birth date was correct, the personal details tallied. There might be a dozen reasons for his daughter's disappearance, he told himself. But he knew, in his heart, that she had eloped with this John Randall Harley, and was perhaps by now married to him. To her own brother — to Stephen's own son.

Fury, despair, terror. He wasn't sure which of these he felt, one or all three. Cursing and damning the God in whom he did not believe anyway, he walked home, pushed open the front door, slammed it behind him.

'You'll have to see her again now,' said the voice inside his skull. 'You've not finished with her yet, after all. You'll have to go and grovel to the witch, you'll have to beseech that woman's

287

assistance, won't you?'

Stephen ground his teeth in rage, and, reviling his wife, cursing his daughter and execrating his unknown son, he went into his study and sat down at his desk, wondering what on earth to do now.

Anna and John had taken a train to Carlisle, made their way over the border, married, and returned to England. They had booked into a hotel room in Carlisle, and they wasted no time in consummating their union. The pent-up frustrations of the past few months were being ecstatically released at about the same time as Stephen was sitting, John Harley's file open before him, in the records office.

Sitting in the train going back to Carlisle, Anna twisted the bright gold band on her finger. As she stared out of the window, she wondered what she'd let herself in for now. 'He'll be disappointed in me,' she thought miserably. 'I'll never be able to let him do — that! But he'll expect it! He'll make me do that — thing; it's why men get married, after all.'

Wondering, now, for what reason decent women got married, she looked at her new husband. He sat, relaxed and contented, on the seat facing her. 'Shall we go and have some coffee?' he asked.

She nodded stiffly. 'Very well.'

They reached Carlisle where they took a cab to a hotel. Anna was growing more terrified by the minute. As she watched her husband tip the porter and close the door behind the boy, she felt her whole body shrinking with fear and would have given anything to be back in the cool silence of the Bodleian library, in her own bedroom — anywhere but here ...

'Anna, what's the matter?' John, seeing her frowning, came over to her and untied the ribbon on her hat. 'Is anything wrong?'

'No.'

'Why so solemn, then?' He took the hat from her head and laid it on a chair. 'Won't you smile at me?'

She tried to do so but only managed a grimace which did not reach her eyes.

So John kissed her. To some extent, the familiarity of the kiss reassured her. She relaxed a little and told herself that perhaps there was nothing to dread, after all.

John took off his own coat and pushed Anna's travelling cape back from her shoulders. He felt her shudder then and so he put his arms around her, held her close to him as if she'd been a child to be comforted, rather than a wife to whom he was about to make love. 'It's new to me, as well,' he murmured, into her hair. 'I'm just as scared as you are!'

'What?' In amazement, Anna stared up at him. 'You've never —'

'No, I've never.'

'I thought all normal men did!'

'Did you indeed?' John laughed at her. 'Well, darling, I suppose all normal men like to kiss girls in boats on rivers; and all normal men try to get as far as they can inside that armour plating in which you women wrap yourselves. But I don't think it's a universal law that all normal men go to their marriage beds as fully fledged seducers.' He slid his hand inside the back of Anna's dress, and tugged at a ribbon he found there.

'That doesn't untie,' she said.

'What?' He gave another pull, and frowned at her.

'I said, that doesn't untie. It's just for decoration.'

'Oh.'

Anna directed him to another ribbon. 'Try this one.'

Five minutes and a great deal of kissing later, Anna was out of her dress.

'You do something as well, now!' John took her hands and laid them on his chest. 'Make a start on my buttons while I try to make sense of all this damned underclothing of yours. I never realized women wore so much! What's it all *for*?'

By this time, Anna had relaxed completely. 'Decency's sake,' she replied, giggling.

'Oh, damn decency! Please, Anna — take all this horrible stuff off!'

So Anna did, discarding her voluminous undergarments as unconcernedly as if she undressed in front of a man every day.

'Was that all right?' asked John, half an hour later. 'Did it hurt you?'

'Yes.' Anna smiled up at him. 'Yes, it hurt a bit. But I could tell you were trying to be careful, so I didn't mind it. I liked it, even,' she added. 'I really did.'

'Did you? Honestly?'

'Honestly.' Anna blushed. 'But perhaps I shouldn't have told you that.'

'Why not?'

'Well — women aren't supposed —'

'Oh, rubbish!' John laughed out loud. 'By that, I assume you mean that *I'm* supposed to be an insatiable lecher, and *you're* intended to be the mere passive vessel for my lust?'

'I didn't mean that at all!'

'Liar.'

'Well —' Anna shook her head, and laughed. 'You think it's all right for a woman to enjoy it?'

'Well, I'd hate to force myself on one who loathed it!' John pushed the bedclothes back and studied his wife. 'Your skin is golden,' he observed. 'It's absolutely beautiful, it seems to be dusted all over with little golden specks. Anna, you're beautiful.'

Anna sat up and put her arms around his neck. 'I love you,' she said. 'You don't know what you do to me! It was wonderful.'

'Was it?' He kissed her and suddenly his face became serious. 'Yes, it was. Oh, Anna — it was!'

He lay down next to her then, yawned, pulled Anna into his embrace and fell asleep almost at once.

Anna ran her index finger down his spine, and smiled when he stirred slightly and muttered something unintelligible. She studied his face, noticing how the hairs of his eyebrows grew in such a neat, fine line, how his lashes were dark although his hair was so blond and had so many different colours in it, giving an overall impression of gold. His skin was many degrees fairer than hers, white on his back and shoulders, almost translucent on his neck and inner arms where the blue veins showed through it, making him look so very vulnerable.

She put her hand inside his, and pulled the bedclothes over them both. Curled around him, she slept herself, perfectly contented to be lying next to him.

They stayed in Carlisle, an uninteresting town dismal in the August downpours, for three days. They spent much of their time in bed, retiring there ridiculously early and getting up far too late for breakfast.

John was particularly fascinated by Anna's long, blue-black hair, which he played with endlessly, plaited and unplaited, and liked to brush, sweeping through the thick, heavy tresses with firm, hard strokes. 'It's so long — three feet at least,' he remarked one morning. 'Have you ever had it cut?'

'No, never. I have the fringe trimmed, of course, but otherwise not.'

'I wondered if you could sit on it.'

'Oh, I see. That's why you married me, is it?'

'Yes, of course — what other reason would I have?'

She caught his hand and wrenched the hairbrush out of it, threw it on the bed behind her. 'There must have been something more?' she asked.

'No, I don't think so. Unless —' John slid his hands down her neck, across her shoulders. 'Come back to bed,' he murmured.

'Why?'

'You know why. Come and make love to me.' He flopped backwards on to the bed and held out his arms to her.

Such a direct invitation was impossible to resist. Anna stood up, pulled her nightdress over her head and let herself fall into her husband's embrace; she spent the following half hour doing just what he'd asked her to do. She kissed him just as passionately as he kissed her, she covered his face with her kisses. 'Do you want to eat me?' he asked, laughing.

'Yes!' Anna pushed his head back on to the pillow, stared at him fiercely, baring her teeth. 'Yes, I think I shall do just that!' And she kissed him again, a long, slow, lingering kiss which began at his jawline and ended on his forehead.

He lifted her away from him then, and rolled her on to her back. 'I want you!' he said, his eyes huge with desire. 'Oh, God, Anna — I want you! Now!'

And Anna wrapped her arms around him, pulling him close to her; she felt again the familiar electric charge go through her, as his body was joined to hers. She heard herself sob with the need of him, heard herself saying his name, over and over again. She'd shed the inhibitions and misconceptions of years as easily as she'd shed her restricting corsets and tightly-laced dresses.

'Perfect,' he remarked later, as he traced a line around Anna's shoulders, down her chest, and let his hand lie comfortably on her stomach. 'You're perfect, Anna.'

'How can you tell?' Anna laughed. 'How many other women have you seen naked?'

'None at all. But I've seen the woman I wanted in my mind's eye and you're my ideal, made flesh and blood. So I know you're perfect, don't I? Darling, come and lie on me, keep me warm.'

'I think we ought to get up. It's gone nine.'

'There's nothing to get up for.' John pulled Anna across him, wrapped his arms around her and held her there. 'I'm going to persuade my mother to let us have a house of hers,' he announced. 'It's in the Midlands, near Worcester — it's very pretty, and I'm sure you'll like it. There are a few acres of land with it so we can keep cows or something.'

'Cows?' Anna tickled his face with a lock of her hair. 'You don't know anything about cows, do you?'

'No, nothing at all. Which is probably about as much as you know, so there.'

'*I* am a farmer's daughter!' Anna retorted. 'So there yourself!'

'Are you?' John laughed at her. 'I didn't know the old tartar had a few rolling acres tucked away somewhere.'

'You're not to speak about my father like that! You're not among your half-witted college friends now!'

'No, I'm not, am I?' John grinned up at his wife. 'Sorry, Mrs Harley. I'm going to have to learn to love the old fellow now, aren't I? What a ghastly prospect! Anyway,' he added, 'this house will be mine when I'm twenty-five, so I don't suppose my mother will mind if we live there now. And we'll travel, shall we? We'll go to America, would you like that?

Again the vision of a bombazined old woman rose before Anna's eyes. 'You don't think your mother will be too annoyed with you?' she asked.

'She'll probably be a little put out at first.' John smiled reassuringly. 'But when she sees you, she's bound to love you as much as I do. And I'm sure you'll like my sister. She's a bit stupid, as all girls are — except you, of course, don't glare at me like that — but she's fairly amiable. Don't worry about my family.'

Anna lay awake much of the following night, considering what she had done; and would now have to do. John had to be told all

292

about her early life; nothing could be left out. She realized, too, that she really ought to send a telegram to her father. For the first time in days she thought about him, understood how much he'd have been worrying about her; and she felt a terrible pang of guilt about what she'd done.

'I think,' she said, as they lay in bed together the following morning, 'that we really must go back to Oxford. Today.'

John sat up and rubbed his face. 'Very well,' he agreed. 'I'm going to have to explain myself to the old — to your father — sooner or later.' He grinned ruefully.

Anna did not smile. 'He'll be very angry, you know,' she said dismally. 'He'll be rude to you and he'll shout at me. We'll go back on the eleven o'clock train,' she continued. 'And get it over with.'

'Darling, it won't be as bad as that.'

'Yes, it will.' Anna sighed. 'We'll confront him together — he can't kill us both, can he?'

'Cheer up, Anna. He might even like me.'

Anna had been expecting an unpleasant scene, but nothing had prepared her for the expression on her father's face that summer evening when she walked back into the Summertown house. Defiantly hand in hand with John Harley, she was ready to justify herself and ask to be forgiven so that life could go on again, just as before.

She looked again at Stephen, and felt her legs weakening. Her prepared speech died on her lips.

He wasn't just angry. The expression on his face wasn't the one which he assumed when Dora had scribbled on some of his notes, when someone in college had upset him, when a publisher had mangled one of his manuscripts — all things which were guaranteed to put him in a foul temper for days, to be cajoled out of his ill humour by Doreas when she thought fit. Now he looked truly frightening. Furious, yes — but stricken, drawn and extraordinarily weary as well.

'Is my mother better?' asked Anna nervously.

'Your mother? She seems to be getting stronger, I think. Well, Anna — and Mr Harley, would it be?'

'Yes, Papa. I — we —'

'Go upstairs to your mother, Anna.' Stephen's tone was mild enough, but the look in his eyes told Anna that if she argued now, he would certainly lose his temper. 'Mr Harley — come with me.'

Stephen pushed open the door of his study and went in. John, flashing Anna a fleeting smile followed by a pantomimed imitation of a condemned criminal, shrugged and followed him. Stephen closed the door firmly behind them. Anna, left alone in the hall, took off her outdoor things and went upstairs.

Scared as he now was, feeling that a lion's cage might be preferable to this terrible old man's study, John prepared himself to face an explosion of righteous wrath from an outraged father.

He had decided what to do. He'd let the old man rant and rave and then he'd simply tell Dr Lawrence that he'd fallen in love with Anna; that he had behaved honourably towards her — and that he was very sorry for all the worry that her disappearance must have caused her parents. He intended to dwell on his future prospects, which were excellent.

He looked across the desk at the older man, and decided that, divested of his gown and smart black tail coat — for Dr Lawrence, without a jacket, had received his visitor in shirt sleeves — the chap wasn't quite so terrifying at close quarters. He was simply a rather tired-looking middle-aged usher, a fellow who spent his life pushing useless information into students' reluctant heads. John was about to begin his speech when Stephen asked him, 'Are you and my daughter married?'

'Yes, indeed, sir — we are.' John tried to look contrite, earnest and responsible, all at the same time. 'We are married — and, sir, I can assure you that before we became man and wife, nothing improper —'

'Had passed between you. I daresay not.' Stephen rubbed his tired eyes. 'Oh, I don't accuse you of abduction, seduction or anything like that,' he went on drearily. 'I merely needed to know how things stood between you.' He picked up an envelope and slid it across the desk towards John. 'You recognize the writing?' he asked.

John saw his own name scrawled across the paper. So that was it; there had been some contact between Anna's parents and his mother. It wouldn't have been too difficut for Dr Lawrence to find out if his daughter had been seen with a young man; and then to put the pieces of the jigsaw together. He felt something like relief.

'Yes, it's my mother's hand,' he replied brightly. 'Have you met her, sir?'

'I've met her.' Stephen grimaced. 'You'd better read what she has to tell you. And I think you should prepare yourself for a shock.'

John unfastened the envelope, unfolded the single sheet of paper inside and began to read, thinking that Anna's father was making rather more of a melodrama out of all this than was really called for.

Stephen rose to his feet and went to the window, stared out at the rain-soaked garden. When he turned round again, John's face was ashen. 'Is this *true*?' he asked incredulously.

'I went to see your mother.' Stephen shrugged. 'It wasn't a pleasant meeting. She feels it is high time I took a closer interest in you.' Stephen gestured towards the letter. 'Is that what she says there?'

'More or less.' John looked again at the sheet of paper in his hand. His mother had made herself perfectly clear — she wanted nothing more to do with him, she forbade him ever to come near her again, she informed him that as far as she was concerned he was now without a family and all that went with it.

But it was what she had written after that which plunged him into the middle of a nightmare, which was making him feel physically sick. It couldn't be true! Such bizarre and ridiculous coincidences do not take place. It was surely impossible that, out of hundreds and hundreds of undergraduates, Anna should have been drawn to the only one — but it seemed that she had.

John looked at Stephen again; he saw, now, his sister Judith's dark features — her slanting eyebrows, her narrow, dark eyes; her well-defined jawline, her wide, determined mouth. These characteristics were, of course, softened and feminized in her young woman's face, but they were recognizable as her father's all the same.

'And she's so like Anna!' he thought. 'So very like!' John wondered how he could ever have missed the resemblance. Judith was built on a larger scale, her features lacked the finely-moulded beauty of Anna's, but it was obvious that they were sisters. They might even have passed for twins.

Stephen sat down again. 'What else does your mother say?' he asked, gently, breaking into John's nightmare — wondering if, perhaps, he was going to have to tell the young man whose son he was after all.

'She tells me that you and she are married.' John's voice was expressionless now. 'She tells me that you left her and your two small children when those children were babies. She tells me that Anna is the daughter of your — your mistress.' Elizabeth had not used the word 'mistress'. John stared at the man facing him. 'Well?' he demanded. 'Is everything my mother says true?'

'Yes.' Stephen shrugged. 'Yes, it's as she tells you.'

Never before severely tested, John's self-control wavered and then gave way. Shock and anger made him quite unlike his normal, pleasant, courteous self. 'Is that all you can say?' he cried, his voice very loud in that quiet house. 'Don't you have any regret at all for what you've done?' He drew breath, looked wildly round the room as if searching for a weapon of some kind.

'You're to blame for everything!' he shouted, beside himself now. 'You've behaved abominably; your treatment of my mother has been shameful! Now you've ruined my life, you've ruined Anna's — and yet you sit there perfectly calmly, looking as if you don't care at all!' He had risen to his feet, and accompanied those last four words with the hammering of his fist on Stephen's desk.

'Naturally I should prefer that none of this had happened.' Stephen looked mildly up at John, who now looked perfectly capable of committing murder. 'I've had time to think about this,' he added placatingly. 'You haven't. So sit down and listen to me for a minute or two.'

John remained on his feet, 'I don't want to hear anything you have to say!' he retorted. 'I'm going to find Anna. I shall take my wife away with me now. And you won't be able to stop me!'

'Don't dare speak to me like that!' Unused to being addressed so curtly — particularly by a person who had, until a month or two ago, been a mere undergraduate — Stephen glared at the young man. 'Sit down! Do you hear me?'

There was an edge to Stephen's voice which had made John flinch and, angry as he was, he bit his lip and looked down at the ground. 'I don't owe you any obedience,' he began. But then he slumped into his chair again, lolling against the arm with his legs thrown over the side. 'Well?' he demanded, as rudely as he dared.

'What did you wish to say?'

'You tell me that you and Anna are married,' replied Stephen. 'You really are man and wife? Everything is legal? You have a marriage certificate, I assume — may I see it?'

'We are married. But I'm not obliged to prove it to you.' John's light eyes were hard with anger. 'We've spent the past week together as a married couple, if that's what you mean to ask,' he continued. 'And you don't imagine that I'd have taken your daughter to bed unless I'd married her first, do you?' he added, unable to stop himself.

'Don't be so bloody insolent, boy!' Stephen was on his feet, glaring at John; so furious now that the young man shrank back in his chair. But then Stephen made an effort to control himself. 'Look,' he went on, more gently, 'don't make this more difficult for yourself than it will be anyway. You realize, don't you, that we shall have to try to arrange an annulment? It ought to be possible, in civil law at any rate.'

John stared. 'Annulment?' he asked, astonished. 'I don't want my marriage annulled! Anna is my wife — I love her, and she loves me! We are married, don't you understand? And we shall stay so, whatever you say!'

Stephen sighed. 'There's no possibility that Anna can live with you,' he said, in a more conciliatory tone than he'd used so far.

But John merely frowned back at him. 'My mother told me that you had been killed in a riding accident, when I was a little child,' he muttered. 'I wish now —'

'Yes, John? You wish what? Be careful what you say to me.'

'Oh, I don't know what I wish! My God, I don't know what I'd like to do to you, damn you!' He stood up. 'You may think you can force your will on Anna,' he cried. 'But you'll find that you can't. She belongs to me now; she's my wife. Anna is mine, and will be for the rest of our lives — do you hear me?'

Stephen rose to his feet and walked towards the door. 'I make allowances for your state of mind,' he remarked coldly. 'Come back here in a few days' time — we can discuss your future then. And John —'

'Yes?'

'You will gain nothing by behaving like a lout, so try to act like a gentleman when you come to my house again. You will never speak to me again as you have done today. Do you understand?'

John walked through the open door. 'I hope I shall always be at least as much of a gentleman as you are yourself — or ever have been,' he replied. And he left the house.

Anna was to remember that evening as the most traumatic of her entire life. She had refused to believe her father at first, for her mother had said very little to her, merely commenting that she was glad that Anna had returned, since her father had been so worried about her. So, when she was eventually called down to his study to talk to Stephen, nothing had prepared her for that awful interview.

'Where's my husband?' she had asked. She'd heard John's voice raised in anger, which had surprised her; for she'd imagined that any shouting would have been done by her father. But then there'd been a calm, so she'd supposed that the two men had resolved their differences.

'Papa — what's the matter?' she asked, for Stephen was sitting in the chair by the fire, holding his hands out before the blaze, and the August evening, though not hot, was far from chilly.

She went up to him and kissed him. 'I'm sorry,' she said. 'I've behaved very badly; I've upset you. I should have known that I was doing wrong. Please will you forgive me?'

Still Stephen said nothing. He took one of her hands in his and held it tightly. Anna gave him a little shake. 'Papa!' she said, in exasperation. 'Where's John?'

Stephen looked at her. 'I've sent him away for the time being,' he replied, in a dead, flat tone of voice. 'He's coming back here in a day or two. I couldn't let you see him again this evening.'

'You sent him away?' Anna was incredulous. 'Why did you do that?' she asked. 'Papa — we may have been foolish, but we've done nothing wicked! You must believe me!'

'Oh, I believe you.' Stephen looked up from his contemplation of the fire. 'Anna, I don't know how to prepare you for this,' he said. 'I've thought of nothing else for the past three days, but the idea of it still makes me cold. And I can't make it any less appalling for you, whatever I say. You remember that I have two other children? That is, apart from you and Dora and Anthony?'

'Oh, yes. Mama did mention it once, years ago. A boy and a girl, wasn't it? Why? What about them?'

'I haven't seen my daughter since she was a baby. I've just spent a very disagreeable half-hour with my son.' He put his arms around Anna's waist, and held her. 'Don't look at me like that, child!' he cried. 'Try to take it in! It's terrible for you, I know —'

'You said that John —'

'Yes, yes, I did — you did hear me correctly. Don't ask me to say it again!' He looked at her anxiously. 'Anna — are you going to faint?'

Anna was trembling with shock. 'No,' she whispered, at last. 'I won't faint. But don't let me go.'

So he held her close to him, leaning his own head against her shoulder, for he needed comfort and support as much as she did. The interview with John had left him feeling so cold and light-headed that he needed simple human warmth now. 'Oh, my darling child,' he cried, 'I'm so sorry! Anna, Anna — why didn't you tell me about him? If only you'd brought him here! If I'd met him, we'd have found out in time! Why didn't you say anything?'

Anna blinked. 'There were all kinds of reasons,' she replied tonelessly. 'Oh, I was afraid you'd dislike him. He's not much of a scholar, you see ...'

'As if that would have mattered to me!'

'He thought it would. And I was afraid that if he knew about me — about us all — he might not want me.'

'Ah. I see.' Stephen pushed his hand through his hair. 'As my son told me, everything is my fault.'

'No, you're not the only one to blame.' Anna kissed Stephen's forehead, taking upon herself the role of comforter which he had assumed he would have to play. 'Shall we go into the drawing room?' she asked. 'Or into the garden? The rain's stopped now.'

He didn't move. Still holding Anna tightly, he began to talk. 'It's almost as if she had arranged it all,' he began.

'She, Papa?'

'Elizabeth.' The name came out like a snarl. 'Listen to me, Anna. I'll tell you everything. Don't hate me for it, if you can help it. Oh God — where shall I begin?'

Chapter Nineteen

'So, YOU SAW YOUR WIFE again?' asked Anna, her voice perfectly expressionless. She was still half-stunned by the revelations of the last fifteen minutes.

'Yes. I met Elizabeth.' Stephen closed his eyes momentarily, grimacing as if in pain. 'Anna,' he muttered, 'do you know if Hell exists?'

'I don't think there's any such place.'

'I didn't, either. But now I think there is, and for me damnation will be to spend it with that woman, locked up with her for all eternity!'

Anna stroked his forehead, as if soothing a child. 'Don't say things like that,' she murmured. 'Just tell me what happened.'

'Well — I went to the house ...'

Stephen had taken the address from the file in the records office, wondering, even as he scribbled it down, how she could have lived so close to him without his being aware of it. Had she never visited Oxford? Why had he not known she was there, in the same county, poisoning the very air he breathed?

When he arrived at the house, it had seemed as if Elizabeth had been expecting him. He was shown into a prettily furnished sitting room, where he found his wife lying on a chaise-longue, idly flicking through a set of fashion plates. As he entered the room she'd looked up — throwing the magazine aside, she'd looked straight at him, and given him a ravishing smile.

'Stephen!' she cried, jumping up and smoothing her dress. 'I've been waiting for you to come!'

He folded his arms and looked back at her.

He saw that his wife had lost very little of her former beauty. There was a certain blueness under the eyes, a faint line or two around the mouth, but she was still quite lovely. The blonde hair was luxuriant, her skin was luminous, and her translucent, pale eyes, so like John Harley's, shone clear and sparkling. She stood still for a moment before she crossed the room to him, swaying slightly as she walked.

'How are you, Stephen?' She held out her hand to him but he did not take it. She shrugged, unconcerned. 'You look worried,' she remarked. 'I suppose you have cause to be. I've heard some very strange rumours recently, all kinds of odd things. I've been told that your daughter has run away from home! And, what's more, that she's been seen in the company of my son! Now, what do you think can have happened?'

'I don't know.' Stephen glowered at his wife. 'But you evidently do. So tell me.'

'Tell you?' Elizabeth folded her hands together and began to walk around Stephen, watching him with glittering malevolent eyes. 'Why should I tell you? It's such a disgusting business that I don't really feel I should discuss it with anyone.' She stopped walking and looked at him archly. 'Don't you agree?'

For a moment he couldn't trust himself to reply. Feeling like an animal in a cage, he stood in the centre of his wife's drawing room, aware that she was examining him minutely, watching him, calculating, deciding where to strike next.

She began to walk around him again, still looking at him intently. 'I do hope you're not going to remain dumb, Stephen,' she remarked. 'You presumably came here to talk to me?'

He returned her glance then, allowed his gaze to sweep over her for a second or two. She was wearing a pale blue satin dress which became her very well, showing off the curves of her beautiful figure. But, standing so near to her, it wasn't the sight of her which disturbed him. It was the faint but cloying, sweetish smell which hung about her that made him feel nauseous. He couldn't decide what it was — but his head was now spinning and he felt that he needed fresh air. 'I want you to tell me where my daughter is,' he muttered. 'As you know very well.'

'Ah, I *see*. You want information. Why should I give you any?' She came closer still now and looked up into his face. 'You've become somewhat notorious, haven't you?' she asked conversationally. 'Over the past few years you've become very well known. In your own rather limited field, that is. I've seen your name in *The Times* upon several occasions now, and I must admit that it's rather exciting to have such a famous husband.'

She grinned at him. 'If certain matters were to become public now, you could be more famous still!' she added. She lowered her eyelids and regarded him flirtatiously. 'Oh, come now!' she cried. 'Don't glower at me so! Can't we speak pleasantly to each other? We must have plenty to talk about after so long.'

'There's only one matter I wish to discuss with you.'

'Oh, Stephen!' Elizabeth raised her eyes to heaven, sighing in mock despair. 'Still such a surly man! You won't speak nicely to me — you won't even look at me! Now, how can I relax you, how can I set you at your ease? I know! Shall I send for some tea? Shall we sit down together and have something to eat and drink? It would be quite in order, wouldn't it, for a husband and wife to discuss their children over a light meal?'

Stephen folded his arms. 'Elizabeth, stop all this play-acting,' he said. 'If you can't tell me what I want to know, I shall leave now.'

'Ah.' Elizabeth leaned against her chair and picked at a loose thread in the upholstery. 'If I do know where your daughter is, why must I tell you?' she enquired sweetly.

'You know perfectly well why.'

'Do I? Mmm.' Elizabeth pulled out the thread and began to wind it around her fingers. 'Well, suppose I do know what has happened. Suppose I know that they've made their bed — a figure of speech, Stephen, merely a figure of speech — is there any reason why you or I should prevent them from lying upon it?

'What is it to me? Or to you?' Her smile became quite ghastly. 'Yes, what is it to you, lecher, adulterer, father of God knows how many bastards, you who prefers the society of an illiterate peasant to that of a woman of your own class? Oh, I know all about your menage in Oxford; I know you're so lost to any sense of decency that you pass that woman off as your wife. I don't know whom you think you deceive! You must be the laughing stock of the university!'

She smirked at him provocatively. 'I suppose that if you want to make an exhibition of yourself, that's your business,' she continued. 'You know — it occurred to me only a day or two ago that it was only to be expected that one of your misbegotten brats should chance on something like this to start her off on a career of debauchery to match her father's! You must admit that she's done something quite spectacular! I doubt if even you ever bedded your sister!'

Elizabeth turned away from Stephen and looked at herself in a glass, watching him in its reflection. 'You may have your son back now, Stephen,' she said. 'Well — doesn't that please you?'

He looked at her, at the reflected, mocking grin. His visit had been an utter waste of time. He turned towards the door.

Elizabeth, however, was there before him, leaning against it. 'Do you think me much altered, Stephen?' she asked.

'Altered?' He sniffed derisively. 'No. You haven't changed at all.'

'But you have!' Reaching out towards him, she pulled out a couple of his side whiskers and examined them. 'Grey,' she observed, sighing. 'Quite grey. Not to be wondered at, I suppose, considering the life you have led!'

He willed himself not to lose his self control. She'd confirmed what he'd feared, and he knew now that she would never voluntarily tell him where his daughter was. He wouldn't have believed that even she could have connived at such a marriage — but it seemed that she had. To spite him she would, it appeared, do anything. He could feel her hatred burning off her as she stood there, still looking at him, still with that awful smile upon her face.

'Look at me,' she commanded, feeling herself in control now. 'Look at your wife. I'm beautiful, aren't I? Very beautiful, in fact. My looking glass and the stares of people everywhere I go tell me that.

'Stephen, I've heard that the peasant has grown coarse and fat. Isn't it time that you returned to me, isn't it time you weaned yourself from your addiction to common sluts?'

She touched the cuff of his jacket. 'You know you loved me once,' she wheedled. 'You could love me again! Oh, I know I was young and foolish when I married you. I know I drove you away from me. But look at me now. I've grown up. There have been men who wanted me but I've stayed alone, hoping that one day you'd come to you senses and want to return to me —'

'Oh, for God's sake, shut up!' Stephen glared at her. 'Get out of my way!'

303

Elizabeth stood her ground. 'If you will kiss me, just once — as you used to — I shall tell you where your daughter is.'

Stephen hesitated, well aware that she was still teasing him. But if, on the other hand, she did know where Anna was, if he could find his daughter, it might not be too late ... He leaned forward, and brushed her cheek with his lips.

'Oh, kiss me *properly*!' she cried, pouting. She took his hand and laid it upon her breast.

So, reluctantly, he kissed her open mouth, pulling away immediately. 'Well?' he demanded.

'They've gone to Scotland of course; how very predictable of them!' Elizabeth began to shake with laughter. 'They were married last Wednesday!' she crowed. 'Will there be a honeymoon baby, d'you suppose? Oh, Stephen! Your *face*! It's a picture!'

To support herself, Elizabeth grabbed a chair-back. 'Oh, I swore I'd have my revenge on you!' she cackled, leaning against it. 'I always said I'd make you pay, and now I have! It'll ruin you when this gets out; and I shall make sure that it does, you may be certain of that! You'll have to resign your fellowship, won't you? Adultery's one thing, but incest is quite another! I doubt if even *your* licentious friends will countenance that!' Convulsed with giggles, Elizabeth clutched her side and grinned at Stephen in triumphant delight.

He wanted to slap her. He wanted to take hold of her shoulders and shake her, to dig his fingers through to the bones, to hurt her, to make her scream. He could feel sweat prickling his shoulders and back, and he fought to hang on to his temper, telling himself that there was nothing at all to be gained by injuring Elizabeth — a relief though it would have been to hit her just once, really hard. 'Will you move?' he demanded angrily. 'I want to leave now.'

'I want to leave now!' she repeated, still sniggering. 'I want to go back to my fat little whore, I want to find my dirty draggle-tail daughter! Oh, dear, dear husband — stay and have some tea before you go?' She reached out and stroked his arm.

He pushed her away as disgustedly as if he'd been touched by a poisonous snake. 'Take your hands off me, you bitch!' he cried, his face ugly with rage. 'Move, damn you! MOVE!'

But Elizabeth only smiled. She put her hands on her hips. 'It's my house,' she remarked. 'I shall do as I please.'

She had become very pale now, obviously afraid of him, but excited, too. Her eyes sparkled, her bosom heaved, and she was breathing far too heavily. 'Stephen, Stephen,' she gabbled, 'don't be so harsh and unkind! You can be so charming when you want to be — I remember the first time we met, you were so pleasant to me that I fell in love with you there and then! Listen to me. I didn't mean what I said about making all this public, I didn't have any intention of hurting you. Can we not be friends?'

'Friends?' he cried incredulously. 'You're mad! Insane! At this moment I hate you! Don't you realize what you've done to our son, and to my daughter? Does hurting me mean so much to you that you'd sacrifice our *children* to your desires? Oh, get out of my way, curse you, I shan't tell you again!'

She did not move, so he took her by the wrist and dragged her away from the door. Then he left. He shouted to a manservant to bring his horse round, and was mounted and ready to ride away when a maidservant appeared, holding a letter. 'Madam says,' she announced, grinning, 'that you will be seeing Mr Harley — and that she hopes you will be so good as to give him this. If you please.'

Stephen hesitated for a second or two but then he took the envelope and stuffed it into his jacket pocket. It was not until he was half way back to Oxford that he remembered that he had a daughter, Judith, about whom he should have at least enquired. He shrugged, and wondered if she were at all like her mother.

He told Dorcas what Anna had done, explained things as gently as possible. But he could not tell if she understood him, or even heard him, for she simply gazed up at him as he spoke, her great dark eyes full of unshed tears. He sat with her in his arms, watching the room darken. Wanting some comfort from her, he stroked her hair.

She laid her head on his shoulder then and began to cry uncontrollably, weeping as if her heart would break. 'Oh, the baby, Stephen,' she sobbed. 'The poor little baby! I never held him in my arms — I never even saw him!'

He realized then that she hadn't heard anything he'd said; hadn't taken it in at all.

Chapter Twenty

JOHN SEARCHED HIS POCKETS AND found that he had thirty-seven pounds, some odd silver and a handful of copper coins. He wondered what on earth he was going to do to support himself. But — before he considered his own future — he had to see Anna. If her father made any objection to their meeting, he'd simply knock him down.

But a week passed before he could bear to go to the house in the Banbury Road. The idea of being with Anna, but being forbidden to touch her, to kiss her, was terrible. He had to see her, however, if only to tell her that he still loved her and that he would go on loving her. She should not feel degraded on his account.

He put on his jacket and went out. The bright sunshine irritated him — he made his way to the north end of the city along shady lanes and alleys.

John had sent a message to Stephen, so had waited a decent interval before leaving his room, to give his father time to think of anything he might wish to say to his son, or to go out and avoid him all together. 'And if he sends word that he doesn't wish to see me, I shall visit Anna anyway,' thought John sourly.

He arrived at the house, was admitted, and found Anna, alone, in her father's study. Her face was too pale and there were dark circles staining the skin beneath her eyes. She allowed him to embrace her but after a minute or two, she eased herself out of his arms and walked over to the other side of the room. 'He's explained everything to me,' she said, looking out of the window.

'He's explained, has he?' John kicked viciously at the fringe of the hearthrug. 'I suppose that you mean he's told you what he did,' he muttered. 'I hope he didn't try to make excuses for his disgusting behaviour?'

Anna flinched at the scorn in her husband's voice. 'My father explained that, before he was married, he was my mother's lover,' she replied coldly. 'He told me that he and his wife separated when you and your sister were babies. Oh, for God's sake, John! It wasn't easy for him to tell me that! He's suffering just as much as we are, you know; he hasn't slept properly for weeks, you only have to look at him to realize that. He looks ten years older than he did last month, poor man.'

'Poor man! Oh, Anna, you break my heart!' John crossed the room, took Anna's arm and shook her. 'My God — I don't care how much he suffers! He ought to feel it — it's all his fault! Oh, Anna, don't let him separate us!'

Anna bit her lip and would not look at him. 'We can't stay together,' she said. 'You know that. My father's arranged something — I don't know quite what, but I'm sure he has the best interests of us all at heart. So don't be unpleasant to him.'

'I expect he intends to offer me money to go away.' John laughed bitterly. 'Well, that would be in *his* best interests, wouldn't it?'

'Please, John!' Anna stamped her foot in irritation. 'Don't be difficult! And don't make him angry, don't refuse to consider anything he suggests just because the idea was his. When you get to know him better, you'll find he's a good man. He's very kind, he's generous —'

'Yes, indeed he is! He's a good, kind, generous adulterer, seducer, deserter of his wife and family! Anna — my sister and I are his own children; but he's taken no interest in us, none whatsoever. He drove our mother away, he abandoned his wife to take up with a mistress; with a woman who was already married to someone else, at that! What do I owe him?'

'There were reasons why things happened as they did.' Anna touched John's arm — but he pulled away from her, scowling.

At that moment, they heard Stephen's footsteps crossing the hallway. When he came into the study, he found his daughter and her husband at opposite ends of the room.

He muttered a cursory greeting to his son, who did not reply to it. 'What do you intend to do, John?' he asked, as he sat down at his desk.

John shrugged. 'I don't know,' he replied ungraciously. 'Obviously, my expensive classical education hasn't prepared me for anything useful. And at the moment, I can't think very clearly anyway.' He frowned at Stephen, determined not to seem at all cooperative, unwilling to show any enthusiasm for anything the older man might suggest.

'Do you see yourself as a merchant?' asked Stephen.

'Is that what you've decided I shall be?'

Anna sighed inwardly; Stephen's face showed that he was making a great effort to keep his temper. John stared defiantly at his father, put his hands in his pockets and, with the toe of his shoe, began to scuff the corner of the desk at which Stephen sat.

'I've no wish to force you to do anything you will dislike,' said Stephen eventually, breaking a heavily charged silence. 'But I have, as it happens, discussed the possibility of an apprenticeship with a wine merchant of my acquaintance. I've offered to vouch for you, and to pay the premium involved. Naturally, I didn't mention our relationship.'

'Oh, naturally.'

Stephen ignored the interruption. 'I think,' he concluded, 'that you ought to consider leaving England for a year or two, for all our sakes.'

John took his hands out of his pockets and folded his arms. 'How much is the premium?' he demanded. 'I only have about two hundred pounds of my own.'

'I shall see to the premium. I have no intention of casting you adrift, destitute and penniless — I have responsibilities towards you as my child, and I don't hold your recent behaviour against you. Don't imagine, either, that I send you away to spare my own feelings.'

'Your feelings, my behaviour.' John looked at Stephen as if the older man were some kind of loathsome reptile. 'You don't hold my behaviour against me. Well ...'

Anna reached out and touched John's sleeve. She shook her head very slightly but Stephen saw her, and frowned.

John shrugged his shoulders and rose to his feet. 'I shall go and see this wine merchant of yours,' he said. 'That is — if Anna thinks it best.'

'Anna?'

'Yes, Papa.' Anna noded. 'Yes, I think that would be a good idea.'

Anna and John went out into the garden, keeping a careful distance of several yards between them. 'There was no need to be quite so rude to my father,' said Anna. 'There was no need to go out of your way to be unpleasant.'

'Oh, shut up, Anna.' John glared at her. 'If you mention that man again, I shall hit you.'

'You wouldn't dare!' Anna glared back at him. 'You wouldn't want to hurt me, would you?' she asked, more gently.

'No.' John shrugged his shoulders in a hopeless, helpless gesture. 'Anna, will you write to me?'

'Of course I shall.'

'That's something, then.'

They walked past the trimmed lawns, on past the shrub borders, down to a wilder part of the garden which lay out of sight of the house. They stopped among some old and useless apple trees, which had stood there before the Banbury Road had been lined with the red-brick villas which now disfigured it. Anna reached out to touch John's sleeve. He jerked his arm away, frowning at her. 'Don't touch me,' he snapped. 'I'm going soon — I'll leave you to your precious Papa.'

'Oh, John! Don't be so cross!' Anna looked at him piteously. 'We shouldn't part in anger.'

'If it hadn't been for him, there'd have been no need to part at all! If it hadn't been for your marvellous father, I'd have always known you as my sister and I'd never have fallen in love with you!'

'Or fallen out of love, as you evidently have.' Anna folded her arms around her body as if she were in pain, and looked hard at the grass beneath her feet. 'Oh, I suppose it's all for the best,' she added. 'It couldn't have lasted, anyway.'

'Whatever do you mean by that?'

'Oh, don't be so cruel!' Anna blinked, refusing to let unshed tears fall. 'It's obvious that you regret ever having set eyes on me!'

'How can you say that to me?' John looked as if he might cry now, for his face was tight with the effort to remain calm, and he was blinking as hard as Anna was. 'Anna, Anna, don't say such things!' he muttered. He looked at her. 'Do you regret meeting me?' he asked. 'I suppose you must ...'

Anna burst into tears, covered her face with her hands. So John took her in his arms and held her very close to him; he began, finally, to kiss her. Anna, her first outburst of passion over, started to cry steadily, hopelessly, unable to help herself.

'Please don't cry,' murmured John, after a while. 'You'll make me cry, too.'

'I'm sorry.' Anna looked towards the house. 'What time is it?' she asked.

'I don't know. The clocks were striking three when I came up the road, and I imagine I've been here for half an hour or so. Why?'

'Half-past three. Then my father will have gone into college — he had a faculty meeting at four. My mother's certain to be asleep, and Fanny will have taken Dora to her dancing class. We can go into the house.' She slipped her hand into his. 'Come with me,' she said.

'I don't think I should. Really, I ought to go now.'

Panic filled Anna's eyes. 'Please don't leave me yet!' she cried. 'Please! Look — we can go up to my room, and talk — no one will ever know!'

John looked hard at her. 'You don't mean that,' he said. 'You know I can't come.'

'Can't?' Anna's narrow eyes flashed. 'You mean you won't! Why won't you?'

John looked at the hand which rested in his. He increased the pressure of his own grasp, held Anna's fingers so tightly that the bones were crushed together. 'I *can't*!' he repeated fiercely. 'Don't tease me like this! If you knew how I feel at this minute, you'd pity me, not torment me.'

'Tease you? Torment you?' Anna glared at him. 'It's you who is tormenting me!' she cried. 'You've probably spent the past few days pitying yourself, but have you thought, have you even begun to imagine, what it's been like for me?'

'Well, I —'

'Of course you haven't! It hasn't even occurred to you that I've been lonely, and wretched enough to consider if I might not be better off dead!'

'Anna, don't talk like that! It's not that bad!'

310

'Isn't it? Why isn't it?' Anna shook his arm. 'Have you wondered what I am going to do for loving for the rest of my life?' she demanded. 'You may have lost your wife — but do you think that *I* am content to see the remainder of *my* days stretched endlessly ahead of me, to be spent alone?'

'You won't be alone! Anna, you won't —'

'Yes I shall! But *you* won't! You know perfectly well that you will find someone. There'll soon be another woman to console you for the loss of me, and in a matter of months you may have forgotten me completely. But as for me, what can I expect? Who would want me as a wife, were I ever to become free to marry? How *am* I to free myself from you, without dragging my family through a stinking mire of scandal and defamation?'

'Anna, you forget that I, too, am tied —'

'Tied!' Anna laughed. 'You're not tied! You'll take a mistress, you'll have children, you'll not suffer — men never do! But as for me, shall I hope one day to be set up as the harlot of some man or other, to be kept or abandoned at whim?'

'You'll be no man's harlot! You're my wife, Anna, and as my wife —'

'Yes, I'm your wife. That's security indeed, isn't it? Do I inspire the same depth of affection in you, as my own mother does in our father? I doubt it! I shall become a poverty-stricken spinster, unless I become a whore. But you are still my father's heir, you're a legitimate son. All he owns will one day come to you. And yet you expect me to pity you! Oh, I never want to see you again.'

'Don't talk to me like that!' John took her by the shoulders and pulled her against him, for she'd become so pale that he feared she might faint. He began to kiss her again, tasting the saltiness of her tears, and he could feel her heart hammering against his own. 'We'll go indoors now,' he murmured. 'Don't cry any more. Please don't cry.'

It was as quiet as a graveyard in the house. Anna listened outside her mother's door, heard the soft, regular breathing of a sleeper. She led John down the landing to her own bedroom.

'I know it's wrong,' she whispered. 'I know it's wicked. But I want you. I love you so much it's killing me.'

John took off his jacket, loosened his tie. He unbuttoned the

311

fastening at Anna's wrist, but in his wretchedness he was clumsy and tore the cuff. 'Don't do that,' she snapped, anxiety and unhappiness making her sharp. 'I know how to undress myself!'

At that point, John lost his temper. 'You know everything, don't you?' he retorted, glaring back at her. 'You're so bloody clever that I wonder you can stoop to doing something so mindless and bestial as what you're contemplating now!' He took her other wrist and, this time, he pulled open the sleeve by ripping the buttons away from the material. 'If this is to be the last time, we'll do it the way I want,' he muttered. He caught the sides of Anna's collar and jerked open the neck of her gown; he pushed the garment back from her shoulders, then kissed her very hard, biting her lips.

She squirmed, but he held her so tightly that she could not get away. 'You hurt me!' she cried, when he finally released her. She licked her lips. 'My mouth's bleeding!'

'Is it?' John now began to pull off his own clothes. 'Get yourself undressed,' he snapped. 'Or I'll tear that precious dress of yours from your back and give you something more than a few bloody buttonholes to moan about!'

'Damn you!' Anna hissed, tears coming into her eyes again. 'Damn you, damn you!' She pushed him, hard, so that he slipped on a rug; and, losing his balance, fell heavily on to the floor. A split second later she was on top of him, pulling at his clothes, scratching him, biting him and hitting him as hard as she could; wanting to hurt. Then, however, she was kissing him; kissing the marks her nails had made on his white skin, crying tears of grief and wrapping her arms around him.

But John was still furious that Anna had dared to attack him like that. Hardly aware that she was already sorry for hurting him, he tugged the rest of her clothes from her body, pushed her on to her back and fell clumsily on top of her, pinning her to the floor.

He really hurt her then. He took her so violently that he bruised her both inside and out, rubbing her shoulders painfully against the hard wooden floorboards, and raising weals on her arms where his nails bit into her flesh.

But Anna had not minded the pain. She treasured the sensations she was feeling, knew she would never experience anything like them again. 'I wish I could absorb you,' she cried, as she lay amid the heap of tumbled clothing, clinging to her husband. 'I wish I could take you inside me, keep you locked away in my heart!'

She opened her eyes and pulled his face close to hers, looked at him as if memorizing his features. 'I'd like to kill you, I think,' she said. 'I'd like to take your life away, then you couldn't ever be with any other woman. I really think I want you to die.'

'Do you?' John reached across the room, jerked a workbox open and took out a pair of scissors. 'No,' he said, seeing Anna's eyes widen. 'I'm not going to provide you with a weapon.' He cut off a long lock of her hair and wound it around his wrist, where the natural curl kept it in place. He looked at the angry red marks on Anna's chest and shoulders. 'I'm sorry I hurt you,' he said, in a tone of real contrition. 'Darling, I didn't intend to be so rough!'

Now, his face was as pleasant and kind as it usually was. All the anger and bitterness of the past hour had been washed away. He kissed her, very gently, on the lips. 'Don't remember me as a brute,' he said. 'I don't know why I hurt you just now.'

She touched a gash which her own nails had made, disfiguring his arm from shoulder to elbow. 'These are the wounds of love,' she said sadly. 'I wish they'd never heal!'

They lay in each other's arms for five minutes more. 'You really must go now,' said Anna. 'They'll all be back home soon, and then —'

'Old Capulet will run me through and feed me to the dogs. Darling —'

'What?'

'You could come with me.'

'Don't say that. You know I can't.'

John sat up and looked at her. 'I shall come back for you,' he promised. 'There won't ever be another woman for me, I know that.' He touched her face and kissed her for the last time. 'I shall work hard,' he added. 'I shall surprise him. When I can offer you a home, I shall come and fetch you. So don't forget me.'

'There's no possibility of that.'

He dressed, checked his pockets for the various envelopes Stephen had given him, then went. Anna lay under the pile of disordered bedclothes, her sobs muffled, wondering if it hurt as much as this to die.

Chapter Twenty One

JOHN WALKED TO THE RAILWAY station and caught the London train. He could not have borne spending another night in Oxford. In his pocket, already crumpled and despised, was a draft for five hundred pounds and a letter addressed to his father's banker, authorizing the payment of a monthly allowance. *That* he would rip up and throw away. The only document which he needed was the letter to Mr Andrews, his prospective employer.

At the memory of Stephen, John scowled. 'I won't be bought off,' he thought.' 'And I won't owe *him* anything!'

He found a corner in a third class compartment and slumped into it, oblivious of the fat countrywoman next to him who was jabbing her umbrella into his side, and of the stares of the other people in the carriage, all gawping at him and wondering audibly why a gentleman like that should be in a cheap seat.

'Bin gamblin', I 'spec,' whispered a man to his companion. 'Lost the lot, I reckon. Looks as if he's had it up to 'ere, don't 'e?'

The other man nodded. He looked at John, and snickered. After all, it was always pleasant to see a gentleman brought low ...

It was dark when the train drew into Paddington. John made his way into the foetid blackness of the warm summer night, feeling as if he were walking into the mouth of Hell but not particularly caring where he went, and not seeing anything very much at all.

He roamed the streets of London most of that night, pushing away hands which grabbed at his clothes, ignoring the smiles of women who stood in his path, inviting him to go with them. 'He looked stark mad, that one,' muttered a rejected harlot, watching John walk on down the Haymarket. 'Must've escaped from somewhere.'

At eight o'clock the following morning, Mr Henry Andrews, a director of Marshall and Co, Wine Merchants and Shippers, was informed that there was a man to see him. 'He hasn't shaved, sir, and he looks very rough,' remarked Mr Andrews' housemaid. 'He says his name's Harley. Shall I let him in?'

Henry Andrews pulled a face. Stephen Lawrence had promised him a bright, intelligent young lad — not an unshaven lout ...

Dorcas gradually recovered her strength. As she did so, she rediscovered a will to live. 'I think I'll get up today,' she announced one fine September morning. 'Stephen — can you take me down to the drawing room?'

Helped out of bed and well wrapped up in a dressing gown and some extra shawls, Dorcas leaned on Stephen's arm as she walked carefully down the staircase. She lay upon the drawing room sofa, looking out into the garden. She played a few games of cribbage with Fanny Lewson — and she ate a proper meal that day, chewing her way through a small plateful of meat and vegetables instead of merely picking at a bowl of bread and milk.

'Still as light as a feather,' remarked Stephen, when he lifted her up to take her back to bed that evening. 'You need a few cream cakes, don't you? A meat pie or two?'

But he was relieved to find that although she was still so light and fragile that he could feel her ribs through the layers of nightclothes and shawls, she was not as insubstantial as she'd been on that horrible day when he had taken her back to her bed nearly fainting, when she'd been exhausted by the effort of walking the few yards along the landing to Anna's bedroom.

All the same, it was depressing Stephen unbearably to be in the same house as two ailing women. Dorcas was so feeble in body that she seemed unable to take much interest in anything but a piece of plain sewing, a dress for a newborn baby which she would now, he presumed, give to someone else's child. Anna roamed the house like a lost soul, hardly speaking, her eyes swollen from secret bouts of weeping — unable to sleep, and scarcely eating anything. Stephen hated to see them both so. Since he was never ill himself, sickness frightened and upset him. Although he no longer feared that Dorcas might die, Anna's misery made him feel very, very guilty.

'So, Stephen — you'll be coming, I hope?' Humphrey Charlton, a fellow of All Souls who had been invited to go to Rome that November in order to read a paper to a conference of classical scholars, grinned at Stephen over his glass of port. 'Should be a jolly little spree,' he added encouragingly. 'And you more or less promised to prepare a paper.'

Stephen shook his head. 'I don't know if I can get away now,' he replied.

'Why can't you?' Dr Charlton refilled his own glass and motioned to Stephen to empty his. 'Come along now, man — drink up. You're very gloomy these days! Carson can take over your classes for a couple of weeks.'

'It's not that.' Stephen rose to his feet and walked to the window. 'I'll see what I can arrange,' he muttered. 'And I'll let you know in a few days' time.'

He walked down the staircase, through the courtyard and out into the High Street. The invitation to go to Rome had seemed a heaven sent opportunity to get out of Oxford for a week or two, and Stephen was chafing to go, but he didn't dare leave his family in its present state ...

Now, resentment at having his plans spoiled made him extremely bad-tempered. While he was tenderness itself towards Anna and Dorcas, three weeks into term his students had thought of a whole new set of uncomplimentary nicknames for him. The old monster, the old devil, the sarcastic sod were now rendered totally inadequate. And all the members of his tutorial group eventually gave up trying to produce essays which would not be returned splattered with red ink.

'Have you ever considered a career as a novelist, Mr Freeman?' Stephen asked his most promising final year undergraduate, as he handed back a piece of work which was now liberally embroidered with scarlet.

'No, sir.' Alec Freeman, realizing that he was in for another unpleasant hour, tried to be conciliatory. 'Sir, I hope to become an historian.'

Stephen grimaced. 'I think, Alec,' he said, 'that you ought to be prepared to modify your plans. An historian needs some powers of analysis, you see — some ability to sift through the — ah —

unwieldy mass of his sources, and to get to the heart of the matter in hand. And, to date, you don't display very much aptitude for any of that.'

Stephen waved his hand towards Alec's essay. 'You do, however, have a great talent for invention,' he added. 'That thing you have in your hand, which purports to be an account of the reign of Tiberius, is pure fiction.' He rose to his feet and opened the door of his study, indicating that the tutorial was at an end. 'I wonder — could you perhaps let me have something a little more thoroughly researched by next week?'

By the end of October, however, Dorcas was almost completely recovered. She surprised Stephen one morning by actually running up the garden path with Dora. And, as she came into the drawing room, breathless and clutching her sides, he was delighted to see that she was laughing, that her colour was better, that she looked pretty again. Her skin had regained the dusky, rosy translucence which had so attracted him to her all those years ago and she was putting on weight again. He now had no qualms about leaving her for three weeks.

But there was still Anna to worry about. 'She's wasting away, you know,' he remarked to Dorcas one evening, when he had asked for and received her permission to go on what she insisted on calling his little holiday. 'She's not eating enough to keep a baby alive, and she's so snappish I hardly dare talk to her!'

'She snaps at you, does she?' Dorcas shrugged her shoulders and gave Stephen a rueful smile. 'Well, she isn't exactly talkative with anyone. And she won't reply to even the most simple question if it comes from me!'

'Won't she, indeed? Dorcas, I won't have her being rude to you. I shall speak to her about that.'

'No, Stephen, don't. It wouldn't be any use.' Dorcas looked up from her needlework. 'Couldn't you take her to Italy with you?' she asked. 'There's no reason, is there, why she shouldn't go? I'm no company for her. And I'm sure she'd like to go to Rome.'

'So, Anna, will you come with me?' Stephen, laying the whole scheme before his daughter the following day, did his best to make the expedition sound as exciting as possible. 'You'll like Dr

317

Charlton,' he added. 'And, since he's taking his valet, you'll have an escort with whom you can do some sightseeing while we old men are shut up together.'

'I'll come.' Anna sighed and looked out of the window. She had responded to her father's proposition with minimal enthusiasm. 'At least,' she thought, as she walked upstairs to look at her travelling clothes, 'at least while he's closeted with all those other old men, arguing, I shall have some time to myself. And that will be better than staying at home with Dora and *her*.'

Before he left for Italy, Stephen set about finding a new governess for Dora. This turned out to be more difficult than he'd expected it to be — he was obliged to interview half a dozen young women before he found one whom he thought might be even barely competent. Two days before he was due to leave for Rome he engaged Miss Jane Thomas, the least ignorant of the bunch; telling himself that it was for a year only, and that next September Dora would go to school whether she wanted to or not.

In spite of her father's misgivings, Dora liked Miss Thomas at once, finding her air of gentle melancholy coupled with her tall, spare figure and gaunt, hollow-eyed face, most appealing. 'She's very nice, isn't she?' Dora asked Fanny Lewson, a few days after Miss Thomas had arrived.

'Oh, she is. She is!' Fanny, too, had taken to Miss Thomas, and was soon shadowing her around the house, gazing at the new governess as adoringly as any spaniel. Miss Thomas took this adulation in good part. Between them the two women played with, educated and loved Dora.

With Anna out of the way, the atmosphere in the Summertown house was much lighter. Dorcas reproached herself for being pleased to have got rid of her elder daughter but, all the same, she decided to make the most of Anna's absence. For a few weeks, at least, decorum could be set aside — she could sit in the drawing room with Fanny Lewson beside her on the sofa, could enjoy a comfortable, aimless chat with the children's nurse without Anna chiming in with some other sarcastic remark, without her daughter glaring at poor, inoffensive Fanny and wishing her away …

Dorcas went to the window and waved to her younger

daughter, who was playing in the garden. 'Dora!' she called. 'Come and have some tea!' As Dora came running up to the french doors, Dorcas turned to Fanny Lewson, who was sitting upon the sofa and winding wool. 'We'll have tea together in here, shall we?' she asked. 'Crumpets and cinnamon cake, by the fire. Go and see to it, will you? And call Miss Thomas down.'

Stephen had told Dorcas to open his post while he was away, just as she usually did. Most of the letters were from other academics — that particular week several had arrived from Russia, addressed in both English and Russian script, and Dorcas reflected that Stephen seemed to correspond with this Dr Gordon a great deal. Most merely needed an acknowledgement, or could be put on one side until he returned. But one day, there was also a letter from Stephen's daughter Judith.

Dorcas did not think about those two children of Stephen's marriage. She hated the very idea of John Harley, and Stephen had never discussed his legitimate children with Dorcas. They were a part of his life which was no concern of hers. Like his wife, like his work, like his estate, like his family there — like so much, in fact... Dorcas skimmed through Judith's letter very quickly, holding it at arm's length as if it might contaminate her.

'My dear Papa,' it began. 'I watched you leave the house when you visited Mamma last summer; and I was a little sad when I discovered that you had not asked to see me.

'Perhaps you did not know I was at home. Perhaps you would not have wished to see me again if you had known I was there — for I understand that you and Mamma parted no better friends than when you left us before. I must say I was amazed when she told me who her visitor had been. We children had always supposed you to have died when we were very small.

'Since you visited her, Mamma has been very unwell. John's dreadful behaviour almost broke her heart; she was so very angry with him that I quite feared for her reason. And to this day she will not hear his name mentioned in her house.

'Two weeks ago, Mamma's lawyer came to see me. Mr Ferguson told me that Mamma has made a new will, leaving all her property, everything she possesses, to me. John is not to receive a farthing.

'Mr Ferguson also told me that, in spite of your treatment of her, you remain Mamma's legal husband — and, as such, have a claim upon her property which might well be upheld in a court of law. All the trusts, settlements and agreements notwithstanding, it appears that much of her wealth could be said to be yours, as well.

'There is something I could do for you, if I choose. If you knew what it was, I am sure you would be glad for me to do it. But, before I discuss it with you, I need to receive your written agreement that you formally give up all claim to Mamma's fortune.

'We ought to meet, to talk about this. Please write to me here, and I shall explain further. Meanwhile, I remain your dutiful, obedient daughter,

'Judith Elizabeth Harley.'

Dorcas placed this curious letter on top of the pile she had been reading. She had hardly taken in its contents, and now she slit open the next letter. But at that moment, the sound of Dora screeching attracted her attention; the child's shouts grew louder, and Dorcas put down her paper knife.

She went out of Stephen's study, through the french doors of the drawing room and into the garden, just in time to see Fanny Lewson helping the little girl into the house, a handkerchief clasped to her bloody knee. Seeing her child in such distress put Stephen's letters quite out of Dorcas' mind.

Swabbing the grit and dirt out of Dora's wound took ten minutes or more, and by the time the invalid was seated upon the drawing room sofa, a glass of milk in her hand and an impressive bandage around her injury, Dorcas had forgotten all about Judith Harley's letter.

She never saw it again. As Dorcas had walked out of Stephen's study, a draught of air had caught the pile of letters, flicking the one from Judith Harley across and behind Stephen's great mahogany desk, where it lay unmissed.

Anna returned from Italy looking much better than she had when she'd gone away. Her colour was healthier, and she was eating properly now. The constant nausea she'd felt since the middle of September had subsided, and in its place she had backache — and an enormous appetite. Even her father had commented upon how much she ate. And she was fatter, so much so that her clothes would scarcely fasten round her.

Dorcas noticed the change in Anna's shape as soon as the girl walked through the doorway. She saw that her daughter was holding herself in the way in which all pregnant women do, shoulders back, stomach out. So she was surprised that Stephen had not, apparently, realized that his daughter was going to have a child.

'Poor Stephen,' she thought, looking at him during dinner. He was so obviously glad to be home; he was beaming round at everyone, and inviting Dorcas to observe how much better Anna looked; was congratulating himself, no doubt, on the fact that all his troubles were over. Dorcas shook her head at him. 'Poor man — he won't get the professorship now,' she reflected. 'The Dean's wife will see to that! And he'd set his heart on it ...'

'I really don't know how I can bear to go off and leave you,' murmured Stephen drowsily, as he lay comfortably next to Dorcas later that evening. 'I missed you dreadfully while I was in Rome!'

'Did you?' Dorcas smiled at him, and snuggled herself closer to her lover. 'Well, I missed you, too.'

'Next time I go away, then, you must come with me.' Stephen stroked her hair back from her forehead. 'I ached for you, you know,' he added. 'Positively ached.' He kissed her, closed his eyes and settled down to sleep.

Dorcas sat up, pulled her nightgown over her head and began to fasten the little pearl buttons. No, it couldn't really wait any longer. 'She's pregnant, you know,' she told him. 'Did you hear what I said? Stephen — your daughter is going to have a baby!'

'What?' He opened his eyes wide and stared at her. 'Oh, God. Are you sure?'

'Practically certain. She was eating enough for two this evening and she's lost that greenish look she had all the autumn. Oh, I ought to have known then! Haven't you noticed that she's fatter? No, I suppose you wouldn't have. I expect you were too busy poking around your Roman remains to look at your own daughter.' Dorcas sniffed. 'Men are so unobservant!' she added severely.

'Have you talked to her about it?'

'No, of course not. She wouldn't want to hear anything I have to say.'

'You're her mother, for goodness' sake!'

'She still wouldn't listen to me. We haven't had what you might call a conversation for years.' Dorcas sighed, and pushed Stephen's shoulder; for, in spite of the importance of her announcement, he seemed to be on the point of falling asleep. She handed him his nightshirt. 'Put this back on,' she said, 'then sit up and talk to me. Tell me what we must do with Anna.'

'Do?' Stephen sat up, took his nightshirt from Dorcas, rubbed his eyes wearily. 'Oh, I don't know,' he muttered. 'What *can* we do?' He looked at Dorcas and read her mind. 'And I didn't want that job anyway,' he said. 'Too much administration, not enough teaching.'

Dorcas found her dressing gown and put it on. 'Shall I make us both some tea?' she asked. 'Then we can discuss it.'

'There's nothing to discuss.' In irritation, Stephen thumped his pillows and lay down again, pulling Dorcas down beside him. 'Go to sleep, dear,' he murmured. 'It's very late and I have a faculty meeting at nine tomorrow.'

Dorcas lay awake long after he was fast asleep, wondering how he could take this latest blow of fate so calmly. For, since he was a man who was capable of flying into a rage if his clothes were badly pressed, if a housemaid disturbed the papers on his desk, she wondered how he could be so stoical in the face of a major catastrophe like this ...

Dorcas turned down the lamp. Eventually, she shrugged and told herself not to fret — and she, too, settled down to sleep.

John Harley wrote to his wife, sent her long, informative letters. He was now touring the wine-growing regions of France. Well, he'd always said he wanted to visit foreign countries ...

Anna half dreaded the arrival of his letters for the sight of his large, childish handwriting sharpened her longing to be with him to an almost unbearable degree. As she read the scrawled pages, she would rest her hand upon her stomach and feel the movement of the child inside her, deriving some little comfort from that.

Anna was, on the whole, glad to be pregnant. She was almost certain that the child must have been conceived the last time she and her husband had been together, when she had known that if she was to keep anything of him, she had to take it from him then.

But she did not tell him she was expecting a child. She would write about that, she decided, after the baby was born. 'If it dies — if I die — what will there be to tell?' she asked herself. 'Why worry him unnecessarily now?'

Stephen resigned himself to the tide of gossip, innuendo and speculation which ebbed and flowed about his family and himself. Sudden silences whenever he entered the Senior Common Room told him that he had been tried, judged and found guilty; and he now gave up all hope of the professorship he'd wanted so badly.

'It's one thing to carry on as he always has,' remarked the Dean, who had been well-tutored by his wife. 'But to countenance such disgraceful behaviour in his daughter is quite another matter all together.'

'He's still the best candidate for the job.' Alfred Carson looked around him for support. 'Well — whatever you say of the man himself, none of you can deny that!'

No one did. But, all the same, Stephen knew that he would not be the next Regius Professor of Greek.

He told himself that he did not care. His work was published, and Archbold would not live forever. He could wait another ten years . . .

Stephen noticed that John drew no money from the bank account opened for him; he had not even cashed the draft his father had given him on parting. He supposed that the young man must be living on his paltry wages.

Winter at last became spring. The middle of March was cold and blustery, keeping Anna indoors when she would have preferred to be walking in the Parks, retracing her steps to the places where she and John had strolled together less than a year ago.

Dorcas, however, felt relieved that her daughter was obliged to stay at home. 'Really, child,' she remarked one morning, 'I wish that, when you next go out, you would walk somewhere else! It's not healthy, going round and round the places where you were together, like some girl in a ballad, pining for her lost lover!'

She frowned at Anna, who was lolling on a sofa across the

room, reading a book and pretending not to hear.

'People look at you,' continued Dorcas, irritated by the girl's studied indifference to what she was saying. 'They know who you are! They gossip about you, and they laugh behind your back!'

'Do they?' Ostentatiously, Anna yawned and turned over another page, noisily rustling the paper. She raised the book so that it obscured her face completely.

'Yes, they do!' Infuriated by Anna's nonchalance, Dorcas rose from her chair, crossed the room and snatched the book out of her daughter's hands. 'It's because of you that your father didn't get the job he wanted — and deserved!' she cried, beside herself.

Anna looked up and gave her mother a look of such absolute contempt that Dorcas winced. 'I'm sorry, Anna,' she said meekly. 'I didn't mean to say that. All I meant was that you ought to consider *us*. Please!'

'And you ought to consider me!' replied Anna coldly. 'Don't talk about my *lover*! Remember that I have a husband. My baby will be legitimate. I have nothing whatsoever to be ashamed of so I don't care what idle, stupid people say about me.

'And why should it matter to you where I go? You didn't think it a disgrace to walk about the very same Parks when you were carrying your lover's children, did you?'

Dorcas reddened. 'As far as other people were concerned,' she murmured, 'I was an ordinary married woman who happened to be pregnant!'

Anna nodded. 'Oh, of course you were!' she said. 'How stupid of me.'

Dorcas wondered how she had ever got into this. 'Anna,' she began beseechingly, 'I didn't mean to be unkind just now. I was merely suggesting that it might be better if you —'

Dorcas did not finish, for Anna retrieved her book and walked out of the room. A few seconds later her bedroom door slammed shut.

'She seems to be coping very well,' remarked Stephen, one evening, when Anna had gone to bed.

'Is she?' Dorcas looked up from an extremely complicated piece of embroidery. 'Stephen, she's as nervous as a wild animal these days — how can you say she's coping well?'

'I mean that she's behaving sensibly; she's looking after herself and eating properly again. She must be sleeping better, and she's lost that dreadful haggard look about the eyes.'

'Oh.'

'We did some work together this afternoon,' Stephen went on. 'She corrected some proofs for me.' He smiled at Dorcas and patted her hand. 'If she's sometimes a little snappish, it's only to be expected.'

'Is it?'

'Oh, yes. It's a very trying time for her.'

'It's a trying time for me, as well.'

Stephen leaned across the sofa and took the needlework out of Dorcas' hands. 'She needs you,' he said. 'She doesn't mean half the things she says, you know. And if she's rather abrupt at times, try to overlook it.'

Dorcas said nothing. 'A little snappish, rather abrupt,' she thought sourly. 'If he could hear some of the things she's said to me, he'd be horrified! If she spoke to him as she speaks to me — but, she wouldn't dare ...'

The baby, a boy, was born easily and safely one spring afternoon. In her relief that Anna had come through childbirth unscathed, Dorcas hugged her daughter and found that she was hugged in return. For a short period, Anna needed her mother — to look after her, and cherish her. So an uneasy reconciliation took hold.

Marcus — a terrible name, thought Dorcas, although she did not dare say as much — was a large, healthy child. Born with his mouth open, he was hungry from his first hour. He fed greedily and grew rapidly. Anna adored him, her lovely child, her husband's gift to her.

Marcus was, in fact, adored by everyone. Dorcas behaved as if no baby had ever existed before. 'He's such a smiler!' she said one evening, taking him in her arms and beaming at him in grandmotherly pride. 'Oh, he's so sweet-natured, isn't he?' Turning to the baby's mother, she shook her head. 'You weren't like this,' she added. 'You scowled at me, all the time!'

'Did I?' Anna, less prickly nowadays, smiled at her mother. 'I'm sorry to hear that! Well — he'll be hungry now, so I shall go and feed him.'

Feeding Marcus was a private ritual from which Anna excluded everyone. Now, as she watched the baby feeding, as she felt the milk drain out of her and flow down his throat, she realized that she must write to his father. 'Shall we tell him, darling?' she asked the smiling baby, who chewed his fist now and grinned at her in reply. 'Shall we tell him about you?'

Anna observed that these days her little sister appeared to be somewhat bored by her lessons. She saw that Miss Thomas would soon become redundant; and she told her father as much. 'She's a proficient enough teacher of all the basic skills,' remarked Anna dismissively. 'But she hasn't the flair to inspire anyone as fidgety as Dora. Papa, it's time I took over my sister's education.'

'You fancy yourself as a governess?' Stephen raised his eyebrows at Anna. 'I had intended to send her to school in September, you know.'

'Let me teach her in the meantime, then. Oh, Papa, I could make a much better job of it than Miss Thomas does! That woman is far too easy-going. My sister does no lessons at all some days. But Dora would work for *me*!'

'No doubt she would.' Stephen shook his head. 'Yes, you're probably right. Very well, then. We'll put together a syllabus for her.'

Dora, who had persuaded Miss Thomas that the day was too warm to work indoors and was lying under the apple tree reading a story book ('and I shall write you a summary of each chapter, Miss Thomas, upon my honour I shall') closed her eyes and prepared to take a little nap, unaware that a period of sustained hard work was about to begin ...

'Latin and Greek, of course,' said Anna. 'And some French and German. I can give her a basic grounding in mathematics. First of all, though, she will improve her handwriting and her command of her own language.'

Stephen nodded. 'Don't push her too hard,' he said. 'She's not academically minded.'

'She's clever enough,' retorted Anna sharply. 'But she's extremely lazy. A little hard work will do her good.'

Miss Thomas was affronted beyond measure when Anna

informed her that she intended to teach Dora Greek.

'*Greek*, my dear! What earthly use is *Greek*?' she had asked Fanny Lewson, as they lay on Fanny's bed that evening. 'Look at Miss Lawrence — a mother but certainly not a wife! I don't suppose we'll ever get to the bottom of that mystery, but anyway, what's the good of all her learning? Where's it got *her*?'

'Shush, Jane! Don't criticize Miss Lawrence!' Fanny glanced round fearfully. 'Whatever would Dr Lawrence say if he heard you talk like that?'

'Dr Lawrence!' Miss Thomas snorted. 'He can't hear me, not while he's tucked away in his study down two pair of stairs! And, my dear Fanny, you're quite needlessly frightened of him. He's just a bad-tempered old man, he's not the monster you make him out to be!'

'Isn't he?' Fanny pushed her friend's hair back from Jane Thomas's high, white forehead. 'I was thinking a day or two ago, dear,' she murmured, 'that perhaps we almost have enough money now. We don't need to stay here much longer. Why don't we go and discuss it with Mrs Lawrence tomorrow?'

Miss Thomas frowned. 'There'd be linen to get, china to buy,' she replied. 'We can't go yet.'

Fanny snuggled closer and took her friend's hand. 'I'm sure we could almost manage it,' she said persuasively. 'And I saw just the place in a house agent's window a few days ago. The rent was very reasonable. Just think of it,' she added wistfully. 'Our own place.'

'We can't afford it. Not yet.'

Fanny tightened her grip on Miss Thomas's hand. 'I'm sure we could!' she cried. 'And I'm sure that if we asked her, Mrs Lawrence would lend us some money!'

Jane Thomas bit her lip. She considered for a minute or two, then looked at Fanny again. 'It's what you really want, isn't it?' she asked. 'Oh, very well. We'll go and talk to Mrs Lawrence tomorrow.'

The following morning Fanny and Miss Thomas presented themselves to Dorcas and told her, hesitantly, that they wished to leave her employ. 'We've been saving hard,' said Fanny.

'And we had it in mind to establish,' added Miss Thomas.

'A boarding house for young ladies. In the Iffley Road,' they said together.

They fidgeted and looked embarrassed while they waited for Dorcas to reply.

Astonishment and relief prevented Dorcas from expressing the proper regret at this news. She had long been aware that this pair of Sapphists had ceased to earn their keep, let alone their wages. And Stephen had remarked, just a few days ago, that he thought it was time they went. But Dorcas, who had never yet dismissed a servant, had replied that while they made themselves so useful and agreeable she could hardly throw them out of their home.

'Fanny has been with us for years, Stephen,' she said. 'She's almost a friend — and she was so helpful when I was ill! It would be unkind to dismiss her. And as for Miss Thomas, she's very good with Dora. Recently, her arithmetic has improved beyond recognition!'

'They are both *servants*!' Stephen had put his book aside and frowned at her. 'My dear Dorcas, Anna can make a much better job of teaching Dora than Miss Thomas does. And the Lewson woman has been in my house quite long enough.' He grimaced. 'It's beyond my understanding why you ever engaged *her* in the first place!'

'I like her, and she's been very useful to us. Surely you must see that? Why do you wish to make her destitute?'

'I'm not suggesting you put them out in the street,' replied Stephen tersely. 'Give them a good reference each, and a month's wages as a gratuity. They won't be upset, I can assure you.' He pushed his hands into his pockets and stared into the fire. 'If you won't tell them they must go — and, Dorcas, it's your province to do so — then I shall. Ring for some coffee, will you, dear?'

So, as the three women sat together in Dorcas' own little sitting room, discussing china and towels, all three were conscious of a sense of elation. Dorcas was able to wish them success with the utmost sincerity; in her relief that they were going, she told them that she would buy them a present of all the tableware they would need.

Fanny, overcome with gratitude, wept. Miss Thomas looked anxiously at Dorcas, blinking in order to prevent tears from coming into her own cold blue eyes. 'I do hope, dear Madam, that Dora will be allowed to visit?' she asked.

'Of course she will, Miss Thomas!'

Dorcas left them then, and went to tell Stephen of her triumph of diplomacy. 'You've told them to leave?' he enquired, looking up from a page of something which he was scoring with green ink.

'Yes — they're going in a month's time!' She beamed at him, waited for his congratulations.

'They are, are they? Good.' Stephen put down his pen and smiled at her. 'What was it you wanted to see me about?' he asked.

Her father might have been glad to get such a couple of parasites out of the house, but Dora certainly didn't want them to go. She made them a pile of presents — pincushions, bookmarks and hideous embroidered place mats. 'I don't want them to leave, Mama!' she moaned. 'Anthony's at school, and even Papa's going to Greece soon. And I expect Anna will go with him; they were talking about it only last night. You and I will be the only people here, we'll be all by ourselves!'

'That's true.' Dorcas thought for a moment. 'Well, Dora, we'll go somewhere, shall we?' she asked. 'We'll spend our summer at the seaside.'

'The seaside? Oh, yes! What about the others, though?'

'I expect Anthony will come unless that friend of his asks him to go up to Scotland again. Anna will do as she pleases, but we can look after Marcus, can't we? I know Papa won't give up Greece; he's meeting some men from Cambridge in Athens, and they're going to spend all September talking to each other about sites and excavations.'

'Are they?'

'Yes.' Dorcas laughed. 'It all sounds very dull, doesn't it? But you and I will have a nice time here in England. We'll go to Weymouth, shall we? I'll write to some hotels in the morning.'

Dora's eyes sparkled. 'Yes, Mama, that'll be splendid!'

It was like having Anna a little girl again, thought Dorcas, as she watched Dora race off down the garden path to tell Fanny. But whereas Anna had, even as a child, been waspish and critical, Dora was always pleasant company. She was looking forward to spending a few weeks in a nice English coastal resort in the society of her younger daughter.

As it turned out, quite a large party eventually went to Weymouth that September. Dorcas took Dora, Anthony — whose friend had unsociably caught the measles — Anna and Marcus away with her. She was quite proud of herself for having organized such a large family expedition so successfully.

Stephen had seen them all off at the station, still somewhat disgruntled because Dorcas had refused to go to Greece with him. She had turned down his suggestion that he and she should transport Anna and three children all the way across Europe in the summer heat, to a country on the verge of a war.

'Why don't you come to Weymouth with us?' she had asked him, when he'd looked annoyed and pointed out that he'd miss her. 'They can do without you at this conference, or whatever it is, surely. Wouldn't you like a real holiday for once in your life?' She had laughed at his sulky expression. 'Come to sunny Weymouth,' she had added wickedly.

'*Weymouth*!' Stephen managed to pour an extraordinary amount of scorn into those two syllables, before getting up and going into his study and slamming the door behind him. And Dora and her mother had looked at each other, and giggled ...

So, while Stephen went off to Athens by himself, the rest of the family had an English seaside holiday, putting up with uncertain weather, uncertain food, and uncertain entertainment with the fortitude only to be expected of English women and children.

Anna wished she could have gone to Greece, Turks or no Turks. Marcus was almost weaned and her mother would, she knew, have been only too glad to look after him while she was away. But Anna could no more have abandoned Marcus than she could have cut off her own right hand.

So she was obliged to endure a month of shrimping with Anthony, of running races on the fine Weymouth sand with Dora, and of eating huge, fattening meals with her mother. 'That must have been why she married a grocer,' thought Anna, watching Dorcas stuff down another unnecessary cream cake — and feeling relieved that there was only one more week of this monotony to go ...

Anna had gone to Stephen's desk one day, in search of a decent pen. When she had found one, she laid it down while she looked for a piece of scrap paper upon which to try it. As she pulled open a drawer, the pen rolled across the desk and fell behind it. Annoyed, Anna looked in all the other drawers for a similar one, but with no success. She realized that she would have to shift the desk.

A great, heavy, cumbersome thing, the desk was only moved once a year; during the summer, when the room was thoroughly cleaned. That year, however, Stephen had been writing a book, and had given instructions that his study was to be left alone; he didn't want housemaids throwing away his notes and disturbing his papers.

As Anna heaved the desk away from the wall, she saw all the dust and mess behind it. Fat spiders scuttled away from the light, and disgruntled woodlice rolled into little grey balls. Anna retrieved her pen, several sheets of scrap paper and what looked like a letter, written on heavy, scented paper.

Anna smoothed it out and read it. Judith's letter was dated more than a year ago, evidently written while Anna and Stephen were in Rome together. Anna wondered if Dorcas had hidden it. But then the more likely explanation for its being there crossed her mind. It had simply fallen behind the desk, and not been missed. As soon as her father came in, Anna took the letter to him.

He had obviously never seen it before. His forehead creased as he scanned it and it became clear that he was very put out by what his daughter had to say. 'You've read this — this thing?' he enquired curtly.

'Yes I have.' Anna reddened. 'I wondered what it was,' she added lamely.

'The first line would have told you that it is a private letter — and it *is* addressed to me!' Stephen glowered at Anna. 'Couldn't you control your curiosity?'

He folded the paper and put it in the top drawer of his desk, banging the drawer shut. He went out of his study and stumped upstairs. Anna heard another door slam. He was morose all through dinner, and for once Dorcas and Anna were united in agreeing that Stephen was becoming very bad-tempered in his old age.

'It was only a letter, Mama,' said Anna crossly. 'Only some silly rubbish from a person I don't even know — it meant nothing at all to me! And he doesn't respect *my* privacy. He looks over anything I happen to leave lying in his study, without asking me first! And he sent some of my work off to Mr Liebermann without even telling me!'

Dorcas shrugged. 'It's my fault,' she said. 'I forgot all about the stupid thing. Anna, shall we have our coffee now? I don't suppose we'll see your father again tonight.'

Anna nodded. 'I'll fetch some,' she said.

Although she had dismissed Judith's letter as silly rubbish, its contents had worried Anna. She wondered what Judith had meant by it all. Finding it had reminded her that she ought to do what she'd been putting off for months now — she must write to John and tell him that he had a child.

But he hadn't written to her for six weeks or more now. She wondered if there were any particular reason for this. Had he, perhaps, found a woman to replace her? Had he made up his differences with his mother, and decided to have nothing more to do with his father's other family? Was he, perhaps, back in England?

She decided that she would ask him to come to Oxford. 'It can't hurt to see him, just the once,' she thought. 'And I must know what Judith meant.' She looked at Marcus, asleep in his bassinet. 'He really ought to see the child, as well.'

She found some writing paper. 'My dearest John,' she began. 'I am very anxious that you should come to England — that you should come to Oxford, and visit us. You will be made very welcome by everyone here; and I, of course, am longing to see you.'

She looked at what she had written. It was the kind of thing she had promised herself she would never write. She would never make him feel guilty that he had left her. As for assuring him that he would receive a warm welcome at the Summertown house ... 'Do not be alarmed by my request,' she added quickly. 'We are all in excellent health, all well and happy.'

She drew a deep breath. 'About a year ago, your sister wrote to my father,' she continued. 'But for various reasons the letter only came to light last week. Judith wrote to him asking if he would meet her. She told him that your mother is ill, and she also hinted that she could do my father a service, if she wanted to. I don't think, however, that he will see her; her letter irritated him rather than aroused his curiosity.

'Obviously, you know your sister well. What could she have meant by her request? It worries me that she may know something which could result in harm to you, or to me, or' — Anna bit her pen — 'or to others I love,' she added inconclusively.

'Please, my dearest, come to see me. I need to talk to you.'

Anna signed, sealed and stamped her letter, enclosing with it a mounted photograph of herself for which John had asked and which Anna had only recently been able to have taken. She posted it the following day, to the latest address which John had given her.

But he had moved since he had last written. He was now travelling in another part of France, was meeting shippers and learning the export side of the business. Anna's letter followed him from Burgundy to Rhone, then on to the Gironde, failing to catch up with him. Finally, a careless postman lost it, together with a pile of other correspondence. Anna's letter came to rest in a ditch, where it mouldered, chewed by mice and insects, until it disintegrated completely.

John Harley was kept very busy. Aware that he would have to rely entirely upon his own wits for the rest of his life he worked extremely hard. Quite deliberately he wore himself out, so that by the end of the day he was too exhausted to do anything but sleep.

At the time Anna had been writing the letter in which she besought him to go and see her, he had been wondering if a clean break with her might not be best for them both.

She obviously regretted meeting him. Her letters were, after all, quite cold, quite formal; so much so that after all they'd been to each other it hurt him to read them. For Anna's letters contained no mention of her emotional state, made no professions of affection, never told him that he was loved or needed — or even missed. Instead, they gave tedious recitals of the outings she took, and she droned on about her work and her publications in the most tiresome fashion.

She never said what she thought about things, never told him anything about the state of her heart. He had asked her to send him a picture of herself, but she had written back to say that she had none suitable. 'I shall have a portrait done in the spring,' she had promised. But nothing had come of it.

'She never did love me,' he thought bitterly. 'And her father's probably convinced her that I'm a half-wit, not worth remembering, let alone loving.' He kicked a stone across the path along which he was walking. 'I'll show the old man,' he vowed. 'I'll do well, in spite of him. I might not be able to turn a page of that bloody bore Sophocles into what the learned Dr Lawrence might call good English. But I'll be the youngest managing director this firm has ever had. I'll succeed in this profession if it kills me!'

Chapter Twenty Two

DORA SPOTTED THE LETTER ON her father's desk before he did. It bore several foreign stamps and seals; it was defaced by various inky purple franks, it was torn in several places, and it had evidently been opened ... Wanting to beg the stamps, she took it to the morning room where the rest of the family was still at breakfast. 'Is this from Russia?' she asked.

'Oh, yes. From Dr Gordon. Looks as if the cat's had it!' Stephen smiled at his younger daughter. 'Thank you, Dora,' he added. Realizing what she wanted, he tore off the stamps and handed them to her; then he unfolded the tattered sheets inside and began to read through them, raising his eyebrows now and then.

He handed the letter to Anna. 'What do you make of all this?' he asked.

Anna glanced through the pages. 'Do you know this gentleman well, Papa?' she enquired.

'I've corresponded with him for several years, merely upon academic matters.' Stephen rubbed his eyes. 'I'm surprised that he should write to me with a request like that. He sounds absolutely desperate, poor man — I'll have to do something, I suppose.'

'Such as what?'

'I'm not sure.' Stephen looked at his daughter and shrugged. 'I'll have a word with the Master, I think, see if the man can be offered something here. In the meantime I'll send him some money, and hope he can make his way out of Russia, then get on a boat at one of the Baltic ports.'

Stephen grimaced. 'Damn fool,' he muttered, pushing back his chair and getting to his feet. 'He should have had more sense than to get involved with these so-called liberators! What have politics to do with scholarship? If he can't get out of Russia now, he'll starve to death — and all for the sake of a pamphlet I don't imagine anybody's read anyway!'

Dorcas, who had sat and listened patiently to this exchange, caught Stephen's hand as he walked past her chair. 'What's this all about?' she asked.

Although she was well aware that her mother did not understand German, Anna handed the letter to Dorcas. 'A correspondent of Papa's, a Jewish gentleman, has been dismissed from his post at the university,' she said. 'He is anxious to leave Russia and come to England. He wants Papa to use his influence to find him a teaching position at Oxford. That's all.'

'Oh — that's all, is it?' Dorcas looked up at Stephen. 'You and the Master are not the greatest of friends at present, are you?' she enquired, unable to resist shooting a meaningful glance at Anna.

'We never have been *friends.*' Stephen shrugged his shoulders. 'But he owes me a favour, so I shall go and see him anyway.'

Dorcas heard nothing more about the matter of five or six weeks. Then Stephen told her that the man who had written to him in such despair was to be offered a teaching post at the university provided, of course, that he could get to England.

'He's a very clever fellow,' remarked Stephen wryly. 'I really shouldn't have had anything to do with this. Dr Gordon's in my field, and he's done far more research than I have. He didn't spend ten, fifteen years messing around in excavations — well, of course, he never had the opportunity to do that. But there it is.'

He put his arm around Dorcas' shoulders. 'They could stay here, couldn't they, dear?' he asked. 'Just for a couple of weeks?'

Dorcas looked up at him, her eyes wide with alarm. '*They?*'

'Dr Gordon, his wife and daughter.'

Dorcas shrugged. 'I suppose so,' she agreed. 'When will they arrive?'

'I don't know. That's the point. When they do get to Oxford, the university will find them somewhere to live. It would only be for a short time that they'd need to stay with us.'

So Dorcas went away to worry about sheets, rooms, and meals. Especially meals. These people were Jewish. What did Jews eat? Dorcas seemed to remember that there'd been a Jewish family at the hotel in Weymouth the previous summer but, as far as she could remember, they'd eaten the same food as everyone else ...

A few days later, another letter came, this time from Denmark. Dora was informed that some visitors were coming.

'They'll be staying with us for a fortnight or so,' said her father. 'I want you to be especially pleasant to their daughter. I don't know if she'll speak any English, but she may know French. So it will be a good opportunity for you to practise your languages.'

Dora wasn't sure that she welcomed the idea of practising her French. She decided that if she had to be in this girl's company, she'd teach her English.

Dorcas looked forward to the arrival of these people with some degree of apprehension. She knew perfectly well that if Stephen found his guests uncongenial he would probably take himself off to college, and stay there for days on end, leaving her to do all the work.

Isaac and Sonia Gordon came to England in the spring. As their ship sailed down the English Channel, and into Southampton Water, it seemed to Isaac that he was at last looking upon the Promised Land. When they had docked and been given permission to leave the ship, Isaac took his daughter Miriam in his arms and held her aloft, so that she might gaze upon the dirty acres of docks, at the cranes, cargoes and the oily water.

'There is no persecution in England,' he told her. 'Here, there will be nothing to fear. They will not burn our house, destroy my books and terrorize my family just because I am a Jew.'

Miriam smiled at him, and said something in Yiddish. 'You must learn to speak English now, daughter,' chided Isaac in the English which he had taught himself, and which was so heavily accented that it was hardly recognizable as English at all.

Miriam stood between her parents now, and gazed suspiciously at the somewhat grubby Paradise spread out before her. It seemed years since she and her father and mother had packed some borrowed clothes and those few of his precious books he had been able to save from the fire before fleeing through the night like a trio of thieves, leaving their home town for ever.

Somehow, they had reached one of the Danish ports, and been able by offering him money to persuade a sea captain to give them passage to England, albeit without the proper documentation and identification papers.

Now, at a loss what to do next, the Gordons waited. Eventually a man in uniform approached them. 'You're from the *Marie-Louise*, aren't you?' he asked curtly.

Isaac nodded. 'We are.'

'Come with me.'

The man led them away to a building where they were interrogated by officials whose English even Isaac found hard to understand.

The attitude of the customs men towards these three Russian Jews, whose papers were obvious forgeries, and who had hardly any money at all, was far from friendly. Sonia shrank against the back of her chair and tried not to cry. And Miriam scowled at these men in extreme distaste, thinking that this species of police was just as disagreeable as the Russian variety.

'I am offered a job at the university of Oxford,' explained Isaac patiently, repeating himself for the third or fourth time. 'I have letters confirming this. Look. I know the rest of our papers are not in order. We are refugees.'

The Gordons were kept in suspense for several days. But, eventually, they were given clearance and informed that they could stay in England for the time being.

In spite of the coolness of their initial reception, the Gordons were apparently resolved to like England, and to be pleased with the English. Isaac had been offered a junior lecturer's post, and he now endeavoured to perfect his English in time for the beginning of the new term. His wife and daughter, whose knowledge of English was yet very limited, tried as hard as he did. The Lawrences found the Gordons the most amenable and pleasant of guests.

Miriam, a slim, dark, sad-eyed child, tall for her years, was very quiet and reserved, but she had a most captivating smile. Dora, interested by her strange, foreign manners and her exotic appearance, took to her straight away. The English girl was charmed to discover that the Russian family had come thousands of miles with only those few possessions they could carry in a couple of carpet bags.

'But why did you have to leave your home?' asked Dora, to whom the concept of racial persecution was quite alien. 'Why did you have to get out of Russia?'

'Why?' repeated Miriam, puzzled.

'Why? *Warum?*' added Dora hopefully, for Miriam seemed to understand German.

'Ah.' Miriam smiled, sadly '*Polizei*,' she explained bitterly. 'They go to our house, you know — they burn it. And they tell my father that unless he leaves, they do the same thing to us. So we come here.'

'I see.' Dora shrugged, and smiled in sympathy. 'Never mind,' she said inadequately. 'Come and have some tea.'

Stephen spent much of the following week in his study, talking to Dr Gordon. Anna was sometimes invited to join them, but no one else was admitted. Dorcas had her hands full, trying to understand, and make her cook understand, what the Gordons could and could not eat, and in what combinations.

Isaac, who had bought himself English clothes, and who now — although he still looked like a foreigner — was not so obviously a Jew, privately told Sonia that there was no need to observe all the dietary laws now. 'To insist upon special arrangements being made just for us makes us look different and difficult,' he remarked. 'So don't be so fastidious in future!'

Sonia shook her head, frowned reproachfully at her husband. 'Mrs Lawrence has asked me most particularly what her cook should prepare for us,' she said. 'She understands that we must not eat things which are forbidden — she has even sent her cook out to buy special food —'

'Exactly!' Isaac glared at his wife. 'I know she has! And you still insist on checking up on her, you still visit the kitchen to make sure everything is properly prepared! Don't you realize that it's impertinent to do that?'

'But Mrs Lawrence told me —'

'Yes, maybe.' Isaac scowled at Sonia. 'But you mustn't put her to so much trouble! You mustn't turn our only friends against us!'

Sonia walked across the room and took her husband by the shoulders. 'You will turn our God against us!' she cried, beside herself. 'Just look at you! Look at you, in your smart black suit, in your white shirt and fancy waistcoat! You've trimmed your hair and shaved off your beard — you don't look Jewish any more!

'We're English now.' Isaac frowned at his wife. 'Or, at any rate, we soon shall be. So you must adapt, you must change! Grow your hair, learn to like English food, and behave like an English lady!'

'No, I shan't!' Sonia's dark eyes flashed. 'I'm not an English lady! I'm a Jew!'

Miriam, taken for a walk in the garden, showed a talent for climbing trees which impressed Dora. She dragged Miriam off to her bedroom, and showed her a vast collection of postcards, pressed flowers and cuttings from picture papers, making her a present of some of her treasures.

Miriam, who had learned very early in life that kindness is not to be taken for granted, responded to Dora's friendliness. Over the next few weeks the two of them became very attached to each other, so much so that Dora was in tears when Miriam left the Summertown house to move into the flat in Norham Gardens which the university authorities had found for her family.

'You can visit, Dora,' said Miriam. 'I shall like to see you there.'

Anna offered to take charge of Miriam's education. With two little girls to teach, she had less time to fret for John, less time to wonder why he had not answered her last letter, and indeed had not written to her now for six months or more.

He wasn't coming to England, that was obvious. She thought that perhaps he'd left Europe altogether, had maybe given up his job and gone to America. He'd said he'd like to go to America ...

'Where is he, darling?' she asked Marcus, bouncing the child on her lap. 'What's become of him?'

'Mama,' replied Marcus, wisely, beaming at his mother. 'Mama.'

He was so like his father. Anna now saw that her son's straight, fair hair would never coarsen and darken, and that those light grey eyes would remain pale. She touched the smooth, white flesh of his forearm and remembered the texture of John's finely-grained skin. She shook herself. 'I'm becoming maudlin,' she told the baby. 'It's time I went to give those girls some work. Shall we take you to Grandmama?'

One winter morning Anna told her pupils that she had a sore throat and that she did not feel up to taking them for lessons. She

340

gave them some work to do and went back up to her room, carrying Marcus with her.

Miriam and Dora lounged around the dining room, unwilling to work by themselves. 'It must be time to have something to eat,' remarked Dora.

Miriam glanced up at the clock on the mantelshelf. 'Yes,' she agreed. 'It must be. Let's go and get something.'

With the speed and determination of any hungry children, they dashed out of the dining room and across the hall — cannoning into the young man who stood, as if lost, in the gloom.

The man disentangled himself from the arms and legs of the two girls, and set them upon their feet again, anxiously brushing their clothes and checking them for scraped knees. Eventually their sniggers died down and they could examine him without giggling. He asked them, very gravely, if Miss Lawrence or either of her parents were at home.

Dora looked at the man. He hadn't said who he was. Ought she to ask? Although he spoke like a gentleman, he was rather too shabbily dressed for her to feel entirely at ease with him. He was a little too old to be a student, she thought, and his face was sunburnt, even in December. She decided that he must be a workman of some kind.

Miriam appeared to have come to the same conclusion. 'Would you like to see the housemaid?' she asked.

'No, I don't want to see the housemaid.' The man smiled at Dora patiently. 'I should like to see Miss Lawrence,' he repeated. 'Or either of her parents.'

Dora shrugged. 'Well, Papa's in college,' she told him. 'And my mother is at her Ladies' Charity meeting. Anna's ill, but I expect she'll see you. Who shall I say wishes to speak to her?'

There was, as it happened, no need to fetch Anna. Dora's elder sister had heard the commotion in the hallway, and she now came to the head of the staircase with Marcus in her arms. When she saw who the visitor was, she lurched forward and grabbed the stair-rail, to support herself. Marcus, frightened, squealed loudly.

At the sound of his son's cry, John Harley looked up. 'Anna!' he cried. 'Anna! Oh, Anna!'

He ran up the stairs two or three at a time and he drew Anna into his arms, locking her inside a passionate embrace, kissing her

341

with uninhibited fervour — and making Marcus yell all the more.

Mesmerized by the shock of seeing him so unexpectedly, Anna stood perfectly still and let him kiss her. 'What are you doing here?' she faltered when, finally, she could speak.

'I've come back for you, of course!' John Harley beamed at her, evidently delighted to see her looking so pretty and, in spite of her sore throat, so well. 'Oh, darling, it's just not possible to live without you! I've tried, and it's almost killed me. I shan't do so any more.'

He looked at Marcus who, recovering from his surprise, gave his father a wide smile. 'Especially now,' he added. 'Why didn't you tell me about this one?'

Down in the hallway below, Dora and Miriam gazed up at the scene above them, too enchanted even to giggle.

John's superiors had decided that he needed a holiday. Enthusiasm in a trainee was all very well, but young Harley overdid it. Up at five or six every morning, spending all the time before noon on paperwork, then out until nightfall or later, he seemed determined to work himself into an early grave. They had never known an apprentice like him.

Certainly he worked to good effect. He had become fluent in French, had learned the business thoroughly and from scratch; and he didn't even mind taking off his coat and helping with the harvest itself. Ambitious, determined, he would probably be a partner in the firm one day. And he'd be the sort of boss who would understand his workforce, having done most of their jobs himself.

But, apart from the few hours' sleep which everyone must have, or die, he didn't appear to take any rest at all. Although he was a good-looking fellow, he appeared to have no desire for the company of women. Nor of men, come to that. Pleasant and sociable enough, he made no enemies, but neither did he make any friends ...

Then, one day, it occurred to John's supervisor that he must have a sweetheart in England. That was it, of course! The poor lad was pining away with longing for her. That was why he worked so hard, that was why he often looked so miserable, that was why he spent no money on clothes, why he always looked like one of the cellarmen!

'I'm sending you over to England for a short holiday,' he told John the following day. He stood back and waited for the delighted smile which he was sure would now come; for the young man's cold grey eyes to light up.

But John Harley merely shrugged. 'I have no use for holidays,' he said shortly. 'I don't want one.'

The supervisor frowned. 'Surely you'd like to see your family and your friends?' he asked.

'I have no family — nor any particular attachments — in England.'

A few weeks later the supervisor — now having conceived the idea that John Harley nursed an affection for a young woman who did not love him in return — tried a different approach. One November morning he called John into his office and presented him with a folder. 'I want you to take the report on the Bordeaux vineyards to the firm in London,' he said firmly. 'Mr Andrews will want your comments. I've booked you through to Southampton, and I don't expect you back here for six weeks.' He handed John the documents and his tickets and turned away to speak to his clerk before the young man could argue.

John slouched out of the office, realizing, sourly, that if he wanted to keep his job he had no choice but to do as he was told. He would have to spend Christmas in England — the last place on earth he wanted to be.

He tried to spin out his work in London, to make it take as long as possible. But, if John had no use for Christmas, other members of the firm had, and they were anxious to deal as promptly as they could with the matters which John had been sent to discuss. So, by the middle of December, his business was concluded and he had nothing to do but walk around London on his own, until the time came to return to France.

After a week's indolence he decided that another three like it, with no work to distract him, would drive him insane. He wrote to a college friend now living in Worcestershire, and was pleased when he received a cordial reply, together with an invitation to spend the holiday at his friend's house near Evesham.

He accepted the invitation. Staying with the Athertons, he'd be forced to talk. He'd have no time to brood about the past. If he drank enough, he might even be able to get to sleep at night

343

without thinking of Anna until it hurt.

'Worcester train, sir? Change at Reading.' The inspector clipped John's ticket and grinned. 'Looks like we're in for some snow, don't it?'

'It does.' Not particularly caring if there were to be blizzards or even avalanches, John opened his newspaper and began to read.

His knowledge of the geography of England was, to say the least, sketchy. It simply had not occurred to him that, after Reading, the train would pass through Oxford. And as the train drew into the station there, as he saw the familiar city outline looming through a grey December mist, John cursed under his breath. He shut his eyes, determined not to open them again until the train was steaming on through the Cotswolds.

But there was a delay. The train waited for a connection. It waited. And waited.

It was too much for John. As the guard's whistle went, he wrenched open the door of the carriage. The train was moving out of the station as he fell on to the platform into the arms of a startled porter, who swore at him. 'Bloody hell, mate!' he grumbled, rubbing his arm. 'You barmy, or what?'

'I'm sorry. Here —' John pushed a coin into the man's hand and strode back along the platform. He walked under the subway in a daze, and presented his ticket to the collector — aware that his luggage was still on the train which had steamed off up the line.

'Worcester train half-past three, sir,' intoned the collector, without interest.

Walking towards the town, John found that his heart was thumping. 'Barmy,' the porter had said. No doubt he was. But he plodded on, not stopping until he came to the house in the Banbury Road. When he rang the bell, no one came to answer the door. He pushed it — found it was open. He had stepped into the hall and been knocked flying by two little girls.

Anna disengaged herself from her husband's embrace and called to Dora. 'Take Marcus,' she said. 'This gentleman and I have something to discuss.'

Miriam and Dora exchanged glances. They were both now consumed with curiosity, not a little doubtful if it was right that Anna should take her friend into her bedroom. Who on earth was he? He seemed to know Anna very well, but Dora was certain that she'd never set eyes on him before.

She did know, however, that it was pointless to argue with her sister. Seeing the determined glint in Anna's narrow eyes, she obediently took her nephew in her arms, and promised him biscuits if he'd come with her. She heard Anna's bedroom door close.

'I suppose that was your sister's husband?' asked Miriam casually.

Dora put Marcus down upon the sitting room carpet. 'She's not married,' she muttered.

'Of course she is!' Miriam let out a shout of laughter. 'Of course she's married! How could she have a baby otherwise? Come on, Dora — tell me what's going on! Please?'

'What's going on?' Dora, unwilling to admit her own complete ignorance of the whole business, pretended to be tying Marcus' pinafore strings.

'Your mother told mine that Anna's husband was abroad,' continued Miriam. 'Has he come back for good now?'

'Oh, I don't know!' Dora looked up at Miriam. 'You seem to know more than I do,' she said huffily. 'They never tell *me* anything!'

Dora was looking through the window observing the lamp-lighter when she saw her father coming up the drive. 'Papa's coming, Anna!' she called, going to the door to let him in.

At the moment that Anna, looking defensive, emerged from the drawing room, Stephen stepped into the porch. Catching sight of his daughter, he walked quickly towards her and took her by the shoulders; he kissed her cheek, and then enfolded her in a bear-hug of an embrace.

'What's the matter?' she asked, smiling at him. He didn't usually greet her so fulsomely. For a moment, she forgot about her fear of what he was going to say when he saw John. 'Papa!' she cried, shaking him. 'What is it?'

Stephen released her and took off his overcoat. 'I have something to tell you,' he replied. 'It's good news — well, it is for you, at any rate.'

But then he stared past her, towards the drawing room door. Anna realized that her husband must have appeared behind her, and was now looking at her father.

She turned, gazed anxiously from one man to the other, wondering what would happen now, praying that her father would not lose his temper.

Stephen's expression, however, was one of simple surprise. He did not look angry at all. To Anna's utter astonishment, he went towards John and held out his hand to him. John, equally surprised, took it.

Stephen turned to Anna. 'Is your mother back yet?' he asked.

'No, not yet. She usually gets back about five on her charity days.'

Stephen looked at his watch. 'Then she'll be here in about ten minutes or so,' he remarked. 'Anna, I could do with some tea — I expect we all could.' He saw his younger daughter peering around the banister. 'Dora?' he asked. 'Would you go and arrange it?'

He walked into his study, leaving the door open, so that John and Anna could follow him.

Dora, watching from her vantage point on the stairs, remained completely mystified. She shrugged, and went to ask the housemaid to send in some tea. As usual, she was going to be left out of things. She decided that she would walk over to Norham Gardens, and grumble to Miriam.

'Sit down, sit down — both of you!' Stephen crouched by the fender and stirred up the fire, which had been left unattended all day. Then he stood up, and put his hands behind his back. 'It's nice to see you, John,' he said evenly. 'Are you well?'

John frowned. 'Yes, I'm well,' he replied. Having been expecting to be asked to leave the house, he found this cordiality somewhat unnerving.

'I've been speaking to my wife today,' continued Stephen. 'I've learned some most surprising things.'

Anna stood up. 'What are you talking about, Papa?' she demanded sharply. 'You don't look at all well. And where have you been all day?'

Stephen went over to his desk. 'I have some papers here,' he said. He beckoned to John. 'Come over here, boy — the light's better. Now, where did I put them? Ah.'

He fished in his inside pocket and pulled out a large blue

envelope, out of which fell some torn, yellowing documents and scraps of paper. He let the whole lot tumble upon his desk. 'Certificates — the Guardians' letter to Elizabeth — yes, it's all there.' He raked his hand through his hair. 'Have a look at it all,' he invited. 'You as well, Anna.'

Stephen sat down by the fire and smiled apologetically at both of them. 'You must excuse me if I seem incoherent,' he said. 'At this moment, I don't feel at all like myself — my head's spinning. And when I saw John here, I thought I was imagining things!'

He looked anxiously up at Anna. 'I do wish your mother would come!' he said. 'Will you tell them to hurry up with that *tea*?'

Chapter Twenty Three

STEPHEN NEVER KNEW WHY HE had chosen that particular day to visit Elizabeth. It was several weeks since Anna had found that threatening little missive from Judith, but *that* had merely served to convince him that his only legitimate daughter was probably as unpleasant as her mother, and he had no intention of opening any sort of negotiations with *her*.

She had, however, told him that her mother was ill. How ill, he wondered. He remembered the blueness which he had noticed beneath Elizabeth's eyes on the last occasion that he'd seen her. There had been that strange smell which clung about her, too — and now he knew what it was. There were, he decided, matters which he and she ought to discuss.

Finding himself alone in college one winter afternoon, sitting at his desk there with nothing to do except mark a pile of first year essays, Stephen put on his coat and went down the stairs. He walked across the road to the livery stables and hired a horse. Then he set off for Stanton St Nicholas.

The journey from Oxford was cold and dirty. A bone-chilling east wind blew, and the winter slush was melting into the puddles on the roads, making the going treacherous. Stephen was almost glad when he reached the village and the horse could pick its way along the rutted, unswept gravel drive which led to his wife's house.

He noticed the unkempt grounds, the dead flowers of the previous autumn standing brown and lifeless in the borders. The air of desolation persisted up to the front door of the house, its paint dull and the brass unpolished.

He pushed open the unlocked door and he stood in the hall, looking about him. A smell of damp permeated the chill air, the dust lay thick upon the furniture. He'd had a wasted journey.

Obviously, Elizabeth no longer lived there. He wondered where the caretaker was.

'Can I help you, sir?' A scurrying sound made him turn round to see the cook coming towards him. She was hurriedly wiping her hands upon her apron, a look of panic on her face. She screwed up her eyes and peered at him. 'Mr Lawrence?' she asked. 'It is Mr Lawrence, isn't it? The gentleman who came before?'

She pushed a strand of hair out of her eyes. 'I saw you coming up the drive, sir — but I thought I must be imagining things.'

Stephen attempted a reassuring smile. 'Is Mrs Harley here?' he asked.

'Well, sir — she is. But I'm sure she won't see you. I'm sorry, sir — but I've had instructions not to let visitors into the house.' The cook leaned towards him and dropped her voice to a whisper. 'Since you were here before, sir, there've been such goings-on! The mistress isn't herself at all these days. She's turned away all the staff, saving me and Martha — that's the housemaid, sir — and she stays in her room all the time.

'As for Miss Harley, she's been sent to Switzerland for the winter, and Mr Harley — well, he's abroad, too, as far as I know. I think they should be sent for, but the mistress won't hear of it.' She sniffed. 'Are you a relation, sir?' she enquired.

'Yes.' Stephen nodded. 'Yes, I am. I heard that your mistress is ill —'

'Ill?' The cook shrugged, raising her hands in an expressive gesture of bafflement and despair. 'I don't know if she's ill, sir,' she said. 'Certainly she's altered a great deal in the past year or so. She's definitely out of sorts. There's a doctor from Oxford comes to see her three or four times a week now; a young chap he is, walks in here as if he owns the place.'

'Doctor?' asked Stephen, expecting the cook to supply the man's name.

But instead she snorted, and folded her arms. 'Doctor! Yes — well, that's what he calls himself!' She bent towards Stephen, confidential again. 'Spends all hours of the day and night here, he does! There's something odd about it all though it's not my place to say so. Perhaps you, sir —'

She looked hard at Stephen and saw a plain, middle-aged man, the epitome of respectability in his sober academic black and grey.

Evidently deciding that he must be a lawyer or a professional man of some sort, a person of some authority, she looked pointedly up the stairs. 'If you're a relative, sir, perhaps you ought to see the mistress,' she said. 'I'll get Martha to show you up.'

Stephen took off his coat and hat, brushed some of the mud from his trousers. 'I'll find my own way,' he told her. He went up the stairs.

He knocked upon the door of a room from which a succession of muffled sounds issued. At his rap, there was a sudden silence — then some scuffling — then a sharp laugh, and a shout from Elizabeth to go away. He hesitated for a second or two but then he pushed open the door and walked into the room.

It was almost dark inside, for the curtains were closed against the pale light of the December afternoon. A solitary lamp glowed feebly from a table near the disordered bed, upon which Elizabeth was sitting ...

She appeared to be dressed only in a thin silk robe. Quite probably she had been in bed for her hair was untidy, and her feet were bare. The room was oppressively hot, for a great fire blazed in the hearth. A stale smell of old perfumes and cosmetics, together with the musty odour of unwashed clothes and human being, hung in the air stressing that the room had not been aired for some time. Overlying all this, there was the familiar but elusive scent which Stephen had noticed the last time he had seen his wife.

Elizabeth stared at him. Even in the bad light, he could see that the pupils of her eyes were no bigger than pinpricks, and that she looked dazed. She peered at him more closely — recognized him and drew back, pulling her dressing gown more tightly round her.

'What do *you* want?' she demanded. 'I never expected to see *you* again. How dare you come to my house, after the way you spoke to me the last time you were here?'

Stephen walked over to her and looked down upon her upturned face. There was a wildness of expression there — a wide-eyed, open-mouthed excitement which he remembered from years ago, on certain nights when —

'I heard you were ill,' he said. 'And so, I wanted to see you.' He went to the window and made to pull back the curtains.

'Leave them!' snapped Elizabeth. 'Don't touch them!' But he pushed back the heavy drapes, then let up the blinds, so that what light the dull day outside could provide might flood into the fusty room.

Now, he found the sight of Elizabeth, who sat blinking in the cold daylight, oddly moving. He sat down beside her, looked enquiringly at her, waited for her to speak.

'I heard you sent him abroad,' she remarked at last. 'He's a merchant's underling, so I was told. That's a fine thing! An excellent thing for someone of his class and education! He's a real credit to me now!'

Stephen reached across and took her hand in his, felt her pulse. It was far from normal. 'How long have you been ill?' he asked gently. 'What does the doctor say is wrong with you?'

She jerked her hand away. 'I don't want to talk about that with you!' she cried. 'As if you have any right to know anything about me! Ah — I see it all now! You've come to find out if I'm dying. And if I am, you'll go back to the peasant whore and tell her that she can look forward to becoming the squire's lady! And that those bastard brats of hers will be legitimized!'

Elizabeth made a feeble attempt to toss her blonde locks in a gesture of contempt — to assume an expression of haughty disdain. 'Well, I'm sorry to have to disappoint you,' she sneered. 'I expect to live for many years yet. I may well outlast you!'

He felt her body swaying slightly as she spoke. She was slurring her speech, and tripping up over the longer words. As she finished talking, she lolled up against him, trying, vainly, to focus her eyes upon his face.

'Do you take opium for the pain?' he asked.

'Opium? I don't take opium!' She made an effort to stand up, but her feet refused to support her and she sat down again, heavily. 'You've been told what you came to find out,' she muttered thickly. 'Now go away. The sight of you sickens me.'

'I can't go yet.' Stephen's voice was low and level. 'I think,' he said carefully, 'that there are some things which you and I ought to discuss. We must, for instance, decide how our estates will be divided between those two children we were so foolish as to produce. I can't believe that you mean to disinherit our son all together.'

'What?' Elizabeth grabbed at his arm, shaking him. Her face was white with anger now. 'The children we were so foolish as to produce? How dare you say such a thing to me! You obliged me to conceive those children!'

'Elizabeth, that's nonsense —'

'Is it? *Is it?*' She ground her teeth. 'I can remember it all as if it were yesterday,' she muttered. 'I can remember you holding me down, forcing me — when I pleaded with you, you hit me. Beast.'

Leaning across him now, Elizabeth slapped his face as hard as she could. 'My God, I hate you!' she spat. 'I once swore that I'd kill you! I wish I could do so now!'

She glared at him, her face a picture of pure hatred. 'And to think I took him from the gutter,' she cried. 'Poor, nameless bastard that he was! To think I loved him, cared for him, believing that he, at any rate, would never be anything like you! Oh, he would have made you sorry for the way you treated me! But then he had to meet your slut of a daughter!'

'My daughter?' Stephen took Elizabeth's hand from his sleeve. 'You took John from the gutter?' he asked her, puzzled. 'Why did you say that? What did you mean?'

Elizabeth looked away from him. 'Mean? I didn't mean anything. Go away.'

Stephen took her wrist. 'What did you mean?' he repeated, shaking her. 'I won't leave until you explain that remark.' He turned her round to face him, caught her chin, tried to make her focus her eyes upon his. His face was stinging from the slap, his temper was rising, and now he was in no mood for prevarication. He took her other wrist, and tightened his grip. 'Tell me what I want to know, Elizabeth,' he said reasonably.

She winced, tried to squirm free, but he held her firm. 'Let me go, adulterer,' she muttered, looking past him. 'If you hold me any longer, I'll scream. I'll have the police sent for. I'll say you attacked me.'

'And if you do that, I shall say that I was merely trying to persuade my wife to explain herself.' He let her go. 'Tell me what you meant by those last few remarks of yours, and I'll leave. I'll never see you again. But you have to speak to me now. Otherwise, Elizabeth . . .'

'Otherwise you'll what?' She rubbed her chafed wrists. 'I won't tell you *anything*,' she cried. 'You can't make me, can you? Go on — force me to speak. What will you do? Beat me? Rape me? You've done that before. Will you kill me? What will you learn then?'

She knelt up against him, letting her gown gape open, rubbing herself against his arm. 'Why do you hesitate?' she jeered, laughing. 'Take whatever you want from me. As you said, I'm your wife. You can do just as you please with me!'

Stephen could feel the soft weight of her bosom against his side; a strand of her silver-blonde hair was lying upon his shoulder, and her white hand, the wrist above it reddened where he had held it, was resting on his sleeve like a dove. He knew he was powerless. At a loss, he sat on her bed, her mocking laughter ringing in his ears. She lay against him for two minutes, three, four, before she understood that he was not going to respond in the way she'd anticipated. But then, to his astonishment, she began to cry.

Elizabeth was weeping. 'Oh, Stephen, Stephen!' she sobbed. 'Stephen — why did you hurt me so?'

'Hurt you?' He looked at her now and saw, to his surprise, that her eyes were full of tears. They overflowed and rolled down her cheeks, splashing on to her robe. 'I never meant to hurt you!'

'You did!' she choked. 'Oh, you did! You hurt me quite deliberately — you were cruel to me! But when you first knew me, Stephen, you loved me.'

She looked at him pathetically. 'Why did you change?' she asked. 'Why did you poison my life? You spoilt everything for me, who'd meant to be so happy with you!'

'I didn't change.' Stephen shrugged. 'When you first met me, you flattered me; and I imagined that you loved me. I was wrong.'

'But I did love you! I did!' She smiled through her tears. 'I remember when I first saw you; I thought then, 'that man shall be my husband'! Oh, you weren't like all the others! You were a man, among all those overgrown boys! I dreamed about you every night, you know. I saw your face in my mirror, even though I was looking at my own. You're still in my heart — you always will be!'

Stephen grimaced. 'Don't talk such nonsense, Elizabeth,' he said sharply. 'We were both stupid. We hardly knew each other when we were married but it didn't take long for us to discover that we were completely unsuited. We could never have made a success of things. You know that.'

'We could! Oh, we still could!' Elizabeth caught Stephen by the shoulders and shook him. 'When you first knew me, you did love me,' she insisted. 'I know you did. Women know these things, so there's no point in your denying it. You had the air, the look of a man in love! You were so gentle with me, so kind …

'I don't know how you could have turned against me. How could you have left me, young and beautiful as I was then; the mother of your children? You left me and went off to Europe, like a vagabond. Then you took up again with that — that slut!'

She sighed. 'Will you get me a drink?' she asked.

Stephen, moving carefully to avoid distracting her — for she seemed to be almost in a trance now — got up and poured her a glassful of spirits. She drained the glass. 'I was so beautiful,' she repeated. 'And yet you left me. You wanted a dirty little peasant instead. Why, Stephen? Why?'

Her tears began to flow again, and she rocked herself backwards and forwards, sobbing. 'You did love me once. You did! Stephen, you loved me — didn't you?'

He said nothing. He who is silent, consents. And that seemed to satisfy her.

'When I left Ashton Cross,' she said, 'I brought the babies here. I didn't care for them much when they were tiny. But when they started to get older, I began to love them. Judith was a beautiful little girl; she's grown up to look very like you, you know, she's very dark. John was always sickly. He died when he was three.'

Died? Stephen's heart jumped. He did not dare to speak.

Now Elizabeth was crying as if her heart would break. Great, gulping sobs shook her body and Stephen, pitying her, took her hand and held it in his. 'When they buried him,' she whispered, 'I thought I should go mad. Stephen, there's nothing so terrible as the grief which a mother feels for a dead child. It cuts into her heart. The memory fades a little with time, but still it's always there, hurting her, spoiling her pleasure in everything …

'My doctor told me I should marry again, have more children. Then, when I said I'd never remarry, he brought me an infant from the union workhouse. A skinny little brat it was, dirty and horrible. It would take my mind off my loss, he said. As if it could have, some filthy pauper's bastard!' Elizabeth sniffed and held out her glass. 'Get me another drink,' she pleaded.

Stephen poured more brandy.

. 'I saw it one day in the garden,' she went on. 'The servants had cleaned it up and dressed it decently — they'd made quite a pet of it, you see. The sun was shining on its hair, I remember I thought it had a golden halo around its head. And then he turned round, and he smiled at me.'

Elizabeth steadied herself and looked into Stephen's eyes. 'I decided that he would be my son,' she said. 'And he was. I loved him. I thought, one day he will do everything he can to hurt Stephen. I shall have a man to fight for me. And with his help, I shall have my revenge.'

'But he met Anna.'

'Yes.' Elizabeth laughed, a horrible, mirthless sound coming from the back of her throat. 'I heard about him and your bastard a few days before he was due home from seeing a friend in Yorkshire — where he never went, of course. One of his friends from college came over here to return some books. He was a silly, talkative idiot, who told me that John had said he was getting married.

'I was very clever, Stephen. I pretended that I knew all about it — although when I heard who his bride was to be, my heart almost stopped beating. How did he meet her? *How*? What did she do to him, to make him fall in love with her, to make him go off with her like that?'

It seemed to Stephen that Elizabeth was now talking to herself. But, suddenly, she was aware of him again. She tottered over to her bureau, opened it and watched while a great disorderly mess of papers spilled all over the floor. 'There's a blue envelope amongst all that stuff,' she said. 'Find it for me.'

Stephen sorted through the pile of documents, and found one which appeared to be what she wanted. He unsealed the envelope and took out the papers inside.

Headed writing paper bore the legend, 'Oxford Board of Guardians'. Attached to this letter was a birth certificate relating to a boy born in the care of the parish three years before; parents' names unknown, mother deceased, child as yet unnamed. Also in the envelope was a death certificate in respect of John Randall Lawrence, aged three years, two months and four days.

'Why did you not tell me?' asked Stephen softly. 'What did you gain by separating them? I can understand you wanting to hurt me

— but at John's expense — well, that seems harsh.'

'What did I gain?' Elizabeth laughed. 'I had the pleasure of seeing you as miserable as you'd made me,' she said. 'Your face, when I last saw you, was the very picture of despair. I remembered your expression for days. And I wanted to hurt him, the wretch! I'd planned to leave him half my estate but now he'll get nothing. I've willed everything to Judith, and told her why.'

Elizabeth leaned against the door frame, grinning at Stephen. 'It's almost as gratifying to have told you the truth,' she observed. 'You'd have found out some day, anyway. It will be such a comfort to you, the great and famous Dr Lawrence, to know that your bastard is married to one of the same — to a penniless pauper!'

She giggled. 'He'll never *be* anything, you know,' she added. 'Oh, he's good-natured enough, but he's idle, he's stupid, he hasn't the brains to succeed. He's been bred up to be a gentleman, you see. I don't doubt he'll be a drag on you for the rest of your days! Oh, God, I wish you'd get out of my sight!'

Stephen picked up the blue envelope, pushed the papers back inside it, and put it into his inside pocket. Ignoring Elizabeth's protests, he went through the rest of the papers she had tipped on to the floor, satisfying himself that there was nothing among them which related to John's parentage or history. Then he walked through the doorway and back down the stairs.

As he rode back to Oxford, he found that his eyes were smarting. He blamed the wind. He should, after all, be happy now, for soon his favourite child would be as ecstatic as she'd been miserable before.

Chapter Twenty Four

DORA HAD COME BACK FROM Miriam's house and gone slowly upstairs to her room, hanging over the banister as she went, straining to catch whatever was still being discussed in her father's study. Faint murmurings reached her. There was her mother's soft voice again, but Dora could not make out what she was saying. They had been talking now for at least two hours ...

Dora lurked on the first floor landing for another twenty minutes and was finally rewarded by the sight of the young man and Anna coming through the door of Stephen's study, hand in hand and grinning like a pair of Cheshire cats. Then Dorcas came out looking almost as pleased as Anna had. But she was followed a minute later by Stephen, who looked anything but delighted. He walked across the hall, his hands clasped firmly under his coat-tails, scowling just as he usually did whenever anything had particularly annoyed him.

Dora grimaced. She just had time to duck into her bedroom as Anna and the young man came up the stairs. They went into Anna's bedroom and Dora heard the key turn in the lock, followed by the extraordinary sound of Anna actually giggling.

'Well,' thought Dora. 'So strange men can walk into the house, slobber all over Anna — and then go to bed with her!'

Feeling that she was entitled to some sort of explanation, Dora decided that she would go and find her mother. She had no sooner pulled off her clothes and got into her nightdress, however, than she met Dorcas coming to look for her. 'Come into your bedroom, dear,' said Dorcas. 'I've something to tell you.'

They sat in Dora's bedroom, on Dora's bed, their heads close together. 'I know she's married,' began Dora sulkily. 'You told Mrs Gordon so.' She glowered at her mother. 'Miriam knew!' she cried.

'But you didn't tell me!'

'I'm sorry, dear, it wouldn't have been very easy to explain.'
Dorcas looked down at her hands, then at her daughter. 'All I told
Mrs Gordon was that Anna's husband had gone abroad, which was
true. There wasn't any need to tell her anything more, you see.
But now, I'll tell you everything.' Dorcas sighed. 'It's all so very
complicated ...'

At first Dora assumed that she was being fobbed off with some
fairy story. 'How could he have thought he was our brother?' she
demanded. 'Did Papa have another wife?'

Dorcas frowned. 'Yes, he did,' she replied. 'He still has. But, you
see — after he and this lady were married, they found that they did
not like one another. They tried to live with each other for a while,
but they found it was impossible. So they decided to part.'

'And then Papa married you!' Dora narrowed her eyes. 'But
how could he have done, if his other wife is still alive? Did he have
two wives at the same time?'

'Well, you see ...' Dorcas drew a deep breath. She had known
that she would have to explain all this to her younger children at
some time; but now that the time had come, she found herself
blushing and tongue-tied, thoroughly embarrassed. 'Before your
father married the lady I spoke of, he and I were lovers,' she said.
'You know what that means, don't you? Anna was born when I
was eighteen, but by that time I had married someone else.
Stephen's wife had her twins about a year later.

'My husband and I did not get on very well. When Anna was
ten I left him, and came to live here in Oxford with Papa. He had
separated from his wife years before that, when her children were
babies.'

Dorcas looked hard at Dora. 'Try to understand, child, that
Stephen and I love each other,' she said. 'We both made mistakes
when we married other people.'

'Well, why didn't Papa marry you, then? Is he wicked?' Dora
looked reproachfully at her mother. 'I don't understand all this,'
she muttered. 'I thought we were just like everyone else — I
thought you were Papa's wife. Everybody thinks you are! Why
didn't Papa marry you in the first place?'

'I can't tell you that.' Dorcas shrugged. 'You don't need to know why. What matters is, that we're together now.'

'You said you'd tell me everything!' Dora scowled at her mother. 'What about John Harley, then?' she demanded.

'Ah. John Harley.' Dorcas frowned. 'Well, your father's wife didn't forgive him for leaving her.'

'Why not? If they agreed to part?'

'I can't go into that. Just listen to me. Now, this lady had two children, a boy and a girl. The boy died when he was very small, but she did not tell your father this.'

'Why?'

'I don't know! Dora, stop interrupting — this is hard enough to explain without you asking me *why* every minute!'

'I'm sorry.'

'Very well. The boy died. Years later, John Harley met Anna, quite by chance. They liked each other enough to wish to get married. And when Papa found out about it, he went to see his wife, who let him believe that Anna had married her half-brother. She didn't tell him that she had adopted John soon after her own son had died and had brought him up to think he was her child.

'She wanted to hurt us all. She let Anna and John believe that they were brother and sister. She wanted to make them miserable, you see. But today, Papa went to see her, and she told him the truth. That's why Anna and John are so happy now.'

Dora chewed her lower lip. 'How did Papa find out about John, in the end?' she asked.

'He went to see his wife, as I told you. She lives near Oxford, you see. I suppose he must have persuaded her to tell him the truth.'

'How?'

'Dora, I don't know! And I shan't ask him!' Dorcas took her daughter by the shoulders. 'He's rather upset about it all,' she said. 'He's going to need a few days to think about things. You mustn't ever mention any of what I've told you just now to him. Promise me that you won't?'

'Why not?'

'Dora, just *promise me!*'

'Oh — very well. I promise.' Dora looked at her mother. 'So Anna, Anthony and I are bastards,' she observed calmly. 'And you are a mistress. A kept woman; isn't that what it's called?'

'How do you know such words?' Dorcas stared at her daughter, shocked. 'Oh, Dora, you mustn't ever think of yourself as a — what you said! You are all three of you our precious, much-loved children! Always remember that! Always!'

Dora sniffed, not convinced. She lay awake most of the night, thinking about it all, and for the next few days she was uncharacteristically subdued. She wished Anthony were coming home for Christmas, so that she could discuss it all with him. But he was spending the holiday with a schoolfriend. Heaven alone knew when he'd be told …

The following day, Dora took herself off to Norham Gardens and stayed there. She needed to discuss her mother's revelations with someone — she needed to be reassured. Miriam, she knew instinctively, could be trusted to keep her confidences. 'You won't tell anyone, will you, Miriam?' asked Dora anxiously. 'It's all a secret, you see …'

'I shan't tell anyone at all. Not even Mama.'

'Good.' Dora smiled tearfully. 'I had to tell you!' she cried, beginning to sob. 'Oh, it's all so horrible! Why couldn't I have normal parents, like everyone else?'

There was an air of holiday in the Summertown house over the next couple of days. The mood of gaiety persisted, despite the fact that Dora's father did his best to spoil Christmas by shutting himself up in his study and refusing to have anything at all to do with the usual seasonal activities.

'Leave him alone,' said Dorcas firmly. 'He'll talk to us all again when he's ready. If we bother him now, he'll just become angry and upset everybody.'

But nothing could have upset Anna. Too happy to notice that her father was unusually surly, she laughed and even sang — one morning, Dora was astonished to see her sedate elder sister actually dancing across the landing, and singing one of the music hall songs which Anna had always pretended to despise.

Dora, still trying to digest the significance of her mother's recent revelations, took to going into her father's study and sitting in the window seat. Hidden by the curtains, her thoughts were disturbed only by the scratch of his pen on paper, or by the soft rustle of pages as he turned the leaves of a book.

'*Is* he wicked?' she wondered. He didn't look wicked. Just very sad. One morning she went to sit on the arm of his chair and leaned against his shoulder. 'What's the matter, Papa?' she asked.

'Nothing, Dora.' He put down his pen and took her on his lap. 'Do you like John?' he enquired, after a few moments' silence.

'He seems quite nice.' Dora shrugged. 'Anna likes him,' she added. 'And Mama says he's charming.'

'Does she, indeed?' Stephen rubbed his eyes and sighed. 'So he's a favourite with you all, is he? Ah, well. Perhaps that's just as it should be.'

John caught Dora one day, just as she was about to slip into Stephen's room where she'd intended to have a quiet read. 'Come for a walk with me, little sister,' he invited, smiling at her. 'You can tell me all about yourself.'

'Is Anna coming too?'

'No — she's sorting out some clothes. We'll take Marcus, though, shall we, and show him the snow? He hasn't seen snow before.'

Dora found that her new brother-in-law was indeed very nice. Telling him about herself did not mean — as she'd feared — that he wanted to ask her all kinds of embarrassing personal questions, for he kept their conversation very general and light-hearted. By the end of the morning, however, Dora felt that she had come to know John Harley rather well. And she had established that he was a dead shot with a snowball, and could skim a pebble across the ice much further than she could — both of which talents recommended him to her.

'I must make allowances for him,' she thought, as she watched him swing his baby son round and round, as Marcus giggled in delight. 'Anyone who can be so besotted with Anna as he is, must be soft in the head, after all …'

John, who knew that he would never be at ease in Stephen's company, was determined to go back to France on the date originally planned. He was equally determined to take his wife and son with him, and he told his father-in-law so. Stephen had

361

shrugged and nodded his head. 'Just as you wish,' he'd said indifferently.

But Dorcas fretted over this, and asked why her son-in-law needed to go abroad to work. 'Surely he could find something to do in England?' she'd demanded crossly. 'He doesn't have to be a wine-merchant, does he? Couldn't you find him something else to occupy his time?'

'I don't think so.' Stephen broke a silence which had lasted for the past three days to inform Dorcas that John Harley should be allowed to decide what was best for himself and his own wife and child. 'He must do as he thinks fit,' he told her.

'Must he?' Dorcas looked sideways at Stephen. 'You just want him to go,' she snapped. 'You're jealous of him — that's what it is! You can't wait to have your daughter's husband out of the house!'

'Don't be so ridiculous!' Stephen's narrow eyes became mere slits. 'It's not that at all.'

'What is it, then?' Dorcas, in spite of her instructions to the others to let Stephen come out of his sulk in his own time, was by now thoroughly tired of his surliness. 'Why don't you like him?' she demanded.

He did not answer her. He went back into his lair and slammed the door behind him.

The whole family went down to Southampton to see the emigrants on their way. Dorcas hugged Marcus and wept, while Anna clung to Stephen and made him promise to write to her every week. 'And you will come to see me this summer, won't you?' she asked him. 'Promise me you'll come! Promise!'

Stephen looked across at his son-in-law. 'Well —' he began doubtfully. 'I'll come if I can. If you're sure I'm invited.'

'Of course you are!' Anna wrapped her arms around his neck, and hugged him. 'Of course you're invited! Anywhere that I am, you are welcome! Surely you know that?'

John and Dora walked away from the group of weepers and clingers to look at the ship. 'I hope I won't be as ill as I was coming over,' he remarked wryly. 'I'll feel such a fool. I don't suppose Anna is ever seasick!'

Dora laughed. 'Anna has no human weaknesses,' she said. 'Surely you must know that by now?'

'Hmm.' John grinned. 'There are one or two, you know,' he said. 'But I must admit that it took me a long time to find out what they were.'

'I'll bet it did!' Dora looked up at her big, handsome brother-in-law and hoped he could cope with Anna, could handle her moodiness and irritability. He was, after all, so nice — he didn't deserve to be made unhappy. 'Don't worry if Anna gets a bit cross sometimes,' she said confidingly. 'She *is* a little bit grumpy now and again.'

John patted Dora's shoulder. 'I'll just put her across my knee if she's grumpy with me,' he said, grinning. 'I shall get a big stick and threaten her with it if she's a naughty girl!'

Such irreverence made Dora giggle delightedly. John could obviously manage Anna.

Dorcas, feeling that her younger daughter needed some society — for she was still very moody and prone to long periods of introspection — arranged for Dora to attend a school in North Oxford, at which Miriam Gordon was already enrolled.

But now, Dorcas herself had nothing much to occupy her time. She wandered round the Summertown house like a ghost; eventually, at a loss for anything more positive to do, she began a campaign to improve her appearance.

She put herself on a strict diet, and she lost a good deal of weight; she ordered some new, pretty clothes; she put her hair up, and she waited for Stephen to compliment her on the transformation.

He didn't. As far as she could tell, he didn't even notice the change. But, worse than that, he had been very preoccupied lately. He had hardly spoken to her for weeks; he was in college all day, and when he did come home he went to bed early and slept all night.

Late one evening, lying propped against her pillows and bored with the magazine she had been idly thumbing, Dorcas decided that she would be ignored no longer. She turned up the bedside lamp so that it burned more brightly. 'Stephen?' She pushed his shoulder, shaking him. 'Stephen!'

He stirred, opened his eyes. 'What is it?' he asked dazedly.

'It wasn't anything, really. I was just lonely. I wanted to talk to you.' She found that she couldn't say what she really meant, couldn't ask him to kiss her, to take her in his arms and to make love to her as he used to do but had not done for at least a month now.

'Couldn't we talk in the morning, Dorcas?' He gave her a weary smile. 'Come on, dear, lie down. It's past midnight.' He laid his arm across her waist, and pulled her down beside him. Within a few moments he was asleep again, breathing regularly. Dorcas stared into the darkness; comforted, but only a little, by his embrace.

Stephen had told her that he would be going to Ashton Cross for a few days that summer, probably at the end of the academic year. Naturally, Dorcas never accompanied him there, tangible evidence that she was of the landlord's irregular way of life which must, she supposed, still grieve his family.

She didn't *want* to go to Ashton Cross. She knew perfectly well that had Stephen taken her to the Manor House with him, she would have been snubbed by his family and jeered at by the tenants, as the landlord's peasant whore.

'But it's not fair,' she thought resentfully, brooding. 'Things are different now. It's nearly the twentieth century. Why shouldn't I go to Hereford with him? What right have his relations to look down on me, just because my ancestors worked for his? They had no choice — the landlords enclosed the common lands, they took away my grandparents' means of getting their own livelihoods!

'Oppressors of the poor! That's all the Lawrences are! And as for him, I've been more of a wife to him than that woman he married ever was. And he still despises me!'

Eventually Stephen noticed how irritable Dorcas had become. Looking up from his littered desk one evening, he asked her what was the matter. 'I think you might be anaemic,' he said. 'You're so pale these days, and you always seem tired.'

'I'm not anaemic,' she replied shortly.

'Well, perhaps not. But you have been very fidgety lately, and that's not like you. Is there anything bothering you at all?'

She looked at him, saw that his pen was still in his hand — that he expected a brief answer from her. 'No, there's nothing bothering me,' she replied. She went back to the drawing room.

'Nothing that you'd be able — or would wish — to do anything about,' she added bitterly, to herself.

The year dragged on. The damp, cold weather of that spring depressed Dorcas' spirits still further. And then, at the beginning of May, the nightmares began.

Dorcas knew what had caused them. A few days before the first bad dream, she had been walking through Cornmarket, not looking where she was going, and she had blundered into a butcher carrying a pig's carcase into his shop.

'I'm sorry, Madam!' The man had put out a hand to stop her falling. 'I didn't see you!'

'What?' Dorcas had stared at him — looked at the steadying hand upon her sleeve, a coarse, red, butcher's hand ... The man was tall, stout, fair-haired. He had smelled like Daniel, too. He had smelled of blood.

She'd pushed the butcher's hand away, and run quickly up the street, trying to rid her mind of the images which now flooded her brain, making her head spin. But it was no use. The damage had been done. The idea of the dead animal, its eyes glazed and its stomach split, would not leave her.

Every night now the same kind of dream came to disturb her sleep. Every night she would wake up sweating and trembling, willing the pictures in her mind's eye to go.

At first, the dream was always exactly the same. She walked through the Summertown house on a bright sunny day, going about her usual tasks, but when she opened the door of the drawing room, there, dripping blood on to the pale carpet hung the carcase of an animal suspended from the ceiling.

That was horrible enough. But worse was to come. The night that Dorcas dreamed that she walked into the room and found the naked, gutted bodies of her three children, hanging upside down from hooks driven into the white ceiling, she had woken up screaming in terror. She clutched Stephen's arm tightly, burying her face in the folds of his nightshirt.

'Whatever is it?' he had asked, alarmed himself.

'A nightmare! Oh, Stephen — it was horrible! Horrible!' She was still shaking as he sat up and turned up the light. 'You won't let him hurt me, will you?' she asked, still clinging to him.

'I'd never let anyone hurt you.' Stephen, wide awake now,

reached for a shawl and wrapped it around her shoulders. 'Look,' he said. 'You're in your own bedroom with me, you're perfectly safe. Darling, it was only a dream; that's all. You should take your chloral,' he added. 'It will help you to sleep better.'

But, whether she took chloral or not, the nightmares continued, although most nights now there was a solitary dangling corpse, and it was always Anna.

The regularity of this gruesome pattern was in some way comforting, for Dorcas went to bed knowing that she would probably be spared the sight of either Dora or Anthony dead and mutilated, their feet pierced by blood-stained hooks, while a shadowy figure went to work on them with knives which Dorcas knew he always kept razor sharp, honed to a thin-bladed precision...

And Dorcas would wake most mornings now, knowing that she had had the dream, but that she had coped with it. But then she would feel wretched and ashamed — guilty that she had watched Anna being butchered and done nothing to help her. 'I must make everything up to Anna,' she thought. 'I must show her that I love her. But how can I do it? What can I do?'

Stephen finished the book upon which he'd been working, cleared away the last batch of the examination papers he had had to mark, and told Dorcas that he and she needed a holiday.

'We'll go up to the Lakes,' he told her. 'Just the two of us. I've had a word with Gordon; he says that he and his wife will be happy to take care of Dora for a couple of weeks. She likes being with them, doesn't she?'

'Yes, she does.' Dorcas stirred her coffee and watched the liquid swirl around the cup. 'He might have asked me before he arranged everything,' she thought sourly. 'But then, that's just like him — whatever he wants, I have to accept.'

The holiday was not, initially, a great success. Dorcas felt morose and Stephen, not an admirer of the grey-green English countryside — which he saw with a farmer's and not an artist's eyes — was bored. The hotel was half empty. Outside, the rain poured down the bleak, stony hillsides.

It was obvious to Dorcas that Stephen wanted to be back in Oxford, where the proofs of his new book would now be lying on his desk, awaiting correction. On waking up one morning to yet another grey downpour, she was not surprised when he suggested that they cut short their stay, and that they return to Oxford. 'We could go by way of Chester, if you like,' he added.

Dorcas shrugged, annoyed that she was being ordered about yet again. 'The weather might improve here,' she began, looking out of the window. 'It's still raining, but the sky isn't so dark now. Perhaps if we ...'

'Oh, it'll pour down all day,' cut in Stephen dismissively. 'This sort of rain goes on for weeks without stopping. And in any case, if we start to make our way home, I can get most of that correcting done before I go to Hereford. Anna might come over in July and I don't want to be shut up in my study all the while that she is with us.'

He stood up and buttoned his jacket, unaware that Dorcas was glaring at him. 'Anna!' she thought. 'Always Anna, Anna, Anna! When did he last arrange his work so that he could spend more time with me? He wanted to come here, he dragged me to this horrible place without even asking me if I'd like to come! And now he wants to go home again — and I have to do as he says!'

Unaware of Dorcas' mounting irritation, Stephen talked on. 'You'll be glad to see Anna, won't you, dear?' he asked, as he fastened his cuffs. 'I expect that's why you've been rather low lately. You've been missing her and the child.'

Dorcas could contain herself no longer. With unwonted viciousness she jammed in her last hairpin, and she went over to the window where Stephen stood, hands in his pockets, looking out at the drizzle. 'Anna!' she cried vehemently. 'As if Anna wants to see me!'

She drew breath and went on, her voice rising. 'You know perfectly well that it's you she's coming to see, not me! So don't talk to me about missing Anna!'

She frowned at Stephen's startled expression. 'Oh, don't look at me like that,' she snapped. 'You know what I'm talking about! Anna's always preferred the company of almost anyone else to that of her own mother!'

'What?' Stephen glanced at Dorcas. 'Oh, don't be silly, dear,' he muttered.

'I'm not being silly! It's true!' Dorcas scowled at him. 'When she was born, that man stole her from me; she wasn't half an hour old before she was in his arms! He loved her, and she loved him. She would spend hours in the shop, just watching him — anything rather than be with me! Then you took her from me, you with your books and your learning, you filled her head with fancy ideas, encouraged her to cherish ambitions way above those any normal woman should have!

'I know you both sneer at me. I know you both despise me for an illiterate, ignorant peasant, while you're both so clever! Don't bother to deny it! Anna treats me as if I were some kind of servant. My own daughter looks down on me as if I were no better than the dirt beneath her feet! And you're to blame for that, Stephen!

'And then she met John. He left her, but she wouldn't let me comfort her, much as I understood how she felt. And now he's taken her from me for good. She kept asking you to visit her. But she hardly even kissed me goodbye. So why should I be missing *Anna*?'

'Dorcas, stop it!' Stephen folded his arms and looked out at the rain again. 'I'm going to have breakfast,' he announced.

'No, you're not!' Dorcas grabbed his arm, pinching it hard through his sleeve. 'You'll hear me out! Oh, you're just the same as Anna,' she cried. 'You despise me, you hide me away, you're ashamed of me! You're going to Hereford soon — why can't I come with you? I belong to you — I've borne you three children, I've been faithful to you! Oh, Stephen, you're heartless! Heartless! You shut me out — you always have, and you always will!'

She began to sob, chokingly, at this point. Leaning against the chest of the man who allegedly despised her, she soaked his shirt-front with her tears. 'It's only a matter of time, I know, before you abandon me,' she wailed. 'I shall end my days in some nasty little slum of a cottage out in the back of beyond, or in the Parish workhouse. I dare say you'll find someone to replace me soon as I'm not young any more, and I never was particularly pretty, so I don't know why you've put up with me for so long!'

Stephen, who had only half-listened to that tirade, put his arms around Dorcas and kissed her forehead. 'What's the matter, darling?' he asked. 'What's upset my dear little trollop?'

That was a terrible mistake. Dorcas wrenched herself out of his embrace and glared at him, grief and anger contending for the upper hand in her emotions.

Anger won. 'Trollop!' she cried. 'Exactly! That's all I ever was to you! That's all you ever wanted me for, to be your trollop! The master's trollop, that's what I am! The squire's harlot, the landlord's whore! Except that these days I'm not even that any more! Oh, I hate you, bloody Squire Lawrence! I hate you!'

She looked up at him, her face blotched with tears and red with anger; wanting to hit him. But instead, she covered her face with her hands and abandoned herself to a violent fit of sobbing, while Stephen shrugged in bewilderment, for he couldn't remember ever seeing her in such a mood before. 'Don't cry, darling,' he soothed, taking her in his arms again. 'Whatever I've said to upset you, I'm sorry.'

'You despise me!' she wept. 'You call me a trollop! That's what upsets me!' As months of pent-up agony was released, tears overwhelmed her again. 'I've wasted my whole life in loving a man who hardly thinks of me!' she sobbed.

'Is it a waste, then, loving me?'

'I sometimes think so. You don't care if I'm with you or not. The children don't need me any more. I'm no use to anyone. You can tell me you're tired of me,' she concluded, sniffing. 'There's no need to pretend!'

'Oh, stop talking like this, Dorcas!' Stephen thought for a second or two. 'Would you like to come to Hereford with me next month?' he asked. 'I'd be happy to take you if you want to go.'

'What did you say?'

'Do you want to go to Hereford?'

She stared at him. 'You'd take me to Ashton Cross?'

'If you want to come. You must admit that you've never shown any interest in going there before today. Not that I blame you — it's very dull.'

'I could stay at the manor house?'

'Naturally. Where else would we go?'

'But what would the tenants think? What would your relations say?'

'Oh, for goodness' sake, Dorcas! As if it matters to me what the tenants think or my relations say!' He took out his handerkerchief and wiped away her tears. 'Is this all that's bothering you?' he asked. 'Don't you want me to go off to Hereford by myself?'

'Partly that. But mostly it's that I know you loved me once, and you don't love me any more.'

'Nonsense!' Stephen hugged her. 'Of course I love you! And you must know I do, otherwise you wouldn't dare to try my temper like this! Dorcas, how could I not love a woman who's loved me as you have, who's given me three lovely children —'

'Three bastards,' interrupted the devil in Dorcas. 'Three bastards.'

'Three beautiful, intelligent children. Whose mother, as far as I am concerned, is my wife. My dear Dorcas, no one at Ashton Cross would dare to insult you! Everyone there knows perfectly well that I'd evict any tenant who so much as whispered about you. And as for my relations — they have much better manners than you suppose!'

'Have they?'

'Yes.' Stephen kissed her face. 'And as for all that rubbish about not wanting you, that's ridiculous. It's been a very trying year for me — haven't you realized that? I'm tired when I come home, but I do look forward to being with you. You comfort me, and lying down at night with you next to me soothes me to sleep. And I'm not twenty years old now. I can't work all day and make love half the night! You had only to say if you wanted me. Dorcas?'

'What?'

'Shall we go back to bed?'

He began to pull the pins from her hair, scattering them one by one all over the carpet. He shook her hair free and let it tumble down her back. Dorcas put her arms around him and kissed him, as much in relief and gratitude as in desire. When, half an hour later, they lay contentedly in each other's arms, she knew how very silly she'd been to doubt that he loved her.

At ten o'clock they observed that the sun had come out, and was shining, half-heartedly, on the waters of the lake. 'Dorcas, you're an *idle* woman!' said Stephen. 'Will you get up? Or do you intend to lie there all morning?'

Dorcas smiled at him, lazily, as she trailed her hand across his chest. 'I'll stay here,' she replied. 'I'm so very comfortable! Yes, I think I'll stay here all day.'

'No, you won't. Put your clothes on and we'll go for a drive.'

'Drive?' Dorcas propped herself up on one elbow and pushed his hair out of Stephen's eyes. 'What about the proofs?' she enquired. 'And the estate?'

'Damn the proofs. Anna can do them. And the estate can manage quite well without me!' He lifted her away from him and reached for his clothes. 'Come along, hurry up,' he said. 'They might give us some coffee if we're quick. Oh, and Dorcas?'

'Yes?'

'You won't want me to give you any more demonstrations of affection like the one I've just provided, will you? Or at least, not for a few days? You will remember that I'm an old man now— that if I neglect you, it's not because I don't love you?'

He laughed at the expression on her face. 'Promise me that you won't leave me for a younger man? Not just yet?'

'Oh, Stephen! What an idea! As if I'd ever want to leave you, for anyone!'

They hurriedly pulled on their garments and went downstairs, to a very late breakfast. As they walked into the dining room, Stephen put his arm around Dorcas' shoulders. 'You're looking very pretty these days,' he remarked. 'You've lost some weight, haven't you? And I like that dress — the pink and grey in it suit you.'

They extended their stay in the Lake District, enjoying the fine weather which had eventually deigned to arrive. They walked for miles, scrambling up the fells under a cloudless blue sky. They looked at all the views mentioned in the guidebooks and told each other, facetiously, how fine all the prospects were.

'Oh, yes, it's all very picturesque,' agreed Stephen, lying on his side and skimming pebbles across a lake. 'But it's unproductive. Nothing but those scruffy little sheep. Must be a terrible life for the shepherds. I wouldn't farm here if I was paid to.'

'Oh, be quiet, Stephen.' Dorcas gave him a push. 'Let me gaze.'

They returned to Oxford rested and relaxed, contented with each other. The following week Stephen went off to Hereford by himself. Dorcas said that she could not possibly go with him, for Dora had to have some new dresses and she would need her mother to supervise the dressmaker. And they had imposed on the Gordons for far too long as it was. And Dora would be bored at Ashton Cross.

As the excuses came tripping off her tongue, Dorcas tried hard not to blush ...

Chapter Twenty Five

THAT SUMMER, ANNA CAME TO Oxford for a month. She found the photograph album a week or so after her arrival. Searching for some coloured pencils for Marcus, she had come across it in the bottom drawer of her mother's bureau. She sat back on her heels and began, slowly, to turn the pages.

Recognizing herself in late childhood — there were no pictures of her before she was eleven — she tried to remember the names of all the people who crowded the photographs.

Most of the pictures were, of course, formally posed. There were records of birthdays and other special occasions, and there were group photographs taken on excavations, showing her father scowling into the camera among a crowd of other men.

But some of the pictures, taken by Stephen, were more casual. Anna turned over pages of likenesses of her younger brother and sister, and of her mother with her children by her side or on her lap. And she laughed at one of herself in fancy dress, a self-conscious water sprite.

Right at the back of the album she found a large manilla envelope. This contained a much bigger, older picture. Once sepia, it was now pale brown with age. It showed a quite different group of people, all clustered together.

In the centre of the photograph was the landlord's family. The farmer himself stood frowning, planted foursquare in the dead centre of the picture; one hand rested upon his gold watch-chain, while the other was firmly holding his seated wife's shoulder, as if he were afraid she might bolt. Mrs Lawrence sat in state, unsmiling, with her three children around her. Looking closely, Anna saw a rather plain girl and two dark-haired boys. They all gazed gravely at the camera, as did the personal servants grouped around them. To the right and left of these house servants, kept well away from the gentry lest they should contaminate them, were ranged the tenants and farm labourers.

Anna saw that, pencilled in above one of the scruffy, shoeless little girls at the edge of the picture, there was a faint cross. Examining the likeness, she recognized Dorcas, obviously uncomfortable in the borrowed finery of a clean, white pinafore which served to conceal most of her ragged dress.

Pale sepia does not flatter anyone, and the picture was very faded. Almost all the people in it seemed to have a crumpled, seedy look about them. The farmer's family looked prosperous enough, Anna supposed. But the others! What a collection of scarecrows! There were young women, young mothers holding babies in their arms, who had the pinched, drawn faces of elderly crones. Raw-boned labouring men peered blearily at the photographer, their thin wrists dangling beneath the frayed cuffs of their threadbare corduroy jackets. Their children were, without exception, thin; scraggy little creatures all of them. Here and there Anna could see the over-bright eyes and unnaturally rosy cheeks of those tubercular infants who would inevitably decline and die, wasting away before their tenth birthdays.

The long, long exposure had fixed glazed expressions on all the faces in the picture. Anna looked at her mother's image again. She saw a slight, dark-haired child who was screwing up her face in a desperate attempt to keep still for the required length of time. It was impossible to say if she had been pretty — but she must have been, for even in middle age Dorcas was still winsome, with her fine dark eyes, abundant brown hair which would never entirely lose its youthful colour, and her sweet, heart-shaped face.

Then, suddenly, Anna's heart ached for her mother. She knew, now, what a dreadful life the child must have led and she realized that, far from being the rosy-cheeked little milkmaid of her daughter's imagination, Dorcas had been nothing more than a peasant's brat, a creature of no more account than a beast of burden, worked like a slave from dawn to sunset, always tired, always hungry, ill-housed and ill-clad, near starvation in the midst of plenty, poor in the richest country on earth. 'Poor child,' thought Anna. 'Poor little Dorcas Grey.'

She did not hear the door open behind her, did not notice that her mother had come into the room. Anna looked up to see

Dorcas gazing down at the photograph. 'Goodness, Anna,' she said, 'where on earth did you find that old thing?' She dropped to her knees beside her daughter. She took the picture from Anna's hands and began to look at it, exclaiming as she recognized faces from the past.

'There's Mrs Collins,' she said. 'She was the rector's wife; but she hadn't a scrap of Christian charity in her whole skinny body! Oh, and there's the carter — he took me into Hereford when I first went into service. I can't tell you how scared I was! There's Luke, and there's Annie — and my mother, look, across here. And there's me! What a sight! You'd have thought someone could have put a brush through my hair!'

Dorcas shook her head, laughing at herself. 'And there's your father,' she continued. 'Wasn't he a nice-looking boy?' She went on like this for a few minutes more, no emotion but pleasure apparent in her face.

Anxiously, Anna touched her mother's sleeve. 'Mama — it's not like that nowadays, is it?' she asked.

Dorcas looked up from the picture. 'Like what, dear?' she asked. 'How do you mean?'

'Well, the people are all so thin; just look at them! So poor, so hopeless; they all seem so miserable. The children are pathetic. And look at these women. They're as wrinkled and bent as grandmothers but most of them can't have been more than thirty years old!'

Dorcas looked. 'Mm, well — yes, I see what you mean. It was a hard life, you know. But things are better now. Your father isn't like the old squire. Stephen's always treated his tenants fairly. No one could say he was a bad landlord, not like his father was.'

She smiled at Anna. 'Things are different everywhere now,' she added. 'After all, this picture is more than forty years old.' It was obvious that she did not feel the pity for herself which was wrenching Anna's heart. 'What's the matter, dear?' she asked, still looking at the photograph. For Anna had begun to cry.

Then, to her mother's great surprise, Anna threw her arms around Dorcas' shoulders and hugged her, sobbing as if she would never be able to stop. 'I didn't know, Mama,' she cried. 'You never told me — and I didn't know!'

Dorcas patted her arm. 'There, there, Anna,' she said, still somewhat puzzled by her daughter's sudden display of emotion. 'It's all over, you know. It's all better now.'